HUNTER'S FOLLY

GALILEO'S LEGACY
BOOK ONE

S. R. GASCO

ISBN: 979-8-9911659-2-1

Library of Congress Control Number: 2024915962

Editing: Writer's Journey Services

Cover Design: Miblart

Acknowledgments

This novel would not be possible without the support of many wonderful people.

I appreciate the beta readers who gave me valuable feedback to fine-tune my story. Conor, Steve, Krystyn, and Jude.

Thank you, Laura and R.B., for cleaning and polishing my words with your editing skills.

The detailed planetary distances listed are courtesy of the resources provided by NASA and the Jet Propulsion Laboratory.

My family and friends whose encouragement said, "You Can!" when others might say, "You Can't."

Finally, thank you to my loving wife for putting up with me the last few months. I love you, baby doll.

Dedication

To the teachers who said I was good enough to write. It took me a while, but I listened.

Contents

The Curse of the Hunter's Folly

2145—Undisclosed Asteroid

The old explorers' spacesuit scraped against the sides of the alien tube tunneled into the asteroid. The obsidian-black surface was sleek yet constricting on his chest. Crawling through the narrow tunnel would be a living nightmare for a claustrophobic. For Fred Stonington, it brought exhilaration.

Getting stuck in the narrow passage was a deadly danger. No one knew Fred's destination, not even his close friends. Future artifact hunters might discover his mummified remains lodged in the tunnel.

Those close to him would recognize his irreverent humor. *I hope they get a damn good price for my mummy.*

Confident that his destiny didn't lie as an exhibit in a museum, Fred pushed ahead. The treasure trove of artifacts he expected could mean renewed life for those in need. Fame and fortune for himself would be an added bonus.

A hacking cough reverberated through his chest. His intense cough that echoed in his helmet was the only sound he could hear with the silence of the vacuum surrounding him. He tasted blood as the cough intensified. He knew he couldn't delay seeing a doctor much longer.

A gleam caught Stonington's attention at the end of the narrow tube. He crawled to the circular hatch, built of the same black metal with alien writing on its surface. If he hadn't been wearing gloves, it would be warm but not hot to touch.

With a practiced hand, he located the emergency manual release handle. He smiled, ready to explore an undiscovered artifact site. He grasped the bar and twisted the lever...nothing happened.

His eyes widened in astonishment, stunned by what he saw. Releases always worked, even after millennia of disuse.

Experience taught Stonington always to *be prepared*. He may have shared the Boy Scout Motto, but he never worked well enough within a set of rules to join. His preparation included carrying a specialized single-use power pack.

With a steady hand, the hunter attached the power pack to the lock. A slight vibration traveled up his arm as he made the connection. A small screen on the hatch began to glow in the dim chamber. Symbols materialized on the screen, their meaning unknown to any human. Yet, with his years of study, the hunter knew which symbol to press for "open."

Shock rolled through Stonington as the reaction was far more dramatic than he had expected. The hatch failed to open. Instead, violet lights began to flash in a rapid strobe-like fashion, alternating shadow, violet, and the white light of his own helmet lamps. A low, vibrating shutter resonated through the tube, which caused a shiver to run down his spine. Behind him, another door had sealed shut, imprisoning him.

This time, panic consumed him, and he felt trapped like a helpless rat. His exhilaration and stoic calm vanished. Pressure enveloped him, squeezing him in a tight grip.

The source of the energy to power the lights and door was unknown. Stonington's powerpack burned itself out from the initial drain. A power source came to life somewhere deep within this dead alien station. The situation seemed impossible and caused his mind to spin in a frenzy of alarm and incomprehension.

The pressure that clutched Stonington's chest was the gradual influx of air filling the tube. Realizing he was in an airlock eased his panic and enhanced his excitement. As pressure increased, sounds flooded in the rush of air, the hum of equipment, and faint electronic beeping from his spacesuit.

Once the pressurization process was complete, the portal before him opened with a soft whir sound.

The mysterious experience astonished Stonington. Every Artificer site ever found was dead, devoid of power and air. A fully functional site would be like finding El Dorado. Artifact hunters spread legends of such a site for decades, and Stonington found it.

As he emerged from the cramped tube, he crashed to the floor. *This room had gravity! How can this be possible on an asteroid only a kilometer wide?* Stonington thought. He didn't experience the distinct feel of artificial gravity but the natural feel of the surface of a planet. It defied logic and reason.

His next action was risky and stupid. He removed his helmet and expected a musty smell. Instead, he smelled spring wildflowers. It evoked memories of a long-ago childhood.

In the first chamber, vibrant displays illuminated the room and cast a soft glow on the sleek consoles. The air hummed with the sound of machines running. The displays showcased a myriad of intricate charts, graphs, and data, all written in the enigmatic alien language. His intuition told him this room was a control center, guiding operations he could not understand. He touched the consoles and saw colors shift under his fingers, which showed the controls being highlighted. His bravery did not extend to pressing these unknown buttons.

He ventured into the next chamber, and what he found there could change how humans understood the alien Artificers.

As he entered the third chamber, Stonington felt a sense of solemnity. The room was a tomb. The contents shattered the foundation of humans' historical knowledge of the Artificers.

He convinced himself that people would soon speak his name alongside Heinrich Schliemann for discovering Troy and Howard Carter for discovering King Tut's tomb. Another coughing fit hit him as he continued to explore.

Six weeks later—Jupiter's moon Callisto

Ensign Kristina Chen-Ramirez wiped the sweat off her brow and leaned back in the pilot seat. The excitement of the chase sent adrenaline coursing through her veins. She spent the last hour matching course and then snagged an out-of-control vessel.

"Excellent piloting, Ensign," the patrol ship captain said. "I hope you know the reward for good work."

"More work?"

"Exactly. Gather a team and search that ship. I want to know why a survey boat nearly crashed into Callisto station."

Kristina boarded the survey boat with a small team. Pungent odors assaulted their noses, and they sealed their helmets in defense. They passed an empty sleeping area and galley and entered the cockpit. A space suit helmet lay on the floor, smashed by a blunt object. In the pilot seat was the body of a man. The man was naked from the waist up and had wild, unkempt hair and beard.

"I'll let the doc know we have a stiff to take back," said one of the crew.

"Hold off." Kristina took a step closer to the man. His right hand held the wrench used to smash his helmet and a pendant in his left. His eye popped open as she reached to check his pulse.

"Back, Witch! You can't tempt me, Circe!" The man jumped up and swung his wrench at her head. The crewmember jumped to help, but he was too slow. Kristina plucked the wrench from his hand and twisted the wild man's arm behind him.

"We're here to help you, not hurt you," she said. She turned to the crewman. "Call the doc, but we don't have a stiff. We have a delirious patient with a high fever."

The frenzied man continued to babble. "I passed Scylla and Charybdis and ventured to the underworld to elude you. Even the Land of the Lotus Eaters could not stop me. Penelope, I will return home to you in Ithaca."

The doctor boarded and examined him. "We can't help him here. He must go back to Earth if he has any hope."

Kristina met the crazed man's gaze and tried to calm him. "Don't worry, we will get you home. You will be with your Penelope soon, brave Odysseus."

Her words calmed the man. "Please place the crates in the cargo area. They must make it home to Ithaca. No matter what. Calypso, if you have any love, do this for me."

The doctor gave him a sedative, and he was out. Upon entering the small freight area, Kristina noticed multiple sealed boxes. The man confused her for two different Odyssey villains, but she saw no reason to deny him. She wondered what was so important about these containers.

Kristina turned to her team. "Load these boxes onto the ship. We'll take him to Earth."

"Should we search them first?"

"Of course not. We have no probable cause for a search. This man is a victim, not a criminal. We are here to help people like him."

1
Friends, Family, and Crisis

July 23, 2155—Scotland

Doctor Megan McCord blotted out the world's distractions while she studied a research paper. Megan was so engrossed that she failed to notice a looming figure until a hand touched her shoulder.

"Bloody Hell, Sergio. You scared me," Megan said as she jumped in her seat at the outdoor café.

"Permit me the pleasure of amending tonight's misstep, my dear." Sergio guided Megan out of her seat, stroked her fiery red hair with calculated tenderness, and kissed her lips.

"You are forgiven." Megan still could not believe this handsome and charming man wanted to court plain old pudgy Megan. Logically, she knew those terms were no longer entirely accurate. But the damage from a particularly cruel nanny never went away.

"What captivated your thoughts so deeply? I called your name, but my words must have been lost in the wind," Sergio said as he sat near her.

"I reviewed the notes for my upcoming journey. Remember, I'm departing for Jupiter." Megan indicated the holographic screen on her forearm bracer cuff computer and turned it off. "Now that you have arrived, you have my full attention."

"Tesoro, my treasure, how can you run away from me to another planet? How shall I endure these endless weeks without your radiance?" Sergio's-sweet smile was intoxicating. It made her feel giddy, like a teenager.

"You're a grown man. I think you will survive." Megan sounded confident but worried that Sergio would not wait for her. "Where is your sister? I thought she planned to meet us here."

"Here she comes now." He pointed down the street.

Crowds strolled the streets on this warm summer day. People gawked as a figure in white leather on a pink and black electrocycle sped down the Main Street of the quiet village of Gorebridge. The driver spun one hundred eighty degrees and stopped on the sidewalk. The large rear wheel released a cloud of smoke and the stench of burnt rubber.

"Mia, sorellina," Sergio shook his head but smiled. "My little sister, Bianca, has a flair for grand entrances."

The woman vaulted from the cycle like a 17th-century dragoon leaping into battle. She removed her helmet and revealed a cascade of shimmering platinum-blonde hair. She tossed the helmet to a stunned waiter who stood nearby.

"Ciao Bella. Girlfriend, I will miss you dreadfully. What must I do to convince you to stay here and party with me instead of flying off to Pluto or somewhere." Every step Bianca took had a playful bounce as if she were dancing through life. She greeted Megan with vivacious air kisses, the customary Italian baci on each cheek.

"Ma'am, you can't park there. We have a parking lot around back," the waiter said. Bianca ignored him except to remove her jacket and give the man a glimpse of her tight, low-cut top. She sat in a chair and displayed a devilish smile.

Megan rolled her eyes at her scatter-brained friend. She handed the waiter some money and said, "Brodie, be a dear and move it for her. I'd be ever so grateful."

"Yes, my lady." The waiter nodded and backed away, always deferential to the daughter of Viscount Primrose in nearby Carrington. Megan relaxed and was satisfied that the incident was behind them. The locals always treated her family with the respect they deserved. Megan reached over and held hands with Sergio.

Bianca blew Brodie a kiss as he moved her bike. The man's face flushed as he drove around the building. Bianca laughed and put her feet on the table. "I love how everyone in this town jumps at the command of *Princess* Megan."

"Bianca, behave yourself," Megan pushed Bianca's feet off the table.

Bianca gave Megan a playful pout but kept her feet on the ground. They chatted, drank wine, and ate for the next half hour. Bianca dominated the conversation with a vibrant energy, exuding enthusiasm and liveliness. She spoke about travels around the world and romantic flings. Bianca was as exuberant as a child promised ice cream.

Sometimes, Megan wondered how they had become friends so quickly. The siblings swept into her life like a force of nature a month ago. The wild and bold Bianca could not be more different than the studious Megan. While Bianca partied on the French Riviera, Megan earned her PhD in exo-archaeology to study the alien sites found in the solar system.

"Megan, must you fly away from us?" Bianca asked. "To chase after some silly alien relics. They're not even pretty. Relics are useless."

"They're called artifacts, Bianca. The technology we obtained from the Artificers is not useless. Where do you think the power for your electrocycle comes from?" Megan's voice had an edge, the tone one takes when one's life's work is belittled.

"Boh, I don't know." Bianca waved her hand in disinterest.

"Starshells. We tap alien artifacts called Starshells for power. Only two provide power to the entire United Kingdom. And most of the tech in your bike comes from other alien technology."

Megan beamed. "With my research, we think we are on the cusp of another great leap forward in understanding the ancient aliens."

Bianca stared off into the distance, bored. Sergio gazed at Megan, captivated by every word.

"Are you ready to tell me what you found? You tease me but never give details. Of course, I appreciate teasing occasionally," he said with a gleam in his eye.

"No, I can't tell you yet. I gave my word to my father that I'd keep the details secret, but I do have some news you won't like. The departure got moved up. I leave in the morning."

Sergio and Bianca sat up straight, eyes wide at the unexpected news. Then, they relaxed their postures after a silent look.

"Already? But I dreamt of a scandalous night out in Milan where we could stir up trouble." Bianca's eyes sparkled at the prospect of mischief.

"Maybe when I get back."

"Fantastico. I'll make plans. We will have a fabulous time," Bianca beamed. Megan wasn't sure how *maybe* became *definitely* in less than a second.

Sergio touched Megan's chin with a feather-light touch and kissed her lips tenderly. In a melodic whisper, "Tesoro, allow me the joy of hosting you to a farewell dinner tonight."

"I can't, Sergio. My shuttle flight is early in the morning."

"I promise not to detain you unduly. A quaint, romantic dinner, perhaps followed by a nightcap at my residence?"

Bianca chimed in. "You absolutely must give Sergio this one last date. You don't want to leave him remembering his last date with you, as shared with his sister. I feel like a third wheel now." Her lips jutted out into a pouty curve.

Megan held up her hands. "Ok, I surrender. Pick a restaurant. I'll be there."

Bianca threw her arms around Megan. "Oh, Girl-friend, you will make my brother so happy," Bianca whispered in Megan's ear. "Solve the early morning departure problem by staying at Sergio's apartment. Leave for the shuttle from there. A sister shouldn't say this, but he can give you a proper send-off."

Even with her quirks and boldness, Megan liked Bianca.

Later that evening, Megan entered her father's study. Roger McCord, CEO of Ettrick Logistics and Viscount Primrose, was so absorbed in work that he didn't register Megan, who stood nearby.

"Dad, I'm leaving. Have a good night. Don't wait up for me."

Roger jumped a bit, startled by his daughter's sudden appearance. A wide smile crossed his face, and he stood with arms held wide.

"You cannot leave without giving your old father a hug and kiss." He wrapped his arms around Megan and kissed her on the cheek. "Don't be out too late. You have an early flight tomorrow."

"Oh, I'm sure Captain Anderson will wait a bit for me. I'm the boss's daughter, after all." Megan waved a hand dismissively, her tone slightly haughty.

"Captain Anderson most certainly will not. I am the boss, and you are just a passenger. The Highland Bounty must maintain a schedule. Megan, I'm quite disappointed. I thought you had outgrown this attitude." Roger's voice hardened. His words sliced through the air with unmistakable disapproval.

"I apologize, Daddy. You're absolutely right. I'll make it an early night and catch the morning shuttle. Tonight's date will be delightful, but I must confess, I'm even more excited about this trip."

Roger's smile returned. "I'm so proud of you. You're brilliant. You solved a riddle I worked on for years. It is the first genuine lead on The Folly."

Rumors of an intact Artificer site had spread for years, but no one had found it. They called it "The Hunter's Folly." Some called it cursed, and those who found it would die. Some considered it a fable and a futile hunt. The legend may now become fact, and she would be there.

For Roger, collecting artifacts has become an expensive hobby. Several years earlier, Roger bought the property of an old artifact hunter at an estate auction. Like many other projects, he could never comprehend the man's notes and lost interest. Time was the one resource he couldn't spare for pet projects. As part of her PhD thesis, Megan found the box of notes and trinkets and unraveled the man's ramblings. In his last days, the old explorer found an active Artificer site.

The prospect of the voyage filled her with a thrilling anticipation. It was the kind of discovery she had dreamed of since choosing her path in exo-archaeology.

Megan tried to downplay her excitement with a smile. "It will be a rather uneventful journey to Jupiter, just more research on the next step. I won't climb into an alien base."

She picked up a section of white alabaster stone etched with alien letters in black metal. She traced her fingers across the symbols, her touch delicate and reverent. A faint warmth radiated into her fingertips. "This was the first artifact you let me hold. Was I about seven? The first time I felt the warmth in the alien metal, I was utterly captivated."

After holding that relic as a child, she developed a deep-seated passion for history and myths about ancient aliens called the Artificers. Megan dedicated her life's work to studying them.

"I know you'll be able to decipher the alien writing once you return from your expedition," Roger said.

"Oh, Dad, while we may disagree on the ease of that feat, I appreciate your optimism." They had debated the subject repeatedly. Roger envisioned discovering a Rosetta Stone that would unlock the language of the Artificers and usher in a new era of knowledge. Megan recognized the potential but believed such groundbreaking discoveries could take decades.

"I should be on my way. Sergio will be waiting."

"You look beautiful tonight. He better treat you well."

"Thank you, Daddy. I can only hope he will be as good as you were to mum." Megan touched her pendant. It had once been her mother's. She kissed him on the cheek. "Prissy, would you be a dear and summon my car?"

"Of course, Doctor. It's pulling around now," a voice said. Prissy, short for Priscilla, was the estate's AI butler and handled the day-to-day running of the estate.

"I love you, Daddy. I have to go now."

Megan gave her father a kiss on the cheek and said goodbye. After she left, he took out a holo-projector and looked at images of his late wife. He still missed her every day.

"Sergio, I'm afraid I really must go. I need to rise quite early in the morning," Megan said to her persistent date. They'd had a wonderful dinner, but it was late.

"Tesoro, the summer sun just descended beyond the horizon. Surrender yourself to a night of music and dancing to daybreak with me. Treat this like your last night on

Earth. Technically, it is." Sergio's voice was almost as soft as his caress. His eyes and smile twinkled in the light of a rising moon.

I am tempted. Sergio is gorgeous, but the flight is dreadfully early, she thought. She touched her cuff computer built into a fashionable bracer. A holographic display appeared, and she entered a command to summon her autonomous car.

"Goodnight, Sergio. Save your enthusiasm for a welcome home party. We will both have a reunion to look forward to." She kissed him and slid into her Tesla Benz. A smile lingered on her lips. As she drove home, thoughts of Sergio and the promise of a celebration upon her return offered a pleasant distraction. Yet even the allure of the evening couldn't overshadow her growing excitement about what lay ahead.

The trip was only a research expedition to find leads on Stonington's destination, but it was all her. No professors, team supervisors, or teaching assistants. Megan would act as the Principal Investigator for the expedition. The fact she was the only expedition member was beside the point.

On returning home, Megan headed to Roger's study. *A last nightcap with Daddy will make this day perfect.*

"Dad, I'm home," she said. A pungent odor met her as she entered the study. Sensing danger, every muscle in her body tensed like a coiled spring.

A hooded figure rummaged through her father's desk.

"Who the Hell are you?" Megan shouted.

The masked intruder looked up, startled at Megan's presence. They grabbed a handful of data chips and bolted out the patio door.

Megan charged the burglar before they could escape. The person shifted to intercept Megan and body-checked her into a bookcase.

Surrounded by an avalanche of books, Megan fell forward, catching herself with her hand before she hit face first. She now saw a ghastly sight that caused nausea to wash over her.

"No, Daddy, no."

Behind the desk, Roger McCord lay in a pool of blood. Sightless eyes and his own Fairbairn–Sykes dagger in his chest told Megan the steady rock of her life was gone.

Megan's eyes narrowed on the intruder's slim frame. The figure ran across the lawn to the outside wall.

Almost instinctively, Megan yanked open the cabinet where Roger kept the double-barrel hunting shotgun used for skeet shooting. Her fingers closed around the cold grip and loaded two shells. The weapon's weight in her hand felt like an extension of her will, embodying her wrath. Megan aimed and fired at the murderer. She ignored the weapon's bucking force in her adrenaline-fueled haze. She pulled the trigger again, and the intruder yelped in pain but vaulted over the wall.

Megan tossed the shotgun away and ran to Roger's body. "Prissy, call the police." The household AI didn't answer.

She didn't know how long she lost herself in grief until she regained her composure enough to call the police.

The piercing sound of sirens filled the air as the police arrived from the nearby town of Gorebridge, which served as the police for the tiny village of Carrington, where the Primrose estate was located. The responding officers called for backup when they saw the horrific scene.

Despite being surrounded by people, Megan felt very alone. The police shuffled her into the sitting room to wait for an inspector. She desperately wanted to talk to someone, but they took her comm.

"He can't be gone. He just can't. How can I go on without him?" Megan said aloud to no one in particular.

"Imagine your father would want you to close your eyes and remember the laughter and joy of the happy moments," A man in a tweed jacket stepped into the room and showed her a badge. "Inspector Owen MacDuff, Police Scotland out of Edinburgh. The locals summoned me to assist in the investigation."

Megan stood, straightened her glasses, and took a deep breath. She focused on the Inspector and summoned her most aristocratic tone. "Thank you, Inspector. What are you doing to find my father's murderer?"

"We relayed your description, but without specifics, there will be little we can do. The household AI went offline before the break-in. Our techs got it back online, but there were no recordings of the attack."

Megan breathed a sigh of relief that Prissy was back online. The AI had been part of the family since childhood, but she refocused on Inspector Macduff.

"I ask again. What are you doing?" She glared at him, hoping her stern posture would prevent her from crying.

"Forensic specialists are examining the crime scene. You and I will sit down and go over the events again. Perhaps you will remember more. Maybe a spot of tea will help." He gestured to a chair when Prissy's voice interrupted.

"Doctor McCord. Inspector MacDuff. Another group of officials are arriving now."

A group in suits stormed through the front door. The air filled with a mix of urgency and tension.

"Good evening, everyone. I apologize, but everyone needs to leave right now," the lead man said. "This location is now under the authority of Coalition Security."

Inspector MacDuff stepped forward, challenging the intruders.

"Who are you? What are you doing here?" MacDuff's voice tinged with frustration.

"Inquisitor Keller, United Coalition of Earth Security," the lead man introduced himself, his tone polite but unwavering. "I appreciate the work you have done, Inspector. This scene is under our control. You can return to your normal duties."

The tension escalated as the Inspector's phone rang, the shrill sound cutting through the room. His expression shifted from frustration to a mix of anger and disbelief.

MacDuff hung up the call and glared at the Security agent, his eyes filled with intensity. He turned to his team and ordered them to leave.

Megan rose and cried out; her voice dripped with irritation. "This is my home, and someone has murdered my father. You have no right to burst in here!"

"I'm sorry, but we are the Coalition. We have determined this is a global matter. We will return your home to you after completing our investigation."

The Inspector approached Megan. "Doctor McCord, let's step outside, shall we?"

Megan's face hardened, but after a moment of consideration, she said, "Fine, let's go. I will make some calls and sort this out."

Inquisitor Keller bowed slightly. "Of course, do what you must."

While leaving with Inspector MacDuff, Megan received a strange message on her smart glasses.

Trust no one and watch for hidden agendas. Coalition Security is not Inquisitor Keller's only employer.

"Doctor, I don't think we need to review your statement anymore. You have my condolences. Take some time for yourself. A trip to allow yourself to grieve seems like a good idea to me," MacDuff said as he handed her back her cuff computer.

"You won't tell me I need to stay in the area like they do in the movies?"

"*I* won't be the one to tell you, and I didn't hear anyone else tell you either." He glanced at the entrance to Primrose estate and Inquisitor Keller inside. The inspector walked away to join his officers.

Megan got in her car and drove several kilometers until she realized she had nowhere to go. Her maternal grandparents lived in the highlands. Too far to drive at nearly midnight. Megan's old school roommate, Emily, was back home in England, and Megan didn't want to pull Emily into her problems.

She opened the car's roof and spoke to the stars. "I'm frightened. Some devious plot even bigger than Daddy's murder is going on. I feel it in my soul. Why would Coalition Security be involved?"

Of course, the stars didn't answer, but Megan's cuff computer received a new text message from an unknown source.

We know you have Stonington's logs. Give us the location and live. If not, you will be gutted like your father. The police can't help you, and Coalition is in our pocket. Send the information, and you can walk away. A link to a dark web file drop accompanied the message.

The message also showed an image of a long-curved knife with a gut hook on the spine. Someone laser etched the words *Megan McCord* on the blade. Megan's stomach twisted with the implication.

"I don't have the information. Dad had it on his desk. The killer must have it." She made a connection to the estate. "Prissy, did dad store the decoded Stonington files on your systems."

"I'm sorry, Doctor. He did not. He only said it would be safe so you could succeed in your quest."

"My quest? I planned to research some ten-year-old records, not make a grand odyssey."

"Your father was a romantic. He loved epic stories, and he loved you. He personally loaded your equipment in the vehicle. Would you like me to play a message he left for you?"

Megan's eyes went wide. "Play it. Play it now."

A holo image of Roger McCord appeared. "Megan, I asked Prissy to deliver this when you are on the shuttle. I wanted to make one simple statement, I know you are nervous, but you can do this. This is your destiny. I love you now and forever. You are the light in my heart. Go and make me proud."

A tear rolled down Megan's cheek. "Prissy, book me on a different shuttle. I need to find a new ship scheduled for Jupiter."

Inspector Owen MacDuff stood in front of the Chief Constable of Police Scotland in her office in Tulliallan Castle. MacDuff had never before met privately with the Chief Constable.

Inquisitor Keller sat nearby, sipping coffee silently, so it might not have been considered a *private* meeting.

"The Inquisitor tells me you allowed Megan McCord to leave the area after her father's murder. Why didn't you detain her?" Chief Constable Morag Stewart asked.

"Yes. The poor girl lost her father. She needed time to grieve. I took her statement and saw no need to detain her," MacDuff said.

"The Inquisitor believes she is the logical suspect." The chief furrowed her brows in annoyance at Keller. Keller continued to sip coffee and didn't react to the chief's stare. "She is Roger McCord's sole heir and had the means to disable the household AI system."

"Her vehicle showed she was traveling when the AI went offline. Also, Roger McCord possessed a heart monitor prescribed by his doctor. This monitor showed his heart stopped before she arrived."

"Regardless, I am requesting a person of interest warrant for Doctor Megan McCord. Inquisitor Keller has *graciously* offered Coalition Security's aid to track her down. You are dismissed, Inspector." Another glare of disdain in Keller's direction showed how she felt about interference in her territory. The fact she couldn't stop the intrusion showed the power of Coalition Security.

Keller lifted his coffee cup in a silent salute as the Inspector walked out with a smile of the victor on his face.

Outside the office, MacDuff sent a message from his personal comm-pad. *Danger increasing. Suggest other assets to aid McCord while we can.*

2
Meeting New Friends

July 24, 2155—Earth Orbit Space Station Three

Megan sat on the hotel bed with her knees to her chin. She rocked back and forth with her arms wrapped around her knees. With trembling hands, she flipped open the holo locket built into her mother's pendant. The holo-projector displayed an image of her parents looking young and happy. A tear rolled down Megan's cheek, the salty droplet left behind a glistening trail on her porcelain skin.

A day before, Megan had been thrilled to be on a solo adventure. Now, she felt more alone than ever. Her family was gone, and her friends were left behind. She had no idea how she would charter a ship in time. The killer escaped and could hunt her down at any moment.

She glanced around the ordinary little hotel room—a plain bed with rough sheets, a hard chair, and a small bathroom. The dull beige walls and plain blue blanket perfectly matched her somber mood.

Such a drab place, she thought. *No, that's not fair. This is a simple and average room.* Megan had never stayed in any room besides a suite before. She was ashamed to admit that she longed for the luxuries she had grown accustomed to.

Megan examined the hologram of her parents dancing at their wedding. The holo flickered strangely when it looped to the beginning. The file size of the holo was much larger than it should have been, causing it to hesitate when loading. A file embedded in the image opened at her command. All of the research related to Hunter's Folly appeared in the air. The killer had not stolen it. *Daddy, thank you. You always knew how to plan ahead.*

Her father's forethought filled her with determination. She would secure passage on a ship and solve the mystery. If her father's killer wanted Hunter's Folly, she would find it first and, with it, find them. *I won't let you down, Daddy. I'll make you proud.*

Upon reaching the ground level, Megan realized she still did not know where to find a ship to charter. Her family owned a shipping company, and hiring a third-party ship never occurred to her. She went into the hotel bar to get a drink to calm her nerves and think of a solution.

Megan ordered wine instead of scotch, which she preferred, but it was essential to keep her wits now. Every few seconds, she glanced about at the other patrons, grateful for a thin afternoon crowd.

"Miss, you look nervous. Are you in trouble? Maybe I can help." A stocky man in a well-cut suit sat on the stool next to Megan. He had been talking to a woman a few stools away.

"Oh heavens no. A little flustered, is all. It's my first trip off old Mother Earth," Megan drawled in an exaggerated American southern accent in the hopes to hide her identity.

"Really? Well, no need to worry. Station Three is safe. If you are worried, I do private security. My name is Axel Vega." The rich softness in his voice displayed an earnest worry.

"Delighted to meet you. I'm Emily Spencer, straight from the heart of Savanna Georgia. I ventured up here for a conference. Bless your heart, but I reckon they have the security buttoned up real tight," Megan smiled at the nice man but hoped he would leave. She stole the name of an aristocratic English friend, who was about as far from a southern belle as a woman could be.

The woman he had been speaking with came over and wrapped her arm around him. "Axel, darlin, time is money. You're wasting it talking to this one."

"Kandi, this lady just looked like she needed some help. I'm being a gentleman."

Kandi chuckled, and the two women studied each other. The age lines framed Kandi's eyes and mouth, while the low-cut dress and makeup would be more appropriate for a woman thirty years younger at a nightclub. Her poorly dyed red hair paled next to Megan's natural locks.

"I charge extra for three, especially with an amateur," Kandi's eyes narrowed at Megan. "Or are you an amateur? You could be a high-end girl trying to steal a real working girl's clients."

Megan's eyes went wide. "What? No. I think I need tae go. Please excuse me."

She got up and retreated to the safe solitude of her room, but she didn't realize she had let her accent slip at the end.

The casual walk she intended turned into a hurried dash from the bar to the lift as nerves took over from reason. The slow hotel lift gave her a moment to decide paranoia got the best of her.

As Megan entered her room, a large hand thumped on the door to prevent it from closing. The matching mitt pushed Megan into the room. She stumbled with the force but caught herself from falling. She spun around to see Axel Vega slamming the door to her room closed.

"Hello 'Emily,' I think you are the girl I'm looking for."

Megan's eyes danced around for an escape. The hotel room had a video screen instead of a terrestrial window. Axel blocked the exit and towered over Megan in both height and bulk. She narrowed her eyes and reverted to her self-defense training.

With a loud shout, Megan snapped a kick with all her might. Her almost perfect aim delivered a blow to his nether regions. Instead of the ball of her foot hitting as she had planned, her toes struck first.

An acute spike of pain went through her foot. It felt like stubbing a toe on a heavy object. This time, she stumbled and fell.

"Nice try, Doctor. I learned long ago against that particular attack. My pants go rigid when a blow is coming. An auto-cup. Like I said, I need to take you."

"Ye bastard. Dinnae expect me tae just let ye force yersel' on me," Megan said in a voice laced with venom and spite. During times of stress, Megan lost her refined accent. She slipped into a thick highland brogue learned from her maternal grandfather.

Axel stepped back in surprise. "What? No. I'm not a rapist. I'm a bounty hunter. There is a large private bounty on you."

Megan deflated a bit but knew the danger was not gone. Just changed. "You called me Doctor just now."

"Yeah, Doctor Megan McCord. A redhead Scottish woman on the run who someone wants back. An aristocrat, too. What did you do? Run off with a local farm boy?" He loomed over her as she lay on the floor next to the bed. She held one hand in front of her and the other under the bed.

"Know what? I don't care. I need to deliver you safe. No funny business from you." Axel grabbed her arm under the bed. He yanked her to her feet by the arm.

In her hand, she held the Sgian Dubh knife her father gave her at her graduation. The knife blended her Scottish heritage with her future. A small oval artifact with a fractal design capped the knife's carved bog-oak handle. The hunter Fred Stonington once wore that same oval Artifact as a necklace.

"Good instinct, but I can't let you play with sharp objects." He squeezed her arm hard and smiled.

Megan yelped in pain and dropped the knife. When he lessened his grip, she scowled in a fury and jabbed out with her free hand. His reaction was not fast enough to block her fast punch. He let go of her and stumbled back a few steps, holding a hand to his face.

A grimace crossed his face. "I tried to be nice, but you are coming with me."

He balled his fists and stomped forward. A loud buzz and flash came from behind him. His eyes glazed over, and he fell onto the bed.

Behind him was Kandi. She held a small object about the size of a lipstick tube.

"Hi, Honey, you look like you could use a friend."

Megan looked about in confusion. "What happened? He just fell."

"Compact neuro-stunner. Only two shots, but an essential for any safe hooker." Kandi held up the tube and tucked it into her shirt between her breasts. She pushed Axel onto the floor and sat on the bed, then patted the bed for Megan to sit.

"Sorry if I came off rude earlier."

"Why did you help me?" Megan asked as she sat down.

"Because you needed help. Whatever you are running from, it is your right to run. In my profession, you need to be a good judge of character, and you're not a criminal. Just scared."

"Thank you, Kandi."

"My real name is Jessica. What's yours? Your lovely Scottish accent tells me you are not Emily, the southern belle from Savannah." She put her arm around Megan's shoulders.

"Megan." She leaned into the older woman. A bit of genuine kindness was welcomed.

"Beautiful name. Tell me where you are running to. You don't need to say why, but I know people who might be able to help."

"I'd planned to go to Titan. It's a moon of Saturn." Megan was not trusting enough yet to reveal her actual destination.

"Oh, I know it's a moon of Saturn. Unfortunately, I don't know anyone going there. Too bad your destination is not Jupiter. I know a ship headed to the moon Callisto in the morning."

Megan's eyes opened wide, but then she tried to control her expression. Callisto was the last place Stonington was seen and where she would start her investigation.

"Callisto shall work. I must get away. What is the name of the ship?" She decided keeping up the unintentional runaway rich girl ruse might help.

"Sure, Red. It's the *Elizabeth*. Her captain is Adrian Kostas. I've met him, although unfortunately not professionally. He is a good man. Give him a call, and I'm sure you can book a passage."

"Thank you. What about Axel? When will he wake up?"

"In about an hour. The zap from this stunner is strong, but obviously, you can't stay here."

Megan smiled. "I have an idea. When he wakes, can you tell him you saw me on my way to the shuttle bay?"

"Sure."

Megan pulled up a shuttle schedule and bought a ticket for the next shuttle. A flight to Luna station left in less than an hour. She then sent a message to *Elizabeth* requesting a meeting to discuss the passage.

"Clever, Red. You still can't stay in this room. Axel already reported to his contacts that you were spotted. Looks like I've lost my date for the night. I have a couch you can sleep on if you want. I assure you no one will know where you are."

"Thank you. I'll take you up on that." Megan didn't relish the idea of sleeping on someone's settee, but it was better than being on the run all night.

"Fantastic. My rates are normally two hundred an hour, but I will give you a special of one thousand for the entire night." Jessica grinned as Megan's mouth opened in shock.

"One thousand for a night on a settee?"

"I need to make a living. As I said, I lost my date for the night. You would pay for the time, so you're welcome to share my bed. I'm a full-service provider. Plus, I saw you drop two grand on a last-minute first-class ticket you don't intend to use. I bet you can afford it."

Megan agreed she could afford it, and buying first-class was a waste. The idea of buying anything less than a first-class ticket never occurred to her.

A message came from the ship captain, Adrian Kostas, offering to meet her to discuss booking passage. He sent a location.

"Looks like you have a date of your own. Call me if you need a place to sleep. Adrian has a bit of a reputation. He might offer you his bed to share. I won't judge. I'd give him a freebie in a heartbeat," Jessica said.

3
Travel Negotiations

July 24, 2155—Earth Orbit Space Station Three

The door to the meeting location had only a number, not a name. Megan stepped through the nondescript door and found a surprising sight. The nostalgic scent of peaty whiskey and a real wood fire wafted through the air. The tavern's design spoke of traditional craftsmanship. It portrayed a time when wood and stone were common building materials. The room had tall, oval-shaped ceilings supported by giant pillars created from logs. On the interior side of the doorway, an archway of smooth alabaster stone framed the door. The arch's surface almost glowed in the firelight.

The centerpiece was a sunken lounge surrounding a fire pit. It radiated comforting warmth from within a circle of high-backed chairs. Megan had never seen such a realistic holographic fire. Anyplace other than a space station, Megan would be confident it was a real fire.

She never imagined finding such a rustic old tavern here amidst the sleek metal and plastic of the space station. Its presence here defied all logic.

Perched on the polished counter of the bar sat a tall woman with long braided hair in pink and blonde streaks. Sleek black leggings clung to her legs, ending in sturdy boots and a fitted tank top. A name tag introduced her as Angelica.

With a graceful hop, she descended from the bar and greeted Megan with a warm embrace as if they were childhood friends. "Hi there. I'm Angie," she said, her voice resonating with a captivating blend of mystery and familiarity.

"Welcome to my Tavern. Don't be shy. We're a friendly bunch here," Angelica handed Megan a glass of wine. "This wine will suit your taste. A sweet Crimean muscat."

I didn't get to see a wine list, Megan thought. She sipped it and didn't complain. The wine tasted fantastic. Sweet and chilled perfectly.

"Hakim, we have a new guest. Find her the perfect spot, won't you?" Angelica wrapped an arm around Megan's shoulder and swept the other arm in a wide arc as she led Megan deeper into the Tavern.

A distinguished man with a trimmed gray beard, dressed in a tailored suit, approached Megan. Hakim's eyes hinted at a lifetime of diverse experiences.

"Welcome, my dear. You honor us with your presence. Please, follow me," Hakim said politely in a crisp but undefinable accent. He took Megan to a seat in the lounge by the fire.

Megan took a sip of her wine, her hand trembling as she reached into her purse to grip the sgian-dubh knife her father gifted her. She pulled out a mirror to check herself. No matter how often Emily and her father called her beautiful, she couldn't help but think of herself as homely.

Megan closed her eyes, allowing the fire's heat and familiar scents to sooth and lull her into a peaceful trance while she waited.

Adrian Kostas, captain of the light freighter *Elizabeth*, strolled through the alabaster arch at the entrance. Far from a roguish space cowboy many expected from an independent spaceship captain, Adrian wore a professional ship uniform with a prominent ship logo on his tunic. A long scar across his square jaw was the only testament to his adventures.

"Adrian, darling, it's always a delight to see you. You get more handsome every time I see you." Angelica sauntered over to give Adrian a kiss on each cheek in greeting.

"Angie, always a pleasure," Adrian said, the corner of his mouth lifting in a playful smirk. His tone carried a hint of jest. "You also say that to every man who comes in here."

She leaned in closer, her voice dropping to a teasing whisper. "Not every man, just most, but with you, I mean it," she winked.

Angelica wrapped her arm around his waist and tilted her head toward Megan, her voice playful, "Come with me. A certain lady has been waiting for you."

Angelica led Adrian to the lounge, breaking Megan from her trance.

"I will make introductions. Doctor Megan McCord, this is Captain Adrian Kostas. I wish you both success in your business," Angelica said.

Megan stood to shake Adrian's hand but could not help but glance at Angelica with raised eyebrows. *When did I tell her my name?*

Angelica touched both their shoulders as they shook and winked at Megan. "Don't worry about it."

A tingling sensation of warmth went into Megan. Though she didn't know why, she put the issue from her mind.

Adrian and Megan examined each other while shaking hands. Both their expectations failed to meet reality.

Megan expected a grizzled gray-haired captain like most Ettrick Logistics skippers. Adrian had brown hair with just a touch of gray. He appeared young, even for an independent ship captain. Megan guessed the captain was only a few years older than she was. It indicated he was competent, lucky, or a trust fund kid rewarded by nepotism. Megan ironically feared the last, but she proved you could be a trust fund brat and capable.

Adrian imagined a bookish, middle-aged academic. Instead, he shook hands with a vibrant redhead younger than him. Her round wire-rim glasses, unusual in this century, marked her with a scholarly air despite her youth. Adrian wondered if they were a rare necessary vision correction or a style choice.

Her stylishly tailored outfit hinted at a life of privilege. A tramp freighter like *Elizabeth* didn't offer the luxurious transportation Adrian assumed she anticipated.

They sat in the comfortable chairs by the fire. The warm glow of the flames lit Megan's hair in a beautiful light and caused Adrian's eyes to twinkle. Hakim delivered a beer.

"Nice to meet you, Doctor. Your message said you needed a ride to Callisto, and we are going that way. I want to make it clear we are not a passenger liner. You will have a small cabin and meals in the crew galley. No fancy dining rooms or stewards."

Megan sucked in her breath. She felt insulted, and he assumed she could not handle life on a ship. After all, her father ran a major shipping company. She could buy his freighter out of her trust fund.

"I assure you, Captain, I am quite capable of managing. I'm an exo-archaeologist and have been on numerous digs on Earth and asteroid habitats. If I can handle sharing bunks with fellow graduate students, I daresay I can handle a cabin on a freighter." Her posture stiffened, and her voice cooled, betraying her irritation at his doubt.

"Of course, Doctor. We can do much better than bunk beds. The cabins are comfortable but small. I think the worst thing you will face is when it is my turn to cook dinner. After one of my casseroles, the last passenger wanted to be let off in deep space."

Her expression softened after his self-deprecating joke, and she smiled. She closed her eyes for a moment and thought about her own words. The staterooms she stayed in were owners' suites, and they did have stewards. The bunking with grad students was a one-time occurrence. She usually stayed in hotel suites. She felt a bit ashamed and tried to change her spoiled rich girl behavior.

"Captain, please call me Megan. I'm still getting used to being addressed as a Doctor. I've just earned my PhD. My grandpa says, 'The ink ain't dry on the sheepskin.'" She lifted her wine to take a sip.

"Then I'm Adrian. Even my crew forgets to call me Captain. The trip will be more fun if we keep it casual." He lifted his beer and held it out. They clinked glasses as a toast to settled differences.

"Can you tell me about your plans?"

Megan couldn't tell him everything, but Adrian's natural charm led her to give him some half-truths.

"I have some hints on the location of an unknown Artificer site. It is mostly a research trip, but if it pans out, I will find the information I want most in the world." Megan could not admit what she wanted most was to find the killer, get justice for her father, and prevent them from acquiring the Artificer's secrets.

She leaned in close and spoke in a whisper. "I do ask for discretion. Archaeologists and artifact hunters prefer to keep our secrets close to the vest."

The knowing look in his eyes conveyed he understood she left a lot unsaid. He stayed silent while considering his options.

Megan looked down at her glass and took another sip of her wine. Without looking up and a subtle tremble in her voice, she said, "When can we depart, Captain?"

A concerned look appeared on Adrian's face. Her urgent tone was too obvious. Adrian took a deep breath and reached a decision.

"My crew is prepping to leave. Supplies will be loaded by morning. Send me the payment and meet me at dock

5C in the morning, and we will depart. Until then, enjoy a fantastic meal here."

She transferred the payment to him from her cuff computer. "How can I view the menu? I don't even know the name of this place."

"Oh, that's not how the Tavern works. They always know what will be perfect for your mood. Trust me, whatever Esperanza brings you will be superb." Adrian rose as Hakim approached.

"Ma'am, I have a lovely private booth for you to dine."

"You're not staying for dinner?" Megan asked Adrian.

"I'm sorry, Megan, but I am meeting a date here in a few minutes. Hakim will take care of you. I will see you in the morning." Adrian gave her a very businesslike handshake.

Megan's shoulders slumped ever so slightly as a shadow of disappointment crossed her face. Without realizing it, she compared him to Sergio. Sergio's looks and charisma were undeniable, but Adrian had an authenticity she couldn't ignore.

Megan, why are you even thinking like this? Daddy was killed yesterday. It's not time to think about men, she scolded herself. Hakim led her to the booth and acquired a fresh glass of wine.

An elderly woman, Esperanza, appeared with a covered plate after Megan took her seat in the booth. The lady smiled at Megan with the genuine warmth of a grandmother. She passed the plates to Hakim, spoke in Spanish, smiled, and vanished into the kitchen to work on her next culinary miracle.

"For the lady, sarburma, traditional Crimean meat pie, and a side of dolma," Hakim said and left her alone. As Megan took a bite of the unfamiliar dish, she savored the explosion of flavors on her taste buds.

While Megan relished the meal's flavors, Adrian studied her from the bar and pondered where this trip would take him.

The door to the Tavern opened, and the woman who entered drew everyone's eyes. Adrian's date had arrived. The blonde woman of blended heritage wore a stunning red dress.

"I see why he ditched my plain face," Megan whispered. She thought no one could hear, but Hakim frowned in disapproval nearby.

Hakim stepped away and returned with a small vase and three roses. He placed it on her table.

"My dear, these are for you to enjoy as a welcome to the Tavern." He pointed to each rose in turn. "A green to celebrate your life. A pink to honor your elegance and refinement. Last, a blue, representing the mysteries and adventure before you."

With a tear in her eye, Megan touched Hakim's hand. "Thank you. You have no idea how much this means to me."

4

The Lioness' Mating Dance

Commander Kristina Chen-Ramirez was the captain of the Customs and Patrol ship *Zeta Sierra*. She had an entire crew to chase suspects. Yet somehow, here she was, running through maintenance tunnels, chasing a pair of criminals.

These dumb criminals thought distilling moonshine on a space station was a good idea. Then, they tried to sell it and smuggle it to other stations. That attracted the attention of the Customs and Patrol Service. The homemade still bursting into flames got her running after two of the fools.

Why make moonshine, of all things? Booze is available in any liquor store. Kristina thought. The answer was age-old. The United Coalition of Earth government heavily taxed liquor on space stations. No one in history wanted to pay taxes, so this group planned to cut out the tax person and make some extra cash selling to others who wanted cheap booze. The fact it was higher proof than anything else sold on the station helped market the illegal hooch.

Fueled by desperation and stupidity, the suspects raced through the remote passage. Kristina ran after them, her determination overriding her burning muscles.

She rounded a corner and smiled at the sight before her. The morons had stumbled to a dead end. Sweat beaded on their foreheads, their gazes flicking from shadow to shadow in a desperate search for escape.

Both men looked a little unsteady on their feet, the result of tasting their own wares. One was large, flabby, and bald. His fists were massive, balled-up slabs. Kristina mentally labeled him Fat Fool. The other wore a formerly white jacket, now scorched black from the fire. He also carried a cheap steak knife as a weapon. He became a Blackened Bozo in Kristina's mind.

She smiled and thought, *this might be fun, but let's see if they will see reason.*

"CPS. You're under arrest. It's the end of the line, boys. Nowhere else to run. Lie down, face first, and make it easy yourselves."

Blackened Bozo lunged at her. Kristina sidestepped with lightning speed as her training kicked in. A swift punch to the gut caused him to sprawl onto the ground and gasp for air.

Fat Fool grabbed Kristina from behind and squeezed tight. He was faster than his bulk implied. His rank breath on her neck. His arms were as strong as his breath.

"Take a breath, mint." She snapped her head back in a head but. The man grunted but didn't let go. The rotgut he drank caused him to feel no pain. She solved that problem.

Blackened Bozo rose and stepped forward to stab her. Kristina used Fat Fool's grip to her advantage and lifted both legs. With a massive two-leg kick, she sent Blackened Bozo flying back into an overhead pipe, hitting his head. He fell in a heap.

The momentum sent Kristina and her new companion into the wall. An elbow in the gut knocked the breath out of him. With a single sweep of the legs, the man crashed down to the ground.

Gasping for breath, Kristina stood tall, allowing herself a moment of triumph. Her blonde hair came loose from her not-quite-regulation ponytail to fall in her face, but she still showed her euphoria after the chase.

A slow clap resonated from behind her. Warrant Officer Phillips walked up, not breathing hard. He glanced at the two men on the ground and said, "You know, you could have simply stunned them."

Kristina pulled a neuro-stunner out of her holster. "No, that would've been cheating. What happened to you? Took your time getting here."

"You're too fast for an old man like me to keep up with, Skipper." Phillips was twenty years older than her but was in better physical shape than most of the younger crew. He tried to mentor his young commander. She rose fast in the ranks by being by the book and dedicated, but sometimes, in action, she tended to be impulsive. His subtle question about stunning was a teaching moment. He hoped to teach her caution and forethought before a more capable opponent taught her the hard way.

A few other agents approached and restrained the two criminals.

The pungent odor of smoke assaulted Kristina's nostrils. It reminded her of the burning still. "What happened at the still?"

"The fire is under control. Two more geniuses were hospitalized due to smoke inhalation. No injuries to our people."

"Good, let's get the two into lockup and start collecting evidence—" Kristina pulled out evidence collection gloves when Phillips interrupted her.

"Skipper, don't you have plans for the evening? We can take care of the cleanup."

"Thanks. I need to hurry back and change." Grateful for the reminder, she turned and jogged toward the ship.

As she departed, Phillips called out, his words laced with amusement. "Don't forget to shower. He will appreciate it."

The single finger hand signal she flashed as she walked away told him what she thought of the comment. He smiled, knowing she would not make such a display to a subordinate she did not trust completely.

Phillips returned to the ship half an hour later and spoke to Lieutenant Frank Davenport, the patrol craft's executive officer, when their captain emerged from her cabin. She transformed from a dedicated officer into a stunning woman off to enjoy the evening.

"Gentlemen, I assume you will have everything under control for the evening? Remember, we leave in the morning," Kristina asked.

"We'll take care of everything, Captain. Enjoy your evening," Davenport said.

Phillips smirked at his captain. "Enjoy yourself, but don't behave yourself, Skipper."

"Oh, I have no intention of behaving. Don't wait up for me." Kristina strutted forward, her eager energy on display.

Phillips leaned closer to Lieutenant Davenport. "I almost feel sorry for her date. After her chase, she has so much energy I don't think he can keep up."

Kristina sashayed across the station with confident strides and a radiant smile. The admiring stares from both men and women only fueled her delight as she reveled in the attention she received. She dressed not to impress her date but for her own pleasure. What woman doesn't enjoy getting dressed to the nines and feeling glamorous occasionally? Driving Adrian Kostas wild was a pleasant side benefit.

The stalwart officer swapped her crisp patrol uniform for a traditional Chinese cheongsam dress in red silk. A gift from her mother on her last trip home to Hong Kong and a subtle wish for Kristina to date more. Her Chinese mother could be very traditional for a Vice President of international trade married to a Mexican man.

An antique Mexican hair clip secured Kristina's signature blonde ponytail. The hair clip was a gift from her grandmother, and the blonde hair came from a distant Norwegian ancestor. Her normally plain face became exceptional with the skillful application of makeup.

The childhood insecurities Kristina felt over her differences were long gone. Now, she was a confident multicultural woman of the 22nd century. Tonight, she exuded an elegant, feminine energy different from her usual commanding presence.

Kristina stepped into the Tavern and marveled again at the classic elegance of the wood and stone architecture. She took a deep breath to savor the hearty aroma of the fire and the ancient oak construction.

Adrian sat in the warm glow of the fire, but before Kristina could join him, Angelica intercepted her.

"Kristina, you look even more ravishing than usual. I'm jealous Adrian has you all to himself." Angelica stroked Kristina's hair and kissed her on the lips. Kristina knew Angelica always greeted her guests warmly but never to a level they would find uncomfortable. Kristina secretly enjoyed the kiss.

"Angie, are you trying to embarrass me or make Adrian jealous?" Kristina asked with a frisky smile and a glance at her date.

"Both, if possible." Angelica winked and wrapped her arm around Kristina's waist as she led her to Adrian.

Adrian rose at the women's approach. Angelica pushed the two lovers together and winked.

"Have fun, you two. Wish I had time to join."

"She always ramps her flirting up to ten when we are here together," Adrian said.

"As opposed to the eight or nine, she's at most days. Now shut up and kiss me." Kristina pulled him in close with a deep, passionate kiss.

Kristina broke the kiss and asked, "How do I look, Adrian?"

"I agree with Angie. Absolutely stunning. Otherwise, I have no words to describe your beauty." He gazed into the eyes of his too-infrequent lover. "I'm happy you were able to make it. Tonight will probably be the only opportunity we have to get together. I leave for Jupiter in the morning."

"We start a patrol in the morning. We will have to make the best of tonight, won't we?"

Adrian was among the select few to see the adorable, crooked smile Kristina only produced when out of uniform, untroubled, and content.

"As you please, Commander Chen-Ramirez." Adrian presented her with a coy smile of his own.

"No need for the rank, Adrian. Just concentrate on the pleasing part." A mischievous glint in Kristina's eye, her words dripping with implication.

"Our patrol will take us to Jupiter, but we stop at Ceres first. It's almost directly between Earth and Jupiter right now. I imagine you will move on before we get there." Kristina sat in a lounge chair next to Adrian. The same chair Megan was in minutes before.

"Cargo vessels don't make money by sitting in one place, but I have a passenger who seems in over her head. Her research might take her to a few of the Jovian moons. We can be flexible in our destinations and make a profit. Sooner or later, she will meet someone unsavory."

Kristina raised a curious eyebrow over the passenger Adrian planned to follow around. Before she could ask, they were interrupted.

Hakim carried a tray holding two glasses with a taste of dark liqueur.

"An excellent Mexican Tequila for the lady and gentleman, a Metaxa special reserve from Greece. Esperanza will bring an appetizer soon." He bowed slightly and walked away.

Esperanza, the Tavern's culinary artist, exited the kitchen with a tray of oysters. When she handed it to Hakim, Kristina stood to greet the elderly Mexican chef. They spoke in Spanish, and Kristina returned to her seat after hugging the diminutive woman.

Kristina smiled warmly. "She reminds me of my own Abuela. That's grandmother to you ignorant Americans."

"I'm half Greek."

"Your entire life was either in Orlando or on a spaceship," Kristina stated, allowing no argument.

Kristina and Adrian sat quietly for a few minutes, slowly sipping their drinks and eating oysters. The soothing ambiance of the fireplace filled them with a deep sense of gratification.

"Tell me about this passenger," Kristina asked. Her tone was closer to the questioning authority of a CPS officer than date small talk.

"We are taking a scientist on an artifact hunt. She says it's a research trip, but I know a Hunt when I see one. She is an exo-archeologist not long out of school."

"Watch out, Adrian. Trafficking artifacts without permits will result in heavy fines and potential seizure of *Elizabeth*. She is far too pretty a lady to be sold at auction."

"My passenger has all the proper paperwork. She sent a copy of the permit, approved a month ago."

Thoughts swirled in Kristina's head. Her mouth opened slightly, words ready to escape, but she closed it again. She knew the information bordered on confidentiality. Whether to tell Adrian or not conflicted with her.

Before she could decide, Hakim approached and said, "Please follow me, and I'll seat you for dinner."

Hakim led Adrian and Kristina to a cozy booth made of live-edge oak, giving off a forest-like atmosphere. She ran her hand over the smooth table surface to experience the earthy and smokey essence in the wood's natural curves. They settled onto the buttery-textured leather bench. The booth felt timeless and romantic.

The soup course was served. Adrian was presented with a warm New England Clam Chowder bowl while they graced Kristina with a Norwegian fish soup. They tasted each other's soups from the other's spoon. They shared laughter as Adrian spilled soup on his clean jacket.

Hakim brought the couple wine before the main course, a French Chablis for her and a Welsh Rose for him.

A serious look appeared on Kristina's face as they sipped their wine. She came to a decision. She would not withhold information from a man she cared about, even if it stepped on the line.

"Adrian, I shouldn't be telling you this. We have reports of an organized group backing a resurgence in artifact smuggling. Known killers are linked to the group. Now is not the time to be involved in Artifacts."

Adrian took her hand and kissed it. "I trust you, and I trust my crew. Everyone else gets my full skepticism."

Kristina's playful, sweetheart face returned. She reached across the table and caressed a scar on his face.

"I've seen you fall for a pretty face with an artifact before. Remember how you got this scar?"

Adrian continued to caress her hand. "Totally worth it. That was the day I met you."

"I plan to check out this archeologist's paperwork. Con artists have disguised themselves as academics before. What's her name?" Kristina's words cut through the air with unmistakable authority.

"Her name is Doctor Megan McCord." His eyes shifted to the side to see Megan leave. He knew Kristina was not prone to jealousy. Still, he felt it unwise to point out a beautiful woman he just had drinks with to the beautiful woman he was having dinner with. His glance did not escape the notice of the trained CPS officer.

"Be careful, Adrian." Kristina's words had dual meanings. Be careful when trusting his new passenger and looking at another woman while on a date. Kristina didn't know they were the same woman.

"I'm always careful, Kristina. You don't have to worry about me."

Hakim brought them their dinner dish.

"The gentleman will dine on another New England favorite, Maine Lobster served with steamed asparagus. We have prepared the lady's classic Hong Kong dish, Hairy Crab, with stir-fried bean sprouts. Your Chablis will pair beautifully with it."

"Oh my god. I haven't had that in years," Kristina said. "How is it possible? Hairy crab isn't in season in July."

"Esperanza never reveals her secrets." Hakim tried to step away, but Kristina stopped him long enough to kiss his cheek.

"Share that with Esperanza for me."

Adrian and Kristina relished their meals. Once again, feeding the other little morsels. They would remember this heavenly meal for years.

Hakim approached again and said, "I hope your meal with us tonight has been satisfactory."

Kristina dabbed her napkin on her lips before dropping it to the plate. "Oh yes, completely. It was fantastic."

Adrian was a little confused. "This is where you normally bring us dessert."

Hakim glanced at Kristina and then addressed Adrian's question with a smirk. "We aim to present the dishes our patrons need, yet certain desserts, it seems, are beyond our ability to provide."

Adrian shifted his gaze to Kristina. Her eyes smoldered with an intense, predatory hunger reminiscent of a lioness fixated on her prize.

"Hakim has a point. I have a special dessert in mind back in my cabin."

Adrian's pulse quickened at the promise in her stare. Kristina trailed a stockinged foot up Adrian's leg beneath the table. Her toes traced swirling patterns on his thigh while her eyes enticed him.

With a sultry gaze, she rose gracefully, her fingers entwined with his. With a tantalizing tug, she led him toward the doorway, leaving the world behind.

The next morning

Together, they filled the memorable night with passion, but when morning came, they both had duties to perform.

"Wake up, you dirty old pirate. It's time for duty," the blonde commander teased, her eyes twinkling with mirth. She caressed his arms and exited the bed to pull on her uniform.

"Pirate? I take offense. No eye patches or peg legs here."

"How about dirty smuggler?" Kristina regretted the jab immediately.

A worry of Kristina's had long been that Adrian might cross a line with smuggling artifacts. She heard rumors of shady deals during Adrian's grandfather's time as captain of the *Elizabeth*. Profit margins were slim on small ships. The temptation for an easy score was difficult to resist.

"Our cargo is always legitimate. The only dirty thing is my thoughts involving you."

After swatting away a few playful advances, Kristina walked to her small closet, providing Adrian a view to remember.

"Well, Captain Kostas, I mean this with the greatest affection and tenderness.... get out."

"Next time, come to the *Elizabeth*. I want to be your host for a change."

The invitation hung in the air. Kristina always hesitated to go to Adrian's home. It would make the relationship too real. With a deep breath, indecision transformed into resolution. She paused, a hesitation flickering across her face. With a soft, almost imperceptible nod, she said, "Okay."

She shook off her timidness and switched back to a professional stance.

"This ship goes on duty in an hour. If you're still on board, I think I must hang you from the yardarm." Kristina finished buttoning her fresh uniform.

"They don't hang people anymore. It's a more enlightened time. And hanging in microgravity is kind of pointless." Adrian, dressed in his wrinkled clothing, picked off the floor.

She opened the door and saw Phillips. "Ahh, Mr. Phillips, I need someone to take out the trash. I mean, please escort Captain Kostas to the docking port. I'll be on the bridge."

Kristina kissed Adrian passionately, etching the night in both their memories. Neither knew when their paths would cross again. "Stay out of trouble, Adrian. Until we meet again."

Lieutenant Commander Chen-Ramirez walked away without a word, leaving Adrian stunned.

Phillips smiled. "Adrian Kostas—speechless? The skipper deserves a medal for this."

A few hours later

As Kristina and her crew prepared the *Zeta Sierra* for departure, she remembered something she had neglected to do.

I hope Adrian knew I was serious about checking on his passenger, Kristina thought. *I should trust him more, but I must do my duty. His small ship is what smugglers would want to stay hidden.*

She turned to her executive officer, Frank Davenport. "Frank, before we depart, file a request with headquarters. I want a background check on Doctor Megan McCord. She registered for an artifact hunting permit and is traveling on the *Elizabeth*. Destination one of the moons of Jupiter," Kristina asked.

"Yes, sir. Is Captain Kostas in trouble again?"

"A hunch right now. Probably nothing."

"Want me to make it a priority? HQ might want to delay our departure."

"No, use routine priority. Like I said, no big deal."

5

Elizabethan tour

July 25, 2155—Earth Orbit Space Station Three

Megan and Jessica shared a delightful evening. Despite the vast gulf in social standing between the aristocrat and the prostitute, they laughed like girlfriends while they told fun stories. A half bottle of Scotch encouraged Megan to share about her father and his loss. Jessica, in turn, shared the events that led to the path she lived. As people should be, neither had judgment over the other. Ultimately, the pleasant company helped Megan keep her mind off her sorrow until she left to meet the *Elizabeth.*

Megan approached a T-junction of the docking level corridor and narrowly avoided Adrian, who came from a different direction. He wore the same clothes as the day before but gained a food stain on the jacket. The wrinkled appearance indicated the clothes were more likely to spend the night on a floor instead of a hanger. Adrian's date went well, Megan concluded.

"Captain Kostas, are you here to escort me to your ship?"

"Good morning, Doctor McCord. Of course, that's why I'm here." He bowed and pointed his hand in the direction they needed to go.

"How gentlemanly of you." She smirked at his white lie.

"Did you have a pleasant evening?"

"Thank you. I met a delightful new friend." She didn't provide details, and Adrian didn't ask for any.

"Well, we're here. Let me give you a view of your temporary home, the *Elizabeth*." He stepped over to a viewport on the bulkhead and touched a button to open the shutters to show his ship.

A mesmerizing mural sprawled across the ship's smooth exterior. It depicted a mountain lake surrounded by pines and rugged peaks. The lifelike realism of the scene invited one to stroll into its tranquil beauty.

"The *Elizabeth* is a modified Light Cargo Vessel but not a flying box like most modern freighters. She has style," Adrian puffed out his chest in pride.

"It's spectacular. I don't think I've ever seen such fantastic art adorning a ship. As you said, most are just large cubes with thrusters attached and filled with containers. The *Elizabeth* looks like an artist painted an old ocean steamer and put her in space," Megan said. Her family owned twenty-six much larger ships, but none compared to this in style.

"That's an apt description, except, of course, the thrusters are where the keel would be on a sea vessel." Adrian pointed to the bottom of the ship. Our array of thrusters can give us a steady acceleration of .55g."

Megan rocked back on her feet and looked at him, eyes wide in surprise. "Very impressive for a civilian ship. Most can't do more than .45g, maybe .5."

This time Adrian cocked an eyebrow. "I'm impressed with you. Few non-spacers know details like that."

"I study artifacts, but I pick up other knowledge along the way." Megan pointed at something directly in front of the superstructure to shift subjects. A glass half-dome covered a vibrant garden of plants. "I don't think I've ever seen anything like that."

"We call it the conservatory—kind of a greenhouse combined with a sunroom. A place to relax on long voyages."

Though an accurate statement, most of her knowledge of spacecraft came from the family dinner table. Ettrick Logistics captains and engineers frequently visited her home. The conversations bored teenage Megan, but she learned things despite herself.

"Tell me the story about the art on the side." Her desire to keep the subject away from the information she should not know caused her tone to be more commanding than she expected.

Adrian smiled, pride for his family vessel clear on his face. "My grandfather painted it himself. He named the ship after my grandmother, Elizabeth. The view was from the mountain cabin where they spent their honeymoon. He wanted her to feel its calming presence always."

"An adorable story. Your grandparents must have loved each other very much."

"They did. Grandpa passed away two years ago, and I took over as captain. Grandma is the owner, but I run things day to day. He left big shoes to fill." Adrian reminisced for a few seconds. "Come on, I'll introduce you to the crew."

They entered through the *Elizabeth's* cargo bay. The hold was small compared to Ettrick Logistics' enormous freighters, yet still impressive to a human standing on the deck. They loaded an assorted cargo of standard fifteen-meter shipping containers, pallets, crates, and other goods to re-sell at the destination. Megan observed the trunks containing her delicate archaeological tools had arrived from the luggage storage service holding them.

Adrian approached a woman in coveralls, black hair in a bun slowly unraveling. "Sarai, how is the cargo coming along?"

"Excellent captain. Everything is loaded, and I will have the last details finished in a few minutes," the woman had a subtle grace and serenity about her.

"Doctor Megan McCord, I want to introduce you to Sarai Rousseau. She is our ship's cargo master and purser."

Sarai bowed slightly. "I am honored to meet you, Doctor. It is a genuine pleasure to have you aboard our ship. I wish you a safe and peaceful journey."

"Don't let her polite demeanor fool you. She haggles like she is in a Baghdad marketplace to get us the best deals on any trade goods we can profit from."

"I'm always polite, but I learned to haggle from my grandmother in a Bangkok market."

"Your haggling always keeps us profitable."

"Captain, the greatest wealth is found within, in the serenity of one's spirit, not in the riches of the earth."

"Excellent outlook, but I have also seen your shoe collection."

Sarai smiled and placed a hand on her chest. "I can have the serenity of the spirit and shoes. A girl's gotta have options. Isn't that right, Doctor? Besides, I'm half French—fashion runs in my veins."

"I agree, Sarai. And please call me Megan."

"Where did you get these beauties? They look like they are fun to fly." Adrian pointed at two sleek asteroid runabouts in the center of the cargo hold. Primarily designed as asteroid mining tools, the runabouts also conjured images of maneuverability and speed.

"I'm good at my job, Captain, but I must keep some secrets. Don't worry. I'll let you take one for a spin before we sell them."

"Let me?"

Sarai rolled her eyes and looked at Megan. "Boys and their toys, right, Megan?" That got Megan laughing.

Sarai became more formal. "Doctor, Captain, excuse me. I still have some preparations. I will meet you on the bridge for departure. May peace be with you."

Adrian nodded to her and looked at Megan. "Let me take you to engineering. I want to introduce you to our engineer."

Megan cocked a questioning eyebrow at the destination. Engineering was not usually a priority visit for prominent passengers on Ettrick ships.

They passed into the engineering space through a hatch at the rear of the cargo hold, opening to reveal the expansive engineering section occupying the aft quarter of the ship. Towering battery and capacitor cylinders stretched from floor to ceiling, connected by a web of catwalks and ladders. Megan gazed up at the massive power storage units, dwarfed by their scale.

Following the echoes of banging, they found a silver-haired woman cursing at malfunctioning equipment. She pushed up her goggles as Adrian approached.

"Problems?" he asked.

Ignoring the captain, she turned to Megan. "You must be Doctor McCord. I'm Elizabeth Victoria Borden - this ship's namesake and engineer."

"Also, the ship's legal owner... and my grandmother," Adrian said.

"Call me Lizzie - we'll drop the formalities," Lizzie took Megan's hand. "I think you'll liven things up around here."

Megan smiled as she instantly liked this vibrant woman.

Lizzie waved off Adrian's departure concerns and then switched to grandmother mode. "Before we leave, you need to call your mother. It has been over a week since she heard from you. And change your clothes."

Adrian protested, but Lizzie shooed him toward the exit. "Talk to her while we are in orbit instead of a forty-minute comm lag. Now go. I'll finish the tour with Megan. We'll have a nice cup of tea after."

Adrian surrendered with raised hands. "Okay, I'm going." He turned to Megan before leaving engineering. "Feel free to join us on the bridge for departure if you'd like."

After he left, Lizzie confided in Megan. "He forgets to talk to his mom, but family is important."

"Now, how about a tour?" Lizzie asked, her voice filled with excitement.

As they walked, Lizzie explained the intricate technology accompanied by the hum of the machinery filling the air.

Lizzie slapped the side of one of the power storage units. "These provide the power for our Magneto Plasma Dynamic thrusters. Engineers like me need to thank exo-archaeologists. You keep finding bits of alien tech, and we turn it into human tech. Without that battery tech, we would never have the energy storage to keep continuous thrust. Otherwise, it would still take a ship this size months to get to Jupiter."

"You're welcome on behalf of the artifact hunters who did the work. I'm still too new to have found anything. I would be absolutely delighted to meet some of the engineers who designed this technology."

Lizzie gave a bow and swept her arms. "I was on a team 'designing this technology' at MIT as a grad student. I handled software for the high-temperature superconductors. You are not the only PhD on this ship."

Megan blushed, very apparent with her pale, freckled skin. She prejudged the engineer of a small ship and made poor assumptions.

Lizzie saw the young woman's discomfort. She smiled and said, "Who cares about engineering degrees? I was also a teen surfing champion in California sixty-five years ago."

Megan laughed. "No surfing, but I was runner-up in zero-g acrobatics during my freshman year at university."

"Fantastic. I'll draft you into any microgravity work I need during this trip. I'm too old for that shit. Let's go sit down and have some tea." Lizzie climbed a ladder to an upper-level exit with a vigor surprising from an octogenarian.

Lizzie led Megan past the crew quarters. The occupants painted the cabin doors to their tastes. An artist had designed murals on the walls between the doors to blend the styles together. The *Elizabeth's* design reflected a family, not a drab corporate ship.

Megan's eyes widened at the lush oasis before her as they passed through a hatch.

The glass-paneled ceiling arched overhead like a greenhouse, angled to let in plentiful light. Rich greens and bursts of color from chrysanthemums, orchids, and other plants brought vibrant life to the room. A staircase led to a second-story balcony overlooking the conservatory.

Wicker furniture with plush cushions beckoned visitors to sit and admire the conservatory's beauty. From this vantage point, the clear ceiling provided a breathtaking view of Earth. The small windows on other spacecraft paled compared to this majestic vision.

"My husband, Charles, designed the conservatory when we had the *Elizabeth* built. He knew I'm an outdoor girl and wanted to give me a place without a 'roof' over my head." Lizzie waved her arm at the planet that filled the "sky" above the dome. Her voice quivered a little, remembering her late husband. After holding her eyes closed for a few moments, Lizzie led Megan to chairs. A wheeled bot brought a pot of tea.

"This is stunning, Lizzie. None of the ships I've traveled on before had anything like this."

Lizzie poured tea. "I imagine so. No offense, but Ettrick ships are a bit on the dull side."

Megan sucked in her breath and went paler than usual. She had not mentioned Ettrick Logistics.

"Now, which story is true? The artifact-hunting archaeologist? Or the daughter of a murdered shipping magnate with a bounty on her head?" Lizzie sipped on her tea and waited for a response.

Megan sighed and realized how hard it had been to hold back. Lizzie listened as she described evading danger after her father's suspicious death.

Lizzie touched Megan's knee. "Don't worry, you're safe here. Whatever these people are after, we will help you find it first and identify your father's killer."

An hour after Megan bore her soul to Lizzie, the engineer led Megan to the bridge for departure. Neither mentioned Megan's secrets.

Sarai and two men were on the bridge with a freshly dressed Adrian. The captain introduced the men.

The first man had a face with gentle lines, creases, and silver hair. A mechanical support exoskeleton encased his body. "This is David Efron. He is our navigator and sail master. He makes sure we don't get lost."

"A sail master? I have never heard of a ship this size with solar sails."

"Ah, more articulated panels than full sails. As a youngster, I was a solar sail racer and convinced Adrian's saba, Charles, to install them when I joined the crew. It gives us a small edge in speed, and every bit counts in this business." The subtle lilt of his Lunan accent explained the exoskeleton to Megan. The first generation of people born in moon gravity needed support for their bones and muscles. Reverse-engineering artificial gravity from the Artificers had solved the problem for younger generations.

A young man stood near David. This man had a weightlifter's body but a librarian's demeanor. "This is Piet van der Berg, a recent graduate starting his apprenticeship."

"Pleased to meet you, Doctor," Piet said. "Let me know if you need anything."

Adrian patted Piet on the back. "Don't hesitate to ask him. As an apprentice, he gets to be everyone's gopher and to handle the tasks no one else wants to do."

"Piet, why don't you walk us through the flight plan? Consider it a pop quiz, straight from the lunar academy." David's tone was reminiscent of a professor putting a student on the spot. But there was a glimmer of mischief in his eyes. "Back on the moon, we used to say, 'A giant leap in the wrong direction will see you lost forever.' So, are we leaping the right way, Kid?"

Sweat rose on Piet's brow as all eyes turned to him. He took a deep breath and brought up a course plot on the screen. "The current distance between Earth and Callisto is 5.9 AU. This is the least time course and will clear us of any asteroids or comets. At our .55 acceleration, the trip will take two-hundred twenty-five hours with a turnover halfway. Nine days, nine hours."

"What is the light-speed communication time to Earth when we arrive," Lizzie asked.

Piet calculated the answer without referring to the plot on the screen. "Forty-eight minutes."

Lizzie gave Adrian a look. He said, "I called Mom already. She sends her love."

Adrian examined the plot with intense scrutiny. Piet stood rigid like an accused, waiting for a judge's verdict. Adrian turned and smiled. "Good work, Piet. Plot it into the nav computer."

Piet let out the breath he had been holding.

"Very well. No time like the present. Everyone get to your stations."

A chorus of "Aye, Captain" filled the air. Lizzie left for engineering, and the others took stations on the bridge.

Adrian sat in the pilot chair and pointed to the captain's chair. "Megan, you are welcome to sit in the big chair. I do double duty as pilot and rarely use it."

Megan took the comfortable seat and watched the crew of the Elizabeth switch from casual to professional.

"Report by station," the captain called from the helmsperson's station.

"Capacitors charged. Fusion plant ready. MPD thrusters on standby. Argon propellent injectors ready. Engineering is a go," Lizzie's voice announced over the speaker.

"All connectors to the station closed. Air level nominal. O_2 scrubbers online with redundant systems checking good. All cargo secured. The environment is a go." Sarai reported from the environmental station.

"Course laid in. The kid did well. Sails ready to deploy. Navigation is a go." A navigation hologram hovered in front of David, showing the course.

Piet looked up from the communication station. "Station confirms we have clearance to depart. Ancillary systems check good and a go."

"Maneuvering thrusters ready to push us away. The main engines are ready. Helm is a go." Adrian said in his dual role as the pilot.

Adrian turned to Megan, "You are in the big seat. What do you see, Doctor 'Captain'?"

Megan smiled and looked at her screen. All items showed green. She tried to imitate ship captains she knew. "All systems are a go. Helm, you may proceed with departure."

Adrian laughed and gave Megan a sloppy salute. "Aye, sir. All personnel prepare for microgravity. Environmental disengage from station gravity."

"Gravity disengaged. Docking clamps retracting." The sensation of gravity vanished with Sarai's announcement.

"Thrusters engaged minimal power." The ship slowly pulled away to a one-kilometer distance. "Deploy sails."

Masts extended from the lower hull with a series of articulated triangular panels furled to the shaft. "Masts extended. Sails ready for full deployment."

"Main engines engaged. One quarter gee. Increasing acceleration to .5g." Once they reached full acceleration, the sails unfurled like a fan. The slight boost brought them to a steady acceleration of .55g.

"Engineering—connect the gravity plates to the fusion reactor." The fusion plant could not power the gravity plates to full gravity on their own. Full power to the plates only happens when connected to a station's Starshell power. The combination of acceleration and gravity plates will allow the crew to ride in a comfortable Earth-normal gravity.

Elizabeth pulled away on the first leg of her long trip to Callisto.

A woman stood gazing out of the station's viewport, her eyes following the departing ship until it disappeared. With a subtle nod, she reached for her comm-pad and started a call.

"They are underway now. No more issues." She disconnected. The Galilean Society preferred short and concise reports.

Good luck, Red. More is happening than you realize. I wish we could help more, but you are on your own out there. Jessica thought to herself as she walked away.

At another viewport, a pair of figures also watched the *Elizabeth* depart.

"Missed her," Roger McCord's killer said.

"Looks like we will have a second chance. We have more instructions from our employer."

The partner's comm-pad displayed a message from Celatum Dominus. *Fast transportation will be provided. Intercept at Callisto.*

6

Dinner with the Stars

To Megan's pleasure, *Elizabeth* had a small library in the second-level common area. Actual paper books lined the oak shelves. The musty aroma of aged paper and the smooth texture of the leather reminded Megan of the old university libraries she had studied in.

She spent much of the trip here studying her notes or reading the old books collected by Charles Borden, Adrian's grandfather. The familiarity of luxurious leather chairs and academics made this place comfortable for her.

Megan refused to admit Adrian was right. Unaccustomed to the simplicity of the modest, compact bed, she longed for something more lavish. The company was friendly, but dining at a metal table in the galley felt awkward.

Megan, get off your high horse. Everyone here is wonderful. You are running from killers, not headed for the palace. You also knew exo-archaeology would not always be five-star hotels. Megan told herself.

Adrian stood in the doorway and knocked to get her attention. "Hi, Megan. It's almost time for dinner. Sarai is making a special Thai Curry tonight. May I escort you, my lady?"

"I'd be delighted, kind sir." Megan put down the book and followed him out.

Adrian led her past the galley. Before Megan could comment on the change of venue, Adrian said, "Tonight, we dine under the stars. We set up picnic tables in the conservatory."

They stepped out of the second-level passageway onto the balcony of the conservatory. Megan took a deep breath to take in the enchanting fragrance of the greenery and turned her eyes upward to the dome.

Most experienced space travelers rarely took the time to gaze at the cosmos except when near a planet or moon. The absence of celestial bodies allowed the sea of stars to shine in a mesmerizing glow. The Milky Way's twinkling gems felt like one could dive into that ocean and swim among the stars.

Megan gaped at the view. "It's beautiful. I should come out here more often."

"It's one of the reasons we are having dinner here tonight. We are halfway in the journey. It's turnover night."

Adrian swept his hands to the ceiling as if painting the Milky Way with a broad brush. "Tomorrow, these windows will face the sun and wash out the stars. Let's enjoy the spectacle."

Descending the spiral stairs, they joined the crew at some folding tables.

"Welcome, Megan. I made a couple of Thai Curries. A spicy Red Curry and a milder Panang Curry. They are traditional family recipes on my mother's side," Sarai pointed at two large dishes on the table. She did not wear her standard coveralls but an ornate Thai Chakri dress tonight.

Megan leaned over the table. "It smells delicious, and you look beautiful, Sarai. Your dress is lovely."

"Thank you. Every now and then, I like to get dressed up. At least I got a compliment out of someone. I think I intimidate the men too much for them to speak up." Her eyes narrowed as she glared at her crew mates. A slightly upturned smile exposed her pseudo-anger for the humor it was.

"Of course, you terrify us. When can we eat? I'm so hungry, I could eat moon cheese." David said, his voice carrying a light, jesting tone with a hint of lunar humor.

Sarai stuck her tongue out at her long-time friend and handed Megan a bowl. "Guests first."

"Thank you. Do you eat out here often?" Megan asked.

David spoke up first. "It's an Elizabethan tradition to have a meal out here on flip day. Ship turnover is a big deal on long voyages. It breaks the monotony. Piet, you are handling the flip tonight. Pop quiz, explain why we turn over the ship to our newbie spacer."

Piet's eyes shot open when put on the spot. He looked at Megan and downcast his eyes. He explained in a soft voice.

"Ship engines push us at a steady acceleration. We would shoot past our destination if we accelerated continuously in one direction. Instead, we accelerate to the halfway point and turn the ship over so the engines point in the other direction. The engine thrust decelerates until we reach zero velocity relative to the destination." Piet gained confidence as he explained and met Megan's eyes.

"Thank you, Piet. That was helpful." Megan didn't have the heart to tell the gentle giant she was familiar with flipping the ship. She experienced ship flips on her father's ships, though they never had special dinners to celebrate. She looked at Lizzie and realized the older woman had not revealed her secret.

"If you have taken a shuttle to the moon, there is always a minute or so of zero gravity in the middle. We will do the same tonight. Unlike shuttles, we have gravity plates. The gravity will drop to about 50% normal but not completely disappear. Still, you might want to strap in before you sleep."

"Good advice. I might stay up and observe your work." Megan patted Piet on the arm as she sat down with her bowl. Piet's cheeks flushed a bit. Megan was the only one in the room who did not notice.

Lizzie clapped her hands to get everyone's attention. "Enough shop talk. Everyone get some food."

The crew sat under the stars and enjoyed the meal with laughter and stories.

Sarai told a story of Adrian when he was a young officer who had a bright idea of shipping live animals instead of frozen meat. He convinced his grandfather it would be more profitable. The chickens were okay, but the sheep and pigs were a mess. In the end, they took a loss. The captain decided the young officer should learn humility by cleaning the hold.

"I call it karma for a certain incident on Luna," Sarai said.

Adrian crossed his arms and looked at Sarai, "As I recall, you were with me on Luna that day."

"I have meditated on that period of my life. I hope I am better because of it." Sarai meditated every morning in a nearby Zen Garden.

Megan wanted to hear the Luna story next.

"No. It is time for your story, Doctor. Everyone here deserves to know the full story," Lizzie's tone was commanding and clear. She had a bottle of Scotch and poured Megan a tumbler of liquid courage.

Megan traced her finger around the glass rim, lost in thought. Her companions leaned in, sensing a revelation brewing behind her distant gaze.

"I'm more than just an archaeologist chasing artifacts," Megan finally said.

In her mind's eye, Megan saw her father's body sprawled on the study floor, the dagger protruding from his chest. She blinked back tears, willing away the gruesome sight.

"My father...someone murdered him six days ago." A chorus of shocked gasps came from the crew.

"He was CEO of Ettrick Logistics and the Viscount Primrose. I found him stabbed to death in our home."

Megan's voice trembled with a raw recounting of that horrible night, from the anticipation of her trip to the chilling shock in her father's study. She told of the fury in her heart as she shot at the killer and the frustration of their escape. The memories swirled together in a tempest of pain.

"Daddy was always the anchor of my life. He inspired my love of discovery. I can't believe he is gone."

Adrian put his comforting hand on her knee when he heard the pain in her voice. Megan stared at him, wishing he could restore the world's balance.

"The killer searched for information we unraveled. I guess I am lucky they never knew I had it on me the whole time." Megan didn't feel lucky at all.

With resolve, she removed her necklace and opened the pendant. A holo-projector was activated. Part of an asteroid flickered into view as she activated it.

"We decrypted this image weeks ago," Megan said. "An explorer named Fred Stonington found this site ten years ago. Sometime after he found this place, his boat drifted to Callisto. The CPS found him onboard very sick. He died en route to Earth for medical treatment. His feverish babbling talked about an intact and functional Artificer base." She paused and took a sip of her whiskey.

"It sounds like you are describing the 'Hunters Folly,'" David said, referring to the legendary "El Dorado" Artifact Hunters had been seeking for decades.

"I am. Stonington convinced himself he found it. My father bought his possessions at an estate sale. We have been researching for years, and decrypting this image proved it was not just a rumor. Other information about the site's contents led my father and I to believe that Hunters Folly is the key to unlocking the language of the Artificers."

Lizzie's back straightened, and her eyes widened as she focused on the implications. "If we can understand the language, we can determine how artifacts function. It would be a tremendous leap. My research team at MIT were blind monkeys trying to put square pegs in round holes. Sometimes, we got it right, but usually we didn't. That is how artifact research has been for a century."

"Exactly, and someone killed my father to find it. I don't imagine they have humanity's enlightenment in mind. I received a threatening message to turn over the information, or they would kill me, too. On the station, I found out there is a bounty out on me now."

"There is more than that," Lizzie said. "I tapped into a security net. The Scottish government issued a person of interest warrant. For some reason, it did not spread past Scotland until after we left. Now, Coalition Security is pushing the warrant wide."

"The night of the murder, Coalition Security took over the crime scene and removed the Scottish police from the investigation. Or at least people masquerading as Coalition Security. I received strange messages telling me not to trust them."

"You shouldn't trust them even if they are real. The CS charter restricts them from Earth-side matters. Not that anything ever stopped UCE administrators from putting their noses where they didn't belong," Adrian said. Lizzie gave him an admonishing glance for allowing his bitter feelings for the unelected de facto solar system rulers to leak through at this time.

"It doesn't matter. My father's murderer will kill me for the information. Coalition Security will drop me in some hole for the same info," Megan said, not trusting CS's motives. "My best option on Earth would be a Scottish jail. I need to follow Stonington's trail to Hunters Folly. It is the only option I see that keeps me alive and out of jail."

"What do you hope to find at Callisto?" David asked.

"I think his boat is still there. If I can find the boat, maybe I can trace where it has been. I planned to gather information and return home to research it, but then they killed Daddy."

Megan had revealed her secrets and finally let herself cry for her father. She lost track of time as she cried. Her head was now on Adrian's shoulder. Her tears had stained his jacket, but he did not mind. The crew huddled together, talking.

"Everyone, I beg your forgiveness." She got up to head back to her room. Her head hung low in shame for burdening these kind-hearted individuals with her problems.

"Where are you going?" Adrian asked.

"I'm retiring to my cabin." Her voice trembled with grief and insecurity, barely audible.

"So, you don't want to hear the plan?"

"What plan?" Megan's head tilted. Her gaze darted around as she tried to piece his words together.

"Did you think we wouldn't help you? We are working on a plan to find this old explorer's boat," Lizzie said.

"No, I will disembark at Callisto. You will never need to hear from me again."

Silence filled the air as the other five stared at Megan like she had spoken an alien language.

Megan sighed and sat back down. "Very well then, enlighten me about this plan."

David spoke first. "I have thoughts on locating the survey boat. It won't be at the dock after ten years. They probably sold it for docking fees by now, or it may be in a parking orbit and forgotten. Do you have any information on it?"

A small smile came to Megan's face. "Ah, but I have something more useful than information. I'm the vessel's rightful owner. The ship registration was part of his estate, and Dad signed it over to me when we planned the trip.

He figured proof of ownership would smooth the process once I found it."

She forwarded David the data on the ship.

"This craft is ancient. The good news is no one would want to buy it if they put it up for auction. The bad news is they might have scrapped it. Let's hope they sent it to the junkyard or CPS impounded it and parked it in orbit.

Sarai placed a hand on David's shoulder. "If you find nothing, I will contact my old underworld contacts. Someone could have stolen and sold the abandoned boat on the black market or a chop shop."

Megan thought of Sarai meditating each morning or bringing Megan afternoon tea into the library. *How would sweet and spiritual Sarai know anyone in the underworld?*

7

The Lioness' Patrol Interrupted.

July 30, 2155—Patrol ship Zeta Sierra—Ceres

The first stop in the patrol took Kristina and the *Zeta Sierra* to the Ceres research station. The crew scanned for trouble while their captain handled irate complaints from the lead researcher.

"Yes, I know they stole an artifact. The problem is you hired unlicensed couriers. They left a week ago. They could be anywhere between Venus and Jupiter by now. Take this matter to your insurance company." Kristina severed the connection without allowing the research leader to respond.

Kristina examined the outpost through the viewport. A domed structure resided on the surface of the dwarf planet at the site of the first alien artifact discovery. In 2045, a multinational group of explorers found proof of non-human intelligent life. Like the fertility goddess it was named after, Ceres offered up a harvest of knowledge. After a century of exploitation, the scientists seldom found new artifacts. The theft of a rare discovery understandably annoyed the lead researcher.

"If only he hadn't been a fool," Kristina whispered. Unfortunately, her executive officer overheard the unprofessional remark.

"You can't fix stupid," Frank Davenport said.

"You're right. I joined the service to protect people like these researchers, but not from their stupidity." She was silent for a moment. "My grandfather was a researcher at a small research outpost. Pirates attacked it, and he was crippled in the attack. It's my duty to stop things like that."

"At least this time, the theft had no violence."

"This time. People want artifacts because of the knowledge that can be discovered. Knowledge becomes power. And power attracts violence." Kristina zoomed the main view screen on an object floating a few thousand kilometers away—the derelict hull of a wrecked ship. "That is a ship destroyed in the Artifact Wars. Primitive compared to ships now. Forces would travel for weeks to fight a battle and die in minutes. Imagine if the same happened now."

"We founded the United Coalition of Earth to stop the wars. As long as the UCE controls space, this won't happen again," Davenport said.

"With the rumors we have heard, the criminals smuggling artifacts don't really care about the UCE. I worry about future violence. You and I will do what we can to prevent it, but I think too many UCE bureaucrats care about consolidating their own power. That thought does not go beyond us, Frank."

"Of course, Captain." Privately, Davenport didn't just think but knew most UCE leadership only cared for their power. People like Kristina Chen-Ramirez were the exception, not the rule.

"Captain, you have an urgent message. An inquiry you made stirred up a hornet's nest," the comm officer said. He forwarded the message to Kristina's console.

She read the message and gasped. "Navigation standby to plot a fresh course to Jupiter. Engineering, please prepare the engines for maximum acceleration."

"What's wrong, Skipper?" the XO asked. Warrant Officer Phillips joined the pair after hearing the concern in his captain's voice.

"Before we left the station, I sent a routine request about a passenger on the *Elizabeth*. Some exo-archeologists are off to explore artifacts. Or so I thought. I wasn't very serious. Mostly, I tried to annoy Captain Kostas. But damn, what kind of shit did you get yourself in this time, Adrian?"

Davenport raised an eyebrow and a smirk. "This time?"

Kristina twisted her blonde hair in frustration, a nervous habit since childhood.

"You probably don't know the story of when I first met Adrian...I mean Captain Kostas. It was before I took command of Miss Zetty."

"You can call him Adrian. Everyone knows he is your boyfriend."

"We don't see each other enough to use labels like that. We are both free to see other people."

Davenport and Phillips looked at each other. The unspoken observation is that she had seen no one else for a year.

"Two years ago, my team turned up a lead on artifact thief at a restaurant on Europa station. We went to apprehend the woman. It turns out she had dinner with Captain Kostas and attempted to book passage on his ship. Let's say the currency she offered for payment was not Coalition Credits." Kristina's nose wrinkled in disgust from the memory.

"Unfortunately for everyone, we were not the only people who wanted the woman. She double-crossed her partners. We arrived just as the band of smugglers attacked the restaurant to kill the woman. Thankfully, we managed to arrest everyone with no loss of life. My point is Adrian Kostas found himself in the middle of that trouble by following a pretty face."

Phillips, who had been a member of her team, interjected. "You forgot the part where Adrian saved the life of a young boy. Adrian took a flechette dart to the face. You may have noticed the scar."

"Point taken. And yes, I have noticed the scar. Plus a few others that I am still trying to get the story on." Kristina gave them a coy, knowing smile.

"Regardless, Adrian is in the middle of a mess again. This Doctor McCord is not just any artifact hunter. She is the daughter of Roger McCord, owner of Ettrick Logistics. He was murdered several nights ago."

Kristina let that sink in for a moment and continued. "The fact that Doctor McCord left Earth the next morning is suspicious. She is wanted as a person of interest. Commonwealth Security had the alert while we were in Earth orbit but forwarded it to the CPS today. Headquarters ordered us to follow and apprehend her."

"With due respect, Captain, doesn't your relationship with Captain Kostas make this a conflict of interest?"

"I'll do my duty, Frank, and I don't think the higher-ups care about our opinions. Jupiter was next in our patrol, anyway. We'll be early," Kristina said.

"According to the flight plan filed by *Elizabeth* before departure, Ganymede is their destination. I hope everyone has been working out. We are pushing up to 1.25g. They have had a head start, but we're faster." Patrol ships had unmatched acceleration and maneuverability; no freighter could match them.

8
Sleight of Hand

August 3, 2155—Callisto Station

Lady Felicity Pembroke sauntered into the exclusive Le Méridien hotel, her jet-black hair cascading down her back like a veil. Her fashionable bolero jacket and matching dress hugged her curves in all the right places. The click-clack of her stiletto heels announced her presence with a demand for attention. Her poise screamed excess and privilege with an air of confidence.

Accompanying her several steps behind was a personal assistant in a sharp suit and a muscular bodyguard.

The assistant approached the desk. "I assume the suite for Lady Felicity Pembroke is ready. We want to enter immediately."

"The suite will be ready momentarily. We have someone going through it as we speak." A squad of cleaning bots and humans verified the room met Le Méridien standards.

"What is taking so long, Constantine? I must get out of these rags and into a warm bath." She opened her Louis Vuitton handbag to take out a silver perfume atomizer and spritzed herself.

A manager came out of the back to greet his guest. The blend of velvet roses and spicy jasmine in her over-applied perfume was almost suffocating. "Lady Felicity, Welcome to the Callisto Le Méridien. Please let me escort you to your suite."

As he led her to a private elevator, she remarked, "I do hope the suite is as impeccable as your reputation claims. If not, I will speak to Daddy about finding different accommodations next time. Bring me champagne chilled to exactly eight degrees."

They entered the massive two-level suite. The manager showed them through the sitting area and bar on the first floor. A wide staircase ascended to a second floor with two master bedrooms, each with enclosed verandas with a view of Jupiter or Callisto.

Lady Felicity waved off the manager without thanking him. She flopped on a couch as the door closed and pulled off the black wig. She threw the wig and bag at a chair several meters away, missing.

"I am glad that's done. I hate stuffy assholes," Megan said.

Adrian sank into another plush chair. "The manager wasn't too bad."

"I was talking about me." She wove her hand around the extravagant suite. "I was born in this world. Justifiably, I've been called 'trust fund girl' many times. I try to avoid pretentiousness. Being a bookworm was all I wanted."

Adrian chuckled. "You did a great job. You played the dumb socialite very well. Though an acting critic might say it was a bit cliché."

"Cliché? Hardly. I channeled the most arrogant and snobbish girl I knew at school. That was exactly how she acted."

She kicked the shoes off in the same direction as the bag, hitting a wall this time. "At least Sarai had these shoes I could borrow to sell the image. My friend Emily is a fashion guru. It would shock her to see me in knockoffs like these."

"Knockoffs? Sarai doesn't own knockoffs," Adrian said.

"You mean to tell me I just threw a genuine Louis Vuitton bag across a room and kicked a pair of Prada shoes against a wall?" Horrified, she ran over to the shoes.

Adrian left the hotel confident with their sleight of hand. After leaving the ship, they rented a cheap hotel room in Megan's name, and she transformed into Felicity. With any luck, anyone looking for Megan will think she disappeared into the station's lower levels.

He walked down the docks to meet David on the hunt for clues about the location of Stonington's survey ship abandoned at Callisto.

The clang of metal and the whir of engines echoed through the bustling docks. Pallets zipped past on robot "mules." A pair of teenagers "surfed" on top of pallets in a form of race. Another group of kids ran after them to see who fell off first—typical wise teenage decisions.

"One of those kids will get hurt. The docks are not a safe place," David said from a table at a nearby coffee shop.

"Let the kids have fun, old-timer. They need to learn caution somehow." Adrian joined the older man and ordered a coffee.

"I remember you learned the hard way the first time you visited Callisto. You were thirteen and joined the *Elizabeth* for summer vacation. Charles took you on a shopping trip, and you wandered off. It threw your grandparents into a panic, and they don't panic easy."

"Oh, it wasn't that big of a deal."

"You showed up hours later with a black eye, a huge smile, and a tale you never told."

"Someday, I will share. My first fight and my first kiss. It was also the first time I met Sarai. Her occupation then was less legal, but she helped me out of trouble and got me back to the docks. The only one that got the whole story out of me was my mother."

"Oh, what did Elizabeth Anne have to say about you getting into the fight." David had known Adrian's mother since she was a teen.

"Her exact words were, 'Next time, duck faster and hit harder.'"

"That sounds like your mom. And that's some good advice. She always won the fights she got in as a teen." David smiled at the little dig into Adrian's ego. "What happened to the girl you kissed?"

"For the next several summers, I snuck off to see her when we were here. She dumped me when we were fifteen." Adrian took a sip of his coffee.

"Oh, Mandy, the girl with the blue hair."

"You knew about her?" Adrian spilled some coffee when he almost dropped his cup.

"Adrian, everyone knew. She dumped you because she found out about your girlfriend in Orlando and the other girl at Mars station. It began your reputation for having a girl in every port."

Adrian down casted his eyes. "Stop trying to embarrass me and tell me what you found."

"I started with the junkyard," David said. Ship junk yards are operated like U-Pull and Pay car part yards on Earth. "Their site listed four survey craft of the model we're looking for. None matched the registration number, so we can scratch the idea the boat was junked—one bit of good news. I found the unit we discussed late last night. I paid them extra to pull it for me and deliver it to the ship."

"That's good. Lizzie called. She checked out the auctions ten years ago. No records of it being auctioned back then. Also, no sign of it in the CPS impound area," Adrian said. Besides being an engineer, Lizzie was a top-ranked hacker.

"I had an idea. CPS removed the cargo from Stonington's boat. The same boxes Megan's father bought at auction. The cargo handlers' guild keeps excellent records, better than the UCE transportation management office."

Adrian jumped to his feet. "Nice thinking. Let's go."

"I already did. That is where it gets weird. A little bribe got me into the records. I found records of the cargo transfer, but after that, it's a blank. The records of the ship got scrubbed."

Adrian stared at his coffee for a minute. "Simplest solution. Someone stole the abandoned ship and made it disappear from the records. I guess we will need to ask Sarai to reach out to her old contacts."

Adrian didn't like the idea of asking Sarai to be anywhere near the life she tried so hard to leave behind, but he knew she would.

With nothing else to do at the docks, Adrian intended to return to the hotel, while David's destination was *Elizabeth*. They took a dimly lit side passage connecting the dock level with a major pedestrian passageway. They chatted as they walked until two men in frayed miner's uniforms blocked the path. One held a length of pipe while another asteroid miner stepped from behind. All had the glazed look of a long-time drug addict.

"Looks like the docks are not just dangerous for teens. Maybe the shortcut through a dark alley was not the best choice?" David said.

"Like I said, everyone needs to learn caution, including these guys," Adrian said with unfelt confidence. Luna-born David could be severely injured in a 1g gravity fight.

"You two have something we want," a short, gaunt man in front of them said. The tall man with a pipe next to him smiled.

"We don't have much cash, but let us buy you a meal. You look like you could use it. We can all part friends." Adrian hoped to diffuse the situation quickly.

"Oh, we will take your cash, Earther, but first, you must tell us where your passenger is. Someone will pay perfect money for a passenger on the *Elizabeth*. We plan on collecting."

"I don't know what you're talking about." Adrian tensed and searched for an advantage.

"Maybe if we break the moonie's legs, you will remember."

Adrian's nostrils flared at the slur to his friend. David gently squeezed Adrian's shoulder to tell his captain to let the insult go.

A scraggly bearded man behind Adrian and David said, "Jax, it's just a moonie and this punk. Let's take them."

"Shut up, Diego. I'm enjoying this. Kostas here messed with my girl years ago. So now I will take his girl," the thug leader said.

"Jax? I thought you looked familiar. You're holding a grudge for something that happened almost twenty years ago when we were kids."

"You know him?" David asked.

"Remember the story of the girl and the black eye? He is the one that gave me the black eye."

Jax grinned with rotten teeth. "You will get more than a black eye this time."

Adrian knew this needed to end quickly. He didn't bring a stunner with him. They were too bulky to escape notice. A pouch in his pants contained an expanding baton. He charged as he shouted, "David, run!"

Jax saw Adrian's charge and took a step back behind his companion. Adrian's plan was to go for the man holding the pipe anyway. The baton expanded to its full length, and a rapid strike to the side of the head took the wide-eyed man down like a sack.

Adrian's momentum took him past Jax, who stuck out a leg to trip him.

Adrian rolled with the fall and popped back up. When he spun to face Jax, the thug had retrieved his friend's pipe. The men stared at each other and leapt like a pair of sword-wielding warriors.

David disobeyed his captain's orders to run. David may not have the strength of an Earth-born person, but he had excellent dexterity.

The scraggly bearded thug, Diego, expected easy prey as he attacked. He didn't expect his prey to dodge so easily. David held out his arm and locked his exoskeleton in place with the rigidity of Michelangelo's marble statue of the same name. Diego's face hit the rigid titanium rods of David's suit with nose-crushing force, while David felt barely a shutter.

David stared down at the dazed man. "Just a moonie, huh?"

Adrian dodged or blocked Jax's clumsy swings and answered with a baton swing to the gut. Jax stumbled back and glared at Adrian.

"Who wants my passenger? Where are you taking her?"

"Fuck off." Jax threw the pipe at Adrian and ran. The strung-out thug ran with shocking speed.

Adrian chose not to follow, knowing David was in trouble. Except David was calmly walking toward Adrian. The other opponent lay flat on his back with blood leaking from his nose.

"How?"

"I did my best Tin Man imitation, but we should get out of here before the constables show up." David walked away while Adrian stood in place, his mouth open in confusion.

Adrian went to the hotel suite while David returned to *Elizabeth*. Sarai joined them at the hotel. Megan was in a hotel robe with still-damp hair.

"My lady, I hope your requested bath was pleasant?" Adrian said.

Megan switched to her snooty Lady Felicity Pembroke voice. "It sufficed. Not as good as the Ritz. I may have to speak to Daddy about booking me in this place." Reverting to her own voice. "It was an absolute delight. After a week of sonic showers, it was nice to use actual water. Not that *Elizabeth*'s facilities aren't nice."

"Well, we're not the Ritz either. We have nothing like this," Adrian opened the champagne the hotel had delivered.

They started a call, and holographic images of Lizzie and David appeared before them. They discussed the day's events, the lack of success finding the survey boat, and the bounty collection attempt. Everyone agreed someone had taken advantage of Stonington's death and made the ship vanish. Being chopped for parts was likely.

"The next step is to find where the parts were sold. We want to know where the ship had been, so we only need the navigation unit. I'm sorry, Sarai, but it means you need to call your old contacts if you're willing," Adrian said.

"Already done. We have a meeting in the Casino's executive lounge at 23:00 with my old boss. If there is information, this man will have it. The cost of information is a different question. Fortunately, I am a fantastic negotiator."

"Okay, you and I'll go and discuss—" Adrian said.

Sarai held up a hand. "You're not invited."

Adrian asked, "What?"

"You were not invited. He doesn't like you."

"Why? I've never even met the man."

"Just accept it, Adrian, you can't go."

"Who is this person?" Megan asked. She sipped the champagne, which had been chilled to eight degrees Celsius as requested.

"The single overlord who controls all criminal activities in the regions near Jupiter. He wants a cut if there's illegal activity in this area. His organization is small compared to the terrestrial organized crime families. They wish they had his level of control. His name is Dwight Wojciechowski, but he likes to be called Zeus."

"Will he give us what we need? Can we trust it?" Adrian asked.

"He may find the information if it exists. We can trust if he says the information is real, it is. For trusting him, I trust him to be true to his nature. Just like a snake, he may bite, but there's always a reason."

"Sarai, I don't like you going alone."

"Don't worry, Adrian. I won't be going alone. They excluded you, but he specifically required Megan to attend the meeting."

"Why me? We are looking for a nav unit, so wouldn't David make more sense?"

Sarai shook her head. "At the moment, the focus lays on the nav unit's location, not its contents. Our friendly neighborhood mob boss can put two and two together. The crew of the *Elizabeth* is looking for a beat-up artifact hunter boat. We've got an exo-archaeologist passenger with a bounty. He wants to know the connection, I'm sure."

"Will Megan be safe? He could be after the reward," Adrian asked.

"He gave his word we would be safe. The bounty is insignificant to him. The answer to a mystery holds more value to him." She looked at Lizzie. "It is cute how your grandson, in 2155, thinks we're helpless womenfolk. Did you let him watch too many 20th-century movies where women are always a damsel in distress?"

"It wasn't me. Must have been his father and grandfather."

Sarai cut him off before he could respond, "Don't worry, we will have a backup. Piet will accompany us, but not in the meeting."

Adrian recognized a good plan, even if he couldn't be involved.

In the late afternoon, Sarai and Megan's outfits arrived. Following a light dinner, the ladies disappeared upstairs to prepare for their mission.

Meanwhile, they had ordered a tuxedo for Piet. He looked uncertain as he entered the room in his new attire, but Adrian smiled. "Looking sharp, Piet."

"Good evening, gentlemen. What do you think?"

Atop the curved staircase, Megan McCord and Sarai Rousseau presented themselves, bathed in the soft glow of Jupiter. Their descent down the steps was a deliberate and elegant affair.

Sarai was resplendent in a long gown, a fusion of traditional Thai style with a contemporary French twist. The dress, boasting a high neck and graceful sleeves, featured vibrant light gold and orange hues. A delicate shawl adorned her shoulders, and a pristine white flower contrasted beautifully with her black hair. Her every step exuded a sense of elegance.

Megan wore a stylish silver gown that accentuated her radiant smile. She wore a green tartan sash diagonally across her body, contrasting with her red hair. A silver, Celtic-designed pin held the sash in place. Her crimson locks had a matching hairpin. Her dress, off one shoulder and graced with a high double slit, allowed her to traverse with confidence in her innate beauty, which she often lacked.

As they descended the staircase, the two ladies said in perfect unison, "Boys, you may now close your mouths."

Obediently, the gentlemen complied.

9

The Olympian Gamble

August 3, 2155—Callisto Station—Olympus Casino

The trio passed through Callisto Station's Entertainment Sector. This section offered wholesome fun for families and adult-focused indulgences modeled after Amsterdam's famed De Wallen Redlight district.

Between these two different spheres lay their destination - The Olympus casino.

All space stations had the same design but unique motifs. The theme of the casinos at the Jovian station was Greek mythology. The designers highlighted the myth of the moon the station orbited.

They entered the casino through a circular atrium. A pair of statues stood in the center of the room. A Greek god embracing a naked woman. The perimeter of the room was alcoves with murals.

The first scene presented a group of nude women surrounding a goddess with a bow.

The statue depicted the god becoming the goddess and seducing the woman.

The next had the woman bearing a child. The goddess with the bow is furious and expels the woman from her entourage.

A stern-looking goddess then transforms the woman into a bear.

Finally, the baby grows up and finds the bear while hunting. Before he can kill the bear, the god transforms them both into stars.

The myth of Callisto and Zeus.

Sarai pointed at the statue in the center and said, "A few last-minute items. Always call him Zeus, never Dwight. He doesn't like the name. We'll have some small talk before we get down to business. Remember, no matter how friendly or charming he acts, he is never on anyone's side but his own. Conversely, if he gives us his word, he'll keep it."

The casino was a throwback to Vegas in the early 21st century. The ding of slot machines, ugly carpets, servers carrying watered-down drinks to players, and no clocks on the walls. The only thing missing was the haze of cigarette smoke.

The casino had three levels. They built it in a faux Greco-Roman style. The first level was the low-limit games designed to bilk money from the miners back from rotation.

The second level was for more affluent customers, mostly tourists from Earth. Of course, the third level was for the High Roller "whales," it was their destination.

A curly-haired blonde woman in business attire met them when they stepped off the lift. "Good evening, ladies, sir. I'm Amanda, and I will be your host."

"It's good to meet you...Amanda," Sarai said. A glimmer in her eye and a crooked smile betrayed that she knew Amanda from some time in the past.

"Mr. Zeus is expecting you. I'll bring you ladies to him right away. I'm sorry, sir, but you will have to stay here. Gamble or enjoy a drink on this level."

The limits at the tables shocked Piet. "I can't afford that."

"Mr. Zeus expected this. The King of the gods offers this modest gift." An attendant appeared with a tray of chips, each bearing a Thunderbolt and value. Piet paled, calculating the sum exceeded his apprentice earnings over several months.

Amanda summoned a nearby casino attendant. "Oliver, please assist this gentleman to one of the gaming tables and ensure he has whatever he desires. Drink, food, or maybe companionship?"

"Which option do you prefer, sir?" Oliver asked.

"I think I'll give Blackjack a shot,"

Amanda used her cuff computer to open a door, revealing a small lounge. A bar stocked with top-shelf liquor was against one wall. Comfortable chairs and tables filled the rest of the room. A video wall opposite the bar showed a moonlit beach somewhere on Earth. A man in his early fifties wearing a well-tailored suit rose and met them.

"Welcome, ladies. I am glad you could make it. You both look stunning this evening. Thank you, Amanda. I'll take it from here." She nodded and left the room.

"Mademoiselle Rousseau and I are longtime friends. It is a pleasure to meet a new friend of hers. Doctor McCord, my name is Zeus. May I call you Megan?"

Megan was prepared to dislike him instantly because of his pretentious name. However, his natural charisma washed it away. "Yes, please do."

He led them to a trio of chairs with a small table between them.

"Megan, for you, we have champagne that I am told is excellent. Sarai, since you don't drink, feel free to have some of my sparkling cider. You stopped drinking for a different reason than I, but I respect it."

"Are you still managing well?" Sarai asked.

Zeus took out a small metal disk and threw it on the table. "I earned my twenty-year chip a few months ago."

Sarai leaned forward to look and beamed. "Congratulations. It's a fantastic accomplishment. You must be proud, Dwight." She flinched and realized her faux pas.

Zeus sucked in his breath but waved it off. "Considering the sentiment intended, I'll let it pass," he said. "You are the one who pushed me to get sober."

He steered the conversation in other directions. They spoke about many topics but did not discuss business.

Once the discussion about football clubs ended, Zeus shifted focus to business. He motioned for a dark-haired woman to approach.

"This is Cassandra, one of my assistants. She took over many of your roles, Sarai." Cassandra glared at Sarai with a raised eyebrow in a clear challenge, placed a data chip on the table, and stepped back.

"Megan, you're looking for a survey ship belonging to a hunter named Fred Stonington." His voice changed tone from the casual one before. "Sarai's assumption about the ship being sold illegally for parts was accurate. The data chip contains buyer names for the parts. It's not an extensive list. As I understand, the ship's condition left little of value."

"Is the navigation computer's location on there?" Megan asked, reaching for the chip.

"No peeking until we reach a deal."

Sarai stepped in at this point, as negotiation was her specialty. "It's simple. After Mr. Stonington's death, Roger McCord purchased Stonington's estate. As the legal owner, she has the right to know the parts' location."

"Her family did not pay the dock fees or the mechanic repairing it. They forfeited ownership." Zeus leaned back and spread his hands wide.

"That would require a legal procedure, which never happened." Sarai focused her eyes on his.

"Sarai, let's stop this little game. Fun as our back and forth has always been. The legalities of ownership have rarely concerned me. You won't get this on a technicality. Megan, I am ready to hand this over. There will be a trade-off.

"I'll start with my most generous offer. You get this data tonight. I'll put you in a suite in the best hotel on the station instead of living on a ship." Sarai felt a little satisfaction. Zeus wasn't as all-seeing as he thought. "Viscountess Primrose should sleep in a luxurious bed." Megan shivered at the reminder that she would inherit the title with her father's death, assuming her father's killers didn't find her.

"I'll provide a modern survey shuttle with all the equipment necessary for artifact hunting. *Elizabeth* will be free to continue business as usual. I even have a lucrative contract for her. I need several containers delivered to a station near Saturn. *Elizabeth* would be ideal." The nine AU distance on that date would place the crew too far to assist Megan if she needed friends.

"I'll make it known no one should attempt to collect on the dark web bounty. If anyone is foolish enough to try, you will have a bodyguard. Lawyers on Earth will work to clear your name."

"There is also information you're not aware of yet that will be helpful in your quest." Cassandra held up another data chip and placed it back in a pocket.

"For all of that, I only ask one simple thing." He stared at Sarai with a devilish smile. "Simply return to my employment."

Sarai sat in silence for a few moments as she held her breath.

"Merde! Le crétin! Imbécile. Mung Luke gah-ree," Sarai let loose a string of combined French and Thai insults. Sarai's loss of composure shocked Megan.

Zeus struggled to contain laughter. "I had hoped to bring a bit of the old you out. It is a serious offer. It is the best option you have. We will protect your new friend here. Hopefully, she'll find what she's looking for. Your old friends will be safe at Saturn.

His eyes flicked to Cassandra, who stood with a passive face.

"I'll respect your desire for non-violence. I know the need to change." He held up his sobriety chip. "You can present a carrot to Cassandra's stick in negotiations. They waste your talents on getting a 10% profit on a run for a tramp freighter. So just come back. Everyone wins."

Sarai closed her eyes in private meditation to return to a Zen state. She repeated her mantras while Zeus talked.

"My friend will not join you, not to help me, not for any reason I can prevent," Megan said. An icy and protective rage laced through her words.

"Megan, this is the best way to meet your needs. I have contacts on Earth. They will drop the warrant if I pull the right strings."

"I changed my mind. You can't call me Megan. It's Doctor McCord." Her voice was steely but even while staring into his eyes.

Zeus met her gaze equally. "Very well, Doctor. You have my respect. I'll not be a hypocrite and use a name other than you prefer."

Sarai, eyes still closed, spoke one soft word, "No."

Zeus and Megan broke their staring contest and looked at Sarai.

"I won't join you, Zeus. Cassandra appears capable. Do you have another offer?"

"Very well. You don't want to do the smart thing—second option. You are obviously on an artifact hunt. I want half. I'll help you move on the black market the other half—no need to pay silly taxes. Doctor McCord will tell me the entire story. I have enough pieces to know it is interesting. I might even volunteer ideas to keep you out of prison. The fact you are still hunting artifacts after your father's death tells me whoever killed him wants these artifacts. Or you were involved, after all."

"If we tell you everything, what stops you from taking it all for yourself?" Megan asked.

"My word. I swear once, I'll not use the information to hunt down the artifacts for myself. I am not a hunter. None are in my direct employment. I profit as a middleman."

"We accept your word. Let's make this simple. 20,000 Coalition Credits for the data. It's more than the junker would have cost in the junkyard it belonged." Sarai countered.

"Well, normally, cash is king. A bird in the hand, as they say. Nonetheless, I'll look at the long game. How about 40% of any artifacts found? I'll get the first choice. Plus, the story."

"First pick? What if we find a Starshell?"

"Starshell? You do dream big. No, if you find a Starshell, you turn it over to the UCE. Like a good little citizen. No one wants to play with hiding those."

"And if we find nothing? That is how most hunts end," Megan asked.

"Then I lose. It's a gamble." He shrugged. "I do work out of a casino, after all. I like my odds with you, Doctor."

Sarai pulled out her comm-pad. "My counteroffer. We get both of your data chips. You get one artifact, our choice. I will give you this." She held up a data chip of her own.

"I might as well take the cash. You're slipping, Sarai." He paused as she showed him a preview of the chip contents. His face drained of color. This time, his icy stare met Sarai's.

"Last offer. You get the chip you asked for. I keep the chip Cassandra is holding. You keep all the artifacts, though my offer to fence them will stand. I want the story. You give me the chip you hold and your word of honor. There are no more copies." An air of finality in his tone.

Sarai looked at Megan, who nodded slightly. Sarai then tossed the chip toward Cassandra, but Zeus plucked it from the air. Sarai pocketed the chip on the table.

Zeus refiled his sparkling cider glass and leaned back. "Well, my dear doctor, please tell me your tale."

Megan recounted her tale to Zeus, summarizing how her father had gained the explorer's estate and the clues that had launched her quest. Zeus expressed sympathy over her father's murder. When asked to see the asteroid projection, Megan refused to share the sole copy.

"One more freebie—I'll quash the troublesome dark web bounty," Zeus said. "Whoever posted it didn't go through me. That needs correcting."

After his dramatic pronouncement, Zeus departed to a private office. A young Italian man awaited him there. "I'm told you bring a message from my counterparts on Earth. My favors don't come cheaply," Zeus noted, his tone laden with implication.

Cassandra escorted them out the door from which they had entered.

"I warned him you won't come back to his service. He needs to learn to listen to my advice." Cassandra spoke for the first time. "A warning to you. Leave Jupiter, or death will come to the *Elizabeth*. I assure you." She closed the door behind them.

Amanda waited for them. "I hope you had a productive meeting. Please follow me to your friend. When I last checked on him, he was alright."

When they reached the blackjack table, Piet was nowhere to be seen. The dealer said he had taken his winnings to a nearby lounge for a celebratory drink with one of the other players. His tone suggested Piet had done better than "fairly well."

Unlike the exclusive lounge where they met Zeus, this was more of a typical casino lounge. The place was mostly empty. Men and women were drinking or talking at a few tables. On the couch was a surprising sight.

"I see Oliver found the gentleman both a drink *and* a companion." Amanda quipped about her earlier offer.

Piet and a platinum-blonde woman were sitting on the couch. She had one arm around his shoulder and the other hand in his lap while nibbling on his ear. On the table was a stack of chips and two drinks.

"Piet, what are you doing?" Megan said. Just as she was about to walk over to him, Sarai intervened by touching Megan's shoulder.

"It's not what it looks like. Look at his face."

Piet's face did not hold pleasure in his situation. Beads of sweat formed on his forehead, and his eyes were wide in terror.

The woman turned, and Megan gasped in shock. Her body trembled, a combination of disbelief and confusion twisting her gut.

"Ciao Bella, Girlfriend. Miss me? We have a lot to talk about." Bianca giggled and grinned as she held a knife to Piet's groin.

10

The Lioness Finds a Target

"Docking complete, Captain," Pilot Thorn said as *Zeta Sierra* connected to Ganymede station. He sagged into his seat. Like the rest of the crew, he was exhausted. Almost four days at 1.25g sapped everyone's strength. Gravity plates were excellent at increasing gravity but couldn't lower the perceived gravity from acceleration.

"Good job, helm," Kristina said. She opened a ship-wide channel. "Zetties. I know it has been a rough few days. You have all done an exemplary job. I'm proud to be the captain of the best ship and the best crew in the service. We still have a duty to do, but as soon as we can, drinks are on me. Chen-Ramirez, out."

She turned to her executive officer. "Frank, it looks like we beat *Elizabeth* here, but they should arrive anytime. Let's welcome them when they arrive and pick up the fugitive. First, I'll speak with station security."

"Yes, sir. Phillips is waiting for you at the airlock," the XO said.

Warrant Officer Philips met her at the hatch, and they took the short walk to the security office.

Kristina approached the desk. "I am Lieutenant Commander Chen-Ramirez of the Customs and Patrol Service.

May I speak to someone for support in apprehending a fugitive?"

"It is about damn time you got here, Commander. Are you aware of the fugitive's importance to the Coalition?" A portly man in an expensive suit approached. Even the fine tailoring could not hide the man's girth.

"And you are?"

"Lead Administrator Roland Hübner. Ship commanders should know the names of their administrators. Now, will you answer my question?"

Kristina chose not to remind him CPS didn't report to him. Unfortunately, bureaucrats like him ran the UCE. "I know how important Doctor McCord is to the Coalition. We intend to take her into custody as soon as the *Elizabeth* docks."

"Not that question. What took you so long?"

"We departed minutes after the arrival of our new orders. The distance was millions of kilometers." *How can a space station administrator not understand physics and travel time?*

Hübner ignored her statement. "About the arrival of *Elizabeth*. A shipping magnate's daughter would never travel on a tramp freighter. The only evidence we have is your hearsay. Most likely, McCord paid off the freighter captain to lie to you."

Adrian would lie to a man like Hübner, but not me, Kristina thought, while struggling to keep a neutral expression.

"The *Elizabeth* hasn't reserved a dock here at Ganymede station. An Ettrick Logistics ship, the *Highland Bounty*, arrives at midnight. My contacts back in Geneva have confirmed she listed that ship in her travel permits. She may have slipped past the officials on Earth but won't get by me." Hübner attempted to puff out his chest but ended in a coughing fit. "Commander, I'll be there to make sure you don't mess this up. Now get out."

Kristina and Phillips left the security office. After walking thirty meters, she said, "No rest for the weary, literally in this case. Get your people geared up. We might have a late night."

Midnight August 4, 2155

Two hours had passed since meeting the administrator. While waiting, Kristina worried about Adrian and the *Elizabeth*. She knew about when they left Earth Station Three and the ship's normal acceleration. The vessel should've arrived a few hours ago. *Where are they?*

A nagging bit of doubt hit Kristina. She knew what Adrian said, but the records indicated Doctor McCord was scheduled for *Highland Bounty*. She didn't like following orders of someone like Hübner, but to search the Ettrick freighter made sense.

Kristina, Phillips, and five of her custom agents were outside the *Highland Bounty*'s personnel airlock. Five station security people supported them. An equal number were at the cargo dock, led by Chief Petty Officer Zhao. The Customs Service agents had neuro-stun carbines and flechette pistols for backup. Station security carried riot shotguns with stun pistols. It surprised her that they even had those weapons on the station. No one wanted to risk losing air with a bad shot.

Administrator Hübner directed the operation from a safe position behind everyone else.

Highland Bounty docked as soon as it had clearance. Phillips squeezed through the opening airlock, surprising the crew. "Everyone against the bulkhead. We are the United Coalition of Earth Customs and Patrol Service executing a search warrant. Don't resist, and this will be quick."

Kristina followed and approached a man in an officer's uniform. "Take me to your captain and your passenger."

Confusion clouded the officer's face. "We don't have any passengers."

"Let's have this conversation with your captain." She nudged the man in the direction of the bridge.

On entering the bridge, Captain Brodie Anderson stood to meet the uninvited guest, "What is happening here?"

"I am Lieutenant Commander Chen-Ramirez. We have a warrant to search your vessel and take your passenger, Megan McCord, into custody. If she peacefully surrenders, you can be about your business."

"What are you talking about? Doctor McCord never arrived for the voyage. Hardly a surprise, considering her father died the day before we left. I said the same thing to the Coalition Security inquisitor, who delayed our departure to search before we left. No one will tell me what this is about," Anderson said.

Kristina opened her mouth to ask about the CS search, which didn't appear in official records. However, Administrator Hübner barged onto the bridge.

"You can't hide her. Turn her over now, or I'll have your license suspended." Hübner wheezed as he pushed past Kristina and stood centimeters from Anderson's face.

"I'm not hiding anyone. What is all of this about? Why are you looking for Megan?" Anderson stiffened his back and glared at the overbearing administrator.

"Captain Anderson, I sent your systems a copy of the warrant. Doctor Megan McCord is wanted as an accomplice in the murder of Roger McCord," Kristina said. She kept her voice level and calm.

Anderson's head snapped to look at Kristina. "Bull shit. Megan would never harm the Viscount. I've worked for the family for years. I have known her since she was a child."

Hübner sneered at Anderson. "You probably think she is your new boss. What has she promised you, Captain? I know you corporate types put your loyalty to the company over the Coalition where it belongs. Maybe we will find her in your bed."

"How dare you." Anderson's fists clenched as his eyes narrowed.

Kristina stepped between the two men who were at least ten centimeters taller than her. Phillips took a step closer and tightened the grip on his stunner.

"Captain, Administrator, let's all take a deep breath. Captain, have your crew step off the ship. We will perform the search. If she isn't found, my crew will buy yours a round of drinks. Either way, your crew members will be free to do their business in a few hours." If Kristina didn't defuse the situation, she might need to arrest the captain for assaulting Administrator Hübner.

After the initial chaos, a calm settled over the scene. The freighter crew stayed off the ship, looking annoyed and resigned. Customs agents and station security searched the boat, exploring every nook and cranny. The Zetties were professionals who caused little disruption. Hübner's people ripped things apart in their search.

The scrutiny lasted two grueling hours. Even Hübner, determined to find something, found no hiding place for an adult human. Instead of admitting his mistake, he left in a huff.

The *Zeta Sierra* agents stayed onboard to help restore order to the *Highland Bounty* and repair damage caused by the rough station team.

Afterward, the two crews enjoyed a few rounds of drinks at a late-night bar. Captain Anderson split the bill with Kristina. She was thankful because the bar tab would stress her paycheck.

Kristina and Brodie sat in a quiet corner of the bar. They formed a friendship over drinks, watching their teams, expecting trouble to brew in the late-night hours.

With a sigh, Kristina leaned in closer, her expression heavy with concern. "Brodie, I wish today had gone better. It should have been more professional."

Brodie nodded, his eyes reflecting a weariness born from decades in space. "I know, Kristina. People like Hübner want to make a name for themselves. I would place money that he thinks a big win would get him out of his 'exile to the hinterlands' at Jupiter. In thirty-five years in space, I've learned people like Hübner are universal constants."

Kristina couldn't help but frown. "Still does not solve my problem. Doctor McCord is a wanted fugitive. I am under orders to find her."

He refilled their beers from the pitcher on the table. "I assure you, Megan McCord didn't have anything to do with her father's death. Megan loved her father deeply. It's just not possible."

She sighed, grappling with her duty. "That is an issue for the justice system and her lawyer. I have my duty to perform. What's best for her? Me finding her or someone like Hübner?"

"I understand," Brodie said, "but I'm not sure I have any answers for you. I don't know where she is. Megan missed her scheduled shuttle to Space Station One. If you want to locate her, check Scotland."

Kristina was desperate, grasping at straws for any clue. "Humor me. A reliable source told me she was on the way to Jupiter. Was there anyone she would have met? Where did she plan to stay on Ganymede station?"

"Ganymede? Her destination was Callisto. We were dropping her off," Brodie corrected. "We came to Ganymede because of a route change from HQ."

Kristina's eyes widened in realization. "What? Callisto? That's where assumptions will get you. All the evidence pointed to Ganymede. Damn, Hübner. I'll be a day behind when I get there."

Brodie stared into his beer mug as he considered if he had helped or betrayed the woman he had known since she was a child.

Kristina stood and held her hand out to Brodie. "Thank you, Brodie. If she is innocent, I have faith in our justice system to clear her name."

"I wish I had your faith." He had one more piece of information to give. "I checked on our change in destination. The order to divert to Ganymede was DNA-coded with the CEO's direct authorization. The timestamp was three hours after his death."

11
Reunion with Old Friends

Megan's open mouth confusion contrasted with Bianca's knowing smile.

"Bianca, what are you doing here? And why are you holding a knife to my friend?" Megan's eyes looked at the other woman as she tried to understand how her bubbly friend came to be halfway across the solar system.

"I like knives. Don't you recognize this one?" Bianca adjusted the angle of the blade to show the words *Megan McCord* laser etched into the blade.

"Ye murdurred mah faither? Why? We were friends." The image of the blade sent with a threat was seared into her brain. Sarai's stronghold prevented Megan from rushing forward.

"No, no. Watch out, Girlfriend." Piet gasped as she dug in the knife, cutting fabric below his belt buckle.

"Your father died of his poor decisions. He would have been fine if he had just given me what I wanted."

Megan tried to charge, but Sarai stopped her. "Calm yourself. Breathe. She has friends." Five customers stood. They wielded spring-loaded batons. Sarai positioned herself between Megan and the three of them.

"You never asked what Sergio and I did for money. Probably assumed we were trust fund brats like you. We are independent contractors hired to acquire the information you had. We tried to do it the fun way, but then you moved up your trip. We took drastic measures. Your father died, and you spoiled my perfect skin." Bianca turned her face to display red welts on her cheek and shoulder. Proof that Megan's shotgun blast found its mark. "Now I'm almost as ugly as you."

Waves of loathing radiated from Bianca. "Give me the decrypted information about the asteroid now. Otherwise, I'll gut Muscles here, and then I get to carve up your pretty face. Like you did mine."

Sarai whispered, "It is time to take control of the situation. Calm and focus and the solution will present itself."

Megan suppressed her anger, taking a deep breath. She locked eyes with Piet, wishing him emotional strength.

Bianca's pride hurt more than her body. The platinum blonde seethed with irrational rage over her damaged vanity.

Megan analyzed her psychotic former friend. A calmness could win this deadly game.

"Don't hurt him," Megan said. "I'll give you the asteroid data if you let Piet go free."

Megan held up her clutch bag. "It's right here. Let him go, and it's yours."

"Hold it right there. No closer. Is this boy worth the price? He does look yummy." Bianca turned to Piet, licked his cheek, and addressed him. "You must be good in the sack. Perhaps I missed out on a delightful little escapade. But alas, one simple twist of my wrist could forever rob us of that chance. So, Megan, if you're serious about keeping him whole, I suggest you toss it over—now."

"You know, *Girlfriend*, I think the scars improve your appearance. They will give you character instead of being a plastic doll." Megan waited for the anger to flare in Bianca's eyes. She shot Piet a look of warning and tossed the handbag at Bianca's feet. "Here it is."

Bianca glanced down momentarily. As she reached for the bag, Megan kicked a shoe at Bianca, hitting the uninjured side of her face.

Piet seized the distraction to twist from Bianca's grasp. He lifted the table as a shield. Chips and glasses scattered about.

Piet preferred a mathematical equation or an excellent book to a fight, but sometimes, he didn't have a choice. His natural bulk somehow drew people who wanted to test themselves. If he could not avoid the fight, he would try to end it quickly.

He charged a pair of Bianca's flunkies, a man with a goatee and a woman who was too small to be a thug. Piet's table shield bulldozed into them, leaving the man sprawled on the floor.

The woman sidestepped the charge. Piet's exposed back took a baton blow, sending him sprawling. He knew now the tiny woman was fast and hit hard.

The woman smiled and advanced on the defenseless Piet to finish him.

With unwavering determination, Sarai maintained a position between Megan and three of Bianca's lackeys. She could not allow them to attack her friend from behind.

Sarai's former career in the underworld gave her a professional paranoia that never went away. She dressed for combat success and brought out some unexpected twists.

She clutched her gossamer shawl in a combat grip. The shawl's fragile look disguised hidden strength and weighted ends to double as a weapon. With the rip of a covert seam, the dress transformed from a long evening gown into a combat-ready mini dress. Slipping off her expensive Jimmy Choos, she stood barefoot and prepared.

In a three-on-one situation, her ability to defend friends while causing minimal harm to others would be tested. She vowed long ago not to take another life or cause severe damage. In this case, she justified that it was not serious harm if a doctor could fix it.

Sarai's first goal was to turn three-on-one into one-on-one.

A swift kick dumped a table and chair tipped over in the path of one attacker. A serving tray thrown like a frisbee disarmed another.

The third held a riot stun baton and sneered as he approached. Any hit would administer a shock to disable a person for at least a minute. *That's a problem easily solved*, Sarai thought.

"You know it's not the size, but how you handle the stick?" Sarai said in an even voice. She didn't fear a man who walked like a bullying oaf instead of a trained combatant.

The slow oaf swung at her, intending to remove her with a single blow. Sarai danced around him and snagged the baton with her shawl. A twist brought the baton into the oaf's face, stunning him. She snatched it from his grip and tossed it.

"Heads up, Piet." as it landed beside him.

Sarai confronted the recovered pair, a bald man and a woman with green braided hair. Dodging Baldy's swing, she launched the weighted end of her shawl straight at the woman's face, who dove out of the way.

I'm glad she was fast enough to dodge. A hit from the shawl's weighted end could have been deadly. Sarai thought. Sarai stepped to the side to keep Baldy between her and the green-haired fighter.

Time for the next trick from The Great Rousseau Magician Extraordinaire.

With a hidden design, the shawl splayed out, mimicking the expansive grasp of a gladiator's capture net. In a move straight out of the Colosseum, Sarai entangled the bald man's face and weapon. With a spin and a kick in the ass, the man was out of the fight.

The green-haired woman had recovered fast and struck Sarai with a life-threatening blow. What could've been a devastating blow to the skull grazed an arm, numbing it. Sarai refocused, recognizing the most challenging opponent. She didn't dare check how Megan had faired against Bianca.

Megan faced off against the woman who had killed her father. Contrary to Bianca's malice, Megan still held a sense of calm. Her focus on protecting Piet allowed her to maintain composure.

He was safe. Well, safer.

Stay alive, find openings. Megan thought. Megan's double-slit dress gave her the mobility to stay alive. Hopefully, her calm would give her openings.

Bianca vaulted from the couch. Blood oozed, forming a scarlet trail where the shoe heel pierced her flesh.

"I'm glad you chose the hard way. I still get paid and get to cut the perfect princess down to size." She held up a wicked skinner knife that had a backward-facing gut hook.

Megan drew her dirk, its modest size a stark disparity to Bianca's imposing blade, yet it fit comfortably in her hand.

Bianca lunged, her blade aiming for Megan's midsection with a fierce speed. The thick weave of Megan's tartan sash prevented a deep gash.

"If you had just gone home with Sergio, none of this would've happened. I would've found what I needed, and you would have gotten laid. You need it, Amica Mia."

Megan attacked, but Bianca danced away with ease. With every parry and dodge, Megan knew she was outmatched. The ditzy party girl revealed her murderous talents while giggling in glee.

In their swift exchange, Bianca calculated her strikes to disable, not kill. A lightning-fast strike sliced across Megan's ribs, causing a hiss of pain.

"Oh no, you got blood on your pretty silver dress. We should soak it right away so a stain doesn't set." Bianca tilted her head and gave Megan a faux-frown of concern.

"Where would I be without a 'dear friend' like you, Bianca?" Her voice oozed insincerity.

"Amici per sempre, cara. Friends forever, my dear." Bianca's eyes went wild as she made another quick attack. As the sharp blade sliced through her flesh, Megan barely registered the pain in her left forearm. Bianca started laughing.

Megan threw a half-finished beer off a table in her opponent's face, and she retreated behind a faux Roman column and a pedestal with a cupid statue.

Fear bore through Megan's calm. Sweat mingled with blood. Megan's heart raced. She needed to find an opening soon, or Bianca would finish her as soon as she grew bored. Megan suspected the real Bianca grew bored just as fast as the image she presented.

Bianca was a cat toying with the mouse Megan—it was time to turn the tables. Megan would be Jerry to Bianca's Tom instead. Channeling the cartoon mouse, she threw Cupid at Bianca.

Piet snatched Sarai's gift baton and blocked a swing from his assailant. He kicked up, and the force of his blow sent the small woman soaring through the air, crashing into the couch.

Piet leapt to his feet at the same time as the goatee man.

Piet held a stun baton, his foe a traditional spring-loaded one. They locked eyes, silently assessing one another. Piet's inexperience showed as he awkwardly gripped the unfamiliar weapon. His talents lay with math and muscle, not weapons.

Piet lunged. The agile henchman dodged, landing a glancing rib blow in return.

Setting his jaw, Piet propelled himself into another rush, "Hya!" His opponent danced away gracefully, landing a baton on Piet's side. The goateed goon laughed as he played matador to Piet's bull.

The momentum drew Piet away from his foe. He took a moment to observe everyone's status.

The woman Piet had kicked into the couch recovered and was about to attack Megan. An immediate threat to his friend.

The apprentice navigator calculated a trajectory and threw the stun baton like a javelin. In slow motion, the baton flew, striking the target's head an instant before she could hit Megan. The tiny female thug convulsed and fell to the ground. Megan never even realized the danger was there, preoccupied with throwing a Cupid statue.

Piet's problems weren't over. Goatee goon approached an unarmed Piet. He jumped behind a platform and formed a plan inspired by Megan's playbook. Two enormous statues, Zeus and Hera, were on the platform.

"Timber!" Piet put all his strength into the pair of statues. They tipped over, Hera falling at the goon.

The man dropped his baton and screamed in terror as he held his hands, hoping to stop the statue. Luck was with the man. The Hera's arm snagged on a cable, halting it just shy of a meter from the man. He and Piet shared a surprised look.

The statue of Zeus fell to the floor and shattered with a massive crash. The entire casino now knew about the fight.

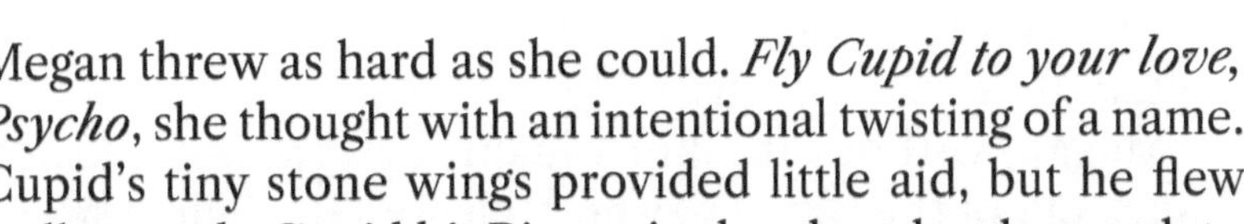

Megan threw as hard as she could. *Fly Cupid to your love, Psycho*, she thought with an intentional twisting of a name. Cupid's tiny stone wings provided little aid, but he flew well enough. Cupid hit Bianca in the chest hard enough to spin her around and send her knife flying.

Megan charged forward and stabbed Bianca's heart—a fitting thing after what happened with Megan's father.

The strike was accurate but only produced a grunt. The dirk did not penetrate the fabric. Bianca's dress was made of an ultra-expensive and thin anti-cut material. The high-neck, off-the-shoulder top protected Bianca's vitals and neck, acting as limited body armor.

Bianca slapped the blade from Megan's hand. She reached her shoulder and pulled out a broken arrow with a heart-shaped head.

"You hit me with Cupid's Arrow?"

"Does this mean you have to love me now?" Megan asked.

Bianca answered by jabbing the arrow into Megan's shoulder. Megan shrieked in pain and fell. They barely noticed the crash of the statue of Zeus. Bianca loomed over Megan.

"Come on, Megan. Best friends should have no secrets. Time to tell me all your juicy secrets." Bianca's eyes darkened, her fingers curling into tight fists as she approached Megan.

Bianca seized Megan's hair, yanking her up. Megan's hands flew to her head, frantically trying to break the grip. Her fingers found her grandmother's Celtic hair comb. She ripped it free and drove the comb into Bianca's unprotected leg.

Bianca yelped, releasing Megan's hair as she stumbled backward. Megan jumped away while Bianca reached to pick up her knife. At that point, the cables the statue of Hera leaned on snapped. The cable supported a statue of Icarus on the ceiling.

The statue plunged straight at Bianca as if the sun melted the wax on Icarus' wings.

Megan, without thinking, leapt forward and pushed Bianca out of the way. They both cleared the falling statue and landed in a heap. Dust and sound filled the room.

On the ground, Bianca asked. "Why did you do that?"

"I just reacted. It's what a good person does."

"Good people are fucking fools."

Bianca flipped Megan onto her back and straddled her like an Olympic wrestler going for a pin. Bianca, in a murderous fury, picked up a broken statue's head and held it high to crush Megan's skull. "Die, Bitch!"

A flechette gun whined, hit the statue's head, and blew it out of Biancas's grip. It was so accurate that no flechette darts cut her hands.

"Stop!" came a command. "It appears some of you lack the understanding of proper guest etiquette when visiting someone's home. I should give you all brooms and make you clean this up."

Zeus, King of Olympus, walked into the destroyed lounge with a flechette rifle resting on his shoulder. Cassandra, a squad of casino security, and Bianca's brother, Sergio, followed Zeus.

12
Returning Home a Little Worse for Wear

August 4, 2155—Callisto Station—Olympus Casino

Everyone froze in their positions. Piet grappled with his opponent, now with the upper hand and both unarmed. Sarai had regained the feeling in her arm and used it to throw the woman she had fought over a couch. She rushed to Megan when Zeus' flechette gun stopped the fight.

Zeus ignored the combatants and stepped to where Amanda hid behind a loveseat. He helped her stand and ensured she was uninjured. After whispering something to her, he turned to the others.

Zeus marched over to Megan and Bianca. He grabbed Bianca and pushed her in Sergio's direction. He helped Megan to her feet as his people checked on those on the ground.

"Cassandra, call the house doctor. She's bleeding." Zeus said.

"Already on the way."

The *Elizabeth* crew gathered on one side of the crashed statues. Bianca's lackeys, those not stunned, gathered near the siblings on the other side. Zeus stood between them both, a foot on a broken statue.

"All of you have tested my goodwill. I have independently promised each group safe passage into my casino. I wish I had known I would need to protect you from each other or protect my casino from you. Hospitality prevents me from ejecting you out of the airlock. Here is what will happen."

He pointed at Sergio and Bianca, "Once your people recover from the stun, you'll leave the casino."

He indicated Megan's team and said, "I will arrange for someone to escort you back to *Elizabeth* after treating Doctor McCord."

The doctor arrived, and Zeus pointed him to Megan. "Please bandage her wounds. Minimize bleeding on the floor." His tone expressed concern that his words did not.

"Why does she get the doctor? She cut me first," Bianca said. Zeus looked at her minor cuts. He reached into the doctor's first aid kit and removed several adhesive bandages. He threw them at her.

"Fix yourself up and get out. If you leave quickly, I won't tell your employer you ruined the chance to make a deal."

While Sergio dragged Bianca away, Megan asked, "Was I simply a means to get to my father?"

"No, we could have gotten to your father, anyway. Tesoro, you were never the treasure I wanted, only the data you hold. I was sure that in my bed, you would babble about everything like most spoiled rich brats. Your father might be alive if you had let loose and given in to your urges. Ultimately, you were a just pleasant diversion," he said, voice dripping with mock sincerity.

Bianca tilted her head and waved at Megan. "Arrivederci amica mia. I look forward to our next meeting, Megan."

Megan saw no point in any more response as they walked away. Armed casino security followed.

"Thank you. You stopped Bianca from crushing my skull."

Zeus picked up Megan's glasses and handed them to her. They had come off in the final skirmish.

"You were here under my protection, and I apologize for the harm caused to you. This shouldn't have happened. Cassandra even warned me having you all here simultaneously would lead to trouble. I should have heeded her words more carefully." He dipped his head to his assistant. Cassandra nodded, keeping the "I told you so" to herself.

Zeus stepped close to Sarai and spoke in her ear. "Once Sergio and Bianca leave my casino, their protection ends. If you return to me, Cassandra and an enforcer team will remove the threat before they reach their ship."

"No."

"They certainly have access to better weapons than these batons. This is a short opportunity."

"Murdering them by proxy would be the same as if I did it myself. I will not do that."

Zeus stepped away and said, "I expected that would be your answer, but I had to ask."

He picked up the remains of the stone head he had blasted. It was from the statue of *Zeus*. "Few live after shooting themself in the head." He tossed the head away.

"Doctor McCord, I'll add this to our deal as compensation for this insult. Cassandra?" He held out his hand. She gave him the second data chip. "Here is information on Stonington's home. Some old shipping containers turned into an orbital habitat. It's in Jupiter's dust rings. He tried to hide it, so maybe it's something valuable in your search, or he was a paranoid madman."

Megan stood up against the doctor's protest and kissed Zeus on the cheek. "Thank you. I changed my mind. Please call me Megan."

"Megan, what I said before is true. You broke hospitality and many other things. You all must leave. A transport downstairs will take you to *Elizabeth*. You won't find the next step in your odyssey at Callisto station."

As Zeus walked away, he stepped on some of the scattered casino chips on the floor. He turned to Piet. "It looks like you did well in my casino, young man. Amanda, get someone to cash in these chips for him."

Amanda cleared her throat. "I planned to mention it later. The pit boss believes this man counted cards at the blackjack table. He cheated."

Zeus glared into Piet's eyes. "Well, did you?"

Piet gulped but met the man's eyes. "Yes. Calculations come naturally to me."

Zeus smiled. "Good. Remember this boy, If you're not cheating, you're not winning. Next time, don't get caught. Give the man his money." With that, he walked away, Cassandra following.

After he left, Sarai picked up Megan's shoes and handbag and returned them to her, "Twice in one day. One does not just fling designer shoes and bags across a room. Adrian showed me where my Prada's hit the wall. Now these. I'm shocked, just shocked. We will discuss the proper care of my shoes."

Megan looked at Sarai and threw her arms around her friend in a mighty hug. She then turned to Piet with open arms to repeat the embrace. One hand extended, the other clutching his side, he said, "I'll rain-check the hug. My rib cage can't handle it."

Megan allowed the doctor to sit her back down without resistance. As the adrenaline faded, the events took form in her mind. "I find it unfathomable she would try to kill us in the casino for some data on an Artificer site. Leads happen with regularity. I intended a fun post-grad excursion, not something serious. How did it spin to mob bosses and knife-wielding psychos? She became my friend."

"Maybe there is something to the 'Hunter's Folly superstitions.' We will help in any way possible. You can continue the hunt, but maybe you should return to Earth. Is it worth the risk?" Sarai said.

"That might be wise, but no. They killed my father for this. There must be a reason, and I saw the hate in Bianca's eyes. She won't stop even if I don't play her game."

"Good. You are right. Too many pieces are moving to avoid them all. You have us to the end," Sarai said. Piet nodded in agreement.

The doctor finished bandaging Megan's arm and checked on Piet. He injected Piet with painkillers and pills for later. He then gave Megan a shot and a bottle of antibiotic medication.

"Young man, you have broken ribs. You both should go to a medical facility soon for a full check-up. Do it at your next destination. The best thing for your long-term health is immediately getting away from Callisto. Doctor's orders if you don't listen to Zeus." He sent over several options for medical facilities on other stations. None were associated with the main base hospital.

Cassandra returned as the doctor finished. She equipped herself with black commando body armor and a holstered pistol. Four men with her had similar equipment.

"Transportation is waiting at the loading dock. Let's get you out of here so they can clean your mess up, and we can bring less destructive patrons in again." She led them to a service elevator. Amanda met them there and gave Piet an envelope with cash.

"Your winnings, sir."

"It wasn't even my money I gambled with. I can't take it." He attempted to push it away.

"Take the money, or you will insult Zeus." Cassandra shrugged.

Two small vans were waiting for them. Independent vehicles were rarely used in space stations outside of cargo areas. Most people traveled on foot or in various public trams. Cassandra reached into the pouch when Megan sat and returned Megan's Sgian Dubh dirk.

She also produced Bianca's wicked knife. "Do you want a victory trophy?"

Megan waved away the prize. "It doesn't feel like much of a victory."

"You lived. That is victory enough. The two are mercenary 'troubleshooters' known to be charming and vicious. They love to convince people to trust them and then frequently and violently betray them. Her pleasure lies in inflicting physical pain, while his lies in emotional pain. You are lucky his game back on Earth did not play out. The rumors have him crushing a woman's spirit and then handing her over to his sister."

After that announcement, silence filled the vehicle for the rest of the trip. Sarai sent messages updating Adrian and the ship while Megan sat lost in thought. They approached their home on the cargo level. Outside the docking port was Lizzie with her arms crossed, staring down at some station officials.

A tall, thin-faced woman turned to them when they exited the van. "I am Junior Administrator Kapeka Belova. Is your captain with you?"

"No, but he is on his way," Sarai said.

"As I explained to this woman, I revoked the docking permit for LCV *Elizabeth*. You won't be allowed to take cargo aboard. You have thirty minutes to depart before we charge fines. The officious woman walked away.

Lizzie assessed everyone's situation and took charge. "David, get to the bridge and prep for departure." Turning to injured strays, she said, "Sarai, get everything buttoned down in the hold and join David. Megan, get Piet to his cabin and make him lie down. I'll call Adrian and tell him to hurry."

Piet tried to stand straighter but winced. "I am fine. I can help." Lizzie responded with a stare. "Umm, yes, ma'am."

"After we leave the station, we meet to discuss the next steps. Now go." the imposing octogenarian commanded. Everyone scattered.

The crew, except Piet, met on the bridge to discuss their next plans. *Elizabeth* departed the station with two minutes to spare from the deadline.

Sarai changed into her usual coveralls, but her hair remained elegantly styled. Somehow, she had kept the flower in her hair the whole time. She reviewed the contents of the data chips they had received from Zeus. For a rare change, Adrian sat in the commander's chair when Megan arrived.

"How is Piet?" Adrian asked.

"The painkillers kicked in, and he is sleeping soundly. He'll be covered in bruises by morning. Do we have anything off the chips?"

"We have two targets now. The parts list from the chopped survey ship shows the nav computer was used on a ferry ship on regular runs between the asteroids and Jupiter. A few days ago, the ferry left an asteroid mine and returned to Io with construction workers.

"The other, mystery chip, contained information on the paranoid old hunters 'secret base.' It's a pair of old cargo containers, air scrubbers, and a mini fusion reactor. It is floating in the Main Ring near Metis." Jupiter's rings were thin and faint compared to Saturn's majestic rings, but they would provide a little cover to keep objects hidden. No one bothered to go near Jupiter's innermost moon because of its lack of value. Occasionally, robot-controlled ships passed by as they dipped into Jupiter's upper atmosphere, collecting gasses. Argon was particularly valuable as propellent in MPD thrusters.

"Megan, do you think the guy likely left anything valuable at these containers near Metis?" Adrian asked.

"Entirely likely. Some of these Artifact Hunters are like Old West prospectors, paranoid that someone will 'jump their claim.' Not without justification, either."

Adrian thought for a few moments. "David, make a course for Europa station."

"Not Io?" Megan asked.

"No, the Io station is under construction. That is why they need construction workers. Plus, Io is close enough to Jupiter's magnetosphere to disrupt instruments. That is why it is the last Galilean moon station constructed.

"Here is the plan. We dock at Europa station and get you and Piet checked out at a medical center."

"I'm fine, but Piet should go."

"No, you need real stitches and Rapid-Heal gel. It will heal better and not scar. Look at Adrian. He tried to be tough and has that scar," Sarai said. Adrian touched the scar on his face.

"All three of you, see a doctor. Then we split. *Elizabeth* stays at Europa. We have the two runabouts we planned to sell," Adrian said.

"David and Sarai will head to Io and meet the ferry. Sarai, negotiate with them to get David a copy of the logs." Sarai and David acknowledged their captain's instruction with a nod.

"Meanwhile, Megan and I search for the old hunter's 'hidden sanctum.' To check for anything valuable left. After ten years, it may have lost power and atmosphere. Good thing to have your EVA suit."

"It makes sense, but I have a concern. Bianca and Sergio will not give up. What is to prevent them from following us to Europa?" Megan asked.

Lizzie smirked and touched Megan's shoulder, "Oh, Sweetie, you should know us better than that. We are full of surprises. Before leaving the station, I filed a flight plan that didn't take us to Europa. I may have messed with other ships' flight plans as well. Junior Administrator Belova will have a lot of paperwork to explain why their system is so screwed up."

13

Employment Review Call

August 4, 2155—Space near Callisto

Bianca, Sergio, and their team boarded the Gulfstellar IX executive transport they used to beat *Elizabeth* to Jupiter.

"There is an incoming call waiting for you in the office," the pilot said.

Bianca and Sergio didn't acknowledge him but went to the plush office. Bianca sat in an executive chair and put her feet on the desk. Her boots scratched the expensive wood. Sergio pressed activated the incoming call.

As with every call, the video wall only showed an image of the solar system above the ecliptic. The words *Celatum Dominus* were superimposed over the image.

"This is a performance review. Please state the mission objective." The voice was completely neutral, betraying no accent or even gender.

"Acquire information from Megan about the location of...Artificer lookout point five or whatever you called it," Bianca said with a dismissive wave.

"We call it Occultatum Populum observationis loco XVI or Artificer Observation Post XVI in modern terms," the voice said.

The image on the screen changed to a still photo of Bianca holding the statue's head over Megan.

"Doctor Megan McCord knows or possesses the information. The mission will fail if you kill Doctor Megan McCord before obtaining this information."

"Rest assured, we'll extract every necessary secret from Megan," Sergio said, his normal silken tone laced with nervousness.

"Celatum Dominus does not worry. If the information is found, you will receive payment in full. We will pay bonuses if this leads the organization to find Observation Post XVI. Suppose Doctor Megan McCord is killed by you before the information is obtained. In that case, employment will be terminated in less than favorable terms."

"Yeah, what kind of terms," Bianca snapped.

A thunk sound came from the door as it sealed. A hissing sound emitted from vents as air sucked from the room. Sergio's eyes went wide, and he ran to a vent in a vain attempt to stop the outflow. Bianca leaned back in the chair and yawned.

The air pressure stopped dropping when it reached 3600 meters above sea level. Roughly equivalent to La Paz, Bolivia. The siblings both got a headache, and Sergio vomited into a trash can.

"Are you clear on the consequences of killing Doctor Megan McCord before we have the location?"

Bianca's breath was labored, but she glared at the screen. "You're are bluffing. You need us."

"Other personnel assets are en route with the same mission. We do not need you. If the other assets find the information, your employment will be terminated, but with future options to rehire."

Air slowly returned to the room.

"Your success is preferable. Our intelligence believes the Galilean Society does not have assets in the area to interfere like on Earth. We are also deploying additional hardware and logistical assets for your use. We have provided your pilot with a new destination."

The communication terminated.

Sergio turned to Bianca. "Sorellina, are you crazy?"

"Obviously. Wasn't that what father's pet psychiatrist said? Except with bigger words."

Sergio ignored the question and asked, "Why go rogue and attack her?"

"Look at what she did to me." Bianca pointed to the wounds marring her skin.

"Mia Bella, That will heal. You won't have a scar. Wear long sleeves and high necks for a while." Sergio sighed at his sister's vanity.

"We planned to keep up the charade of loyalty to lure Megan to us. This opulent vessel suits her taste far better than any decrepit cargo ship. She would have been putty in our hands before long." A conspiratorial glint in Sergio's eye.

Bianca jumped to her feet. "Yes, marvelous Megan spends her life in riches. With all that money, she spends her life with her nose in a book. She was given everything and wasted it."

"Father was almost as rich as Roger McCord. We never wanted for anything either." He sat on the edge of the desk and smiled at his sister.

"You never did. I was just a box to check. They had a boy, and the checklist said a well-off couple had a girl too. So, they had me. They couldn't even be bothered to do it the natural way. Some doctor whipped me up in a lab."

She grabbed her hair with one hand and put the other between her legs. "The docs made sure I had the required vagina and threw in blonde hair and blue eyes for good measure."

Sergio knew better than to interrupt Bianca when on a rant.

"Once I was born, the set was complete. I was just needed when they needed to look like a family. Father wanted you as the heir. I didn't even rate being the spare.

"Our precious Megan could have been her father's heir. She was Daddy's little girl. He would give her everything, even the whole company, if she wanted. Imagine having the power to control Ettrick. Instead, she plays with trinkets. What a fool." Bianca plopped back into the chair and closed her eyes.

"In the end, father kicked us both out. We could not live up," Sergio said.

Without opening her eyes, Bianca said. "Well, you destroyed that maid with one of your games, and I removed the balls from one of Father's business partners who thought I was a plaything. Not exactly nice business conversations."

"And then, my dear Bianca, it's just us against eternity. Once we secure what we need, Megan's fate is yours to decide. But I must confess," he leaned in, a shadow crossing his features, "the prospect of a little... amusement beforehand is rather enticing."

"It's a deal, big bro. You and me forever."

14

Health Check

"LCV *Victoria*, you have clearance to dock. Welcome to Europa Station," the docking controller said.

"Thank you. It's been a long trip from Saturn, and we can't wait to stretch our legs," Megan sat in the captain's chair. She wore one of Adrian's shirts and a beret that covered most of her hair. After disconnecting the video feed, Megan put on her glasses and removed the silly hat.

"Do you think they will believe me as a ship's captain?"

"You are the only one who has never been here. They might recognize anyone else, and we need to keep up the ruse," Adrian said. The ten-hour trip to Europa allowed them to transform LCV *Elizabeth* into LCV *Victoria*. A simple polymer skin hid the hull's mountain mural, and they swapped the nameplate.

"Putting a new name on the hull should not have worked. They should have recognized the transponder."

Lizzie strolled onto the bridge and laughed. "Oh, Megan, I need to tell you more stories of my Charles. Years ago, he equipped the ship with a counterfeit transponder. Just in case someone asked the wrong questions about the *Elizabeth*."

"It also shows Grandpa was not original in his naming. Isn't that right, Elizabeth Victoria?" Adrian asked his grandmother.

Lizzie turned her nose up at Adrian but spoke to Megan. "Now, you, Sarai, and Piet must get to the clinic."

While they were at the clinic, David moved the asteroid runabouts out of the hold and prepared them for their journey. The two sleek, fifteen-meter vessels floated outside the *Elizabeth* like fish beside a whale. They named the identical boats *Castor* and *Pollux*. Adrian admired them through the bridge viewport when Megan and Sarai returned.

"Do you have a clean bill of health?" Adrian asked.

"Yes, they replaced my emergency stitches and coated them with Rapid-Heal gel." Rapid-Heal augmented the body's natural healing processes. "They confirmed Piet has broken ribs. They are keeping him overnight. Sarai only has bruises."

"The clinic surprised me. It's a state-of-the-art hospital, but completely hidden. Not even a sign on the door," Megan said.

"Zeus' organization occasionally needs discrete medical care," Sarai helped set up the network almost twenty years earlier.

Lizzie looked up from a console. "Adrian, you shouldn't wait too long to leave. I have news. Last night, a Customs and Patrol Service ship raided the *Highland Bounty* at Ganymede."

"*Highland Bounty* was the original ship I planned on taking. Why did it get raided, and why was it at Ganymede?"

"I can't tell you why she was there, but I'm certain the reason for the raid was because they expected you on the ship. They were serving a warrant for your arrest," Lizzie said.

Megan sucked in her breath and closed her eyes. "Killer friends, black market bounties, and now law enforcement catching up. Can it get worse?"

"Yes, it can." Lizzie turned to Adrian. "The CPS ship is the *Zeta Sierra.*"

"Shit." Adrian smacked his fist against the console. David and Sarai also muttered something.

Megan glanced from Adrian to the rest of the crew and wondered what they knew she did not. "What? Why does it matter which ship it is?"

"*Zeta Sierra* is commanded by Kristina Chen-Ramirez, Adrian's girlfriend," Sarai said.

"She's not my girlfriend. Our relationship and consent agreement lists us as a long-distance, nonexclusive, intimate relationship."

Sarai placed an arm around Adrian's shoulder and grinned. "In English, he means they can't keep their hands off each other whenever they are at the same station. Unfortunately for both of them, our schedule only matches up occasionally."

"And that schedule might match up again soon. *Zeta Sierra* just left Ganymede for Callisto. She's smart. She might guess where we are going next," Lizzie said.

"Can you talk to her?" Megan looked at Adrian, hopefully.

"She's one of the most dedicated people I know. An occasional date with me won't stop that lioness on a hunt."

15
The Lioness in the Grass Seeks Her Prey

August 4, 2155—Callisto Station

Zeta Sierra departed Ganymede station in the early afternoon after her crew sobered up after drinking with the crew of *Highland Bounty*.

The trip from Ganymede to Callisto took seven and a half hours. Upon arrival, Kristina once again didn't find *Elizabeth*. Station control informed her the ship left a little after 01:00, a less than twelve-hour stay. She asked about *Elizabeth's* destination in the flight plan. The response was Alpha Centauri, and the estimated arrival time was last week. Kristina doubted Elizabeth Borden solved FTL and time travel.

"Junior Administrator Belova, can you explain why flight plan records at your station are in shambles? The ship I looked for had an impossible flight plan," Kristina asked.

"It's not the only one. The cargo vessel *Independence Hall* is due in Philadelphia on July 4, 1776. For arrivals, the *Argo* is arriving to search for the Golden Fleece. You better hurry. You must roll out full presidential honors for Abraham Lincoln onboard the *RMS Titanic*."

"Nothing like this has ever happened before, I assure you. It must be a technical glitch our people will solve soon," Belova said.

"Why did you order *Elizabeth* to leave the station?"

"A concerned citizen expressed his desire for them to depart immediately. The *Elizabeth* crew caused an incident at the casino, so I agreed to evict them. I don't like agitators on my station."

Kristina continued to beat her head against a bulkhead with the administrator and got nowhere. She left and found Phillips, who worked with station investigators, to get a timeline of what Adrian and his crew did when they were here.

"They offloaded cargo on arrival, nothing out of the ordinary. Then four crew, including the suspect, exited the ship unsupervised," Phillips reported. "The captain, the apprentice, and Doctor McCord vanished into the lower residential blocks. David, I mean Sail Master Efron, asked questions on the docks about a ship CPS impounded ten years ago."

Phillips pulled up a report from their files on the survey boat. Seeing the report sparked Kristina's memory.

"I was there. It was a derelict ship, and we towed it back to the station. A very sick man was onboard. We shipped him back to Earth for medical treatment. I'm sorry to say I never even learned his name. The ship was a junker ten years ago. What would Captain Kostas want with it?"

"I don't know, but any records of the ship disappeared a few days later. My bet is it got stolen, and someone scrubbed the record.

"Back to the present. David returned to the ship after they spoke to the cargo handlers' guild." Kristina knew Phillips and David Efron were close friends. "No word from the others for hours, and we found this."

Phillips called up a shaky video clip. "This leaked social media post shows what appears to be the cargo master fighting in a casino lounge. The posts say the fight involved three beautiful women in elegant clothing and several others. A dark-haired woman, a blonde, and a redhead. The casino claims it was just an equipment malfunction. No one filed an official report."

Kristina watched the short video. She recognized Sarai, who looked very different out of her usual coveralls and messy hair bun. Wearing a graceful dress, Sarai fought another figure in a casino lounge.

"Well, that's Sarai Rousseau, but I can't imagine her fighting someone. She is one of the most peaceful people I have ever met. What about the rest of the *Elizabeth* crew?" Kristina asked.

"None show up on this video. There were no videos on any other social media posts. Of course, the casino has provided no footage.

"The *Elizabeth* disembarked about an hour after the casino incident," Phillips concluded.

"I think Lt. Davenport and I need to visit the casino management."

The casino security staff stonewalled Kristina and her XO when they requested a video of the fight.

"I'm afraid we can't provide you with access. It would violate guest privacy. It doesn't matter, as there was no fight in the lounge. The disturbance was an equipment failure. An improperly secured cable broke free, causing a statue suspended from the ceiling to fall. We are fortunate no guests were injured." The security officer said with sincerity.

Kristina crossed her arms and smiled. "If there was no fight, seeing the images shouldn't be a problem."

"I am sorry, Commander, but my hands are tied without a warrant. You are in luck. The station's magistrates are in the casino at a private party sponsored by the casino owner."

Like Las Vegas of the 1950s, Kristina inferred the local magistrates were almost certainly in the casino's pocket.

"No, I wouldn't want to interrupt their party. Perhaps we could speak to some of the staff that may have seen Doctor McCord."

"Commander, we can do better than that. Mr. Zeus has requested to meet with you," a curly-haired blonde woman in a crisp suit entered the room.

"Thank you. That would be helpful."

"My name is Amanda. Please follow me to his office."

Amanda led Kristina and Frank to a small private office. A once athletic man, slowly losing a battle with age and inactivity, sat at the desk. He didn't rise to meet them. A woman with short dark hair stood behind him in a protective stance.

"Good evening, Commander, Lieutenant. Please sit down. I am Zeus. May I offer you a refreshment?"

They sat but declined a drink.

"I understand you're seeking information on my visit with Doctor McCord?"

"You met with her personally?" Kristina asked.

"Yes, she sought some information from me."

"Mr. Wojciechowski, why would she come to the owner of a casino for information?"

"I prefer to be called Zeus. Please do me that kindness. Though I'm impressed, you pronounced the name correctly."

Zeus leaned back in his plush, actual leather chair, an indulgence on a space station. "My business interests are quite diversified. I'm particularly fond of commodities, especially the most valuable of commodities, information. I agreed to meet Doctor McCord because Sarai Rousseau accompanied her. Mademoiselle Rousseau and I were acquaintances years ago when she was a Jovian resident."

"May I ask what information she sought?" Kristina asked.

"Of course, she asked about the location of an asteroid survey ship. It belonged to Fred Stonington, who died roughly ten years ago. His death left the vessel abandoned here. You may recall the incident, as you were the officer who found the ill Mr. Stonington." Zeus proved to Kristina he had access to information that was unavailable to most.

"I obtained information on the vessel's fate and gladly provided it. I like to foster new minds, and Doctor Mc-Cord, for all appearances, is a promising young exo-archaeologist."

"Why do you say for all appearances?"

"After our meeting, I learned she is being sought after for her involvement in her father's killing," Zeus gestured toward them. "I fear she isn't to be trusted and could be dangerous. She may have my trusting friend, Sarai, fooled."

"What about Captain Kostas? Do you think she has him fooled as well?"

"Oh, the captain of the *Elizabeth*. I feel that she may have convinced him in other ways. He is a man with a reputation for having 'a girl in every port'. I'm sure he wasted no time seeking out this woman on his ship." Zeus' slight smile indicated awareness of the relationship between Kristina and Adrian.

Kristina smiled at Zeus' attempt to stir jealousy. Their non-exclusive agreement allowed Adrian to see others if he wished. She also knew Adrian hadn't seen anyone else in the two years they had been lovers. Of the two, Kristina had a few flings with men and women, but the last was almost a year ago.

"What about the survey boat? You found it?" Davenport asked.

"Yes, it was sold at auction due to nonpayment of dock fees. A different Hunter from Ceres bought it. Sadly, that hunter disappeared, and his ship was never recovered. He is presumed lost."

Frank raised a finger. "We looked. There is no record of an auction with the station administration."

"Lesser Administrator Belova's record keeping isn't known to be exceptional."

Kristina, a stickler for detail, said, "Her title is Junior Administrator."

"I stand behind my statement," Zeus said with a dispassionate look. There was no love between him and Belova.

"Tell me about the fight at the casino lounge."

"This isn't some dockside dive bar. The rumors of a fight here are false. We had a costly accident that will keep one of our most profitable lounges closed for at least a week."

Frank produced a tablet and showed the video of the fight with Sarai. "There was this social media post showing part of the fight."

"A fake. That looks like Sarai and even shows her wearing something similar to what she wore last night, but her dress was floor length, not short—bad video editing. Plus, anyone familiar with Sarai knows she is a pacifist and a fashionista. She wouldn't engage in such fights or wear such clothing." That described Sarai Rousseau as Kristina knew her.

Knowing they were being stonewalled again about the altercation, Kristina switched tactics.

"If the survey vessel they were looking for is lost, did Doctor McCord indicate her next plan?"

"I was able to provide her with more information. Mr. Stonington frequently operated out of Ceres and the artifact research center there. She planned to contract *Elizabeth* to go there next, doing old-fashioned research and back-tracing Stonington's steps. I understand they departed the station immediately after they left the casino.

"I am afraid I made matters worse. Early this morning, I met with a man who claimed to be the doctor's boyfriend. He chased her down like a lovesick puppy. I remember what it is like to be young and in love. I provided this compelling young man with the same information I gave you. It's embarrassing I didn't vet him. We discovered he is suspected of multiple crimes...Cassandra?"

The woman sent a file to Frank. He opened it and saw a picture of Sergio and an Interpol file on him.

"This man, in my civilian opinion, is dangerous. I don't care about Doctor McCord, but my friend Sarai could get caught in the crossfire. It's best to arrest both the doctor and her boyfriend."

Kristina thought they had everything he was inclined to give. She thanked Zeus for his time and left.

"Do you think they will follow your wild goose chase?" Cassandra asked.

Zeus smiled. "We can hope. If we're lucky, they will keep Sergio and Bianca busy."

"You did catch me by surprise by portraying Doctor McCord as a villain. I assumed you liked her."

"I will apologize if I see her again. Adding additional chaos to the situation will benefit us."

Kristina, Frank, and Phillips met to discuss the day's results.

"After our talk with Zeus, one thing I know. They did not go to Ceres. He was too eager to get us out of the area," Kristina said.

"So, where do you think they went?" Frank said.

"Not to Ceres. Not here in Callisto. Not Ganymede. They would have arrived before we left. Technically, that leaves the rest of the solar system." Kristina put a chart of the area on a screen and studied it for a few seconds.

"My gut says they stayed in the Jupiter region. Someplace the old Hunter would have a connection. Unfortunately, there are dozens of mining locations in the area. Ten years ago, Io was just a research station studying volcanoes. Some have suspected an Artificer site is hidden under the volcanic sulfur. From our information on Stonington, it sounds like a place he might go to."

"You are forgetting something, Skipper," Phillips said. "The *Elizabeth* needs a base of operations. An LCV would be noticeable at Io or a mining settlement. I think Captain Kostas would want someplace safe. Look at their manifest. They had two asteroid runabouts. They didn't sell them at Callisto. Those give them flexibility."

"Ganymede has the most traffic. They could blend in there. Maybe they did a few orbits to throw off anyone tracking them and headed to Ganymede." Kristina pointed to Jupiter's largest moon on the chart.

"Maybe if Lizzie were making the decisions." Phillips knew the *Elizabeth* crew the best. "Adrian is the captain. He will let his emotions drive him to make this decision and then go to Europa. Adrian may not think about it, but it will feel comfortable."

"What do you say that?" Kristina asked as she raised a questioning eyebrow.

Phillips observed the woman he regarded as his little sister, "Captain, Europa is where he met you."

16

Journey to Metis

August 4, 2155—Runabout Castor en route to Metis

Megan and Adrian left on the runabout *Castor* for Metis. Meanwhile, Sarai and David took *Pollux* to Io to meet the ferry that contained Stonington's old nav computer.

Megan marveled at the strange design of the small craft. They sat in the pilot and copilot seats in a central sphere. On each side were cylinder-shaped wing pods housing mining equipment and a tiny living area. An independent, rotating thruster sat at the end of each wing pod, directing thrust in almost every direction.

Adrian grinned like a small child on Christmas morning. The look on his face brought Megan a smile as well.

"Okay, I know you want to. Tell me all about it."

"The ball turret we are sitting in rotates independently and can match the thruster turrets for any maneuvers they are capable of. This allows precise maneuvers but keeps the direction of thrust we feel consistent." Adrian spoke with rapid excitement. "Watch this."

Megan yelped as the boat twisted through complicated maneuvers but calmed when she realized the acceleration always pushed in the same direction relative to her seat.

Adrian leveled back out. "No ship this size has gravity plates or the energy to use them. This design will keep us from being battered if we need to maneuver."

"Let's try to keep it straight and level when we can. I have another question." She pointed at the navigation plot on the screen. "That looks like we are headed to the wrong side of Jupiter. Metis is on one side, and we are headed to the other."

"The orbital period of Metis is only seven hours. We need to go where it will be, not where it is. Navigation between the moons of Jupiter is a pain. Technically, we do it every trip, but the difference is not as obvious on a trip of multiple AUs."

"I guess I should have paid more attention to Daddy's ship captains."

"Navigation is not your specialty. Anyway, we have a four-hour trip. No one got much sleep last night. If you don't mind sharing, we can take a nap. Sorry, but there is only one small bunk." Adrian opened the small hatch to the living area. He yawned as he climbed through. Megan watched him move in the bed's direction and smiled as she followed. She didn't notice his yawn.

Adrian hadn't slept at all during their late-night run from Callisto. Fatigue from nearly thirty-six hours awake weighed heavily on Adrian as he removed the outer layer of his spacesuit. He lay on the small bunk wearing only the skin suit found under his space suit.

Despite his exhaustion, he noticed Megan's appearance in her skin suit when she removed her outer suit. The skin-tight outfit hugged her in a sultry and captivating manner.

They cuddled together as it was the only way to fit in the bunk. Despite holding an enchanting woman, Adrian fell asleep in minutes.

Sleep eluded Megan as the welcoming warmth of Adrian's body next to her stirred a desire she could not ignore. Adrian's intent to ask her to share a bed seemed evident, but she knew he needed sleep. She held him close, feeling his chest rise and fall in a steady rhythm. He murmured in his sleep, and a distinct bulge appeared that his skin suit could not hide. *I know I can't match Kristina, but she's not here, and I am. He wants me as much as I want him...maybe. I hate to say it, but I need to be bold like Bianca and go for it.* Megan thought with shaky confidence.

Adrian's dreams came in a confusing jumble. A lioness with golden fur chased him through the corridors of the *Elizabeth*. When he ran into his cabin, the lioness stood on two legs and transformed into Kristina. Silky fur still covered her body as she pushed him onto the bed. She leapt onto the bed and pinned him down while giving a sultry but predatory smile.

Moments later, the cabin on *Elizabeth* swirled away and transformed into the luxurious bedroom of the Le Méridien hotel suite from the day before. His partner changed from golden blonde hair to curly red with pale, freckled skin. She leaned down and kissed his neck. He moaned in pleasure.

Adrian's eyes snapped open with the realization the kisses were real. He sat up so fast that his head hit the low ceiling and grunted in pain.

"Are you okay?" Megan asked after his sudden move.

"Yes. I was not expecting to be woken up that way."

"Really?" Megan gave him a coy smile. "You invited me to share a bed. I saw you become aroused. I decided I wanted the same thing."

Adrian examined Megan to see she had unzipped her suit far enough to tease almost everything. "I'm sorry, Megan, but I was being literal. I wanted us to get a little sleep. I'm sorry if I led you to the wrong idea."

"Okay, but we are here. I obviously aroused you." She pointed to the indication she saw earlier. "Stress relief would be good. We both need this. We both want this. Right?"

"Oh, I won't deny that, at this moment, I want this, but it would be a bad idea." Adrian grabbed a pillow and put it on his lap.

The light in Megan's eyes dimmed, and her expression wilted like an unnurtured flower. Her pale skin blazed red in a combination of embarrassment and disappointment. "You said you had a non-exclusive intimate agreement with Kristina. I had hoped for the same deal. Is it because I'm fat and ugly with frizzy red hair? Compared to the golden-haired goddess you had dinner with at the tavern?"

Adrian rocked back at the venomous tone she directed at herself. Kristina kept herself in top athletic condition, but that did not make Megan fat or ugly. When he thought about it objectively, Adrian found Megan to have a naturally beautiful face compared to Kristina's plainer face, which only sparkled with makeup.

Before he could think better of it, Adrian placed a gentle, open palm on Megan's cheek. Megan pressed into it, and Adrian said, "Megan, you are beautiful. And yes, my relationship with Kristina is non-exclusive." Adrian learned as a teenager, painfully, to not hide dating other people. His life kept him on the move, and he never desired an exclusive relationship. From the start, his relationship and consent agreements clarified this to his lovers. Kristina had no problem with this clause. She even told him about several flings in the last two years.

For the first time, Adrian felt no desire to see anyone except Kristina. Until today, at least.

Adrian dropped his hand. "Ordinarily, I'd be a fool to say no to you, but I am. Less than a day ago, you found out your previous lover betrayed you and his sister murdered your father. You are hurting, and I won't take advantage of that."

"Sergio and I were not lovers. He asked, but something didn't sit right. Sergio and Bianca were fun to hang with, but I wasn't ready to leap into his bed." She looked down at the bunk she lay on and realized the irony of her words.

She smiled at Adrian and zipped up her suit. "You're right, though. It's too soon, but I can't say I'll give up. I may ask again."

"I can't promise my answer, but you can ask." Adrian's emotions conflicted with him. Before meeting Kristina, he would not have hesitated. His early reputation of having a girl in every port was not quite literal. Still, it was not a massive exaggeration either.

"We're approaching the Main Ring. I better go up and take manual control." Adrian touched her arm and wavered as he stared into her hopeful green eyes. He turned to go but glanced back as he went through the hatch. "Thank you for understanding."

Though the heat of her excitement had not subsided, she couldn't help but feel a bit crushed. Megan forced herself to give her most pleasant smile.

"Of course, Adrian. I'll join you soon. I need a few private moments."

Castor passed into Jupiter's Main Ring as they approached Metis. Adrian and Megan sat in the control sphere, wearing their spacesuits.

Adrian wore a practical, semi-rigid, orange and silver suit—designed for safety and hard work.

Megan exuded sophistication in her costly yet functional cobalt blue suit. Specially designed for her exo-archaeology work, the one-of-a-kind suit was as tough as Adrian's without the bulk.

Adrian adjusted the flight path to stop above the American football-shaped moon. They scanned for the pair of containers Stonington used as a hideout. Adrian estimated there was a good chance they no longer existed.

"Found it, but we have a problem. Look at your side screen," Megan said.

Adrian's display illuminated to reveal an unexpected sight. The screen portrayed dozens of containers instead of a single set of containers. Old shipping containers were transformed into makeshift space homes—robust steel girders and cables connected clusters of these containers.

The crisscrossing network of wires all led to an old asteroid tug. Emissions from the old ship revealed a working reactor powering the busy living area.

In this strange mix of metal and cables was a sizeable old freighter. Its original purpose had been abandoned a long time ago. Only a framework existed for most of the ship. Someone attached more containers inside the skeleton. These containers created a gigantic structure filled with life.

Adrian saw something he had heard whispered rumors about but had never seen—a space shanty town.

17

Watching Kids Play Catch

David Efron sat in the control sphere of *Pollux*, the twin runabout to *Castor*. He enjoyed a rare moment of peaceful contemplation. He flew the shuttle to Io, and Sarai negotiated for the ferry's navigation logs. She excelled at many things, but piloting wasn't one of them.

Reclining in the pilot's seat and feet resting on the main window, David saw a sight he rarely saw anymore, which was his beloved solar sails in action. These weren't the sail racers of his youth but mundane freight pods.

A stream of containers, which wouldn't appear out of place on a sea vessel, traveled the long void from Earth, guided by an automated sail system. David watched as the complex matrix of fins retracted to the control unit. Each unit entered a series of massive circular bands that generated an electromagnetic field, forming an enormous "catcher's mitt" in space to snare containers.

With a last burst of light, the container glided smoothly into the cradle of electromagnetic energy. The container came to rest among a neatly packed row of similar containers, their sails retracting in synchrony like a flock of folding origami birds settling into roost. A crew removed control units with their bundled sails to be sent back to earth while tugs pulled pods loaded with construction supplies.

Returning the sail control sleds was always a decent source of income for the *Elizabeth*. It's not the most profitable, but it's better than running empty. David fell asleep while thinking of one of those runs.

Sarai accepted the memory chip containing the navigation data of ferry *DW-1876*, nicknamed *Deadwood* by the crew.

"Thank you, Captain Dalton. Our client will appreciate this information." Sarai smiled at the unique captain.

Captain Reed Dalton looked like he was plucked out of the central casting of a Western movie two hundred years ago. The image was built by a Stetson hat, leather vest, denim jeans, and a revolver strapped to his leg. Sarai may have sworn never to use a deadly weapon again. Still, her experience told her it was a Colt Single Action Army. Genuine, not a replica, she guessed.

"No, ma'am, thank you. We gave you old data we didn't even know was there. In return, the Deadwood crew will now eat like royalty. You are a genuine lady." He tipped his hat to her and picked up the box of fresh steaks Sarai had traded for the nav data.

If Adrian wants a steak soon, it will have to be frozen. Sarai thought. Her expertise in negotiation came from learning about the other person. This morning, she removed these steaks from the *Elizabeth's* small stasis fridge. The steaks were as fresh as if purchased from a butcher shop the day before.

The ferry's first mate, a woman named Sally, led Sarai back to the airlock. "He's eccentric, but we get used to him. He needs a break. We all do. Two years of going back and forth to the Asteroids bored us all. Good thing we are taking this thing over to Europa soon for an overhaul. We get to rotate back to Earth for a month."

Sarai smiled, held her palms together, and bowed. "May your journey be filled with joy and serenity."

She reentered *Pollux* to find David snoring in his seat. She laughed and shook awake the man who had become an older brother over the last fourteen years.

"Did you get it?" David asked. She handed him the data chip but noticed something distracted him outside.

"What are you looking at?" Sarai asked.

"I was reminiscing about when Adrian stacked sail control sleds. Back when you first joined the crew, Charles sent sixteen-year-old Adrian to work with you in cargo. Adrian knocked over a pallet full, and you scolded him like a drill sergeant while he gazed at you like Aphrodite."

Sarai rolled her eyes. "I simply explained the proper procedure. He never stacked wrong again, did he?" Her smile faded. "But I should have handled his crush better, like a sister, not..."

David leaned forward. "He fixated on you after that blue-haired girl Mandy dumped him. You handled it well. The liaison between you and Adrian wasn't until two years later when he was eighteen."

Sarai buried her face in her hands. "I got drunk and took advantage of a boy."

"Oy vey, he was a consenting adult. Stop being hard on yourself."

"I wasn't a girl then, and I'm not now, but you're right, he wasn't coerced. What about his mother, Elizabeth Anne? How did she feel about me sleeping with her son?" Sarai asked. Her voice carried a harsh note of self-judgment.

"Lizzie Anne ran off with Adrian's father around the same age. She was in no place to judge."

Sarai shook her head in disbelief. "I can't picture his mother as the wild rebel I hear stories of. She's just a meek software engineer."

"People change. You've grown so much since then." David squeezed her shoulder.

Sarai smiled. "You've been a good friend."

They turned back to the traffic around Io. Sarai's gaze narrowed on the heavy flow of containers. "Is it just me, or is that an awful lot of cargo for this stage of construction? They're hauling some moon side. Odd, isn't it?"

David frowned. "Yes, odd, but let's get back to Europa. One mystery at a time."

As they prepared to depart, a sleek transport arrived, barely noticed by David as he piloted them out. It would soon alter their lives profoundly.

18

The Welcoming Committee

August 4, 2155— Castor near Metis

*C*astor glided toward the space shanty town. Adrian maintained a slow and cautious pace. The low acceleration caused a low perceived gravity. It comforted Megan, who had grown up doing low and zero-gravity gymnastics.

The town resembled a hive of interconnected tubes and boxes. Cables threaded between the modules like spider webs, carrying power across the makeshift station. Adrian whistled in awe. "I've never seen anything like this."

Megan shared his fascination. In all her sheltered academic studies, she never imagined humanity could build such a ramshackle yet ingenious habitat in the void of space. *How desperate must one be to live in the most perilous place known, kept safe solely by the discarded steel of containers tossed away as trash?* she thought.

Megan leaned close to the window and craned her neck to look around. "Where is everyone?"

"Did they abandon it?"

"No." Megan gestured in the direction of the containers. "There were lights and movement. Then the lights blinked out, and movement stopped a few seconds later."

"I doubt they welcome uninvited guests. It's decision time, Megan. We can return to check the nav data or make new friends."

"One can never have too many friends. Let's see if we can give them a ring."

Adrian picked up the radio mike and set a broad frequency transmission. "Hello, my name is Adrian. We were seeking something in this vicinity. We have no ill intentions to you. We would like to talk to someone in charge."

"Bloody Hell, Adrian. Why not just say, 'We come in peace. Take us to your leader.'" She smacked him playfully on the shoulder.

"Well, I can't let you talk. Your upper-crust British accent may make anyone here think you're trying to colonize them. 'The British are coming! The British are coming!'" Adrian smirked playfully.

She smacked him again. "Scottish! It is a Scottish accent. How can Americans not tell the difference? And it's not the nineteenth century. The United Kingdom does not colonize anymore. Now, Captain, return to the radio and contact them in the name of Queen and country." She looked down her nose at him with a perfect aristocratic glare.

"Aye, Aye, Admiral." Adrian gave her a sloppy salute and a silly grin.

Her glare shifted to a smile, and they both broke into hearty laughter.

"Thank you. A laugh was just what I needed," Megan said. She felt warmth inside and was glad they had no awkwardness after the incident in the bed.

Adrian tried the radio again. They only received silence back. They still saw no lights or movement, but the tangle of crates gave many blind spots.

Megan examined the town's layout. It was bigger than they thought. It had a three-dimensional grid of "streets."

The hubs were the old freighter and the power station tug. She brought up a layout for Adrian to study.

"I'll take us in and look around. Don't worry, I'll take it nice and slow. Please, keep an eye out for signs of activity."

Megan used the runabout's limited scanners to search for evidence of life. Adrian slowly moved their little vessel through the maze of containers.

"The scanner is detecting power in the cables going to the container. Heat readings say most of these are warm enough for human habitation." Power cables wound through the containers like veins.

As they ventured deeper into the lifeless town, a chill ran through Megan, conjuring images of Pompeii preserved in its silent demise. Though her expertise lay in exo-archaeology, she had trained in ancient sites, too.

As they floated through the abandoned habitat, Megan felt the same eerie stillness that came to Pompeii's streets when the tourists left at dusk. Someone had painted the containers in vibrant colors. The windows revealed vacant living spaces. Megan shivered, half-expecting to discover frozen figures suspended in time like the victims of Pompeii.

"Was the light cut off an automated response? The movement I saw may have been my imagination. Maybe the people who built this place are dead." Megan's voice wavered, her words laced with uncertainty.

"I don't think so. Look up,"

Adrian had stopped in front of a container. A little girl gazed through a window. She smiled and waved at the strangers outside her home. The child shouted as an adult arm tried to pull her away. Despite the girl's valiant effort to maintain a grip on a grab bar, she was pulled out of view.

"There's our sign of life. Should we knock on the door and introduce ourselves?"

Proximity alarms went off, and they jolted forward. Rear cameras showed a dented asteroid mining "rockhopper" pod attempting to grasp the *Castor* with a claw arm. A piercing screech of twisting metal vibrated through the hull.

Megan shouted a warning when she saw the other arm. That arm had a scary drill bit and a laser cutter designed to cut through iron asteroids. It could burst their capsule like a balloon.

"Remember when I said I would take it nice and slow?" Adrian asked. "I lied."

He slammed on the thrusters and broke free of the rockhopper with a jolt before it could secure its grip.

Megan knew the *Castor* was maneuverable, but this caught her by surprise. Despite the advantages of the rotating control sphere, Adrian turned faster than the sphere could rotate to compensate. The movements felt like a rollercoaster combined with bumper cars.

Megan grunted as Adrian turned almost ninety degrees to avoid a series of cables connecting two pods.

Other vessels joined the chase, blocking escape routes and pushing *Castor* deeper into the town.

The town's exterior lights were back on. People gathered in the windows. This chase had become a spectator sport for the residents. The more cynical took wagers on where the strangers would crash. Cynicism thrived among the castoff people of the shanty town.

G-forces pinned Megan in the seat, but like a fighter plane copilot, she watched where Adrian couldn't. She called out the location of the rockhopper and other craft chasing them.

They were getting deeper into the tangled labyrinth of the shantytown. Adrian's jaw tightened each time a mass of cables or a looming vessel blocked a promising exit route.

Emotions ran high for everyone.

Adrian was determined to protect Megan and escape. His white-knuckle grip on the controls pained his hands. He tasted his own sweat as it dripped down his face.

Megan felt the terror of the violent maneuvers in this strange environment. She trusted Adrian's skills, but this was beyond her wildest experiences. Bile rose in her throat with the unexpected sensations.

The rockhopper pilot felt anger at the invader of their home and fear that their hideaway would be revealed to the outside universe.

The waving little girl showed glee at seeing interesting new visitors. As *Castor* passed her module again, her youthful exuberance sent her spinning in zero gravity, giggling the whole time.

Adrian almost piloted them to another dead end. His thoughts were a whirlwind of calculations as he navigated the metallic maze for an exit.

Finally, *Castor* emerged onto a wide thoroughfare, spanning from the ancient freighter to open space.

Adrian's eyes lit up, and he shifted their trajectory toward the beckoning freedom of open space. "I think we found Broadway. Hold on!"

Megan gripped her armrest as they accelerated faster than she expected. They sped down Broadway like a drag racer running to the finish line. Hope surged past her fear and the crushing pressure. They were almost out.

A group of wrecked containers pushed in their path dashed their hope. Adrian flipped the thrusters one hundred eighty degrees and used full power to stop a dangerous crash. He could not rotate the control sphere and still maintain his desired view. G-forces pushed them into the seat straps, causing pain to their shoulders. The powerful deceleration made the earlier maneuvers feel like a lazy river ride.

Both of them groaned in pain when they saw the barrier approaching. They knew changing direction would cause them to crash into inhabited modules. They slowed to a stop meters from the container wall. Ironically, they were in front of a faded Ettrick logistics logo, her family company.

Adrian turned off the thrusters. Cables flew behind them, blocking their way back. The rockhopper they first met stopped in front of them. Its spinning drill bit was aimed at *Castor's* main window.

They saw the hopper's inhabitants. Two people in ancient, heavily patched spacesuits. The man in the pilot seat controlled the drill arm and gave them a one-finger salute through the window.

A young woman pressed buttons on another control panel. A cable shot out, and they heard a thud as it was magnetically attached to them. The woman grinned at Megan and Adrian and pressed a button. Some electromagnetic pulse went down the cable. All the systems of the *Castor* shut down, leaving them at the shantytown's mercy. The pilot of the rockhopper switched his rude gesture to using both hands.

The rockhopper towed *Castor*, allowing Megan to observe the city.

Many containers had very personal styles and intricate designs, not unlike *Elizabeth* and her mural. The artwork ranged from landscapes, portraits, street art, or simple family names. The people's reactions in the windows ranged from curious stares to unheard shouts and gestures.

This hidden city in space was more sophisticated than its ramshackle appearance let on. The best human ingenuity does not come from a comfortable and stagnant environment. It comes from those striving to rise above adversity and crisis.

As they drew closer, the remnants of the old freighter emerged from the shadows. A fresh layer of paint displaying "Penelope" obscured the faint, weathered letters. The freighter's skeletal framework cradled many containers, nestled against one another, mirroring the design of a space station.

"Your family name may not be welcome here. Look." He pointed to another preserved section of the hull. It had the Ettrick logo, with *Screw McCord* painted over it.

Megan stared at the wreck. "I know this ship. It's the *Beatrix*—one of the first spacecraft in our fleet. They scrapped it years ago."

Their captors connected *Castor* to an airlock. When the hatch opened, the man and woman from the rock-hopper met them. The man scrutinized Adrian like he was a deadly viper about to strike. He blocked the hatch, his boots magnetically attached to the deck, arms crossed protectively. The waif-like girl floated behind him. Her rich expresso-colored locks drift in microgravity while framing her heart-shaped face. Her shy smile contrasted with his angry scowl. Both were young, in their late teens or early twenties.

As the men stared at each other, the girl said, "Hi, I'm Carolina. This is my brother, Rafael." Her low tone was almost inaudible. "We are supposed to take you to the town council."

"What did you do to my boat?" Adrian asked. He continued to look at Rafael, but the question was directed at Carolina. Instinctively, she moved behind Rafael for protection.

Rafael floated up to Adrian. "Trespassers don't get to ask questions."

Carolina answered anyway, still hiding behind her brother. "It's a special EMP scrambler. I made it. It's really cool, isn't it?" This time, she spoke louder and faster, showing pride in her invention.

Adrian's expression remained impassive, and his lips pressed into a thin line. He offered no comment.

The siblings and several armed guards escorted Megan and Adrian down a corridor. They entered a massive chamber that defied expectations.

Without gravity, *floor* and *ceiling* were mere conventions. Cables crisscrossed with geometrical precision, turning the room into a three-dimensional matrix. Traditional furniture becomes obsolete without gravity, replaced by metal vines providing handholds and connections to people floating without gravity.

Adrian inspected the architecture with a trace of skepticism. Having spent his life on an old spaceship, he concerned himself with stability and safety. "This is just a bunch of containers welded together and hollowed out. How does this not fall apart?"

"Ah wid hae preferred nae knowing that," Megan whispered. The stress of the situation caused her accent to thicken.

Carolina started to respond, but Rafael broke in. "Not everyone gets to live in perfect boxes. We make do with what we can get."

They tethered Megan and Adrian to a central column and removed the spacesuit helmets.

The removal of their helmets was the last indignity. Megan longed for the helmet, feeling exposed, floating in midair. It was irrational, yet she couldn't shake the vulnerability of having her head uncovered in the vast chamber. They dangled like a human mobile in a nursery.

Adrian's clammy hand closed around hers, his grip tightening. Silence amplified their shared fear. The room emitted a musty odor caused by air filters used long past their intended life.

"Adrian, whit dae ye think wull happen noo?" Megan's voice cracked.

"They'll let us stew and get anxious. When the town council talks to us, let me talk. I have an idea."

"Ah, hope it is a guid idea because ma hands are trembling." Megan attempted to restore her composure by taking several beep breaths.

Soon, people wearing mismatched spacesuits came in and started flying up cables and latching themselves in.

Microgravity provided a unique alternative Megan wouldn't have considered. The cables within the space replaced chairs.

Meg, you need to think in 3D, not 2D. You may have played games in weightlessness but never lived in it, Megan thought.

Six people wearing marginal spacesuits came together and flew up to cables in front of Megan and Adrian.

A woman in her late middle years stopped before Megan and Adrian. Somehow, even in zero-g, she managed an upright and stalwart posture that showed her as a leader.

"I am Sakura Akiyama. Welcome to Ithaca. This is the town council," she pointed around the circle. "Priya, Jabari, Layla, Felipe, and Fynn. Together, we represent the individuals of Ithaca. We are a sanctuary for the castoffs of the solar system. Please tell us who you are and why you have visited our home uninvited?"

Adrian had drifted to an angle. He tried to steady himself and failed. Megan caught his arm and maneuvered him back into position, anchoring him with the ease of her gymnastics experience.

"I am Captain Adrian Kostas. This is Bonny-Lee Howe. The British Museum contracted me to take Ms. Howe on a survey trip through the rings of Jupiter. None of our data showed anything near Metis. I sincerely apologize for any slight we have made."

"What did you think you would find here? We need to know what pointed you here for the safety of our community," Sakura said.

"Fred Stonington, an artifact hunter, discovered interesting items years ago. Research suggested he had a hiding spot near Metis. We came searching for his hideout, not you. We will gladly compensate you for allowing us to look. This could help increase the knowledge of all humanity." Adrian hoped his face did not betray any lack of confidence in the tale he spun.

"Why should we care about the knowledge of 'humanity'? They forgot about us, left us to rot!" shouted Rafael from the crowd. Carolina was still beside him, curiously floating inverted to everyone else and looking at an old tablet.

Sakura motioned to another leader. "Felipe, calm Rafael down. You sponsored him. No more outbursts."

Felipe scolded Rafael in Portuguese.

Megan felt her heart pound and watched beads of sweat form on Adrian's forehead. *This could spin out of control fast. I hope Adrian knows what he is doing. I'm not sure stretching the truth to the breaking point will help us.*

"Fred Stonington was the founder of this community. If he didn't wish to share something, we should respect his wishes," Jabari, an elderly African man in the leadership ring, said.

"Good point, Jabari. Stonington-San was a good friend. Without him, we wouldn't be here. He was a very private man," Sakura said.

Priya, the youngest member of the leadership ring, drifted forward. "The real question is, should we allow these foreigners to leave? They know about us now. We can't allow them out."

"Rich Earther bastardos like you can walk back to a space station. We don't want nothing to do with you. But your boat, that we can use," the angry youth from the rockhopper, Rafael, interrupted the leaders again.

Even with no gravity, Megan felt the weight of the situation crashing down on her. Her throat dried as if in the middle of a desert.

Adrian tried to speak up, but Sakura held her hand and commanded him to stop. The authority of the woman's willpower caused even Adrian to be silent.

Sakura looked sternly at the young man but addressed the leader who last spoke. "Priya, we don't just murder people who innocently stumble on us. It would make us just as bad as the UCE overlords. We need to have a calm discussion, and we'll determine if they are lying."

A general murmur of conversations reverberated around the room.

A decisive decision came to Megan. *This is not working. We will be tossed out of the airlock unless something radical happens.*

"We are lying!" Megan shouted.

The giant chamber fell silent.

"My name is Doctor Megan McCord. My father owned Ettrick Logistics. It is true we're looking for Stonington's old container home. We expected to find that, not Ithaca.

"Originally, I was a spoiled rich girl on an artifact hunt. Then someone murdered my father for information about artifacts Stonington found." She sucked in her breath and closed her eyes in prayer for her father. Murmurs started in the hall, but a commanding hand from Sakura silenced them.

"I am not here for the British Museum, the UCE, or Ettrick. The Coalition government is saying I was involved in Daddy's death. The person who killed my father is hunting me to get the same data. I'm accused of a crime I did not commit. Captain Kostas is my only ally." Adrian smiled and placed his hand on her shoulder.

Megan looked Sakura in the eyes with an unflinching gaze.

"I ask for sanctuary from the people of Ithaca."

19

Meeting the Neighbors

August 4, 2155—Ithaca

"I hate to admit it, but telling the truth was not a strategy I considered," Adrian said as he paced the floor. Magnetic boots prevented him from drifting away.

As Ithaca had no jail, the council imprisoned them in a standard living cubicle with metal walls and basic microgravity furnishings. A narrow slit of a window provided a view of Jupiter. The resemblance between these lodgings and a prison cell was a sad reflection of life in the town of outcasts.

A few touches showed this was not always a prison. Faded paint and a child's scribbling on the walls showed a couple who once lived here with a young child.

"Desperate times call for desperate measures. Even the truth," Megan giggled at the situation. "At least it got them to listen. We get a private meeting with the council in the morning to consider sanctuary."

They had been in their new home for an hour. After Megan's plea for sanctuary, all Hell broke out in the chamber. Megan feared she had made a terrible error. It took Sakura several minutes to restore order. They escorted Megan and Adrian to this room while the council discussed the matter.

"Adrian, please come here next to me," Megan snapped with a frown. Adrian's pacing annoyed Megan. The clang of his magnetic boots on the deck echoed in the small space.

Adrian strapped himself in next to her. She put her arms around him. Right now, she needed the solace of his embrace.

"Did ah mak' a mistake, Adrian? Why wad they wan-tae help? They view me as a privilegit brat handit every-thing in life. They're nae wrong. Hell, they anchored their community wi' a freighter mah folk cast off lik' garbage." She wiped away a tear that obscured her vi-sion. Even crying in microgravity was a challenge.

He put his hand under her chin and looked into her eyes. "No, you were right. I told lies, and they would not work. The council needed to see us as people in real trouble, not thieves seeking to take from them. They connect to people whom the government has wronged. They will connect with you, Megan."

"Thank you, Adrian." His little words of kindness touched her heart and calmed her.

"What's with the thick accent? It's cute but hard to understand."

"Cute?" Megan laughed. "That's the accent of my mother's family in the Highlands, especially Grandad. I slip into it when stressed."

A noise caught their attention. Old-fashioned keys entered the lock. Megan held a finger to her lips and whispered. "We have visitors."

The door opened, and Rafael and Carolina entered. She held a duffel bag with the *Elizabeth* logo on it.

Carolina said, "We brought some things from your boat."

She tossed Megan the bag, staying behind her pro-tective brother. Inside the bag was a change of clothes for each of them and their toiletries.

"Tonight, I'm your babá, babysitter. In the morning, you go to the council to get the judgment you deserve," Rafael said. Sakura tasked him with guard duty for his outburst. He wanted to keep Carolina distant from the strangers, but she refused to leave his side. He had been forced to put the interlopers in the room next to theirs.

Megan tilted her head to look around him at the mousey woman. "What do you think we deserve, Carolina?"

Carolina's eyes widened, her pupils dilating in sheer surprise as if such inquiries were foreign to her. Carolina shrank back, her posture echoing the timidity of a frightened child, though her age was close to Megan's.

When the girl stayed silent, Megan said, "Don't be afraid. We won't hurt you. My name is Megan."

Gaining the trust of this wary girl could be our key to winning over her brother. Despite his anger toward us, his affection for her is obvious. She seems to deserve a friend beyond just Rafael, Megan thought.

Rafael's words came out in a harsh, staccato rhythm. "Don't you get it? Just being here puts us all at risk. If word gets out about us, the UCE will come and clean us out like the lixo you see us as."

Lixo? Trash? I don't see people as trash. Megan's skin flushed in anger.

Adrian said before Megan could snap a reply. "You are right. The UCE shouldn't be trusted. A 20th-century US president said, 'The nine most terrifying words in the English language are, I'm from the government, and I'm here to help.'"

Adrian balled his fists at his sides and gritted his teeth as he continued. "The UCE should protect those off Earth and guard the Power of the Artifacts. Instead, it views dissenters, including other governments, as enemies.

"Power corrupts, and absolute power corrupts absolutely. Humanity gave absolute power to this one organization. It may have been the stupidest thing we have ever done." His parents and grandparents had raised him with very pro-individual views. His observations of the unelected, bureaucratic UCE government set those views in steel.

The power and conviction in his words surprised both Rafael and Megan. Megan knew he distrusted the government, but the vehemence was shocking. Adrian's eyes locked onto Rafael, and the two men measured each other up.

"I'll take your secrets to my grave before revealing this haven to the UCE," Adrian concluded.

The younger man said, "I believe you," after studying the other for a few moments.

Carolina only half listened to Adrian's words, but the change in her brother's tone and demeanor calmed her. She pulled out her ancient tablet and floated up to the ceiling, typing.

Megan glided up to her and found it surprising Rafael didn't stop her. Megan asked again, "Carolina, will you tell me what you think? Should they allow us to stay?"

"Oh, I definitely don't want them to throw you out an airlock," Carolina said like it was a normal conversation. Her eyes flickered up to Megan but then returned to the tablet. Megan watched the other woman focus on a task. Carolina instinctively curled up in a protective ball, shielding herself from the rest of the universe.

"É isso aí! We could do it," Carolina said, "if we removed the power regulators on the one and three power conduits, it could get 12% more thrust. We would never have caught you."

Megan and Adrian looked confused at the comment.

Rafael chuckled. "She got obsessed with your boat's design. Can't stop thinking about how to improve it. When she starts with numbers, she forgets about the world."

"Power regulators serve a purpose. The engines could overheat or burn out," Adrian said. He couldn't resist his grandmother's training.

Caronia waved away the potential danger. "You would still have two others."

"It doesn't matter now," Rafael said. His words snapped out, sharp and curt. "You won't see that boat anytime soon."

They were taken to use the facilities and locked in for the evening.

"How did it go with Carolina?" Adrian asked. The restroom trip gave the ladies a little time together. He smiled when he saw Megan change into an oversized band shirt to sleep in. Completely casual and different from the modern chic styles she usually wore.

"She opened up a little for me. They are orphans from the streets of Sao Paulo. Fraternal twins. I don't know how they got here. That will take a while. I got the impression something bad happened to her. Her talking to us is likely a significant milestone for her."

"Better than I got out of Rafael. I know he is a good pilot and an angry man."

She looked around and realized the "bed" was a couple's zero-g cocoon. It's like a sleeping bag for two strapped down so you don't float away at night. Her hard mattress on *Elizabeth* would seem luxurious compared to this, and she needed to share it.

"Why don't you take the bed? I will just..." Adrian recognized her discomfort and tried to figure out how he would "sleep on the couch" when there was no couch.

"Don't be silly. You need to be strapped in, or you will hit your head. Your zero-g skills suck." It surprised her how bad he was in microgravity. "We did fine together when we napped this morning. Come in. I promise no funny business."

They climbed into the cocoon and strapped themselves in. Their proximity allowed them to feel each other's heartbeats twice in twelve hours. Her warmth permitted Adrian to work up the courage to ask a question.

"Earlier today, why did you say you were fat and ugly? Just look in a mirror. You always look fantastic."

"After mom died, I had a nanny. She frequently expressed very negative views of my appearance. Not near Dad, only in private." Her features tightened as the painful memories surfaced.

"I completely disagree with your old nanny."

"Thank you. That means a lot to me. When you hear criticism enough, you start to believe it.

"Fortunately, when I went away to school, I met Emily, my school roommate with a flair for fashion and encouragement. She helped me develop a style and gain self-confidence, but obviously, I still fight it." Megan chuckled and pointed at the old, oversized band shirt she wore. "Emily would be horrified if she saw me wearing this shirt."

"Well, I think it looks sexy." Adrian gulped when he realized he said a private thought out loud.

Megan smiled at Adrian's embarrassment. "Thank you. Don't worry. I won't take it as a 'go ahead' sign."

"Not like there could be much funny business in weightlessness."

"You never had weightless sex? You lived a sheltered life."

Adrian looked shocked.

"I took zero-gravity gymnastics and acrobatics up to grad school. Freefall sex was a rite of passage for college freshmen. Good night, Adrian." She kissed him on the cheek and closed her eyes. It was wrong to tease him, but she couldn't resist. It was as if a mischievous fairy of her ancestors had taken hold of her, pushing her to test the boundaries of their connection. It was unlike her, but it felt good.

20

The Lioness Meets the Orca

August 5, 2155—LCV Elizabeth–Europa station

"Captain, I swear, a minute ago, the transponder on the craft said *Victoria*, not *Elizabeth*. It just flipped, but now I query the station's computers, and it says the ship that docked yesterday was the *Elizabeth*. I am certain that until we got in visual range, every electronic source told us the freighter docked was *Victoria*." The confused and frustrated sensor technician said.

What kind of game are you playing, Adrian? Kristina thought. *I know what the Elizabeth looks like. The mural on the ship's hull is unique. Here, I catch you running a different transponder, and suddenly, when we get near, it changes back.*

"The vessel now transmits an ID matching the *Elizabeth's* image. The station computer thinks it's always been that way?" Frank Davenport, the XO, asked.

"Yes, sir."

"Frank, I don't like it. You know running a false ID is illegal. We could arrest the crew and impound the ship. We must do exactly that."

A knot twisted in Kristina's gut. She started second-guessing her decision to stay the night at Callisto. But knew letting the crew rest after several hard days was the right decision. An overnight run would have made no difference. *Elizabeth*, or *Victoria*, docked at Europa before *Zetta Sierra* even left Ganymede twenty-four hours earlier.

"Skipper, it would be our word against theirs, and the station's computer corroborates them."

Dammit, Frank, I don't want to arrest Adrian. It's my duty. Kristina thought. *Why do you even have an ID scrambler, Adrian? I only joke about you being a smuggler. I only want to apprehend the fugitive. You believed everything was legit with this charter.*

"Captain, in my opinion, if we arrest them, the case will drag out for months. It will cost the Coalition a lot of money in court fees. *Elizabeth* will be impounded. The service will need to maintain it until the case is settled. The ship, almost fifty years old, may be sold at auction if guilty. No one will want to buy it. Captain, it's fiscally responsible to let this matter drop on behalf of Coalition taxpayers."

Kristina gave her executive officer a steady look. *Really laying it on thick, aren't you, Frank?*

"Plus, the case would fall under the jurisdiction of Lead Administrator Roland Hübner. You will need to work closely with him for the prosecution." The low blow settled it for Kristina.

"Ok, we will drop it...for now."

Kristina twisted her ponytail in frustration. *Adrian has some explaining to do, but not today. Today, we hunt for a fugitive.*

"Phillips gets two squads together. I guess we get to search another freighter for Doctor McCord. This time with no station security 'help.' By the book and professional. I'll meet you at the docking port five minutes after we complete arrival."

Kristina, Phillips, and one squad were at the personnel lock on the upper level. The other team was at the cargo entrance. Phillips should've been leading the other team as the senior warrant officer present. Still, Kristina had accepted his desire to be her babysitter. She pressed the call button at the dock port, and the door opened without an answer.

I guess we were expected, Kristina thought. The welcoming committee was a small, one-meter-high rectangular box-like bot with six wheels. A small screen said *Welcome* and then *Follow me.*

She remembered Adrian telling her about these bots designed by his grandmother. The tiny machines handled many small tasks and allowed the *Elizabeth* to be run by a small crew.

Kristina and Phillips exchanged glances, and he swept his arm at the bot, "Let's follow the leader."

They exited the airlock into *Elizabeth's* main personal entry path. A passenger liner or more enormous freighter might have a carpeted hallway or elegant purser lounge to greet guests. *Elizabeth* had a metal grate catwalk suspended over the cargo bay. The rails were painted a bright safety orange. Taller men had to duck due to the low roof.

The cargo area was strangely empty. The only item in the aft was a large curved cone-shaped object. Part of an old spacecraft, but Kristina couldn't identify it.

"Sail Master Efron bought something from a junkyard at Calisto. That must be it."

"You can call him David. I know you are friends. Who went drinking with the *Elizabeth* crew before we left Earth?" A look on the teams faces gave the answer—every single one of them.

This mission would test the Zetties' professionalism. After the captains of the two ships became lovers, the crew socialized frequently.

The other squad spread out in the cargo area. Phillips shouted down, "Start searching. Figure out what that thing is. We'll be going up into the superstructure."

They reached an orange metal ladder, and the bot connected itself to a mini lift on the side. The screen displayed *GO UP* with an arrow as the bot rose.

Kristína climbed after the bot as Phillips sent half his team to search that level.

They entered the superstructure at the lowest level. Kristina assumed the long hallway with brightly painted doors and walls as the crew quarters. Before them stood the renowned Elizabethan Conservatory. Kristina stepped through the glass doors and paused, taking in the expansive conservatory. Though she had admired it from the outside, this was her first time inside.

Flower beds occupied sections of the floor in full bloom, their fragrances mixing in the warm, humid air. It reminded her of the arboretums she enjoyed back on Earth.

This oasis of plants and light-filled her with peace. Kristina took a deep breath, letting the tranquility wash over her. She understood why Sarai practiced her daily Buddhist meditations in this serene spot.

Sarai did precisely that and silently meditated beside a small Zen Garden, eyes closed and legs crossed.

In a wicker chair nearby, Kristina noticed a white-haired woman. An empty chair and a table with a teapot sat nearby.

"Come sit down and join me for some tea, my dear. We have so much to talk about," said the one member of Adrian's crew she hadn't met. In her most honest with herself moments, Kristina was terrified of meeting the formidable Elizabeth Victoria Borden.

Kristina told Phillips to start searching this deck for the fugitive. He sent his people to search but stood nearby at parade rest. He intended to stay and support his captain.

"Mrs. Borden—" Kristina started.

"Please call me Lizzie. You're sleeping with my grandson. We are practically family." Kristina's face turned red while Phillips suppressed a chuckle. "Sit down, I insist. This a lovely Oolong tea. Please share it with me."

Kristina sat in the other chair without even consciously thinking about it. Lizzie poured tea into a cup and handed it to Kristina. It was, in fact, an excellent tea, quite like the tea she shared with her grandmother.

"Mrs., I mean, Lizzie. We have a warrant for Megan McCord. The passenger you took on at Earth Orbit Station Three. She is wanted in connection with her father's murder. Tell us where she is, and we will go. Otherwise, we will have to search the ship."

"Megan isn't here. Feel free to search away." She picked up a pad and pressed a button. "Every room, including my cabin, is now unlocked. Mr. Phillips, please tell your people not to linger in my unmentionables drawer."

Phillips narrowed his eyes, not in response to the suggestion of impropriety by his team but in response to how easily full access was given. The crew of the *Elizabeth* were his friends, but he never doubted they had secrets they didn't want CPS to know. Lizzie showed complete confidence Phillip's team would find nothing.

Lizzie sipped her tea and eyed Kristina over the cup. "So, my dear, what are your intentions toward my grandson?"

Kristina tried to keep her composure, "That hasn't anything to do with why I am here. If Doctor McCord isn't here, where is Adrian?"

"It has everything to do with what *I* want to talk about, but to answer your question, Adrian isn't here either. Why have you been avoiding meeting me, Kristina?"

Kristina didn't know the answer to the question. She avoided it by saying, "Lizzie, this woman could be dangerous. Coalition Security lists her as a person of interest. I warned Adrian about the increase in violence in the Artifact trade. Organized crime and con artists will have no problem stabbing someone in the back."

"You're right about a woman who stabs people. That person isn't Megan." She picked up the pad and displayed the image. "This is Roger McCord's murderer. Her name is Bianca."

Kristina saw an image of a blonde woman holding a wicked knife. The woman displayed grinned with deranged joy. This was a still from the casino security video Zeus said didn't exist.

"This woman is the one you should be hunting. Right now, we need to focus on the important issue. Your relationship with my grandson."

"Lizzie, I care for Adrian, but that's not important right now. If this woman is the killer, we should bring in Doctor McCord and let the law take over."

"No, your relationship with Adrian is the most important thing."

"What do you really want, Lizzie?"

Lizzie smiled like a spider with a fly in her web. "What do I want? My dear, I want what every woman my age wants, great grandbabies before I die."

The blood drained out of Kristina's face. Phillips had a coughing fit. Even Sarai, in her meditation, lost her composure.

Lizzie's eyes sparkled with amusement, crinkling at the corners, and her hands clutched her stomach, trying to contain the waves of uncontrollable mirth. Her infectious and hearty belly laugh echoed across the room.

"The look on your face. I'd love to see great-grandbabies, but it can wait." Lizzie wiped tears from your eyes.

"Kristina, I have achieved many accomplishments in my life, surfing trophies as a teen, a PhD in engineering from MIT, and this ship, but the most important thing is those I love—my family. When my husband died, I lost the other half of my heart two years ago, but I still have my daughter and my grandchildren. And the family I have found, like Sarai, David, and Piet. In the short time I have known her, Megan became part of this family. Adrian cares for you, so I hope you can join our family. I'll do everything I can to protect my family. Turning this over to the UCE won't protect them." Lizzie's eyes narrowed, lost in deep thought, gazing at a small tree in the honored garden. A tear rolled down her cheek.

Kristina gave Lizzie a private moment before continuing.

It gave Kristina time to consider her own family. She had been raised to honor her blood family. So much so that her college friends thought she was crazy about spending her winter break helping her distant cousin Bjorn in Minnesota. A blizzard had damaged his home, and the elderly cousin needed help. A Minnesota winter drastically differed from the Hong Kong or Veracruz homes where she had spent her childhood.

She looked at her protective "big brother," Phillips. *I have my own chosen family, too.*

"I am trying to protect Adrian. Just being involved puts him at risk." She held up the picture of Bianca. "A woman's picture in a Callisto casino is irrelevant to a crime committed in Scotland. I must trust in the UCE law."

"Well, I don't, but I'll trust you. I'll make you a deal. I'll answer five questions to the best of my ability. After that, you stay with me and tell me about yourself. I have gotten bits and pieces from Adrian, but I want to know more."

Kristina thought, *I think she pulled more than bits and pieces from Adrian. She knows where to pull my strings, but she is also sincere.*

"Ok, Lizzie. It's a deal. Where are Adrian and Megan?" Kristina asked.

Lizzie perked up at the switch to Megan's given name but shook her head. "Following a lead. An Artifact hunter who died about ten years ago had a hidey-hole somewhere in the rings. They took a runabout to search. It's unclear what will come of it. You should know as an investigator that leads don't always pan out."

Kristina was confident it wasn't the perfect truth. Lizzie could provide a more specific location than 'Somewhere in the Rings' if she wished.

"When are they getting back?"

"The simple answer is 'when they find what they are looking for.' But I'll be nice and give a full answer. A garbled transmission revealed a larger search area than expected. I expect they will return in a few days or send another transmission. The runabout has enough food for about a week. The living arrangements will be cozy."

Lizzie's subtle attempt to spark jealousy from Kristina worked better than Zeus' attempt. Kristina suppressed any outward signs. *Adrian's temporary living arrangements had nothing to do with finding a wanted suspect,* Kristina told herself.

"What happens if you don't hear back soon?"

"Then we charge in after them, dragging you with us if we need. That was question three." Lizzie felt no guilt at her petty gotcha.

Kristina kicked herself for wasting a question. Lizzie was obviously a charge-in-guns-blazing type of woman. After pausing briefly, she asked the next question.

"How can you convince me I should turn aside my duty to arrest Doctor McCord and help clear her instead?"

"Very good. A complex question deserves a complicated answer. Follow the spirit of your duty, not just the letter. Catching the actual killers will honor your duty. Your duty is to protect the people." Lizzie leaned forward and scrutinized Kristina.

"Looking into your eyes, I see your integrity in that pledge. I also looked into Megan's eyes. I saw the love and pain for her father. I saw the anger at the killers. There's more to the story than a dead man in Scotland or a bar fight in Callisto." Lizzie leaned back again and continued.

"Organized crime plays a major role in the illicit trade of Artifacts. They want the information Megan's father found, which goes beyond a little smuggling. That is where your duty should point you. Start finding this Bianca and her brother Sergio."

"Sergio? Zeus mentioned a man with that name, also looking for Doctor McCord," Phillips said. Everyone turned to look at him. Sarai stood beside him now, watching the Lizzie/Kristina show.

He pulled out his own pad and pulled up the document given to Lt. Davenport by Zeus with the picture of Sergio.

Sarai examined the image on the pad. "That's Sergio. After Zeus broke up the fight, we saw him at the casino. He left with Bianca. He romanced Megan in Scotland to get close and betrayed her. A nasty pair."

So, Sarai was in the fight. How did this gentle, funny woman throw someone across a bar? Kristina thought.

"Zeus tried to send us on a wild goose chase to Ceres. He said he sent Sergio there as well," Phillips said.

"Zeus always liked misdirection," Sarai said. Lizzie's gaze sharpened, wordlessly cautioning the other woman's over-share. Sarai shrugged in response. She had too many secrets in the past to conceal things now.

Lizzie held up a single finger. "Only one last question, Kristina."

Kristina's duty called again with another question. "How did you change the ID on the *Elizabeth* to *Victoria*?"

Completely straight-faced, Lizzie said, "I don't know what you're talking about. This ship has been called *Eliza-*

beth since the day Charles embarrassed me by announcing the name."

Okay, four mostly accurate answers and one bald-faced lie. I guess I can live with that, Kristina thought. She could not legally force Lizzie to give up Megan's exact location. Sergio and Bianca added complexity to the case. The chase changed into a waiting and observation game.

"Here's my plan. We will investigate these siblings and see if they are involved in smuggling. I have a higher duty to prevent the smuggling and theft of Artifacts. It is a prime duty of the service. I can't ignore the warrant for Doctor McCord. We keep an eye on the *Elizabeth*. If Megan steps on board, I will be forced to arrest her."

"Sarai, grab a chair. Let's have some girl talk. Phillips, run along and finish searching my ship. Don't break anything." Lizzie poured a cup of tea for Sarai.

"Kristina, I told you about my family. Tell us about yours."

Kristina looked to Phillips to save her. With a smile, he left his captain to fight this battle alone.

21

The Judgment of Father Frost

Rafael pounded on the door to wake Adrian and Megan. "Can you Earthers manage a little walk? Now we go to the council chambers."

A little walk in Ithaca was a spacewalk. They were to travel from the container cluster into the remaining superstructure of the old freighter *Beatrix*, renamed *Penelope*.

Adrian's eyes flickered back and forth as he walked to the airlock. Several doors were stuck open or missing. He touched the seams between internal partitions and noticed many were riveted, not welded. The compartments could not hold an airtight seal if the exterior lost pressure. From Lizzie's example, Adrian learned that one should maintain ships to exacting standards. The haphazard construction of Ithaca terrified him.

Megan noticed the concern in his eyes. *Perhaps my lack of engineering knowledge turned out to be a blessing in this situation.*

Once in the airlock, the system lost power, locking them in. The faint nostril-stinging scent of scorched wires lingering in the airlock made Megan and Adrian nervous. Carolina flicked on a light and opened a panel to fix the airlock before they could exit.

Megan followed Carolina out of the airlock to find cables stretching to other containers and the remains of the bulk freighter. Carolina pointed to a cable and connected her own safety line to it. She pointed to their destination, the superstructure of the freighter.

Megan loved microgravity, but her experience was inside space stations, not in open space. She hooked her safety line and pulled herself along. A few meters down the line, she froze.

Adrian watched Megan freeze, and training kicked in. People unused to spacewalks sometimes panicked and froze. Panic on a spacewalk could be deadly. He moved forward and placed his hand on her to steady her.

With a gentle touch of their helmets, he said in a reassuring voice. "Breathe. Focus on the cable. Tell me what's wrong."

Megan's eye didn't meet his. She stared past the edge of the container cluster and pointed. "It's beautiful."

Adrian followed her gaze and took in the same sight.

Jupiter's dazzling, colorful expanse loomed so close they could almost touch its atmosphere. The majestic sea of clouds filled the view with the dazzling eye of the Great Red Spot looking back at them. Jupiter covers half their view with its grandeur in a view that cannot be appreciated from a viewport.

Both Adrian and Megan took in the view until Rafael pushed them. He pointed down the cable to get them to keep moving. They pulled themselves along but could not avoid staying mesmerized by the view.

At an airlock emblazoned with a faded Ettrick logo, Megan felt like she had returned home, entering the place she had gone as a child.

After removing their helmets, Carolina said, "Are you ok? You seemed so comfortable in zero-g and then froze up on a spacewalk."

"Don't worry, Carolina, I've never seen a sight like that. It was incredible." Megan pointed in the direction of Jupiter.

Carolina looked out a small window. "Oh, I guess it is nice."

"Merda! We ain't got enough pods to chauffeur rich girls around. Can't just stop on the line. Everyone, even kids, gotta get around on their own." That remark earned Rafael a dirty look from his sister.

"I will be fine next time, Rafael. Can you keep up?" Megan asked in a firm challenge.

Megan launched herself down the corridor, floating in a graceful, slow pirouette, arms outstretched as if in flight. Her fingertips grazed nothing but empty air. With a flawless mid-air flip, she landed feet first on a former wall. She gazed up the passageway at them. Tilting her head coyly, she crossed her arms and flashed a sly smile.

"Show off," Adrian and Rafael said simultaneously, the men walking closer in magnetic boots.

Carolina took the challenge on herself. She launched herself to repeat Megan's performance. Everything went smoothly for her until Carolina's hand clipped the side and spun out. Megan caught Carolina just before she hit the far wall, their bodies colliding in a tangled heap.

Rafael gasped and started running. When Rafael reached them, it surprised him to find his sister giggling.

"But it was fun. Megan, will you show me how to do that?" Carolina's face lit up with excitement, like a little kid on Christmas morning.

"Carolina, you coulda gotten hurt," Rafael looked at his sister.

"Yes, Rafael, she could have gotten hurt, but she can make her own choices. I'm more concerned that I saw your prisoner flying down a corridor. Is this how you are maintaining control?" Sakura asked as she approached from a side passage.

"No, Sakura. I lost control of the situation."

"Good, as long as you understand and learn from it." Sakura turned to Megan. "You are about to be judged. Is this all a game to you?"

"No, but a lot has happened in the last two weeks. I have seen my father murdered by a friend, the same friend tried to carve me up like a Christmas roast, a bounty hunter tried to kidnap me, and Adrian's lover wants to arrest me. I thought it was time for a little fun." Megan floated in mid-air with her arms crossed.

"Yes, two bad weeks. Many here have had two bad decades. Rafael, take them to the council chambers." Sakura turned and pushed herself away.

"This way." Rafael let them down the hall. This was all familiar to Megan. These were the standard boring gray and blue walls selected for Ettrick ships years ago.

Rafael escorted them into a conference room. They had removed the fancy furniture, leaving only faint marks on the floor. Shadows marked the walls where artwork had hung for decades. Floor-to-ceiling tethers again took the place of chairs.

The members of the town council were waiting for them.

"Good morning. I hope you had a pleasant evening," Sakura said. Her casual voice showed no indication that she had just spoken to them.

"We met some nice new friends. Sleeping in zero gravity was not enjoyable," Megan said.

"Like McCord's brat would ever have to sleep outside gravity." An American-accented woman spoke up. The woman was silent in the town hall meeting. The animosity confused Megan.

"Layla, most humans live in gravity. Would you choose to sleep without gravity?" a German-accented man said.

Layla didn't answer but gave the man a dirty look.

Sakura held up her hand. "We'll get back to business. Megan McCord and Adrian Kostas, we have discussed your petition for sanctuary. Do you have any statements before the final vote?"

"I'm falsely accused and hunted. My father and I deciphered part of Fred Stonington's discovery, and it got him killed. Let us search and find the rest of the clues. We'll depart and draw the threat away. I swear to guard your secrets."

"You admit you brought danger?" Jabari said.

"The danger was always there. The same clues we followed could lead the killers here. Is denying the danger exists helpful?" Megan countered.

"Enough debate. We will keep talking forever at this rate. I call for the vote," the German man said.

Priya nodded. "I second the request."

Megan grabbed Adrian's hand as their anxiety rose. The next few minutes would change their future. Ithaca could accept them, or the council could expel Megan and Adrian from the city. That option could be them peacefully flying away in *Castor* or them "walking back" as Rafael threatened.

"Very well. We will vote on the Sanctuary request. Please vote For or Against."

"Jabari Mbeya, what is your vote?" Sakura selected the eldest of the council to vote first.

"Against," Jabari said with icy firmness. "I don't trust them."

The first vote jolted Megan's spirit.

"Fynn Mueller, what is your vote?"

His statement was as efficient as a well-tuned German engine. "For."

With the vote tied, Adrian looked at Megan and smiled. Megan squeezed his hand.

"Layla Washington, how do you vote?"

"McCords can burn in Hell. No sanctuary for her." The American woman's eyes bore into Megan's with a venomous glare filled with pure hatred. Megan's nails dug into Adrian's skin, but he didn't flinch.

Layla's tone drew a tight, restrained look from Sakura. "Felipe Da Silva, your vote, please."

"I can't trust anything connected to Ettrick. I might like the pilot, but together? I vote against the sanctuary."

Megan drew in a breath. She looked at Adrian. Deep furrows of worry marred his face. This was not going well—three against and one in favor. Two more votes to go.

"Priya Banerjee, your vote."

Megan's apprehension spiked, making her palms sweaty and her breath shallow. Yesterday, this woman declared they shouldn't be allowed to leave.

"Young man," Priya, the youngest council member, was near Adrian's age. "You came before us yesterday telling lies. Your charm didn't hide these lies. This doesn't earn the trust of people who value secrecy."

Adrian's eyes darted down, lips quivering, as his brow furrowed. His sweaty grip crushed on Megan's hand. Priya's comments had a foreboding tone, hinting at something ominous. Sakura's vote may not matter soon.

Priya then turned her gaze to Megan. "Doctor McCord, you told us the truth. I respect that. The truth was as risky as the lie. Many do not love the McCord name here." She looked at Layla and Felipe. "Your truth outweighs the lies. I vote for sanctuary."

As Adrian's grip relaxed, Megan exhaled slowly, the tension in her body melting away. Sakura Akiyama was the only one left to cast her vote.

She had been the fairest to them, even friendly, but a hard woman to read. Megan could see Sakura's fierce protectiveness for Ithaca would override any personal considerations.

As if she were a mind reader, Sakura said, "Don't worry, I won't keep you waiting. I vote for sanctuary. I am sure you see the problem."

"A tie," Adrian said.

Sakura nodded. "The council is divided on whether to grant you sanctuary. Three votes for, three against."

Megan exchanged a worried glance with Adrian.

The hatch door slid open, and a tall, broad-shouldered man pulled himself through. His graying hair and weathered face spoke of a lifetime of troubles.

"Andrei Petrov is our engineer and seventh council member," Sakura said. "Andrei, I would say you had perfect timing, but it would be a lie. You are late again."

"My apologies. The blasted oxygen generator failed again." The man had a thick Russian accent.

"Andrei, we require your vote to break the tie," Sakura stated. She outlined their plea and Megan's identity revelation.

Andrei eyed Megan. "Little Megan has grown up."

"Have we met?" Megan asked.

Andrei didn't answer but turned to Sakura. "I must speak with you both privately."

Layla objected, but Sakura dismissed her. "This way, please," she said, leading them to the office door. Megan recognized this door. It was the door to the owner's private office. Her father's office.

Adrian watched Megan exit. He didn't want to admit his anxiety over his fate was determined behind a closed door and in the hands of someone he had known less than two weeks. Adrian had trust in only a few people outside of the crew. Kristina was one, and Megan had become another.

As the door closed, Felipe interrupted his worries. "Tell me. Is that runabout as much fun to fly as it looks?"

Adrian smiled as he recognized a fellow pilot.

Megan found herself in a hollow shell of an office, the fine wood surfaces now bare and scarred from removing any valuables. What was once her father's sanctuary now stood cold and barren, like a tomb robbed of everything but ghosts. Tether cables replaced standard chairs.

Andrei looked at Megan again. "The grown woman is also still the lost girl. Will Father Frost help you again?"

Megan felt a wave of confusion wash over her. The man looked familiar, but she didn't know where she had seen him before. "Who is Father Frost? And who are you?"

"Think of the last time you were on this ship." His voice was soft and familiar.

Megan closed her eyes as the wave of memories surged through her. She was back on the ship as a young girl of eight or nine. A funeral made the boat somber, filled with people gathered to honor her great-aunt Beatrix, the ship's namesake. Solemn faces greeted her everywhere she looked.

More than anything, she wanted to be home with her sick mummy. Daddy refused to take her home when she asked. Without him noticing, she slipped away and began wandering aimlessly.

She approached crew members, asked, pleaded, and finally demanded they take her home.

Eventually, she found herself lost in the massive engine room. Strange sounds and metallic smells assaulted her nose. The ladders and stairs made the confusing room more vertical than horizontal.

She remembered the cold metallic floor against her skin, tears streaming down her face, and the feeling of utter loneliness. Amidst her despair, a soft voice broke through her sobs.

A kind-faced man, an engineer perhaps, approached and tenderly wrapped her trembling form in his warm jacket. He sat with her, spinning tales of forest witches and huts with legs. She clung to every word. He finished with the story of Morozko, Father Frost, rescuing a lost girl.

"Little Megan has lost her way. Do not fear. Father Frost will guide you home," his deep, gently accented voice soothed her. Later, it could have been hours or minutes, he guided her to her frantic father, who had been desperately searching for her. The man smiled, giving her one last pat on the head before disappearing.

Megan's mind returned to the present. "You're Father Frost?"

Andrei held his arms wide. "We are one and the same. At least, I used to be. An old Russian fairy tale. A suitable version to soothe a scared little girl."

"I thought it was all a dream. How could you be on the *Beatrix* then and Ithaca now?"

"That is a much longer tale. No mystical being saved us." His cheerful face changed to a bitter frown. He looked to Sakura to explain.

"Doctor McCord, what do you remember of the fate of the *Beatrix*?"

"Not much. It was one of the oldest ships in the Ettrick fleet. We sold it for scrap. I don't recall exactly when, but it was around the time my mother died."

"I wouldn't expect a young girl to know the details. Ettrick decommissioned the *Beatrix* while his wife's death distracted Roger McCord. He entrusted the ship's sale to someone less honorable." Sakura closed her eyes for a moment, lost in the past.

"The crooked Ettrick official schemed to sell off this ship. He cast us out penniless on a half-completed Europa station, at the mercy of outlaws who stripped the *Beatrix*. Neither the UCE nor Ettrick would help us."

"Us? You were on the ship, too?" Megan asked. She paused for a moment, thinking. "You were the ship's purser? On an earlier trip, you gave me a beautiful Japanese doll. I still have it."

Sakura smiled, pleased her gift was treasured. "Yes, Andrei, Layla, Felipe, and I were all crew members. We had nothing but the clothes on our backs. The bitterness we held for Ettrick and your family was beyond measure."

"It makes no sense. My family wouldn't treat people so horribly." Outrage laced Megan's voice as the absurdity of the claim sunk in.

"It happened. Your father had lost sight of everything in his grief. Malice or neglect, we blamed your father for our plight. Roger McCord was a good man, but convincing Layla and Felipe won't be easy," Sakura said.

Andrei continued from there in a pained voice. "Unlike Sakura, I did not know Roger McCord well. Being kicked out created resentment for your family and has not completely disappeared. I dedicated myself to Ettrick for twenty-five years."

He inhaled deeply and closed his eyes to shake off the dreadful memories. "After our abandonment, we met Fred Stonington. He told us of his idea for a home for outcasts. We joined him in creating Ithaca. He traded some artifacts for the remains of *Beatrix*. He renamed her *Penelope*, and we have been growing since."

Megan pondered the impact of the lives destroyed because of McCord's inaction. Despite their shared grief, her father's failure was inexcusable.

"What can I do to make this right?"

"You can't. This is our life and our home. Our story is not unique. Unscrupulous people in power sometimes outnumber the good. We take in those run over by society. You have also fallen victim to the UCE. The question is, do you get to join us?" Sakura said. She looked at Andrei with a raised eyebrow.

Megan asked, "Will Father Frost help me again?"

Andrei gave her a crooked smile. "Did you ever learn the full folk tale of Morozko, Father Frost? It differs from the fable I told you."

"Yes, in the authentic story, the girl's evil stepmother abandons her rather than her getting lost."

"Essentially, yes. Go on."

"There were two girls. The first girl is polite and kind. Morozko returns her to her father with jewels and fine clothes."

"Yes, and the other girl?" Andrei gestured for Megan to continue.

"The stepmother abandoned her own daughter in hopes she would get the same rewards. The other girl was rude and selfish. Father Frost leaves that girl, and she freezes to death." Megan completed the tale.

"So, are you the kind girl or the selfish girl? Should I save you or leave you to freeze?"

"I hope I've become the kind girl. The girl you saved was selfish and rude."

"It was the real world. I wouldn't ignore a crying girl, even if she's a spoiled brat. Layla and Filipe have stories of you demanding they take you back to Scotland. Tell me about you now."

Megan closed her eyes and examined her memories. She recognized the faces of the crew members she had tried to order around years ago. She believed the crew should treat the CEO's daughter as a princess.

"I will stand by my friends, old and new. I want to prove who killed my father and why. I fought alongside my new friends from the *Elizabeth*." She showed the stitches on her arm. "I pledge to improve Ithaca's inhabitants' lives because of my family's previous inaction."

"Most Ithaca residents are not from the Beatrix,"

"It doesn't matter. Ithaca deserves better. If the government will ignore them, I won't."

"Your heart is in the right place, but you can't fix everything." Andrei turned to Sakura. "I vote for sanctuary."

Sakura nodded and led them back to the conference room. The council hovered in anticipation of the trio's return. Megan noted Adrian had a discussion with Filipe and Rafael. They were, without doubt, touting their piloting skills. Exclamations murmured around the room, asking for the results of the private meeting.

"Please quiet down." Sakura grabbed a cable and waited until everyone stopped speaking. "The vote is four in favor and three against the sanctuary."

The room clamored with voices again. With a simple gesture of Sakura's hand, the room hushed.

"This is a unique situation. The sanctuary is conditionally granted." She studied Megan and Adrian. "You will need to prove yourselves. Convince us of your sincerity and truthfulness by your actions, and I will show you Fred Stonington's paperwork."

She faced the council. "You will need to pull your own weight. Any suggestions on work details?"

Felipe said, "We need more pilots. Rafael can teach him the ropes. We can place him in the rotation."

"What about the girl? We have no need for an archeologist," Jabari said.

Layla glared at Megan. "Did you pick up any useful skills as part of a family in the space shipping industry? Other than being overbearing and selfish?"

Megan ignored the slur. She would not win over Layla soon. "I have experience moving in microgravity. Give me a zero-g task, and I may perform it as well or better than I could on Earth. I'm sure I can assist in many ways."

Andrei reached to his tool belt and tossed a wrench in a slow trajectory at a wall. "Catch."

Megan understood the unstated goal. Catch the wrench before it hits the wall.

She grasped a tether cable secured to the ceiling and floor, and Adrian, his magnetic boots, fixed him on the floor.

"Tense up, Adrian."

She shot forward like an Olympic luger, launching herself out of the start gate.

Megan didn't have a direct path to the wrench. She flew to the cable Fynn fastened himself to. Grabbing the cable above his head, she was propelled to a different angle by the centrifugal force. Fynn was unfazed and scrutinized her movement.

She snatched the wrench from the air and landed on the wall, perpendicular to most of the rest of the viewers. Like a billiards master, she then shot herself at a different wall and, in a perfect bank shot, found a new trajectory. She passed by Andrei, handing him his wrench, and returned to her original position by Adrian. He rolled his eyes and said for the second time that day. "Show off."

"You should be careful when dropping your tools." Her lips quirked up in a smirk, eyes gleaming with mischief.

Sakura said, "I ask again for suggestions."

"She can work with me," Carolina said. Everyone fixed their eyes on the usually quiet and reserved woman. Again, Carolina floated at an odd angle relative to everyone else. People sometimes wondered if it was deliberate, but Carolina didn't care about orientation.

With everyone's gaze upon her, she instinctively sought refuge behind her brother, the weight of their scrutiny making her feel vulnerable.

"She's not an engineer," Andrei said.

"I can carry Carolina's tools or fetch the ones she needs. An extra set of eyes and hands make any job faster."

Rafael and Carolina had a whispered conversation. "Carolina is comfortable with Megan. Previously, she only trusted Andrei or me. This is good for her, but I'm not sure about it. That's just me being an overprotective big brother."

"I'm fourteen minutes older than you." Carolina smacked him.

22

First Day on the Job

August 6, 2155—Ithaca

The next day, Megan and Adrian reported to their new jobs. Adrian helped Rafael with transportation and construction projects as a pilot. Megan was Carolina's helper in a never-ending struggle to repair items in Ithaca.

The day started with strength exercises with resistance bands. Life in microgravity requires regular muscle building.

Megan, Adrian, Carolina, and Rafael ate a small breakfast in a communal kitchen near their housing pods. The breakfast consisted of a tube of protein paste with a distinctly fishy taste and a handful of browning collards and spinach.

We're supposed to eat this? Megan thought. It would be thrown away if she saw this in the kitchen back home.

Rafael took a bite of the spinach but noticed Megan's reluctance. In Portuguese, he mumbled, "Our food is not good enough for her."

In English, Rafael said, "Next week, we are in rotation to get the fresh produce from hydroponics, but we ain't wasting any food. Eat it or starve."

Megan bristled at his words but crinkled her nose and ate it. She chewed as little as possible to keep the taste from lingering. The others finished their small meal in silence.

On leaving the kitchen, Rafael led Adrian toward the shuttle airlocks. But Carolina grabbed Megan's arm and pulled her in the other direction.

"Come on. It's only a kilometer across the cables," Carolina said.

Megan's mouth dropped open. *A kilometer? Yesterday, the spacewalk was only a hundred meters.*

After exiting the airlock, they pulled themselves from one container cluster to another. This time, Megan wasn't lost in the beauty of Jupiter. Many other people crossed between sections of the city on cables.

Eventually, they reached the power plant, an old tug with an oversized fusion reactor. The thrusters didn't work, but the reactor provided power to the town. It needed lots of tender, loving care from Carolina, Andrei, and other engineers. Megan's arms hurt, and their workday had not even started.

"Good morning, little ones. I hope you are ready to work," Andrei said. "First stop is the clinic. I fixed the diagnostic med scanner. Drop it off and get to hydroponics. There is a broken pump."

He pushed the scanner and a tool bag into Megan's arms. "In the story I told you, Father Frost gave the girl jewels and sent her home. Today, you get tools and hard work. Off you go."

The items may have had no weight in microgravity, but the bulk still created a challenge. At the same time, Megan pulled herself along the cables. Carolina offered to help, but Megan declined.

The clinic consisted of two cargo containers attached end to end. On entering, Megan examined the space. If she hadn't been here, she would have never believed the dull, metallic walls housed a makeshift hospital. Contrasting to Earthbound hospitals, this held no soft white surfaces. Blankets, taut from the floor to the ceiling, functioned as partitions between the "patient rooms." Only the smell of antiseptic bore a resemblance to a hospital.

Council member Priya Banerjee met them at the makeshift airlock to take delivery of the med scanner.

"Thank you. Mei Lin is in labor. We need to monitor her vitals."

Megan was shocked. "This is the only diagnostic scanner?"

"Yes, Doctor McCord. We are lucky to have this. It is almost 50 years old. You, in fact, are the only one in Ithaca who carries the title doctor and obviously not the kind this clinic needs." Priya may have voted for Megan, but there was no love in her voice.

"You're not a medical doctor?"

"No. I simply do my best to care for people. Also, thank you for your donation." Priya held up a bag containing a tube of Rapid-Heal gel and a bottle of antibiotics.

"Those were prescribed to me. I was cut two days ago. The doctor told me to use them daily." Megan could not hide the indignant tone in her voice.

"Come here." She pulled aside a curtain to see a teen boy with a bandaged arm. "As teen boys do, he did something stupid. Probably to impress a girl. Your Rapid-Heal gel will help the wound close without the stitches he really needs. Plus, antibiotics to prevent infection."

Priya took out a single antibiotic pill and gave it to Megan. "Come back tomorrow, and if the scanner shows any sign of infection, I will give you another. No Rapid-Heal, though. At this point, you would only need it to prevent a scar. Your vanity is not worth it when that gel could heal a fresh wound. All medical supplies that come to Ithaca are shared."

Megan's face turned red, and she tried to hand back the pill. "Of course. Please keep all of it, including the antibiotics. I will be ok."

"No. You are now a resident of Ithaca. Now, if you have signs of infection, we will treat them. Be back here tomorrow. At the end of the month, you will get bisphosphonate, an osteoporosis drug. Anyone in microgravity is at risk of bone loss. We have a source that smuggles the medicine to us."

A cry of pain came from behind a privacy barrier. "Excuse me, Mei Lin is having a contraction."

Carolina led Megan to another lifeblood site of Ithaca. The pair of stubby cylinder-shaped modules floated near the powerplant were initially designed to carry grain. Regularly, bulk freighters like *Beatrix* carried these fat space grain silos to the outer moons.

"These are both hydroponics?" Megan asked.

"No, one is Hydroponics. The other is the fish tank."

"Fish tank?"

"We raise sardines as a source of calcium. The fish are the base of the protein vat to be multiplied into food paste. That is what was in the food tube you ate this morning."

"Raising sardines in space? Ingenious. I'd love to see it." Megan tried not to think of the lab-generated fish paste they ate at breakfast.

"Not today. Now we are needed in hydroponics." Before entering, Carolina said, "We are going straight to the pump. Layla Washington runs hydroponics, and I don't think she likes you."

That's an understatement. Megan thought.

The two found the pump but did not avoid Layla. Carolina nervously slunk behind a piece of equipment.

"Ok, princess. See all this food." Layla waved her hands around the hydroponics beds. "Without this, no one eats. Including you. Carolina, make sure she doesn't break anything."

Layla left without allowing Megan to respond.

"Don't worry. I will do the hard stuff. I need you to turn a valve when I say. Just don't turn it the wrong way, or it will release a muddy sludge," Carolina said as she exited her shelter.

"Sounds simple enough," Megan said.

Adrian returned to their room after a long day of flying shuttles and helping with construction projects. Megan floated in the center of the room, wearing a t-shirt and shorts. She attempted to scrub a black and brown substance from her brilliant blue spacesuit. Her once lustrous red hair was matted down and caked with the same muddy goo.

"What happened to you?"

As Megan faced him, her shoulders slumped, and her gaze dropped in quiet resignation. "I turned it the wrong way."

23

The Lioness and the Lost Lambs

August 8, 2155—Zeta Sierra near Europa

Kristina felt conflicted as she stared at the report she had submitted two days before. Her eyes scanned the lines as she read through each word, searching for discrepancies. Every word on the report was accurate, but also a dance of misdirection and glossing over crucial information. Guilt gnawed at her conscience for sending it.

The conflict inside Kristina's mind spun like a tornado. *The report, as it stood, would appease the higher-ups, but at what cost?*

Internal Memorandum
TO: Admiral Jonas Wells, CPS Headquarters
FROM: Commander Kristina Chen-Ramirez
DATE: August 6, 2155
SUBJECT: Search for Fugitive Megan McCord
Summary:
We confirmed fugitive Megan McCord had been aboard the Light Cargo Vessel *Elizabeth*. She disembarked at Europa Station on August 4. Her current whereabouts are unknown.
Details:

- Boarded and searched LCV *Elizabeth* with a team of customs agents.

- Confirmed from records and crew interviews, Megan McCord booked passage aboard *Elizabeth* with a legitimate charter.

- The crew claimed she disembarked upon arrival at Europa.

- A review of station security footage confirmed her arrival but has no record of her departure.

- Unconfirmed report of a female suspect boarding a private vessel, identity unknown. The source was an anonymous tip from a possible underworld source. The unconfirmed destination was Ceres.

- We held the *Elizabeth* for forty-eight hours. The crew repeatedly told the same story. Our conclusion was they didn't know McCord's location.

- *Elizabeth* was cleared to resume the trade route pending any new evidence.

Recommendation:
- Issue a bulletin to Ceres, and all asteroid facilities will be on alert for McCord or the unknown vessel.

- Pull transmission records from Ceres Station to see if she contacted anyone about her plans.

- Follow up with belt mining colonies to monitor for her arrival.

Commander Chen-Ramirez
Commanding officer - *Zeta Sierra*
Kristina knew the proper thing to do was to report everything. Still, Lizzie persuaded her someone had plotted against Megan and her father. The real threat was Sergio and Bianca.

The *Zeta Sierra* glided through the vast expanse of the Jupiter area. Kristina had other duties to fulfill but remained close to Europa. *Elizabeth* would not leave without Adrian, and he would return with McCord. She wanted to meet the doctor, hear her story, and understand her. Kristina shook her head, forcing thoughts of Megan and Adrian aside.

The words of her communication officer snapped Kristina back into focus.

"Ferry *DW-1876*, This is Customs and Patrol Service vessel *Zetta Sierra*. Please respond. We are on an intercept course." He turned to Kristina. "Still no response, Captain."

In front of them, the lifeless ferry spun out of control toward Europa. A damaged thruster caused sporadic bursts, forcing it to spin chaotically. Only hours remained until it crashed at high speed.

Kristina took the comms. "*DW-1876*, if anyone can hear us. We are on the way. You are not alone. If you can, get to the main airlock or engineering. We will be there soon. *Zeta Sierra* is out. Elias, do your thing."

Fortunately, her pilot, Elias Thorn, had skills matching his ego. The crew strapped themselves in for the unexpected twists and turns he performed to match speed and trajectory with the derelict.

As the *Zeta Sierra* closed in on the derelict ship, alarms blared. Warning lights flashed like frantic fireflies, illuminating the tense faces of the crew.

Kristina's heart pounded in her chest. Elias maneuvered through the debris that broke away from the derelict. The ship's hull groaned under the strain, protesting against the intense forces. Partial artificial gravity did little to reduce the effects of the maneuvers.

With each burst of the maneuvering jet, the derelict craft spun faster, its erratic path resembling a demented dance. It was a dangerous waltz, but *Zeta Sierra* knew the steps.

The *Zeta Sierra* approached the derelict ship with a magnetic docking clamp extended. A metallic clang reverberated through the hull as the two vessels locked together. Elias used Miss Zetty's thrusters to reduce the spin of the paired ships to zero. Despite the challenges, Elias's skills and expertise triumphed.

Memories of a similar situation ten years before were returned to her. She piloted the patrol vessel that snagged the derelict ship belonging to Fred Stonington before it collided with Callisto. She hated to admit it, but Elias' piloting skills exceeded hers.

"Excellent work, Mr. Thorn. Get us stabilized." Elias's grin showed his satisfaction with himself. He would embellish the story manyfold the next time he tried to impress a girl in a pub. The green tinge to some other crew members indicated they were not as pleased.

It took a few minutes, but the paired ships became stable and on a trajectory to avoid colliding with the moon's ice. *Zeta Siera's* gravity plates provided a sense of half Earth's gravity. The maximum possible under on-board power without acceleration.

"Phillips, a boarding party to the airlock. Let's see what happened."

Frank Davenport, her XO, said, "I suppose you are going along too?"

"You know me too well. You have the conn." She stood and bounded down the corridor.

The derelict vessel had been used to ferry asteroid miners to and from the mining stations. This boat was scheduled for overhaul at Europa station.

They would enter the abandoned ship in microgravity, safer without knowing the status of the vessel's interior. The sound of metal scraping against metal echoed as two crew members struggled to pry open the hatch. The unpowered ship was shrouded in darkness, with no interior lights to guide the way. Kristina and Phillips entered first.

They turned on their helmet lamps, shafts of light creating strange shadows.

"Air pressure is at 845 millibars and dropping, about that of Denver. The Air Quality Index is near 200, like in heavily polluted cities of the early 21st century. I recommend we keep on suit air," Environmental Specialist Daniel Miller said.

"Agreed. Everyone proceeds with caution. Chief Zhao takes Doctor Roy and Park to look for survivors. Malik, Miller, and Rossi go see if you can get power back. Phillips, Rogers, you are with me."

As Kristina, Phillips, and Rogers made their way through the derelict ship, they couldn't shake the feeling something was wrong. The silence was deafening, broken only by magnetic boots on metal decks.

Her helmet light cast eerie shadows on the walls, causing the abandoned vessel to look scarier. The light flickered and danced, showing the rusty metal and bits of debris on the floor.

"Phillips, you take the lead. Get us to the bridge, and hopefully, we can find out what happened."

Phillips nodded in acknowledgment, his expression mirroring Kristina's own concern. The ferryboat crew's fate weighed on their minds, making the atmosphere even more oppressive.

They approached a ladder leading to the command section, their eyes scanning the darkness for any sign of life. The air was heavy with tension, their breaths shallow as they moved through the silent corridor.

Kristina's sharp eyes caught something and called out, "Alice, stop!"

Petty Officer Alice Rogers froze, her body stiffening in response. The legs of Alice's suit held a disturbing sight. A vivid red liquid marred the pristine white fabric. They looked around and saw crimson orbs floating in the shadows.

A trail of grizzly breadcrumbs led them to a horrifying sight. Flickering lights illuminated two motionless bodies drifting in a storage compartment. One person, facing away from the door, had a gruesome wound on his back. Multiple flechette blasts had torn through flesh, leaving jagged edges and exposing raw, shredded muscle.

The man died shielding a woman. Her arm, wrapped in a belt used as a makeshift tourniquet, showed signs of a desperate attempt to stop the bleeding. Her right hand was a grotesque sight, reduced to shredded meat and the source of the blood trail. Heat sensors confirmed she was still alive, a flicker of hope amidst the darkness. In an ultimate act of heroism, the man had bandaged her wound and blocked a lethal attack, hoping to save her.

"Doctor, we need you here right now. We found a critically injured survivor," Kristina said over the radio. Petty Officer Rogers put an emergency oxygen mask on the woman. Phillips used a first aid kit to stop the bleeding.

Doctor Maya Roy arrived two minutes later and took over the care, her gloved hands moving swiftly and deftly. "I need to get her back to sickbay. I can stabilize her there, but we must return her to the Europa Hospital as soon as possible."

"Doctor, there could be other survivors. We can't leave yet."

"I know, but there might not be too. Everyone else might be like this man," pointing at the mangled body. "She might be the only one we can save."

"Understood. Take Petty Officer Park and get her to sickbay. Boarding team, this is the captain. I want everyone else to spread out. We have five minutes to look for survivors. Lt. Davenport, prepare the ship for departure. Least time route to Europa station. If we don't find anyone else in the next five minutes, burn like Hell for the station."

"What about you, Captain?" Davenport said.

"We'll keep looking. Maybe we can find out what happened here. If there are any other survivors, we will care for them the best we can until you return. I figure it is about a two-hour round trip."

"I can do it in an hour and a half," Thorn said in the background with his customary pilot arrogance. He could probably do it, too, but at a cost to the engines.

"Don't break my ship."

"Seriously, Captain. That boat is not stable. What if the malfunctioning thruster fires off again? Thorn won't be here to steady it."

"We'll take the chance. Specialist Malik, the first priority after the survivor search is getting the thruster shutdown. Then get power back. I will head to the bridge and see what the status is. Everyone go!"

Phillips followed Kristina to an emergency ladder.

"Donald, I meant it when I said everyone needs to spread out. I can handle myself. We need more people down here searching passenger and cargo compartments. That is the most likely place for survivors." She rarely used his first name. His protective instinct said to stay by her side, but he rolled his eyes and followed her orders.

As Kristina ascended the narrow ladder shaft, her breath echoed through the stillness. The only source of light came from her helmet lamps, intensifying the feeling of isolation that enveloped her. A sense of unease gnawed at her as if something sinister lurked in the shadows, observing her every move.

Reaching the top of the shaft, she paused, her apprehension growing as she contemplated what awaited her on the bridge. Did they seal the doors? If she had been in command, that's what she would have done.

"I am about to enter the bridge level. Anyone find anything?" No one had found anything except eerily empty rooms.

She stepped up onto the command level. Two things were apparent.

In the dark corridor, a lifeless body clad in a black space suit floated. It was no ordinary spacer's suit. This one was armored. The face shield had a hole in the center, the glass now smeared with a gruesome shade of red. Kristina circled around the figure but didn't see an exit hole. She grimaced at the horrific thought of the bullet bouncing inside the armored helmet.

She examined the melted door lock leading to the bridge. "Zetties, be cautious of explosives. Someone used thermite on the bridge hatch."

She held her stunner tightly and entered the bridge. A lingering doubt crept into her mind about boarding the derelict in rescue gear instead of body armor.

Ten years in service didn't prepare Kristina to see the bridge. Tied to the command chair was the figure of a man, presumably the captain. Someone had used a staple gun from a nearby tool chest to staple a cowboy hat to the man's head. Blood from the wounds indicated he had been alive at the time. Two As and two eights were carved into his hand. Someone then shot him in the back of the head with a revolver floating nearby.

The horrors did not end there.

A woman's naked body floated several meters away. The victim endured unimaginable brutality. A leather belt wrapped around her neck had strangled her. An empty gun holster hung from the belt like a macabre pendant. The killers forced the captain to watch. Kristina got a fire blanket from an emergency supply cabinet. She covered the woman's lifeless form with it. The image etched itself into her mind, destined to haunt her dreams forever.

"I am on the bridge. I have two dead here. No survivors." Her voice was as steady and even as she could force it.

"Are you ok, Skipper?" Phillips said on a private channel.

"No, but I am safe. I'll deal with what I see here later. It's horrible, Donald."

"I can be there in a minute."

"Stay searching. I will be fine."

Reports from the other team members came in.

Engineering Specialist Jamal Malik arrived in engineering and started working on his tasks. The other crew members had found three bodies but no more survivors.

"Captain, permission to release? Are you sure you want to stay?" Lt. Davenport asked.

"Go. Just get back to me as soon as you can." A heavy silence settled onto the bridge. The lifeless gaze of the deceased captain appeared to stare with accusatory eyes at Kristina.

"I'm sorry, Captain. I swore to stop things like this. I failed you."

Kristina connected a portable power unit to the bridge computers, hoping to bring them back to life. The faint hum of the power pack was the only sound in the grim room.

The pitch-black darkness engulfed the small cargo area, broken only by the lights of Petty Officer Marco Rossi. His wide eyes darted around, pointing his weapon light at every menacing shadow. As he walked, his magnetic boots made a sharp clang that echoed through the otherwise quiet space.

"Damnit Malik. Why can't you get these lights on?" Rossi grumbled under his breath.

Crates scattered in the area created ominous shadows crushing. Rossi couldn't shake off the feeling anything could lurk in the depths of the darkness. Every sound, every movement, made his skin crawl with unease.

Rossi strained his eyes, hunting for any sign of light or relief. The weight of the blackness seemed to press down on him, suffocating his senses. He knew he had to stay alert, ready to face whatever dangers awaited him in this dim light.

His grip tightened on his stun carbine, his knuckles turning white. Sweat running down his face dripped to his lips, causing him to taste his bitter fear.

A flicker of movement caught his eye. He trained his gun's light on it, heart pounding, breath held. His light didn't reach the far wall, making the space seem even more prominent in the dimness.

Nothing was there. His mind raced, trying to make sense of the impossible. Was it a hallucination?

Yes, Marco, you're just imagining things. Nothing is here. Just finish the search and leave, Marco told himself.

Without warning, the world shifted. The malfunctioning thruster roared to life at full power. A loose crate crashed into Marco, causing his stun carbine to fly from his grasp as he fell face-first. The impact shattered a helmet light, leaving him with only one source of illumination - the light on his gun. The other headlamp only flickered. Darkness encroached on him further.

"Dammit, Malik, get the thruster locked down!" he shouted, desperation lacing with a thick Italian accent.

In the feeble glow of his gun's light, the silhouette of a person emerged from the darkness.

An ear-piercing scream shattered the stillness. Marco Rossi hadn't regained his footing when his faceplate shattered, sending searing pain coursing through his head.

A figure slipped back into the darkness. Until the intruder spoke, he was unsure of the threat. Now, he knew the enemy had returned. He stopped one, but the sound of Sally's screams in his head didn't go away. He needed to find the laughing woman with the platinum blonde hair to do that.

"Sorry, Captain," Specialist Malik said, his voice strained amidst the whirring and clanking of the ship's machinery. "I'm trying to get the thruster isolated."

"It's okay. Just keep working on it," Kristina replied, her voice steady despite the tension in the air. She could hear the distant hum of the ship's engines intermingled with the occasional hiss of escaping steam.

The Zetties commander called out to the team, her words echoing through the metal corridors. "Everyone report in. Any injuries?"

One by one, the team answered, their voices filled with a mixture of relief and frustration. They reported no injuries more significant than bruised egos.

But one voice remained silent. Marco Rossi didn't respond.

"Anyone know where Rossi is?" Kristina asked, her voice tinged with concern.

"He headed to cargo," CPO Zhao replied, his words barely audible over the ship's constant rumbling.

"Get down there and check on him. I'm heading down too," Kristina raced to the ladder as the situation's urgency pushed aside her lingering anxiety.

"I'm closest. On my way." After returning from escorting the doctor to the airlock, Petty Officer Jun-Seo Park pushed off and drifted in zero-g to the cargo bay. In the darkness, the shadows cast from his lights made it appear like the walls reached for him. A glance between floating crates made him think he saw a monster. *It's your imagination.*

Park found Marco drifting near a loose cargo box. The glass from his broken faceplate formed a halo near his head. A single headlamp only blinked, the light sparkling off the glass.

"Rossi is down!" He rushed over to his friend, knocking away the glass and looking through the broken face plate. "He is breathing."

Park removed Marco's helmet and placed an emergency oxygen mask over his friend's face. Marco bled from cuts on his face, but he critically needed oxygen in this thin air.

Park, focused on helping his friend, didn't notice a presence looming centimeters behind him. A hand grabbed his shoulder. With a sudden surge of adrenaline, he twisted his body, positioning himself between his friend and the threat.

The 'danger' was Chief Warrant Officer Phillips.

"Chief, you startled me. I have Rossi on O2 now, but we must get his cuts bandaged soon. A crate must have collided with him and broke his faceplate."

Phillips checked Rossi's vitals. "He is stabilizing. Monitor him. I have to look for something."

Moments later, the captain and Chief Petty Officer Zhao showed up. After they were told of Marco Rossi's condition, Phillips explained the problem.

"Someone was here and attacked him."

"It could easily have been the crate that hit him," Zhao said.

"He got hit by the crate, but it didn't break his faceplate. No glass in the box. The more important question. Where is his stun carbine or sidearm?" They all looked and saw the empty holster.

Kristina didn't hesitate. "Time to regroup. Chief Zhao, stay here with Park and Rossi. Malik and Miller are together in Engineering. The only one on her own is Rogers. Phillips, let's go find her."

Alice Rogers slowly and carefully traveled back toward the cargo bay. She had been spooked by walking through a floating pool of blood.

The lack of light didn't faze her. Though the scattered wreckage complicated the task, she quickly navigated through the darkness. The cold rattled her. Growing up in Bermuda, she developed a strong aversion to the cold.

Rogers heard a welcome noise, the whine of air circulation. Miller must have gotten the environmental controls working. She never admitted it but got a little claustrophobic with a closed helmet.

She stepped to a nearby vent and opened her helmet in violation of regulation. With the touch of a button, the helmet collapsed remarkably small into a compartment on her upper back. As she touched the vent's edges, a rush of air caused her platinum-blonde hair to billow behind her. Taking a moment to breathe, she could feel the soothing coolness of the filtered air on her skin.

"Monster." A shadow in the hall formed into a man in ship coveralls. He pointed a flechette pistol at Rogers and yanked the trigger.

She yelped in pain as a red mist erupted from her left arm. This time, the blood on her suit was her own.

"You stabbed my friend. I heard Sally's screams over the intercom. Die."

She pushed herself out of the way just in time to avoid a string of flechette darts. She tried to raise her neuro-stunner with her right arm, but her aim was off. The man ran off as she squirted stun shots.

Rogers fled as fast as her magnetic boots could carry her. Her left arm was useless, and her right fired her stunner behind her. Kristina and Phillips intercepted her before she got to the cargo bay.

"What happened?" the captain asked.

"A crewman shot me. He thought I was the one who killed the people here." As she ran, a trail of crimson orbs marked her path.

"Let's get back to the others. Phillips covers us. I will help Rogers." Phillips scanned for threats. Utterly cool and collected.

Alice examined Phillips and her captain in action. *Did anything frighten him? Or the captain?*

They reached the cargo area, and the captain grabbed a first aid kit. She cut away the damaged section of Alice's suit to bandage the arm and started giving orders.

"Zhao, Park. Help cover the exits. We have a hostile on the loose. We retreat to engineering."

"Captain, this guy is just a scared crewman. Not a hostile," Alice said.

"Nice attitude, but he shot you. He is hostile until we stun him, and then we can help him."

"Brace for movement!" Malik shouted over the radio.

The team readied themselves and protected the unconscious Rossi. With another sudden lurch, the ship rocked, but Malik's warning allowed them to avoid any injuries. The well-trained unit pulled back and proceeded to the engine room to plan the next move.

Kristina gathered her team near Malik, who had worked on the thruster. Warmth returned, thanks to the functional air circulation and heating system. The smell of burned wires lingered despite the working system. The lights were still out, but they found portable lights to give adequate illumination. These lights and the helmet lamps made crisscrossing shadows on the walls.

Rossi lay unconscious but stable. Chief Zhao, with limited resources, organized defenses. Her voice commanded and sounded determined. PO Park stood watch under

Zhao's direction. The tense set of his shoulders showed his anger.

Phillips, as usual, noticed everything. His mind was already busy thinking of solutions.

Rogers' injury-fueled adrenaline had worn off, leaving her withdrawn.

They were alone until *Miss Zetty* returned. Time to organize. The first thing is to get the team focused.

"Malik, where are you on the thruster?"

"Hold on a moment, Captain. Daniel, on my mark, pull the cable." He pointed at a cable a few meters away. "One, Two, Three, Pull!"

A series of indicator lights flickered out. Malik said, "There you go, Captain. We got the power cut off to the fuel pump for the thruster. The thruster still has fuel. It can burn one more time. It shouldn't trigger on its own, but I suggest we manually trigger it again to be safe."

Kristina was about to tell him to go ahead when Philips said, "No. Hold off, I have an idea, but we must work out some other things."

"What is your idea?"

"Still working on it. Come back to me in a moment." Phillips knew Kristina well enough to know she had a goal. She needed everyone involved and focused to get them away from the individual stressful thoughts they were having.

Kristina recognized the need to pull Alice Rogers out of her shell for her well-being and the team. A task to focus on would do that.

"Petty Officer Rogers, report on your attacker."

"Yes, Captain. The man was in cargo deck crew coveralls and knew the ship well. From where he was when he attacked, he must have been watching me, but I never saw him. After I got a few stunner shots off, he vanished. I bet the same thing happened with Rossi. The man hid in the cargo area and watched us the whole time. For all we know, he could be here now."

Alice scanned the massive engineering department, its vast space stretching above her. Dim lights barely reached the ladders, and platforms seemed to extend infinitely. The team probed the area to find the elusive phantom they expected. Anxieties charged the air.

Their commander knew she must halt this train of thought before it could take root.

Kristina used her best parade ground commanding voice. "Crewman, this is Commander Chen-Ramirez of the Customs and Patrol Service. Your vessel was in distress, and we stabilized the ship. We took an injured crew woman for medical aid. We mean you no harm and are here to help."

Adrian would laugh at my unintentional copying of one of his favorite quotes. Well, I am from the government, and here to help, Kristina thought.

She paused for a moment. "The crewman now knows we are friends. He is not a monster, just a scared man. Dangerous, but still a spacer. We are CPS agents, and our duty is to aid and protect the spacers of Earth. In the face of fear, let compassion guide our actions. For it is in helping others we truly protect ourselves," she quoted.

"Hurrah!" came a chorus of cheers from her team.

"Let's help this man. I want to hear your ideas."

Rogers was the first to speak. "He thinks I am the enemy. Use me as bait and stun him in the open."

"Brave, but too dangerous. You were already shot once."

"Get the lights back on and hunt. The light will cast away any shadows to hide in," Park said, the sharp words slashed through the air.

Specialist Miller shook his head. "Sorry, Jun-Seo. I checked the main lighting panel. Someone blasted the main transformer."

Chief Petty Officer Zhao said, "Captain, the logical thing is to wait for *Zeta Sierra* and reinforcements."

"That's logical," she responded, "but none of us are the type to sit around and twiddle our thumbs. Mr. Phillips, you have had some time to think. What is your idea?"

"First, a question. Malik and Miller, can you get the computer online?"

"Sure. It never went down. No remote terminals have power, but the terminal here does," Malik said.

"OK, let's pull up the surveillance footage of the borders and see if I am right."

A screen flickered to life, revealing a video of the main hatch. Two crew women appeared on the screen. No audio accompanied the video. One of them was the wounded woman they had evacuated.

Kristina's heart skipped a beat. The other woman... it was the same woman, the brutalized woman on the bridge.

A tall, dark-haired man and a platinum-blonde woman in a pink civilian space suit entered through the hatch. Relief washed over the blonde's face, evident even without sound, as she clutched onto one of the crewwomen. Little did the crew of *DW-1876* know a predator had infiltrated their sanctuary.

As the video continued, the unfolding events became clear. A glint of steel caught the light in the blonde woman's hand—a knife hovered against the bridge woman's delicate neck. The man produced a flechette pistol and spoke inaudible threats.

Despite her terror, the bridge woman refused to yield to their demands. In response, the man unleashed a shot from close range, shattering the other woman's hand in a spray of blood. The remaining woman's resistance broke. Without further hesitation, they went to the bridge.

Within moments, five others clad in black armor infiltrated the ship. The injured woman wailed in pain over her mutilated hand, and one of the intruders knocked her down with a swift punch. After the invaders left the area, a crewman ran over to drag the injured woman away. They discovered that brave man's sacrifice earlier.

Phillips stared at the frozen image of the man and woman who had entered. "That's Sergio," he said. "The man Zeus warned us about. And the woman... she matches the image Lizzie provided for Bianca."

"Why would they have done this?" Chief Zhao asked.

"I don't know, but it isn't important now. We need to find out what happened to the hiding crewman." Phillips switched cameras to a hall near a lift where Zhao had found a body.

Two men were on the video. Bianca walked up to them with a big grin. She pulled out a knife and stabbed one man many times. No warning, just repeated stabs while laughing.

The other man bolted away. Sergio fired at him but missed.

Alice pointed at the man running away. "That was the man who shot at me."

"We found his trigger," Phillips said. He pointed at Bianca's silvery hair, an uncanny match for Alice's, creating an eerie similarity between the two.

"Sorry, Captain. We are back to using me as bait to draw him out. I'm what he wants. Let's show me to him."

"No, what he wants is a blonde woman, and you're not the only blonde woman here," Kristina said.

Phillips's back stiffened. "Skipper no. We can't use the ship's captain as bait."

"But we can use Petty Officer Rogers?"

"Yes!" Phillips and Rogers said simultaneously.

"I'm not sending a wounded woman out there to do this. It's me or no one."

"Skipper, your blonde hair is not quite the same."

She retracted her helmet and let her honey-blonde hair flow free. "This will have to do. Plus, a little extra disguise."

She activated her suit's camouflage mode, and its surface changed to a shade of pink exactly matching that of the suit worn by the psychotic killer Bianca.

"If a picture of me in a pink space suit makes it to Adrian, I will find a reason for a court martial."

"We wouldn't dream of it, Skipper," Phillips said, "But you need some protection. The standard CPS space suit has no armor, and he still has a flechette pistol."

"I have an idea for that," Kristina said. She opened a tool locker and pulled out a heavy-duty carbon fiber welding blanket. Pulling off the outer camo layer, she wrapped the blanket around her chest twice. The camouflage net went back on to cover everything.

"It's not perfect, but it might stop flechettes."

As Kristina stepped into the cargo bay, her heart pounded in her chest. She gripped her neuro-stunner, searching for threats. Unsure if he was there, she tried to draw his notice.

"Hey, jerk. You missed me earlier. I'm here to finish what I started with your friends." Saying it made her stomach churn.

Her lights cast ghostly shadows on the walls. Her skin crawled with unease over fear for her crew, herself, and the man she hunted.

Phillips, Zhao, and Park flanked from three directions in an attempt to capture the crew member or drive him to her.

A giant clang reverberated as airtight doors closed at the entrances to the cargo bay, locking Kristina's crew out. To ensure safety, airtight doors had separate power, allowing them to close during emergencies. The lost crewman may have been out of his mind, but he was not stupid. He trapped Kristina in his home territory.

Kristina's senses heightened as she rounded a corner. Her eyes scanned for any signs of movement. A figure bolted from the darkness. The crew member, with a wild look in his eyes, held the flechette pistol in his hand and Rossi's stunner slung on his back.

Time slowed as Kristina reacted, diving to the side as a hail of darts tore through the air. She rolled, her training kicking in, and returned fire. But the man was not there.

She jumped toward some crates and then pushed to the ceiling. Unable to hide in the crewman's home turf, she became a moving target.

The room erupted in chaos. Sounds of flechette fire echoed off the metal walls. Kristina ducked behind a pod, her heart pounding in her ears.

In an energetic burst, she vaulted into the open. Darts flew by, leaving sparks behind. Taking cover behind a support beam, her breath came in ragged gasps.

She fired her stunner in the dimly lit room at a figure lurking in the shadows. Nothing was there. The light once again played tricks on her. The pause gave her opponent an opening.

The crew member charged toward her, his eyes filled with desperation and rage. He fired the pistol and swung a pipe. A barrage of darts struck her right in the chest.

A dozen stings hit Kristina like she had knocked over a hive of angry bees. The welding blanket acted as a pin cushion, saving her from being shredded.

Her problems were not over. The crew member charged toward her, his eyes filled with desperation and rage. With a swift swing, he sent the stun carbine flying from her grasp. As he tackled her, their bodies collided with a resounding thud against the wall, the impact reverberating through the room.

His stolen pistol clicked empty. He threw it away and raised the pipe.

"Now, Malik!" she shouted over the radio.

Another part of Phillips' plan came to fruition. Malik stood by the controls and fired the thruster one last time.

Kristina had activated magnets in her gloves and boots to hold her in place against the support beam. The sudden acceleration hurled the man into a cargo pod. She leapt at him and grabbed onto the stun carbine strapped to his back. A quick twist allowed her to get an angle and fire.

The man was stunned, but she restrained him as her training told her. No more chances today.

They sedated the crew member. He would stay that way until he was in *Zeta Sierra's* sick bay and woken by the friendly face of Doctor Maya Roy.

Kristina, Phillips, and Malik went to the bridge. They planned to restore the bridge systems and find out what Bianca and Sergio were after. Kristina and Phillips covered the murdered woman again. The thruster push disturbed her.

Phillips examined the gun in the holster and belt wrapped around the woman's neck, which was an antique Colt Single Action Army revolver. The captain viewed himself as an old west cowboy. Six shots were fired, and one through the face mask of the invader floating dead outside the bridge.

"Nice shooting, Tex." Kristina somehow thought the captain would appreciate the sentiment.

Phillips pulled up the communication log. The ferry received a distress signal en route to Europa station for refit. He replayed the message.

"Mayday, mayday. Please help. Is this working? Can anyone hear me? The engines just stopped. It's getting hard to breathe. I don't want to die. Please help us." Tears streamed down Bianca's face. She knew how to play the damsel in distress.

"We know how they got on board, but what did they want?" Kristina said.

"Look here, Captain," Malik said.

He pointed her to the navigation section. Someone had ripped apart the panels, and one piece had disappeared. The navigation module was gone.

"Why would they want a ferry boat nav system?" Kristina asked.

"I don't know, Skipper, but I know who to ask. Four days ago, the captain met Sarai Rousseau in Io orbit, who negotiated to buy a copy of the nav logs. Ten-year-old nav logs. If this timeline is correct, she bought these logs while you talked to Zeus at Callisto."

"I think we need to have another talk with our favorite Buddhist, pacifist, ninja cargo master."

24

School's Out

Megan and Adrian developed a routine in Ithaca, working long hours to gain the town's trust. They ate breakfast with Rafael and Carolina before being assigned daily tasks. The day would end with Adrian and Megan exhausted and sliding into separate sleeping cocoons.

They didn't have *Castor* back yet but had been allowed to exchange messages with *Elizabeth*. This alleviated Lizzie's concerns, and everyone was kept up to date.

Adrian's favorite task involved being a bus driver for the children of Ithaca. As he flew the children to the school, Adrian loved seeing them chat and laugh together. It had never occurred to him that a town like theirs would have a school. The town's inhabitants still prioritized the care and education of their children.

The town council didn't give him the task he loved out of the goodness of their hearts. They wanted to show him the people of Ithaca weren't only outcasts and his captors but also filled with innocent children.

"Good morning, Mr. Adrian," a young girl said. This girl was about eight but much taller and thinner than an Earth girl of similar age. Her face appeared puffy, and her eyes were abnormally large compared to an earth child. A tragedy of Ithaca, she was born here and could never live in gravity.

"Good morning, Emma. I hope you have a good day at school."

"We have a spelling test. Yuck, I'd rather be doing art." No matter where they lived, kids never changed.

"I'm sure you will do great." The look on Emma's face showed she was not as optimistic. Adrian smiled at the little girl, his eyes sparkling with genuine joy.

Adrian continued to pick up the other children who lived farthest from the school. He limited the acceleration for the no-gravity children like Emma.

Adrian left the children in the care of their teachers and returned to central dispatch. His next task was to help Rafael build a new quad of containers for a residential unit. Felipe stopped him before he got into a rockhopper.

"Adrian, I changed my mind. Forget the rockhopper, take *Castor*. You're right. It will be much better. With its built-in welding tool, the task will go faster." Daily Adrian insisted the modern *Castor* would be better than the variety of ancient rockhopper work sleds. The council, fearing they would run, denied each request.

"Thank you. I appreciate the trust."

Adrian's face lit up at having *Castor* back - it felt like coming home. Another barrier to complete trust broke down.

Felipe's following news disappointed Adrian. "I need you to stay on the construction task. We will get someone else to pick up the kids this afternoon."

After a morning of repair tasks, Megan and Carolina ate lunch in a shared meal area. With Carolina's extreme anxiety around people, they hovered in an upper corner of the room. Most people *sat* at the tables welded to the floor to give a semblance of normalcy. Carolina didn't care because staying far away from others calmed her.

Megan hoped that someday Carolina would open up about the trauma in her past that triggered the anxiety. She wasn't sure if what happened was when they lived on the streets of Sau Paulo or between leaving there and finding their way to Ithaca.

"I think I'm getting the hang of some of the work," Megan said. She had felt bad for days just handing Carolina tools. Short of a few dirt site archaeology digs, the academic aristocrat rarely performed physical labor. In the first few days, she suffered in silence as muscles she didn't even know she had burned in pain.

Now, the streaks of grease Megan wore with pride provided clear evidence of actual hands-on work. Her father would be shocked and proud.

"You're doing good. I'm so glad to have you with me." Although she didn't say it, she was scared to be around anyone except the few she trusted.

"Where are we going this afternoon?" Megan asked.

"The school needs work on the air filtration system."

That news perked up Megan. "Oh good, I keep hearing about the school. It'll be great to see it. Why don't we finish up and get over there?"

A scruffy-looking man watched the two attractive ladies leave, but not with admiration. Closer to a predator stalking his prey.

The school was a cluster of interconnected shipping containers in the town center. Megan and Carolina started the repairs, but Megan got distracted by the children. Watching the kids eased Megan's weeks of tension.

"Megan, we're almost done here, and school is almost over. The bus will be here soon. Go say hi to Adrian."

"Are you sure you can handle the rest? I don't want to leave you with too much work."

"I can handle it. Go." Carolina disappeared into the ventilation system.

That girl is like a cat. She can fit into any small space.

Megan departed and watched the kids finish their day. As was customary in Ithaca, the null-gravity nature of the school was unconventional. No traditional rows. Instead, teachers hovered amidst a half-sphere of students. Megan hovered outside the class, observing with a sense of wonder.

Just like on Earth, when the end-of-day bell rang, chaos erupted. They scattered from their classes like flocks of birds. Laughter and shouts echoed off the walls as children dashed about. Hugs were exchanged, stories shared, and promises made for tomorrow's escapades.

They were getting into their mismatched spacesuits to walk home. These children were more comfortable in microgravity than Megan could ever imagine. Even the youngest were as natural as a zero-g Olympian. Sadly, the same kids had never learned to walk, but they flew.

Megan entered the long tube-shaped transfer module between the school and a ship hatch. She saw the yellow-painted mining transport used as a school bus approaching. With a mischievous smile, she couldn't wait to see the look of surprise on Adrian's face. *I know I shouldn't tease him like I do, but I can't resist. I need to behave a little around the kids.*

"Are you Miss Megan?" a little girl asked. She flew up and was just inches from Megan's face. In Ithaca, adults didn't crouch to get to the kids' level. Instead, the kids came up to the adults' level.

"Yes, I am. You know who I am?"

"Of course, silly. Everyone knows who Mr. Adrian and Miss Megan are. He is my favorite bus driver. You are lucky to have him as a boyfriend. I'm Emma."

Megan grinned but didn't choose to correct the little girl. "Thank you, Emma. It's nice to meet you. Adrian's your favorite after only a week?"

"Yea! The other drivers don't talk to us like he does. I'm the first one to get picked up and the last one to get dropped off. I used to bug my parents to move closer to the school like other kids, but riding with Mr. Adrian is fun. He talks about you a bunch but also brings up someone named Elizabeth. You should ask him to marry you quick."

This time, Megan's face reddened. "Don't worry, Emma. *Elizabeth* is the name of his spaceship." *He didn't talk about Kristina...*

"I thought his ship was called *Castor*?" A look of confusion passed on the girl's face.

"That's his little ship. His big ship is called *Elizabeth*."

"He has two ships? Wow, he must be *rich*. What's he doing at Ithaca?"

"He is helping me look for something." Megan didn't want to mention her family-owned twenty-six ships.

"The hatch is opening. Come on, will you ride with us? You can tell me all about whatever you are looking for. On the way back, you can smooch with Mr. Adrian."

That's an idea I could get behind. "I don't know if I can. I have a friend I am helping here."

"Go. Have some fun. I'm safe in here." Carolina's voice came from the vents. The school comforted Carolina. She attended this school two years earlier. Her first formal education since she was Emma's age. The teachers and students didn't threaten her much, but Carolina stayed near her twin brother when she attended.

Emma grabbed Megan's hand and pulled her to the school bus. Some of the kids were already moving through the hatch. They waited their turn and boarded last.

"Oh, Hi, Mr. Filipe." Emma's voice dropped in disappointment.

"Good afternoon, Emma. Good to see you again. Ms. McCord, what are you doing here?" His tone reminded Megan that while he liked Adrian, he voted against her. He still held resentment toward her and her family.

"I had hoped I could say hello to Adrian."

"He is still on a construction job. I took the kids myself today. You need to leave."

She came close to him and spoke in a low voice. "Filipe, I'm sorry for what happened back then. I remember you were one of the people I was rude to as a child on *Beatrix*."

In an equally low volume. "Rude? You acted like you owned the company already. Emma here acts more like a lady than the daughter of a Viscount did back then."

While Megan and Filipe talked, Carolina, still in the vents, watched three men enter the school's personnel airlock. Parents frequently pick up little ones, but these were not parents, and that's concerning. When the men entered the transfer tube connecting the bus to the school, Carolina radioed a warning.

"Megan, some people are trying to get on the bus. I don't recognize them."

Megan looked out the hatch and saw the three scruffy men approaching. Hairs on the back of Megan's neck stood on end. Her heightened sense of danger went on full alert.

"Close the hatch! You take the little ones to the back." She pointed at one of the oldest children, but it was too late. The men yanked a young boy out of the hatchway and burst into the bus.

The boy lost grip on his helmet as they threw him back. His helmet drifted into the bus, and the boy hit a tube wall.

The situation terrified Carolina, and part of her wanted to hide more profoundly in the vents. But seeing the attack on the boy triggered memories in her. Too often, she had experienced the strong preying on the weak. Only finding Ithaca brought refuge. She couldn't sit by and watch harm come to the boy, so she scrambled out of her hiding spot to help.

In the bus, Felipe tried to block the men, but the first one pistol-whipped him. He collapsed and floated away.

"Hello, Doc. It's my lucky day. I missed you on Callisto, and that bastard Zeus had it out for anyone who answered the bounty on you. I ran only to find you eating lunch here at the ass end of nowhere. Time to get out of this hellhole and get paid," the man said.

"Who are you?"

"Name is Jax. Don't resist unless you want a kiddie hurt." One of the thugs went to the transport controls, and the other closed the hatch.

Megan stood between the men and the children. She pointed at one of the older boys and said, "Take Felipe and the kids to the back. It's me they want. Nobody be scared." The boys pulled the unconscious Felipe and stood protectively in front of the younger children, putting up a brave face.

Megan activated a unique feature on her suit. The smart goggles she wore with the spacesuit were not just for vision correction. They contained a heads-up display. She interfaced with the bus's communication system and activated the radio transmitter on a general channel.

"I'll cooperate as long as you let the kids back out in the school. Don't hurt the kids, and we can fly away on the school bus," Megan said.

"No, I think I want some extra insurance. The brats stay here. Diego, get us out of here," Jax said. Several of the kids cried.

"We're stuck, boss. The dock clamps have us locked to the airlock. It needs a code to release."

Jax pointed the gun at Megan. "What is the code?"

"I don't know. You knocked out the guy who knows it. Just leave how you came, and we will all forget about this."

"Not a chance. Diego, rip us off that thing."

Megan jumped to the viewport in the hatch. Carolina held the boy, who huddled in the fetal position. "There are people in there! You can't do that."

"Do it, Diego."

The other thug reached for Diego to pull him away from the controls. "I didn't sign up to hurt kids."

A massive crack sounded in the small space as Jax shot his own man. The children all screamed in terror. Blood flew everywhere in zero gravity. He pointed the gun at Diego and said, "Do it."

Diego engaged the thrusters, and the sound of metal twisting filled the air. Megan ran to the window and watched the boy, certain she was about to watch him spill into space. The boy was not wearing a helmet.

Carolina heard the muffled gunshot and the screech of bending metal. The cries of terrified little Shaurya grew louder, and they watched the bus's hatch close. Realizing what was about to happen, she slapped the emergency protocol button. Many things in Ithaca needed repair, but not the emergency systems at the school. Andrei ensured those systems were a priority.

Airtight doors closed on each end of the module, and breakaway bolts separated the danger from the school. The bus lurched to the side as it flung away at full power.

"Carolina!" Megan, holding on to grab bars, watched through the viewport as the module with Carolina and the boy tumbled end over end into the void.

Adrian heard Megan's tense voice come across the radio.

"I'll cooperate as long as you let the kids back out in the school. Just don't hurt the kids. We can fly away in the school bus."

What the Hell is going on? Adrian thought.

He listened for a few seconds and disconnected *Castor* from his welding containers. He twisted the boat around and hit maximum thrusters for the school. Rafael kept pace with his rockhopper.

They heard the gunshot, and Megan shouted Carolina's name. Adrian willed more power out of his little ship.

"Carolina and a child are in the module. They could hit other parts of the city. Save them." Megan's voice came over the radio again, technically speaking to the kidnapper but also delivering a message.

"I'm going after Carolina," Rafael said. His words trembled, carrying the weight of his fear.

"No. You go after the bus. I will get Carolina. *Castor* is more maneuverable. You chase the bus and hit it with the EMP cable."

"I can't leave her!"

"Trust me, Rafael. I will treat it like my sister is over there."

Rafael said with a note of resentment in his words, "Merda. I'm breaking off."

The rockhopper split off and sped after the bus. The transport had a lead in the race, but the rockhopper was faster.

Adrian again willed himself faster while tracking the spinning of the module. He traced the pattern he needed to match to divert the impending collision.

As the surrounding chaos escalated, Megan's thoughts flickered to Adrian. She could almost see him, a knight astride a white horse in some fairytale her mother read to her. But this was no time for idle fantasies. *You need to rescue yourself, princess*, she chided herself. With that, her gaze hardened, and she prepared to do what was necessary to survive and protect those around her.

She comforted the children while watching for her opportunity. Acceleration was at almost one full gravity. The children born in Ithaca were not only terrified but in intense pain. The older ones had been born in gravity but had not lived there for years.

Megan pleaded with Jax to slow down, fearing for the children's well-being. "You'll hurt the children! They can't handle this acceleration!"

"It'll toughen them up. They'll be fine. We will leave them here when we get to our ship," Jax's voice held no empathy.

Rafael's rockhopper homed in on the bus. The bus veered to the side just as Rafael lined up the EMP harpoon cable. He smacked his fist on the console in frustration.

Megan saw the rockhopper zoom by while she held a crying Emma. She discreetly opened a channel to find out the plan. "Qual é o plano, Rafael?"

"You speak Portuguese?" Rafael asked, his jumped and octave in surprise.

"A little out of practice, but yes. When you were my guards, I didn't think it wise to tell you I understood what you were saying. More importantly, now, I doubt this fool understands. So I ask again, what's the plan?" Megan responded in a university learned Portuguese.

"I'm trying to hit the bus with the EMP. Others are on the way, but we ain't got time to set up a trap like we did to stop *Castor*," Rafael said. "Droga, I can't aim the cable and fly."

"I have an idea," Megan whispered.

Adrian tweaked *Castor's* thrusters to match the module's chaotic tumble. He knew he only had time to control the sideways spin or rolling motion. He focused on aligning with the spin rather than the roll. It was the only way.

With beads of sweat trickling down his forehead, Adrian gritted his teeth as time passed. He took a breath and keyed the radio.

"Carolina, can you hear me?" Adrian maintained a calm and level voice.

"Yes, are you coming? This spin is hard on Shaurya." Carolina held the boy with one arm and a grab bar with the other.

"Yes, I'm almost there. I need you to stay calm," Adrian's voice was steady but laced with urgency. "Brace yourself. It'll get worse before it gets better."

"Okay, Shau will be brave and protect me. Won't you?" The boy nodded. He couldn't hear the terror Carolina felt. For the first time in her memory, she was the one protecting instead of the one being protected.

There was no time for preparation. Adrian said, "Ready? One, two, three, go!"

Adrian matched the module's chaotic spin, then fired Castor's thrusters to surge forward. The manipulator arms reached out and clamped onto the module's edge firmly.

Castor and the tumbling module merged into one, locked in a graceful synchronized dance as they spun through space. Adrian gritted his teeth and ignited *Castor's* engines. The burst of power pressed him back into his seat.

Slowly, their deadly dance began to arc away from the habitat containers looming ahead. Adrian held his breath, willing every ounce of thrust to curve them just wide of the cluster. The bonded pair avoided the collision by a hair's breadth, almost close enough to scuff the paint.

Now that the town was safe, Adrian slowed the module and halted the spin. He longed to help Megan but could not ignore Carolina and young Shaurya, trapped inside a damaged module. He eased the module to the cluster of homes, expecting people to help him free the two. Adrian was out of the chase for now.

Gazing into the void, he sent a plea into the vastness. *Megan, please be alright.* The stars offered no reply, only the twinkle of distant light. His heart hung suspended in silence, waiting for the chaos to unfold.

Megan made her voice tremble, acting scared. "Who hired you to come after us? Was it Bianca? I can pay you double, triple whatever she offered if you let us go."

"Who the Hell is Bianca? No one hired me. Even Zeus can't completely squash a dark web bounty. More money interests me, though. Where would you get the money to triple the bounty?"

"My family is rich. Daddy set up a ransom fund in case I ever got kidnapped." Her father had done no such thing. The pitch of her voice increased to a terrified squeal. "I can get more, too! I don't want to die. If the people who want me don't kill me, Diego's driving might. When they stopped us, they put an empty container right in front to block the path. This bus won't stop as fast. It will kill all of us."

She sobbed and made a show of it. Despite hating to frighten the children, she had to keep up the charade. It also allowed her to monitor Rafael's telemetry with her smart goggles. *Just need a few more adjustments.*

She got up and approached Jax. He took a step in the direction she wanted him and pulled up his gun. "Not too close."

"All I want to do is live. Daddy's money won't let me do any good if I'm dead. I'll give you anything you want, anything." She felt dirty just making the implication, but it allowed her to take another step forward.

She pointed out the front window and screamed, "Oh my god, they're blocking us. Turn left now, or we'll die!"

Diego just reacted and twisted the bus left. The sudden movement sent the body of the dead thug at Jax. He attempted to use his arms as a shield, but his victim still collided with him.

This gave Megan time for the next part of her plan. The movement lined up the bus with Rafael. He connected Megan's smart goggles to the EMP harpoon controls. This freed up his hands to fly, and she fired the magnetic harpoon when the crosshairs lined up. A bolt of energy zapped down the cable to disable the bus's controls.

The instant she fired, Megan charged at Jax. With a sudden motion, she jabbed a child's pencil into Jax's hand, causing the gun to fly out of reach. Her knee found its mark with a swift strike between the legs. Unlike the bounty hunter on the Earth station, Jax was not prepared for a hit to the nuts.

Power had failed, thrust had stopped, and microgravity returned. Megan jumped into the cockpit. Her feet landed on a ceiling and triggered her magnetic boots. She hung upside down like a bat over Diego. With a fierce gaze, she pointed the pencil toward his face as if it were her dagger.

"You'll cooperate with me, right Diego?" Faux-fear gone, her voice now a raw, fierce growl.

Rafael towed the bus back to the school. At the same time, Megan secured the bindings around Diego and Jax, their muffled protests filling the surroundings. Still dazed from his awakening, Felipe rubbed his temples, feeling the lingering grogginess in his head.

As they reached the school, a wave of gratitude washed over the scene, with parents embracing their relieved children. The sweet scent of relief and joy filled the air. Sakura and some of the council had also arrived.

"Thank you for saving our children," Sakura said.

A pit of guilt snakes writhed in Megan's stomach, "My presence put them in danger. How can you thank me?"

Sakura pointed at Jax. "These people's actions caused this. In Ithaca, we don't blame people for the actions of others. We evaluate individuals based on their own merits. Your actions have proven you to be trustworthy. Tomorrow, I will take you to Fred Stonington's documents. I hope you will find what you are looking for."

"Thank you, though I wish it didn't need all this."

Adrian arrived with Carolina and the boy. Carolina flew toward her brother, their reunion filling the air with tears of relief and happiness. Adrian, filled with emotion, enveloped Megan in a tight embrace.

"I'm glad you're ok. I wish I could've been there."

"You were where you needed to be," Megan said.

"Kiss him already!" Emma shouted.

Megan smiled and looked Adrian in the eyes. "We don't want to disappoint her. And I really could use a good kiss. Please?"

"After the day you had, I think you deserve it." Adrian's tone was flirty but sincere, and his eyes held an admiration that was a massive turn-on for Megan.

Emma and the other children cheered as Megan gave him the kiss she had wanted to provide since they met.

25

The Lioness and the Tiger

August 10, 2155—Europa station

Kristina, dressed in civilian clothing, waited in the café for her lunch guest. The air was filled with the aroma of coffee and soft chatter. As she idly stirred her cup, a familiar face approached the table.

"Good afternoon, Commander," Sarai Rousseau said, taking a seat opposite Kristina.

"Thank you for meeting me here." Kristina poured a cup for Sarai from the carafe on the table.

"What did you want to discuss, Commander?" The aroma of the delicious French press filled the air as she took a sip.

Leaning in, Kristina began, "Well, there have been some recent developments I believe you should know about."

Curiosity sparked in Sarai's eyes. "Developments? What do you mean?"

Kristina kept her voice low. "This hasn't made the news yet, but we discovered a ship with most of its crew brutally murdered."

"That is sad news. May peace and serenity surround the families of the departed."

Kristina's expression turned grave. "The vessel was ferry *DW-1876*. My issue is that you were aboard it not too long ago, and you purchased old navigation data from them. I need an explanation."

Sarai's eyes widened, her face frozen, while a single tear betrayed the turmoil gripping her.

"*Deadwood*? Captain Dalton? It's my fault. I led lambs to the slaughter. I might as well have killed them myself."

Kindness replaced harshness in Kristina's voice. "No, Sarai, this was the fault of the monsters who did this."

"It had to be Bianca and Sergio."

"Yes, we have a video recording that captured their actions. Their reputation is to never leave evidence behind. They intended to crash the ship into Europa, but we got to it first."

Kristina broke some rules and gave Sarai restricted data. "The Interpol file on those two is heavy on suspicion but light on proof. They work for the highest bidder. Someone pushing for results, making them sloppy and bold."

"So, you have proof. Megan's in the clear now."

"You know it doesn't work like that. I could arrest the siblings for murder, but not Roger McCord's murder. Tell me what you know about the nav computer, and we might be able to find them and arrest them."

Sarai took a sip of coffee, allowing the rich aroma to fill her senses as she pondered for a moment.

"Megan learned that before you found Fred Stonignton's ship drifting, he discovered a place artifact hunters call 'Hunter's Folly.' She came searching for the old ship and its nav data. We traced it to *Deadwood*. Ferry *DW-1876*." New tears came to Sarai's eyes as she saw the faces of the ferry crew in her mind.

"They took the whole nav unit. So now they have the information," Kristina said.

"The information on the nav system was useless."

"What was the problem?"

"In his last year, he visited the Trojan asteroids at Jupiter's L4 and L5 Lagrange points often, but the data was crazy. Something must have corrupted it."

"The data didn't narrow down which asteroid is 'Hunters Folly.' Stonington couldn't delete data from the nav unit, but he added waypoints. For each asteroid he stopped at, he tagged several others at both Lagrange points. We need to hope Megan finds some clues in her search."

"How are our wayward travelers? It's been over the week Lizzie said she would charge in after them." Kristina refilled her coffee.

"We received a few messages. Just enough information to know they are safe. I don't know where they are."

A fresh voice interrupted their conversation. "Zeus said you used to be a better liar than that."

Cassandra, Zeus' assistant, grabbed a chair and sat with them. Today, Cassandra wore a sundress, not the 'tough as nails' image she presented at the casino.

"Good afternoon, Cassandra. I agree I was a much better liar when I had your job. I find truth brings enlightenment. The truth has set me free."

Kristina rocked back in shock at this new revelation about Sarai's past.

"Kristina, I don't know where they are other than somewhere in the rings. I never saw the exact location. And yes, before you ask, I used to be Zeus' chief troubleshooter, like Cassandra is now. I won't lie about it, but please understand that I don't plan on volunteering information to a dedicated member of law enforcement. I have genuine remorse and am reformed. Better than a prison term could have produced."

The more I get to know the crew of the Elizabeth, *the more stress I put on my oath. The right thing is to do nothing, but the 'book' tells me to dig deeper. Lately, I think*

I misplaced my copy of 'the book.' Kristina thought as she made her decision.

Kristina turned to the new guest. "Cassandra, I don't recall inviting you."

"Oh, you will want me here. I am here to pass on information from a concerned citizen about a recent act of piracy and murder."

"Somehow, I'm not surprised you know about that. Why would Zeus care about this attack?"

"Zeus is a legitimate businessman who runs casinos and other entertainment facilities. An attack on the ferry that transports Zeus's customers hurts his business."

Legitimate business people don't need to stress they are legitimate, Kristina thought.

A waiter interrupted them to bring a beer and a plate of cookies for Cassandra.

"Isn't it a little early in the day for that?" Kristina asked.

"It's afternoon and my day off. I'm just here as a favor. And it's never too early for cookies."

Kristina got back on the subject. "So, Zeus is worried about disruption to his crooked casino."

"A casino doesn't need to be crooked. The house odds favor the casino enough to make plenty of profit. Zeus learned from the mistakes of past criminals. Don't cheat people and pay your taxes on legitimate activities. The smuggling then goes under the UCE radar," Sarai said.

Cassandra's piercing gaze bore into Sarai, her eyes narrowing with intensity as if she were revealing trade secrets.

"How can I aid Zeus in protecting his *completely legitimate* business?" Kristina said.

"By stopping these people from causing disruptions. Sergio came to Zeus claiming to represent associates on Earth. We contacted this organization, and they said the siblings are not currently in their employment."

Cassandra paused to take a bite from a cookie and washed it down with a swig of beer. "We don't know exactly who they are working for, but the rumors are these are new players looking for artifacts and something specific."

"That matches with reports we have of violent players involved in artifacts. So, not really new information," Kristina said.

"Well then, you are in luck. I have visuals of the ship Sergio and Bianca are traveling on—a Gulfstellar IX executive transport. No one has seen it in the last week. We also spotted an odd-looking ship. I think it belongs to their employer." She passed over a data chip.

Kristina pulled up the images. The Gulfstellar was expected, but the other appeared capable of an atmospheric landing with its sleek and aerodynamic design. Few designers would make the compromises to allow a ship to do both.

"Sarai, a warning. I'd leave before the siblings make their next move. And if this new ship appears, it will end in tragedy." Cassandra walked away, taking the cookies with her.

"She has a point about the danger from Bianca and Sergio. How long will it take to figure out the navigation data will not take them where they want to go?" Kristina asked.

"A day or two. Does it matter if they have useless data?"

"It's been almost two days since they attacked the ferry. Once they realize it's useless, they'll search for something valuable. They don't know where Megan is but know where she was."

In realization, Sarai's eyes widened as she said, "The *Elizabeth*."

"I'm putting a team on your ship while we keep an eye out for the Gulfstellar and this weird ship."

26

Secrets Found in the Library Stacks

August 15, 2155—Ithaca

Megan hovered in zero gravity, engrossed in reading various papers from Stonington. She transitioned from a brave warrior fighting off kidnappers to a focused academic in research mode.

Megan wore her antique-style spectacles, adding a touch of nostalgia to the scene. It almost felt like being in a university library, if not for her space suit and the papers floating around in microgravity.

This type of environment makes her happy. The worry of the last few days is gone from her face, Adrian thought while watching her work.

True to her word, Sakura led them to Fred Stonington's pair of shipping containers. As Zeus had described, these containers served as Stonington's home and sanctuary. Adrian described the place as a hoarder's paradise, with books and trinkets everywhere. Stonington's books included modern ones on artifacts and Homer's epics.

While Megan worked, Adrian studied the scattered collection of broken alien artifacts. Adrian didn't know that artifacts could sustain damage. He caught a cracked object. It had a concave hemisphere shape with an open bottom.

"What do you think this could have been?" He placed it on his head like a small hard hat. "Some sort of alien mind control helmet?"

Megan turned and lit up with a smile at seeing Adrian holding the object on his head. She plucked it off his head and flipped it to the open side. "I don't think the 'mind control helmet' would work with you. It's a bowl. Like we use for eating."

"Really? What did they eat out of it?"

"Who knows. Soup. Cereal with blue milk. Alien pasta. Maybe we can translate their writing and find a cookbook for you someday." Megan continued to smile wide. She flipped the bowl over again and returned it to Adrian's head. He noticed this lacked the inner warmth of all other artifacts he touched before.

Curiosity compelled him to grasp another ruined relic. This was a half-meter-wide disk with a black surface like other artifacts but lacked the polish or warmth associated with artifacts. A few alien words were on the surface. Something cracked the disk as if it were constructed from delicate porcelain instead of a material more rigid than steel. He traced his figures across the unknown character of the writing.

"My father and I thought it reads something as simple as 'this side up,'" Megan said.

She held onto Adrian's shoulder while pointing at the broken disk. Her touch on his shoulder felt right, but this was not the time to delve into those feelings. After their kiss the day before, his feelings became even more complicated.

"This is a levitation disk. If near a Starshell, this levitation disk possesses anti-gravity properties and can move heavy objects or function as a fancy shelf. Our scientists were able to reverse-engineer our gravity plates from levitation disks. Gravity plates are much cruder and work in reverse. They create artificial gravity instead of anti-gravity. We think the Artificers had another source of true artificial gravity."

She touched his hand and traced the letters on the disk with him. "These characters are always on these disks and always on the side of the disk facing away from gravity. When powered up, if this side is down, it falls to the floor. But if it is up, it will hover wherever it's placed.

"Little bits like this made my father hope to find a Rosetta Stone to decipher the alien language. It was one of our biggest arguments because I said it was unlikely to happen."

"Why?" Adrian asked.

"What do you know about the Rosetta Stone?"

"It's a stone tablet with the same Greek text and hieroglyphics. Egyptologists translated the hieroglyphics using the Greek as a template."

"Correct. What is the problem with finding a Rosetta Stone for the Artificer language?" She had floated back a bit from him and looked at him in full-teacher mode. With her arms crossed and glasses perched at the end of her nose, she looked at him with a slight smile.

Adrian thought for a minute. "All the experts agree the Artificers disappeared long ago. Some say thousands of years, and others say millions. Either way, they were gone long before any human written language. So, it's not possible to have anything in both languages."

Megan beamed and gave him a kiss on the cheek. "Top marks for the student."

"Mr. Green, my history teacher, never gave me my test scores that way," Adrian said with a crooked smile.

"Some students just need a little extra encouragement." Megan patted his cheek and winked. "The impossibility of both languages existing at the same time is the exact argument I used with my father, but he was a dreamer. He was certain we would find a solution someday."

She paused and held up some paperwork. "I'm looking at these notes from Stonington and have made a new conclusion...daddy was right."

"I'm sure your father would have been happy to hear you say he was right, but a million years is a heck of a counterargument."

"Oh, he would have never let me live it down." Megan laughed and lost herself in thoughts about her father.

Megan sifted through the notes, plucking them out of the air and reviewing them.

"To conceal the location, Stonington used code phrases. He referred to the artificer site as the tomb of Hektor and Achilles. The asteroid was small, only about a kilometer across. The site comprised three chambers, but he gives only vague details." Megan's annoyance was obvious, stemming from Stonington's lack of professionalism.

"He describes one of the other rooms as having human books on tables next to alien tablets in their script. His assumption was that human books were being transcribed into the alien language. This is our Rosetta Stone," Megan said. She was thrilled about the potential of the find.

"This is the secret they killed your father over. Aliens were here relatively recently."

"Yes. And because of that, we might be able to translate the alien language." Megan's words gushed out with rapid excitement. "This discovery would be as groundbreaking as the first Starshell or even the revelation of alien existence."

Adrian quirked to the side as he grabbed one of Stonington's notes. "How did these notes get here? I thought he died after the discovery."

Megan thought for a second. "I don't know. I was so excited to see this. I didn't think about it."

"He took two trips. On the first, he brought back notes and a few trinkets. He never came back from the second." Sakura said from the entrance. She held two small food packages. "Excuse me, I came to bring you some food and overheard the conversation."

"Thank you. So, did Stonington tell you where he had been?"

"No. Just some asteroid. Fred was very secretive, even to me. I doubt I would be of much help anyway. I was a purser, not a navigator." Sakura's voice softened, the warmth in her words hinting at a bond deeper than friendship.

"A one-kilometer asteroid is a small needle in a big haystack," Adrian said.

"Well, let's start with what we know. The message from David and Sarai said the nav data showed Stonington explored the Jupiter Trojan asteroids," Megan said.

"Yes, but it didn't exactly show which asteroids he visited. He added a lot of false data."

"Our explorer has helpfully supplied a map."

She pulled out a map. An actual physical map of Jupiter's Orbit. *This guy really liked paper,* Adrian thought.

"Regrettably, he was not helpful enough to mark the spot with a simple big X. The two groupings of Trojan asteroids are called the Greek and Trojan camps after heroes in the Trojan War, right?"

"Yes. The 'Trojan camp' is at Lagrange point L4, and the 'Greek camp' is L5."

"I know this question may be odd for someone who lives in a space habitat. Can you explain Lagrange points? Like I said, I was a purser, not a navigator," Sakura asked.

"Of course. Lagrange points are spots of gravitational balance between two bodies. In this case, Jupiter and the Sun. L4 and L5 are the most stable and exist sixty degrees in front or behind Jupiter in its orbit. These stable spots allow many asteroids to share Jupiter's orbit. Called Trojan Asteroids. We need to find which one."

"I think clues in his notes will show us, but he was cryptic. He gives no dates for his searches, and the locations are all masked by vague references to the 'people' he visited. If we can decipher these clues, we will know where he went. Then we can calculate which asteroid is the Folly." Megan showed them some of the references.

"Look at these examples."

I met A Son of Mars, who led the people that dwelt in Aspledon and Orchomenus, the realm of Minyas.

I yoked the fleet horses, steeds that could fly like the wind. Famed offspring of Podarge.

"These all sound like he took lines from *The Iliad* or *the Odyssey* describing characters," Adrian said.

Sakura nodded. "Fred loved reading Homer."

Megan looked pleased with herself. "Well, I think I can at least narrow it down to one camp. Look at this."

I started my search with the great tamer of horses with the gleaming helmet and his new companion huntsman and keen lover of the chase who was killed by the spear of Menelaus.

"I think 'great tamer of horses' and 'gleaming helmet' talk about Hektor. So that means we need to search in the Trojan camp."

"You're right. That is Hektor in *the Iliad*, but a slight problem with that. The asteroid Hektor is not in the Trojan camp but in the Greek camp. Good thing you have a Greek ship captain here. I'm familiar with Homer and with the Trojan asteroids. Give me a moment."

Adrian pulled out his comm-pad and searched for information he had stored. He smiled and went to Stonington's book pile. He pulled out a copy of *The Iliad* and opened to a page.

"Here we go. '*Menelaus, son of Atreus, killed Scamandrius, the son of Strophius, a mighty huntsman and keen lover of the chase.*' The second part of Stonington's clue refers to Scamandrius, a small moon orbiting the asteroid 624 Hektor. The little moon had an Artificer site picked over twenty years ago." Adrian said. A gleam of pride appeared in his eyes that he was now the teacher.

"So now we need to find out which asteroids match the names in those clues he gave. We need to get back and talk to David." He held up his pad. "This has some navigation data, but not enough. We need to go home."

The town council gave Adrian and Megan permission to depart. Some were likely relieved to see them leave, but they had earned enough trust that no one thought they would betray the town. Sakura, Andrei, and Felipe were present to see them off. Their presence brought a sense of bittersweet finality to the moment. A pang of disappointment tugged at his heart, and Adrian noticed Rafael and Carolina's absence.

Sakura stepped forward, her usual formality replaced by warm hugs that enveloped Adrian and Megan. The touch of her embrace brought a sense of comfort and genuine affection. His gratitude was evident. Felipe extended his hand to shake theirs, his voice tinged with remorse as he addressed Megan. "I owe you my life and the lives of the children I cared for. I apologize for my misjudgment, which was influenced by the actions of others and your past. I'm truly sorry." Megan, understanding, responded with a heartfelt hug, acknowledging her growth from her troubled past.

She then gave Andrei a big hug. "Thank you for bringing back those memories from my childhood. You will always be my Father Frost. I wish Carolina and Rafael were here so I could say goodbye."

Andrei's laughter filled the air as he playfully retorted, "Who says you're saying goodbye to them?" At that moment, Carolina and Rafael appeared, each carrying a bag.

"It is time they saw more of the greater universe. Their experiences have been limited to the chaos of the streets of Sao Paulo or the confined spaces of the containers in Ithaca. You have been good for them, and they need to grow more."

"Can we come? I'm scared but eager," Carolina asked.

"Of course, you are welcome, but it could be dangerous. The secret we are looking for got my father killed, and they will try again," Megan said.

"More dangerous than flying uncontrollably in space?" Carolina spun in a circle for dramatic effect.

Adrian said, "It might be. I might not always be there to catch you."

Rafael placed a hand on his sister's shoulder and reached out to shake Adrian's hand. "If you're not, I will be. You can count on me to be there for both of you. Vamos nessa."

"You will always be welcome here. We consider you citizens of Ithaca now," Sakura said, her typical formality returning.

Megan hugged Sakura. "Thank you. After we solve our problems, I promise we will find some way to help you discreetly, of course."

They all climbed into *Castor*, Adrian, and Rafael in the cockpit and the ladies in the sleeping compartment. It will be a cozy trip back. *I better call ahead to have extra cabins prepared,* Adrian thought.

27

Elizabethan War

Sarai stood on the catwalk above the cargo bay, helping to lower some equipment through a hatch to David inside his almost complete pet project. Petty Officer Park, also on the catwalk, watched Sarai work. Petty Officer Rogers, left arm still bandaged, guarded the main floor with David. He rose from a hatch of the cone-shaped module, occupying much of the cargo bay.

The Elizabethan crew and the CPS agents tried to ignore each other. Petty Officer Rossi sat with Piet on the bridge. At the same time, Lizzie enjoyed quiet time away from the government agents in the conservatory.

"Almost there, David. This is the last piece, right? You can get this thing out of my cargo bay once you are done."

"Yes, Sarai. We can move it into space as soon as we button it up."

"You know, when I collect shoes, I keep them all in my cabin. Maybe next time, pick something smaller than an old ship component to collect."

"This is way better than shoes," David tinged his words with a playful bite.

"Now I know you are delusional," Sarai shot back.

A small shuttle snuck in from deep space, unseen by the people on *Elizabeth*. Its hull, constructed from radar-absorbing materials, ensured its silent approach. The shuttle was the same as the type used by the UCE special forces, an organization that didn't officially exist.

The shuttle docked at an engineering hatch. Six figures dressed in black stepped out into the tranquil and empty engineering section, their presence concealed from the unsuspecting crew. The opening hatch triggered an alert on the bridge.

"That's odd. The outer hatch is showing open, but nothing is attached to the outside," Piet said when an alert illuminated the bridge.

"Must be a glitch. Otherwise, there would be depressurization. I'll go down and look. It's boring here just watching the screens, and I could use a walk," Rossi said.

"I will go find Lizzie. She will be happy to have something to fix." Piet couldn't bear to sit still and stare at the screens any longer, driven by the impatience of youth. They missed when security cams captured black-clad figures moving around the ship.

The sound of the hatch opening broke Sarai's intense focus on her task. Out of the corner of her eye, several figures in black stepped onto the catwalk from the engineering entrance.

Park's reflexes kicked in as he turned and reached for his weapon. But it was too late. The burp of a flechette rifle filled the air, followed by a sickening wet thump.

Blood splattered across Sarai as Park's lifeless body tumbled off the catwalk. Sarai found herself exposed as the invaders closed in on her, their weapons trained on her vulnerable form. She didn't panic as her expertise and training took over. Her shout echoed through the chaotic space. "David, take cover!"

Sarai hurled herself from the walkway as a volley of darts whistled past, nicking her skin with fiery trails. With a loud crash, she collided with the module, and her arm throbbed with intense pain as it broke. She slid down to the floor, leaving a trail of blood.

David reacted to her frantic shout and sealed himself in his pod for safety.

Petty Officer Rogers watched her friend die and unloaded her stun gun at the attackers, to no effect against the armored foes. Ducking behind a crate, she drew her flechette pistol. Before she could fire, a shadow loomed behind her. The person held a stun pistol to her back and fired.

Sarai was now alone and in pain. However, adrenaline fueled her escape as she weaved through the sparse cover, trying to avoid getting shot. Sarai darted inside a storage locker for cover. She slammed the door shut just as a spray of darts hit the surface. She panted in the dark, illumination only from emergency strips. They would need a blowtorch to open the door. But by then, she'd be a ghost in the maze of Charles's secret passages.

Charles Borden installed secret access tunnels behind many of the bulkheads. Sarai usually considered this a waste of cargo space, but today, she was thankful for the paranoid rogue.

Bianca stepped onto the cold metal cargo deck. Her boots echoed each step. The faint scent of ozone lingered in the air, mixing with the metallic tang of blood. A misplaced shot caused some lights to flicker, casting eerie shadows across the scene.

She returned her freshly cleaned knife to its sheath and discarded a bloody cloth. Wary of unknown threats, she placed a ready hand on the pistol at her hip. A far more lethal weapon was magnetically attached to her back.

Bianca walked to Sergio, who stood over the unconscious Alice Rogers. Nearby, Park sprawled on the deck, a pool of blood spreading beneath him.

"Why did you leave her alive? We only need members of the crew taken prisoner." Bianca's words were sharp, laced with irritation.

Sergio's face twisted into a savage leer, telling Bianca what he planned to do with the woman. His interests veered into such dark territories it even disgusted Bianca, a self-aware psychopath.

"We need to focus on the mission. Take your prize if we have time. Otherwise..." Bianca drew a finger across her throat. She almost felt sorry for the woman and her brother's idea of fun. Long ago, she realized that indulging Sergio's desires was a way to subtly manipulate him.

"You're not the boss." Sergio's demeanor hardened, his charm fading in the absence of a target for manipulation.

"The boss put me in charge of this operation. Probably for not keeping the McCord bitch busy in Scotland. I'm still pissed at you. If you had, I wouldn't have these scars." Bianca's voice dripped with bitterness, her fingers tracing the faint marks on her skin. Rapid-Heal was slowly erasing them, but the memory remained.

Bianca's gaze searched the area. "Where did the crew go? We need them to tell us where McCord went."

Sergio pointed toward the white ovoid-shaped object, its surface marred by a vivid red streak. "The navigator sealed himself in this. We have Rousseau caged in a storage locker, hopefully bleeding to death."

"Get the Moonie out of there. It should be easy to get him to talk." Bianca pointed at one of the thugs. "You take a charge and blow that storage locker open. Kill the

woman fast. She is too dangerous to screw around with."
The memories of Rousseau's impressive skills in the
casino flashed through her mind.

"Sergio, Andiamo. Time to hunt for the others upstairs. Mallory, come with us," Bianca commanded, her
voice filled with determination. With Sergio and a short
female goon by her side, they made their way toward the
ladder leading up, their footsteps resonating through
the cold metal deck.

Sarai maneuvered down the narrow secret passage. The
distant sound of a blast and the sharp ding of flechette
darts hitting the back wall of the locker echoed through
the air. *I guess they didn't wait on a blow torch.*

She reached a secret room she had never wanted
to enter again. The long, narrow vault had the musty
scent of a long abandoned crypt. Along the walls stood
cabinets, the metal doors dulled with age.

With trembling hands, Sarai opened the cabinets, revealing the hidden treasures that had introduced her to
the world of the Bordens. The gleam of illegal weapons
caught her eye, remnants of a past she had long left
behind. She ultimately severed ties with Zeus, finding
solace within this new family.

Sarai's eyes scanned the array of weapons, weighing
her limited options. The stunners and flechette carbines
would be imprecise with her injured arm. Shotguns suffered the same limitation. The handguns lacked fire-
power against armored foes.

The mere thought of utilizing the plasma grenade
launcher within *Elizabeth* seemed absurd, leaving her
wondering why Charles had even purchased such a
weapon.

Among the disappointing array of weapons, one viable choice remained—a weapon for close combat, desperate and short-lived. A wave of dread washed over Sarai at the thought of using this weapon, but it was the only viable option.

She took a moment to bandage her wounds and pull on some body armor. Every movement sent waves of pain coursing through her body. Determined, she prepared for battle, aware that it would crush her soul but save her friends.

Emerging from the tunnel through a secret entrance in the engineering room, she found herself near a more conventional entrance leading back into the cargo bay. Her gaze fell upon the lifeless body of Petty Officer Rossi, his vacant eyes fixed on the ceiling. His slashed throat was a chilling sign the knife-wielding Bianca had been there.

Before she reentered the cargo bay to fight the battle, she started a timer in a console to produce a surprise and, with luck, get some help.

Piet wandered the ship looking for Lizzie. He could have called her, but he wanted some exercise. He failed to find Lizzie in her quarters or private office. But decided she might be in the conservatory enjoying the view of Jupiter. His broken ribs pained him enough that his walking pace was slow, so the trip might take a while.

Piet felt a strange chill as he walked through the narrow corridors. In the distance, he heard a sudden, unexpected thump echoing through the ship's metallic walls. A low rumble vibrated the hull.

He ran back onto the bridge. This time, he checked the security cameras, realizing his terrible mistake of not doing so earlier.

The camera captured the chaotic scene as three individuals unleashed a barrage into the storage locker, its door blown open. Thick smoke billowed from the explosive, obscuring their intended target.

He saw three people in combat armor enter the conservatory, where Lizzie sat in a chair. Piet kicked the bridge's back wall. A hidden door opened to reveal several weapons. He snatched up a shotgun and a box of shells.

Bianca, Sergio, and Mallory entered the large observation dome the *Elizabeth* crew called the conservatory. Lizzie sat in a wicker chair, drinking tea.

"Was that explosion I heard your doing? I don't appreciate the damage to my ship. I'll end up fixing it." The tone of her voice was so icy that it was a surprise that the tea she drank didn't freeze.

"Oh, there will be more damage before we are done, and you won't be here to fix anything. You are coming with us until your passenger gives us what we want," Bianca said.

"You must be Bianca and Sergio. I have heard about you. Nothing good, I'm afraid. You're the one who killed Roger McCord, am I correct? Do you plan on killing me too?"

"I killed McCord, but you will be just fine if his daughter gives us what we want."

"But the authorities say she was behind it all. You don't work for Megan McCord?"

"Of course not. That bitch shot me."

Sergio leaned close to Bianca, "Enough with the theatrics. She poses no threat. Take her—now."

"You like attacking defenseless people, don't you? Like when you stabbed Roger McCord," Lizzie said.

"Ha. Daddy McCord wasn't defenseless. He pulled some antique dagger on me. I took it away and returned it to his heart." Bianca's words showed evident pride in her actions. "You have nothing."

"Oh, I have something a little better than an old dagger." Lizzie raised a gleaming silver-colored pistol. Bianca recognized it even though she had never seen one. Lizzie held a genuine laser pistol.

Lasers were usually poor choices for handheld weapons. The energy required and the time to cut with one made them impractical in pistol size. Lizzie's weapon was created with an Artificer focus crystal, which amplified the energy enough to make it practical.

Lizzie pulled the trigger, and it burned a hole just above Bianca's hip. Bianca screamed in pain and dropped to the ground.

Both Sergio and Mallory fired with stunners but missed. With an agility that defied her age, Lizzie dodged behind a large planter as she fired twice more with the laser.

From behind the planter, they heard Lizzie say something odd. "I forgot to tell you when you came in. Smile, you're on candid camera."

The thugs pinned David to the floor with his exo-skeleton disabled. He struggled in vain to defend himself. The same three thugs Sarai fought in the casino kicked him.

Sarai witnessed her friend's suffering, and all reservations dissolved into a fierce determination. She charged onto the cargo deck, wielding the grotesque weapon she chose - a plasma knife.

A plasma knife was a weaponized version of a plasma cutting torch. The short blade existed for only seconds but possessed a brutal cutting efficiency. The weapon was neither elegant nor civilized.

She ignited the plasma and slashed the leg of the same slow oaf she stunned at the casino. The blade flared, melting armor, flesh, and bone as it hacked through the leg. The man's screams would haunt Sarai for eternity.

She twisted and reversed her motion. The flaming dagger pierced through thick chest armor into the bald attacker's heart. The heat from the blade fed back into the handle. Sarai released it a moment before it immolated itself. The risk of catastrophic failure made these weapons as dangerous to the user as the targets.

The green-haired assailant, recovering from surprise, aimed her weapon at Sarai. Before she could fire, the cargo bay's gravity dropped to the level of the moon's surface, 0.166g. This sudden shift threw off the enemy's aim, and Sarai bounded away like an early astronaut.

The reduced gravity gave Luna native David an opportunity. He lunged at the disoriented woman from the side. Overcompensating in the low gravity, the woman collided with a bulkhead and lost grip on her flechette rifle.

Sarai acted on reflex. She snatched up the weapon with one hand and shoved the barrel to the green-haired thug's unarmored neck. The women locked eyes.

Channeling an icy part of her soul she thought was long gone, Sarai jerked the trigger. A final splash of blood signaled the end of the fight.

Overwhelmed by the weight of her actions, Sarai's body finally succumbed to exhaustion. She drifted to the ground. The wounds on her body and the pain in her heart consumed her.

Bianca applied a patch to her suit, ensuring an airtight seal. She pointed at Mallory to go to one side but held up her hand when Sergio wanted to follow.

Mallory is expendable. Sergio is not. He was the only one who had ever been there for me. Our parents didn't care if I lived or died, Bianca thought.

"Eccelente, Borden, but you should have aimed at my chest. This hurts, but all you did is make it so I can't wear a bikini for a while."

"Don't give my aim too much credit. I aimed at your ugly face. I wanted to improve it." Lizzie still sheltered behind a large planter.

Mallory circled to Lizzie's left, trying to get an angle for a stun shot.

Bianca lowered her voice so only Sergio could hear. "You will have an opening in a moment. When you see it go." He nodded his understanding. Combat was her area, and he didn't argue.

Bianca picked up a nearby rock, her fingers curling around it as she gauged its weight. She resumed her conversation with Lizzie, her voice filled with a deceptive sweetness.

"You can't improve on perfection, nonna bella. My face exudes innocence, captivating anyone who lays eyes on it. Your grandson hasn't had the pleasure of meeting me yet. Perhaps after this, we can indulge in a little playtime," Bianca's words dripped with confidence. Deep down, she believed every word, for she was a true narcissist, infatuated with her own reflection. Her looks gave her power over people's lives. Her knife gave her control over their death. Bianca adored both those powers.

With a sudden motion, Bianca flung the rock, employing one of the oldest tricks in the book, but this time, against one of her allies. "Mallory, there she is! Stun her!"

Mallory sprang up, her stunner firing toward where the rock had landed. In that vulnerable moment, Mallory exposed herself.

Lizzie emerged enough to retaliate. The buzz of a laser shot echoed through the air as Mallory let out a scream. The helmet's face mask shattered.

Sergio recognized his cue and lunged toward the planter Lizzie had hidden behind. He swiftly aimed and fired at her back, stunning her before she could react. He snatched up Lizzie's laser pistol.

"Excellent work, Sergio," Bianca praised, her voice filled with genuine approval as she rose to her feet.

"You almost got me killed!" Mallory's voice seethed anger. Her shattered face mask revealed multiple facial cuts, but miraculously, the laser missed her face. She stomped over to Bianca and scowled with fury.

Bianca hid her surprise at Mallory's survival and responded calmly. "The old woman threw a rock. You fell for the oldest trick in the book."

Mallory's expression betrayed her understanding of what had truly transpired. She drew a heavy pistol from behind her back.

Before Mallory could aim, Sergio brought the laser pistol to her helmet and fired. This time, it did not miss her head.

Bianca looked down at Mallory's body. "Damn. Now we need to load the old bitch in the life jacket ourselves."

The 22nd-century emergency vacuum pod was equivalent to a life jacket on a seaborne cruise ship, providing temporary survival in the vacuum of space. As Sergio pulled out a small container, a hissing noise filled the air. The pod expanded to fit a human.

Working together, the siblings maneuvered Lizzie's limp body into the pod.

As they did so, Piet emerged from the superstructure's second level onto the balcony. He lifted his shotgun but didn't have a clear shot without risking Lizzie.

"Call the rest of the crew. We have the best prisoner. They can kill the Moonie and get up here to carry Borden."

Bianca didn't know her other lackeys were fighting for their lives at the exact moment.

Sergio took a few steps as he activated his radio. Movement at the top of the stairs caught Bianca's attention.

"Sergio, look out." Bianca pushed Sergio aside as a thunderous boom echoed through the conservatory. A large planter shattered.

Piet charged down the stairs, certain his shotgun slug would have taken down Sergio if Bianca hadn't pushed him away. Before he could aim again, he saw both raise flechette guns at him. He dodged to the side before they fired.

Piet found cover behind a Buddha statue on a pedestal. *Sorry, Sarai, but the concrete will stop these flechette darts.* Some of those darts hit the outer glass. Fortunately, the "glass" was a durable transparent polymer the flechette would not penetrate. He returned fire, aiming high to avoid the prone Lizzie.

"Ciao, Piet. Such a pity things didn't work out when we met in the casino. I dreamt of your powerful arms. Why don't you come a little closer and let me make it up to you with a kiss?" Bianca's voice cooed, reminiscent of her initial flirtation. Starkly different from the cold menace in the eyes.

"How about you leave Lizzie and run? I triggered the emergency beacon when I left the bridge. Help will be here any minute."

"Alas, amore, we disabled your transmitter in engineering right before I slit the throat of one of those CPS idiots." She was still in her friendly tone, contrasting with her evil words.

Piet blinked rapidly, trying to keep tears over Rossi's death at bay. He didn't want to give the woman the satisfaction of seeing his vulnerability. But the raw ache in his chest grew stronger with each passing moment.

Piet fired several blasts, more in anger than hoping to hit them. He realized he was outnumbered two to one against armored opponents. His shotgun may be more powerful, but they had armor. His simple ship coveralls provided no protection against the flechettes.

"You're right, Piet. We should leave. We'll be taking her with us, making you unnecessary. Have you ever played the old American board game Clue?" Bianca's sudden change in topic puzzled him. He had never heard of the game.

Bianca removed the weapon attached to her back and stepped into the open. Sergio fired before Piet could aim at her, keeping him pinned down.

"Let me spoil the ending for you. The killer was Miss Scarlet in the Conservatory with the plasma grenade launcher." While Sarai wasn't prepared to use a plasma grenade on the *Elizabeth*, Bianca had no qualms. She aimed at the windows and pulled the trigger. The siblings braced themselves and grabbed Lizzie's pod.

Piet watched in horror as the shell soared over his shoulder and exploded into a fiery ball against the window. The room burst with chaos—the shattering of glass and the silence of vacuum. The suction lifted Piet off his feet and out of the hole. His last thought was to admire the beautiful mural on the ship's side.

28

Tearful reunions make the family stronger

Adrian and Megan burst into the hospital room at the secret clinic on Europa station, desperate to get to their injured friend. Rafael and Carolina followed close behind, if only because they didn't know where else to go.

Sarai lay in a hospital bed, her face ashen except for red and puffy eyes. One arm was in a sling, and the other had an IV feeding her body medication. Monitors showing her vitals beeped. The air smelled of disinfectant combined with fresh-cut flowers, an extravagant item on a space station.

"Adrian! I'm so sorry I couldn't stop them." Sarai's voice cracked and faltered. The confidence and serenity that defined Sarai Rousseau abandoned the fragile woman.

Pain and confusion flashed on their faces. Details were too elusive. Lizzie is missing, Sarai is wounded, and Piet is gone forever.

"We're here, Sarai. I'm the captain. It's my responsibility. I failed to protect everyone." Tears welled up as he embraced Sarai on the bed, doing his best to avoid disturbing her bandages.

"I killed people, Adrian. I murdered them, and I still couldn't save Lizzie and Piet." Sarai grimaced in pain as a wave of sobs vibrated through her body.

"No, Sarai, you saved me and Alice Rogers. You saved her from a fate worse than death." David limped into the room, almost dragging his left leg. His exoskeleton had failed on the left side. Megan gave him a hug and helped the struggling Lunan into a chair.

"Where have you been? You left Sarai alone in here." Adrian rarely used such a sharp tone on anyone, let alone a crew member and friend he had known all his life.

"Adrian, stop it. He stepped out for a minute. He was here the moment I woke up." A hint of Sarai's protective nature resurfaced like the distant echo of a tiger's roar.

Megan stood in the center of the room and used a commanding, aristocratic tone. "Everyone, take a deep breath. Adrian, save your anger for whoever did this."

Adrian's gaze fell downward in shame. "You're right. I apologize, David. Can you tell us what happened? Where's my grandmother and Piet?"

"Piet's dead," David said. He stared at the floor and spoke in a relaxed tone to hide the pain over the loss of the apprentice he was in the process of training.

"By the time the CPS rescue team got to us in the hold, they had already recovered his body. They shattered the dome, and he died in space. Donald told me as they were loading us into an ambulance." David Efron and Donald Phillips were close friends.

"What about Grandma?" His voice cracked, each word pleading for hope. He didn't call her Lizzie, the ship engineer, to his captain. She was a grandson's beloved grandma.

"I don't know, Adrian. I don't know." A hushed whimper escaped David's mouth. "They were still searching when they rushed us away. That's one of the reasons I was out of the room to ask the clinic people to find out. They will get back to us soon. I'm sorry, Adrian, we have to wait."

More tears streamed down David's face while Adrian's shoulders slumped as he sat on the edge of Sarai's bed.

Megan took a tissue, wiped the tears from David's face, and asked, "How did you get to this clinic? I would have thought the CPS would bring you to the main station hospital."

"They were supposed to take us there, but our ambulance got diverted here. The doctor said it was Zeus's orders."

Megan gave Sarai a gentle hug. As their cheeks touched, they felt the warmth of their tears mingling.

"Megan, it was terrible. I never wanted to harm a human again. When I worked for Zeus, I killed to help him secure his power. Those were always clean and fast deaths. Last night, I was vicious and brutal. A monster. I...I..." Sarai pulled Megan in close and clung tightly. Her body shook with uncontrollable sobs, the sound echoing through the room. Adrian offered comfort by stroking Sarai's hair. Everyone comforted each other without words for several minutes.

"Um...Adrian, would you mind introducing your friends? Because she is freaking me out. Stop that," David said.

Carolina crouched next to David's left side. She took several medical tools out of a drawer. The reflex hammer became a pry bar, and the forceps transformed into pliers in her hands. Alarm spread across David's face when she poked around in his exo-skeleton with sharp trauma shears. He tried to push her away, but she waved him off like he inconvenienced her engineering problem.

"Carolina, what are you doing?" Megan asked.

"Fixing it." A soft hum and a few indicator lights came from David's exoskeleton.

His eyes lit up. "It's on again! Thank you!"

"The introduction might be a little late, but this is Carolina and Rafael. They are new friends and came back with us, but that's a story for later." Rafael stood in the corner and seemed out of his depth. Content with her job, Carolina simply returned to stand near her twin brother.

"Prazer em conhecer. Nice to meet you," Rafael said. Carolina retreated into herself again and said nothing. Before he could say more, they heard a knock at the door.

"Please come in," Megan said, expecting a doctor.

A blonde woman in a business suit entered. Adrian's eyebrow arched up in recognition and curiosity.

"Good morning. I'm Amanda, Mr. Zeus' personal assistant. As I told Mr. Efron earlier, he has asked me to assist you in any way I can." She held out a package to David. "Here is the item you wanted."

"Thank you, but did you find out anything about Lizzie?" His words were rapid and combined with hope and dread in anticipation of the answer.

Adrian stood but clutched Sarai's hand, expecting the worst. The room was silent.

"Doctor Elizabeth Borden is alive."

The tension held by everyone relaxed. Adrian smiled and kissed Sarai's hand. Megan noticed Amanda didn't look pleased when she delivered the message.

"It's not all good news, is it?" Megan asked.

"No, Doctor McCord, it's not." She stepped up to Adrian and handed him a tablet. Her voice softened. "I'm sorry, Adrian, they took your grandmother hostage. Mr. Zeus received this message to be passed on to you. Please wait till I leave to view it."

Amanda looked at Sarai and said, "Mr. Zeus is on Europa now and would like to call on you later. He wants to wish you a speedy recovery, nothing more. He hopes you enjoyed the flowers."

Amanda paused as she walked out. "Adrian, I wish we could have seen each other again under better circumstances."

"Do you know her?" Megan asked.

"From a lifetime ago and not a story for today. Let's see what is on this video."

"Before you do that. I think we may all need this," David handed Sarai the wrapped package.

Adrian helped Sarai unwrap the box, and they found a small statue depicting a seated Buddha with the right hand raised and facing outward.

"The protection Buddha. Thank you, David. This means more than all these flowers Zeus sent." The room had several vases filled with flowers, each costing as much as an average person earned in a week.

Sarai put the statue on her eating table and waved everyone over.

She said a small prayer for protection. "Faith protects, and blessings abound, as this statue guards those around my table. Now play the video, Adrian."

29

Ultimatum

Evening August 15, 2155—Europa station–Private clinic

Bianca appeared on the screen with a sweet smirk, bouncy blonde hair, and a top cut so low it left nothing to the imagination. This video wasn't intended for a woman.

"Ciao, Captain Kostas. May I call you Adrian? I know you have heard horrible things about me, but I have fantastic news for you. We saved your nonna when those CPS goons detonated a plasma grenade. She's healthy and unharmed." Bianca beamed a smile while she delivered the message. "We didn't want anyone harmed. Those government bastards were holding your ship hostage when we got there. They never give a shit about regular people. Let me prove to you she is okay."

An image appeared of Lizzie sitting in a chair in a comfortable cabin, drinking from a plastic teacup. Lizzie was uninjured but wasn't happy in her surroundings. Adrian leaned closer to the screen to convince himself it was real.

"See, she is doing great. I hope she and I become friends while she is my guest." The video switched to Bianca biting her lip in a slight pout and twisting her hair.

"Everything has just spun out of control. I'm sorry we had to trespass like we did, but I have very demanding employers. Sometimes, the good of all must outweigh the *desires* of a few." She pushed her chest forward and winked at the camera.

Sarai rolled her eyes. "Subtlety is an alien concept to her."

Bianca intertwined her fingers, her gaze fixed with a thoughtful expression. "My employer's simple wish is to protect humanity. The secret the McCords' discovered is dangerous and needs to be protected by the right people. Let me tell you a story."

The screen switched to a picture of the asteroid Ceres. "I'm sure history class taught the first artifact discovery on Ceres in 2045. Humans finally knew we weren't alone in the universe.

"Like most of history, that was a lie. The organization had long known about the existence of the artificers. They allowed the discovery, hoping to introduce alien technology to humans gradually. We are a self-destructive species, and too much knowledge too fast gives too much power to the stupid."

The video switched to a video of a mushroom cloud rising from the ground. "If not for the intervention of my employers, we would have destroyed ourselves in the 20th century. Allowing artificer technology to trickle in seemed the best alternative. But someone stumbled onto the first Starshell. Unlimited power was now in the hands of fools, and the Artifact Wars broke out."

This time, she showed a clip of a ring-shaped space station. An intense flash came from the edge of the wheel as a fusion bomb ripped the station apart. The single most significant loss of life in the Artifact Wars was the Massacre of Luna Station One. David grimaced at the image. One of his earliest memories recalled that massive flash where ten thousand people died.

The camera switched back to Bianca, her face in an angry snarl. "*This* is what all powerful governments and unaccountable corporations can do."

Her eyes widened, filling with desperate hope as if she were a puppy begging for food. "I need your help, Adrian. If we let this knowledge out, we will doom millions of others to this fate. Think of your friends on space stations across the solar system."

Adrian scoffed as the spellbinding witch tried to pull his strings.

"Get me Doctor McCord's information, and the organization will find this artifact site and keep it safe. There are others who want to exploit it, not just the incompetent UCE. They will use it for selfish gain and repeat past mistakes. Your Megan will unintentionally lead them right to this power."

With a sudden jerk, Megan's attention was drawn to the screen, her fury intensifying. Adrian's hand found hers, offering a comforting presence at that moment. "Don't worry about her lies."

"Adrian, I'm sorry about Piet's death. I liked him when I met him at the casino. I thought he was cute. My flirting with him wasn't just an act. I would never have hurt him then, and I didn't want him hurt on the *Elizabeth*. We had to take some drastic action to protect humanity, but the blame for his death is on the jackbooted thugs the government put on your ship."

David snarled at the screen and tightened his fists until the knuckles turned white. In a gesture of solace, Sarai reached out and placed a gentle hand on his arm.

Bianca twirled a finger in circles on her upper chest, drawing attention downward. She licked her lips slowly and said, "Adrian, my employer will compensate you for the damage. Enough for you to buy a new ship if you want. And you will receive my apology in a more intimate way. You can see my sincerity up close and very personal. All you need to do is get me the information on how to find the artificer's site. Then you can have the money and me."

Megan had witnessed Bianca twist men to her desires before. Relief washed over Megan to see Adrian scowl at the seductress's advances.

The image transitioned back to Lizzie, who glared at the camera as if she knew she was observed. The challenge in her eyes spoke of her fire and determination not to give up. "My employers have given me another week to resolve this. Give us the decrypted site data and any leads you have for its location. If not, I can't promise the safety of Elizabeth Borden."

The tone of the last displayed the ice living in Bianca's soul.

Everyone in the room stared in silence as they processed the message.

Carolina broke the silence with a whimper. "That woman scares me."

Rafael pulled his sister in for protection as David said, "That may be the wisest thing I have heard in a long time."

"At least we know Grandma is safe, or was when the video was recorded," Adrian said with relief laced with a current of anxiety. "We have a week to get her back. Any ideas."

"The obvious. We trade this and my notes from Stonington's safe house for Lizzie." Megan took out the pendant containing the holo info for the asteroid site.

Her friends shouted protests, but Megan crossed her arms and stared them down in determination.

"They murdered my father over this. I won't see Lizzie die as well. My quest got Piet killed, Sarai injured, and Lizzie kidnapped. Plus, the CPS troopers on *Elizabeth*." She threw the pendant on the bed. "This has shed enough blood."

Megan knelt next to Sarai and sobbed again.

Sarai pulled Megan in with her unbroken arm. "We don't blame inanimate objects for tragedy. We blame the individuals responsible. In this case, Bianca and this 'Organization' are to blame."

David grabbed the tablet and rewound the video to freeze on Bianca's pleasant grin. He held the tablet in front of Megan. His voice was tight, and with an intensity the gentleman rarely displayed, he said, "You know evil hides behind this smile. I heard her and Sergio talking. Sergio could have killed Petty Officer Rogers but planned on taking her as a plaything. Bianca was the one carrying the plasma grenade launcher that shattered the dome and murdered Piet. Do you really think she will let Lizzie or you live if you trade that to her?"

"No, you're right. But what can we do?"

"Simple. We find this Bianca and rescue your grandmother," Rafael said.

They all turned and looked at the man who had been silent. Adrian said, "This isn't your fight. I can't ask you to come."

"You saved my sister and dozens of others. I'll help save your family."

"Thank you. That means a lot to me. How would we even mount a rescue? There are just a few of us. Sarai, you are injured. David, it would be too dangerous for you to fight. Carolina, you should stay here too. That leaves Megan, Rafael, and me."

"If Rafael is going, so am I. I don't want to fight, but I'm not useless. Remember, I helped little Shaurya at the school." Carolina's conviction told them there was no way they would split the twins. "Plus, the answer is simple. You have friends here. Ask them. Amanda said she was supposed to help. Maybe she can get this Mr. Zeus to help, too."

Sarai smiled at Carolina's innocence. "Zeus did this to help me, not Adrian or Lizzie. He and I were friends and more many years ago. But he doesn't like Lizzie or the *Elizabeth*. It's not logical, but that's the way it is. I have another idea. There is someone we know whose job it is to rescue kidnapped UCE citizens. Ask Kristina to help."

Adrian shifted his weight from foot to foot. His conflicted gaze landed on Megan, revealing the inner battle he currently experienced. "No, she would arrest Megan, and I can't trust the CPS right now. Even Kristina. Her people were protecting *Elizabeth*, and this still happened. I won't ask Kristina."

"It's a good thing I just asked for you." Sarai held up Adrian's comm-pad, which she had slipped from his pocket. Apparently, one-handed pick-pocketing was another of Sarai's mix of skills.

30

The Tigress and the New Boss

August 16, 2155—Europa station—Administration office

An aide escorted Kristina to a private office and fled to his station like the room contained toxic waste. Hübner stood behind a desk with his palms planted flat.

Hübner arrived at Europa station while *Zetta Sierra* was still retrieving the dead and wounded from *Elizabeth*. A man wearing a suit stood in the corner, leaning against the wall.

Who is he? He is not the lower administrator who oversees Europa Station, Kristina thought.

The scowl on Hübner's face showed the direction of the meeting, so she seized the momentum before he could speak.

"Administrator Hübner, I assume you wish to express your condolences over the loss of life among my crew. It is very honorable of you to take time from your schedule to speak to me. We thank you, but I would like to keep this visit short. We have much to do if we want to catch these criminals."

Hübner blinked, and his mouth opened as if the words he was about to speak were stolen from his lips. The man in the corner snickered softly. Hübner gathered himself. "Of course, losing valiant CPS members is tragic. However, we need to discuss these actions. Twice, pirates attacked ships in the Jupiter region during your patrol tour. The second attack had your people on board defending it."

"Yes, I have sent a report to Admiral Wells detailing both situations. Tonight, I will record messages to the families of the men killed. Do you wish to express your condolences as well?" Kristina held her ground against the insufferable man, but it didn't deter him this time.

"Your failures mount Commander. What excuse do you have for not preventing this bloodshed?"

"I don't have an excuse. I have explained it to my chain of command and will answer any questions they have." He had struck on an unavoidable point. Her heart sank for not protecting her people or Adrian's crew, and she would accept accountability for it, but not to Hübner.

"What about the fugitive McCord? You failed to catch her as well. You even thought she was on the *Elizabeth*. Inquisitor Keller traveled all the way from Earth to fix your problem." He pointed at the stranger who had been silent so far.

"That's unfair, Administrator. Commander Chen-Ramirez is a dedicated Patrol Service officer. Her team uncovered invaluable information for the McCord investigation." Keller held his hand to Kristina. "My name is Keller, Coalition Security, and I'm here to help."

Kristina shook his hand firmly and wished she was on the way to Pluto. Anyone who believed a Coalition Security Inquisitor was there to help had lost their grip on reality. After she let go, she felt an overwhelming urge to scrub her hands clean.

Coalition Security's charter provided for the safety of the UCE government, not the people, by any means necessary. They had no oversight Kristina was aware of and operated as an intelligence agency when none should be required.

"I am very sorry for the death of your people, but the pirate will need to wait until we have captured Megan McCord. Sometimes, the greater good of the UCE must outweigh our personal wishes. She has vital information that is a danger to us all. Here are orders from Geneva placing you under my authority in this matter." He sent her an encrypted document.

After examining the document he sent, she realized it was unambiguous. "What information makes one young exo-archeologist be a greater danger than murders attacking ships?"

"You don't have clearance for that information, but I will share with you what I can." Keller sat in a chair and got comfortable. He smiled like a storyteller about to spin a tale.

"We believe you were right that McCord sought passage on the *Elizabeth*. Unfortunately for the crew, Doctor McCord's accomplices planned to silence them after she left the ship. Due to your diligent investigators, we know she met with a known criminal in Callisto, and then she disappeared at Europa. The fact that the surviving Elizabeth crew members disappeared before they reached the hospital makes things more suspicious. I'm sorry to conclude the crew of the *Elizabeth* were all killed to cover McCord's tracks. They are the only ones who might have clues to her location."

Kristina closed her mouth before she could say something that would ruin her career. She reluctantly accepted that she had no alternative but to listen in silence. Ignoring Hübner was possible, but not Keller.

"I disagree with your assessment, but I'm at your service. Our investigation shows these commandos who attacked the *Elizabeth* are likely Doctor McCord's father's murders. We don't know where she is, so following them is still the best lead. We will continue the analysis and report back if we find anything." Maybe she could convince the idiot to do the correct thing.

"That won't be necessary. Coalition Security is taking over the investigation. Your people will leave the *Elizabeth* and no longer be involved. Return to your normal patrol duties. I'm sure it will help your people get their minds off your loss. I'll call you when I need you," he said with a smile and a dismissal.

He flexed enough muscle with command to get me under his authority, only to push me away. What game is he playing? Kristina thought. She left the office and called Phillips to have the team pulled off *Elizabeth*. Now she was officially off the case, she could go to her next meeting with a clear conscience.

31

Long Awaited Meeting

August 16, 2155—Europa station—The Tavern

Megan and Adrian walked into the location where they would meet Kristina. Instantly, a bizarre déjà vu rolled over Megan.

The nostalgic scent of peaty whiskey and a real wood fire wafted through the air. Log pillars supported an oval-shaped ceiling that spoke of traditional craftsmanship using wood and stone. The centerpiece was a sunken lounge surrounding a fire pit radiating comforting warmth from within a circle of high-backed chairs.

I've been in this tavern and sat in one of those chairs. But that's impossible. I've never been to Europa station, Megan thought. Her mind raced, and her heart slammed into her chest as she panicked at the complete illogic of this. She touched the stone archway entrance. The cool, smooth alabaster almost glowed in the firelight.

Adrian's face displayed no concern. His somber mood even improved on entering.

Behind the bar, perched on its polished counter, sat a tall woman with hair in a long braid with pink and blonde streaks. Sleek black leggings clung to her legs, ending in sturdy boots and a fitted tank top. A name tag introduced her as Angelica.

She sprung off her perch and came to greet them. "Megan, Adrian, it's so good to see you again. I heard the news of Lizzie being kidnapped, and my heart sank."

Adrian said, "Thank you, Angie. You have always been such a good friend."

Angelica gave him an enormous hug and a kiss on the cheek. "Lizzie doesn't visit as much as I would like, but we've known each other for decades. I'm here for you and will help you win over Kristina when she gets here."

Megan tried to comprehend everything. Her eyes flitted around the room. Hakim stood by the fire and gave her a warm smile. The fire looked and smelled like an actual wood fire but was three-quarters of a billion miles from the nearest forest. *And how could this young woman have known Lizzie for decades? She knew Lizzie had been kidnapped. How is that possible?* Megan thought.

Angelica's eyes darted toward Megan, her eyebrows furrowing ever so slightly. The frown on her face disappeared, replaced by a warm and inviting smile.

"I'm sorry, Megan. I was so busy with this guy that I forgot the cardinal rule. Ladies first." Angelica enveloped her in a mighty bear hug and kissed each cheek.

"I'm glad you traveled with Adrian. I was worried about how your quest would go if you traveled solo." Angie let go of the hug but held Megan by the shoulders and momentarily peered into her eyes.

This warm embrace must have been what Megan needed. The tension and doubt vanished from her. Like a dream, Megan recalled little of the issue. Maybe it was a nightmare that the daylight glow of Angelica's smile wiped away.

"Let's get you two seated. Kristina will arrive soon." Angelica wrapped one arm around Adrian's shoulder and took Megan's hand. Her firm grip tingled slightly in Megan's hand as they walked to the chairs.

The luxurious wing chairs deserved to have people lounge in the delicate leather and bask in the fire's warmth. Instead, the tension tied Megan and Adrian's stomachs in knots. Megan trembled on the edge of her seat while Adrian slumped in his. They dreaded what would come.

Will Kristina help us rescue Lizzie or arrest me? If the price to pay for Lizzie's rescue is being hauled back in chains for a crime I did not commit, I'm prepared to pay it, Megan thought.

The door swung open, and Commander Chen-Ramirez strode into the Tavern. Adrian stiffened in his chair, but the fugitive scientist studied her hunter.

Kristina's crisp Customs and Patrol Service uniform contrasted with the flowing elegance of the red dress she had worn before. Kristina's plain and unadorned face held none of the glamour Megan saw on that first day. Yet, something in Kristina's focused calm hinted at a deep allure, one not dependent on the trappings of fashion and makeup. Megan felt a pang as she realized the goddess she had once seen was not gone but armored in duty.

Adrian rose to greet his lover as Angelica hugged Kristina at the door.

"Hello, Kristina. Or will it be Commander Chen-Ramirez today?" Adrian said. The sharp and calm edge to his voice was abnormal and unexpected.

A startled expression flashed across Kristina's face, momentarily losing her composure. She had been opening her arms to embrace him but stopped herself at his tone.

"Adrian, I'm not here on official business. I'm here as your friend. I hope more than friends still." Kristina's voice cracked, and a flash of hurt crossed her eyes. "I'm so sorry about the attack. We tried to stop them. I wish I could have done more..."

"You should have done more. Grandma is missing, and Piet is dead! You had people on the *Elizabeth* there to protect them. Or were they just hostages until the UCE got what they wanted?" Megan rocked back in her seat at the bitterness spewing from Adrian. Kristina, the target of his venom, narrowed her eyes and tensed her shoulders.

"I lost people, too! Two of my crew are dead, and a third is hospitalized. A point-blank shot to the head with a neuro-stunner scrambled her brain. She's lucky to be alive. Where was the captain of the *Elizabeth*? Not protecting his crew, but runoff with a pretty face promising artifacts, as I warned you." Her defensive posture switched to the offensive, staring him down nose to nose.

As their tension escalated, the atmosphere grew heavy with their conflicting emotions. Each harsh word used as a weapon became an electric shock into their souls. Megan shrank back in her chair as they drew her into this war.

"Sit down, both of you! You are guests in my place and will behave yourselves." Angelica stepped between the two and pushed them apart. The ease with which flimsy-looking Angie moved them back startled them both. "Sit and don't speak until Hakim has poured tea."

Adrian sat back next to Megan, and Kristina sat across from him. Angie took the fourth chair. Megan noted only four chairs were in the lounge on this visit. They were on one side of the fire, close enough for soft conversation. The small bog-oak table between them added a rustic charm to the scene.

"Thank you, Angelica. I will serve a family recipe for chamomile tea to calm everyone's nerves and soothe the tension." He placed a beautifully crafted brass teapot on the table, its intricate design catching the eye. He filled four crystal glasses of an Arabic design with the tea. Hakim didn't ask anyone how they wanted their tea but added various amounts of sugar or milk to each glass. He served Megan first, followed by the other ladies, and ended with Adrian.

Megan tasted her tea. The warmth of Hakim's masterful brew spread through Megan's chest. She closed her eyes to savor the chamomile's floral scent and clean, honeyed taste. When she reopened her eyes, she found her tension waned. It was exactly how she liked it. *How did he know?*

Adrian and Kristina sipped their tea. They didn't question the tea any more than the sun rising in the east. Confused emotions scrambled their thoughts. Anger, fear, pride, and shame flowed through their guts, but trust and caring won their hearts.

Angelica, who had been studying them, said, "Now, children, apologize, and let's have a civilized conversation."

"I'm sorry, Kristina. My words were uncalled for and unacceptable. I know your crew too well to lash out like that. Jun-Seo and Marco were dedicated agents and good people. I hope Alice recovers soon, and if there is anything I can do for her, please let me know." Adrian had his eyes downcast and waver in his voice.

"No, Adrian, throwing their deaths at you was uncalled for. You're right. I didn't do enough to protect the *Elizabeth*. And accusing you of abandoning your crew to follow a girl was unacceptable, and I hope someday you can forgive me." Kristina sat with the stiff, upright posture of a military officer, ready to accept a reprimand from a superior.

"Thank you both. I think that makes this a good time for long overdue introductions," Angelica said.

All eyes converged on Megan. The insecure girl in her heart wanted to melt back into the chair to avoid notice. The aristocrat in her soul did the exact opposite. Before anyone else could speak, she rose from her chair, stood directly before Kristina, and held out a hand.

"Hello, Commander, I'm Doctor Megan McCord. I believe you have been looking for me." She dared not show her anxiety to the imposing woman who had been hunting. Kristina stood and shook Megan's hand.

"Yes, Doctor, until about an hour ago, it was my duty to arrest you. Now, I have been ordered to resume my regular patrol duties. Therefore, to the best of my knowledge, you are only wanted for questioning in Scotland. That is out of my jurisdiction, so all I can do is advise you to return and turn yourself in for questioning." Megan could almost see her dance a fine line between the letter and spirit of her orders. Kristina took a deep breath, and a resigned tone entered her voice. "However, there is one duty I must perform, no matter how much it hurts. I should have done this the moment I walked in."

Kristina stepped to Adrian, who also stood. The steadfast officer had steadied her nerves but looked to be holding back tears. "Adrian, we recovered Piet's body almost immediately, but we haven't found your grandmother. Everything we could find showed she was under the dome when it shattered. It looks like she must have been pulled into space. I'm so sorry, she is gone, and I can't even bring her body back to you."

Kristina dropped her professional detachment and wrapped her arms around Adrian. She held him tight to comfort him. He returned the hug briefly but then pushed away and smiled. Her confusion about his reaction was apparent.

"Thank you, Kristina. I appreciate it so much, but this is one time you are mistaken. Lizzie is missing but not dead, and I think you very much can help bring her back."

"What? I don't understand. Where is she?"

"People kidnapped her and want information for her safe return. I want your help to get her back. Will you help me?"

"Of course I will. I owe it to you both to help and redeem my failures." This time, Kristina didn't settle for a hug. They kissed each other with the zeal of long-separated lovers.

This is unlike the kiss Adrian gave me as a reward on Ithaca. This is a true passion, not lust and adrenaline, Megan thought. Shame washed over her as she admitted that she had secretly hoped for a chance with Adrian amidst their anger. The thought disgusted her rational brain, and she was happy for Adrian.

Angelica cleared her throat, and Kristina snapped back to reality. She adjusted her uniform and turned a bit red at her loss of decorum.

The most difficult thing an officer can do is inform the next of kin about the death of a loved one. The intense pressure of having to tell her lover had crushed her spirit, only to have it spring back in an instant.

"I'm sorry that was unprofessional," Kristina said. *Time to stop behaving like a lovesick schoolgirl.*

"Well, you did say you were off duty, but I figured I needed to stop you before you started tearing each other's clothes off. Ordinarily, I would love to watch the show, but I think you have some business to discuss. I think the need for a referee has ended, and I will let you talk privately. I will be at the bar if you need me or decide to do it, anyway." Angie gave them a wink and strolled back to the bar. The playful and flirty Angie returned, replacing the surprising authoritarian version they hadn't seen before.

"Adrian, maybe we can pick that up later, but give me the details for now. I'm relieved Lizzie is alive, but how did she survive, and how did you find out? Forgive my blunt phrasing, but station cameras recorded two bodies being ejected. We were lucky to find Piet and assumed the other was Lizzie."

"They sent us a ransom demand of sorts. It included a video of Lizzie followed by thinly veiled threats unless we provide them with all Megan's information on the 'Hunter's Folly.' Here, watch the recording. It will be easier than explaining." He handed her the tablet with Bianca's ultimatum.

Kristina pressed play and saw Bianca for the first time outside a security video. Blaming her people for setting off the plasma grenade hurt Kristina's pride. Still, she saw it as manipulation targeting her fiercely independent lover.

Kristina recognized Bianca as a master manipulator, using her soft face and friendly voice to hide the monster underneath. The image of Bianca gleefully cutting into a crewmember on the ferry replayed in Kristina's mind, causing a shiver to run down her spine.

The thought of Bianca's calculated plan to kidnap Adrian's grandmother and then offer herself up to him baffled Kristina. *Does Bianca believe her twisted scheme will work? Or has she become so adept at influencing men that she cannot fathom any other option?*

"What a fucking piece of shit." Kristina couldn't help but smile when Adrian's mouth dropped in shock. "What? You only thought I use the word fuck when in bed with you?"

Megan put a hand to her mouth to stifle a laugh. The inappropriate humor lets them all relax in the tense situation.

"I think she was off her game in this video. This is rushed. Bianca and her brother took a month to worm into my life. Bianca became my friend. Maybe a goofy friend in a ditzy blonde way, but still a fun girl. She had me completely fooled, right up until..." Megan turned to gaze into the fire, lost in memories.

Kristina leaned forward with questions on her lips but stopped herself. The professional investigator wanted to hunt for more answers, but the woman in her knew to give Megan a moment.

Adrian said, "You heard rumors of a violent organization involved in artifact theft. You were right, and here is the proof."

"Too bad it wouldn't hold up in court, but you remind me of something else," Kristina said. "Doctor McCord, I need to apologize to you as well. Earlier, I made a nasty comment about Adrian running off with a pretty face instead of protecting his crew. I shouldn't have made an implication like that without knowing you."

Megan's face twitched a bit before responding. "Thank you, Commander. I didn't take offense at your remark."

"Bianca is the kind of manipulative pretty face I warned Adrian about, and she wants to find the same Artificer site as you. Murdering the ferry's crew didn't get Bianca the location. She hopes kidnapping Lizzie will. I'm sorry, but this will be very blunt." Kristina's training as an investigator kicked in with intense focus.

"Where have you been, and did you find the information Bianca wants?"

A knowing glance passed between Megan and Adrian, their silent communication deferring to Megan to take the lead.

"I will take your second question first. We found Stonington's cache of information. He didn't make our life easy and give us the location. He gave cryptic clues that should cross reference with the navigation data and get us near the correct asteroid. David is working on it now. We have already decided we aren't giving Bianca the information."

"Of course not. I wouldn't ask you to. I want to know what we have. How about the first question? Where were you for over a week?"

Adrian took the lead this time. "Who is asking, my friend and lover, Kristina or Commander Chen-Ramirez, agent of the United Coalition of Earth? We promised never to let the Coalition know about the place."

"Adrian, you put me in a bad position. I swore an oath as well. I can't ignore it if it threatens the Coalition or Earth."

"They are not a threat to anyone except maybe to some bureaucrats who don't like people not living the way they are told to live." Adrian's distrust rang through with his words.

Kristina stood, removed her uniform jacket, and handed it to Hakim, who had stepped forward with a hanger. Her rank insignia were nano-bonded to her shirt but popped off with the proper touch.

"Sorry, Angie, that's all I'm taking off."

"Oh, you're no fun." Angelica had been watching from the bar top she sat on. As a bartender, she rarely seemed to be behind the bar.

Kristina sat back in the chair and opened her hands wide. "Ok, you just have Kristina. I won't tell Commander Chen-Ramirez if you don't."

"We lived and worked together in a haven for outcasts called Ithaca. They live in the scraps cast off by the UCE. Old shipping containers and scrapped ships. These people built a way of life, and I will help them protect it." Megan met Kristina's eyes with a stern determination.

"Stonington founded Ithaca, and they safeguarded his secrets all these years after he died. We earned their trust enough to allow us to look at his notes," Megan said.

"Ithaca? Well, what he said makes sense now. I was the one who found Stonington ten years ago. He wanted to go home to Ithaca and Penelope. I thought he was delirious and loved Homer."

"Oh, he was a nut for the Iliad and the Odyssey, but how does this help us find Lizzie?" Adrian asked.

"I guess it doesn't for now, but having information is better than not."

Adrian said, "OK, it's your turn to share. How did Bianca and Sergio escape after the attack? No ship bigger than a one-person racer is faster than a CPS patrol vessel."

Kristina's jaw set tight, and her nostrils flared with a sharp breath intake. "This one is."

She displayed a holo video of space near Elizabeth from her cuff computer. The image of the conservatory's shattered dome caused a shadow of distress to cross Adrian's features. However, a determined set in his jaw showed his spirit had not broken like the glass.

A white glow flared in the distance, and the camera zoomed in. A triangular-shaped object surrounded by a corona of fire plunged at the station. The brilliance appeared like looking into a solar eclipse. It approached the station at an unbelievable speed.

"What the Hell! It's not slowing down. How does it miss the station?" Adrian said.

"Sorry, no spoilers, lover. Just wait for it," Kristina said with a knowing satisfaction.

When it appeared far too close to the station to stop, the flare ended to reveal a delta-wing-shaped ship. The arrowhead shape had a three-quarter sphere in the back and a needlepoint in the front. The vessel did a flat spin into a one-hundred-eighty-degree turn. They saw a soft glow at the rear of a giant engine. A tremendous flash filled the screen.

"Did it explode?"

Kristina remained silent and gestured to keep watching. White glare washed out, the video sensors faded and merged into a violet jet as the ship broke hard to settle beside *Elizabeth*. The camera angle didn't see anyone transferring to the new boat. The engine flared again, and it left. After it went, the stealth shuttle still attached to *Elizabeth's* engineering section exploded, leaving a wrecked airlock.

"Before you ask, my team estimated they peaked at 6g on deceleration. It was *only* at 3g when they took off again." She sent Adrian the sensor data, even though the information touched the line of being classified.

"All from one big thruster? *Elizabeth* uses dozens of plasma thrusters to get just .5g. You have four military-grade thrusters to get 1g." Adrian's rapid speech caused his words to run together. His fingers swiped on his screen as he struggled to make sense of it.

"It doesn't make sense to me either. The ship must have advanced grav plates and inertial compensators. Otherwise, the thrust parallel to the decks makes no sense." Most ships had thrusters at the bottom of the vessel, so the acceleration force and gravity plates didn't fight each other. A thruster at the rear of a craft would cause the room's back wall to feel "down" while the grav plates pull the person to the deck.

"True inertial compensators are only theoretical or in fiction. No ship can have that kind of power. And what kind of thrust is that?" Adrian asked.

"They cracked a shell," Megan said. The two spaceship captains gave the archaeologist a bewildered look.

"They did what?" Adrian asked.

"We can tap into Starshells to generate electricity, but inefficiently. Some theorize the raw energy inside a Starshell would be massive, but to get at it, you would have to 'crack the shell.' It is not a widespread theory because no one has any idea how to open a Starshell or contain the energy if they did. Mostly a thought exercise artifact experts talk about with no way to prove it. No more practical than Da Vinci drawing a helicopter in the 15th century."

"So, if this theory is right, these people already have a Starshell, the most valuable object known to humanity, and they broke it open? Which shouldn't even be possible. A nuke hit one during the war and didn't damage it," Kristina said.

"It also raises another question. What value does this Artificer site have compared to a Starshell?"

"Knowledge is power, Adrian," Megan explained the possibility of finding an alien Rosetta Stone on the asteroid for Kristina's sake.

Kristina thought for a few seconds. "Whatever is there, we can't let these people have it. We find Lizzie and stop them. How do we find them? If the Ithaca place you mentioned can stay hidden, so can this ship."

"The raw Starshell energy should have a distinctive signature. I know of research into it, but I don't have it. Some of my tools can be modified into a detector," Megan said.

"Worth a try, but it will probably be short range. We will resume patrol late tomorrow. Maybe we can detect something as we police the area. Sorry, Adrian, but I won't be allowed to get officially involved. Coalition Security took it all over."

"Well, we will just keep things quiet. At least with you leaving, we can move back onto the *Elizabeth* and work out of there. We can set up encrypted communication with you."

"Sorry, but you won't be able to do that either. Inquisitor Keller, with CS, kicked us off and moved his people onto the ship. Even if you got on, you're not going anywhere. Bianca blew up her shuttle and set off several small explosives in engineering."

"Keller? That can't be good. He was the same one who showed up and seized control of my father's murder investigation. I suspect he is connected to everything." Megan didn't reveal why she suspected it.

A shadow crossed Adrian's face after he learned Coalition Security barred him from home. He put his hand on his chin and closed his eyes in thought.

"Adrian, do I want to know what you have in mind?" Kristina asked.

"No, you don't. Let's say I want to pick up a few personal items from the ship," Adrian said as he stood up. "Let's get back to our teams with this information and see if anyone has ideas."

When they exited the Tavern, Adrian and Megan turned one way and Kristina the other. Kristina glanced at the pair as they walked away. *Last time, I was with him and took him to my bed. Will that happen again?*

Megan felt an urge to look at the tavern's entrance but only saw a blank wall.

32

The Prosecution Argument

August 17, 2155—Europa station—LVC Elizabeth

Senior Agent Ashford knew Junior Agents Huntington and Dubois despised each other, so he assigned them to work the overnight shift guarding the *Elizabeth* in an act of vindictiveness. Fortunately for them, Ashford was an idiot.

Bailey Huntington enticed her lover with her nakedness while he dressed. "Jacq, you were fantastic as usual, but tomorrow, let's try to sneak up to one of the bedrooms. We deserve something softer than these old packing blankets."

"Oui Ma chérie, but if the logs show our transponders entering the same bedroom, Ashford and Keller would know something is up. Keller wouldn't care, but Ashford would transfer one of us," Dubois said. He stroked her soft hair while reconsidering getting dressed.

"Don't be so sure. If Keller knew we were screwing on duty, he might shoot us for dereliction of duty. Part of what makes this so exciting." Huntington picked up her pants. The rest of her uniform was scattered around the cargo bay floor. Her games of chase and strip aroused them both. Almost as fun as pretending they hated each other to the rest of the team.

The clatter of heels on the metal deck echoed in the cargo bay. "I hope this excited you enough because it will be the last time," said an Australian-accented woman with an ice-cold and razor-sharp voice. Dubois and Huntington's heads whipped around in unison, their eyes widening at the sight of four silhouettes emerging from the shadows, led by a woman whose authority was unmistakable.

"Who are you?" Dubois said as the naked Huntington jumped behind a crate to put on the pants she picked up. The sudden appearance slashed away any remaining passion and replaced it with shock.

"Charlotte Kingsley, Special Prosecutor Intrasolar Court of Justice, here inspecting the evidence gathered for this case. I find you two rooting around all over it. Get over here, both of you, now!" The woman appeared flawless in a white, high-necked button-up blouse, black bolero coat, and pencil skirt. Her blonde hair was in a perfect bun.

The man beside her contrasted with an ill-fitting, wrinkled suit hanging loose on his frame. His crooked tie, askew and frayed, desperately needed replacement. Dark circles under his eye told a tale of sleep deprivation stemming from stress or overwork. Two other people stood nearby wearing evidence tech jumpsuits.

Huntington poked her head from behind a crate and said, "I don't know where my shirt is, ma'am."

"Do you think I care? I've seen tits before, but I haven't seen two idiots trying to destroy my high-profile case. Williams, give her your jacket."

The man took off his blazer and handed it to Baily Huntington. Bailey's cheeks flushed as she accepted the blazer from the man's outstretched hand. He gentlemanly looked away, though Bailey was confident he had already gotten a complete view.

"I'm Charlie. Just do as she says and keep out of the way. If she gets what she wants, she will forget you exist by morning," He whispered, leading the semi-dressed woman in front of Kingsley.

Prosecutor Kingsley reached into a hidden pocket, and a pair of ultra-modern pince-nez glasses popped out. These armless spectacles were a high-tech 22nd-century version of a 19th-century classic. The eyewear hovered unaided on the tip of her nose. Pressing a button on her cuff computer caused green translucent writing to appear on the smart lenses as they synced together. Bailey assumed that the data she pulled up was their personnel data.

"Give me your names, ranks, and what your team has done here. Maybe I can salvage what you bumbling fools have done. Williams, take this down for the report. You first." She pointed at Dubois.

Her words were a calculated barrage, leaving little room for doubt or argument. Dubois's eyes darted to Huntington, begging to be saved, but Kingsley's imposing stare smothered any reprieve.

"Junior Agent Jacques Dubois. Ma'am, you should wait and talk to Senior Agent Ashford or Inquisitor Keller. It's two in the morning, and we are junior." Fear and worry clouded his eyes as his hands shook with uncertainty.

"I just arrived. It's noon for me. I stay in the Sydney time zone when traveling off-world. Even your senior agents answer to someone, and right now, that someone is me. The ICJ operates on a level that does not bow to Coalition Security. Every second we waste could compromise the integrity of this case. We will work now, so shut up, Dubois." She pointed at Huntington. "You...talk."

Only a fool or someone powerful didn't switch to Geneva standard time off-world, and Bailey didn't think this Solar System Court counsel was a fool.

"Junior Agent Bailey Huntington. Our Coalition Security team took over this crime scene from the Customs and Patrol Service yesterday. We transferred all evidence into our control with a proper chain of custody. Agent

Ashford assigned Agent Dubois and me to guard the ship on the overnight shift." She tried to project confidence, but her voice cracked and faltered as she stammered out her statement.

"It sounds like you had a long day. I guess I am lucky you were screwing on the job, not sleeping on it. Where were you, and what were you doing before that? The CS leadership has neglected to keep me in the loop. Tell me what you know, and none of your team will end up in front of a committee at The Hague," Kingsley said.

"We arrived at Europa station shortly after the attack on this ship. Before that, we were at Ganymede station. Inquisitor Keller had been talking to Lead Administrator Hübner, and the administrator accompanied us to Europa. Before Ganymede, we were on Earth. Keller investigated the murder of Roger McCord, and we hunted his daughter, Megan. The inquisitor interrogated the staff but didn't find Megan. I don't know what Keller's theory was. Some of us think the daughter and her new boyfriend killed her father together for the inheritance." Bailey rambled on her story, hoping to distract the intense prosecutor.

"It is not your place to put forward unfounded theories." Kingsley's words were even more biting than before. "I will review the reports and see if we need to revisit that. Now, you will give us all of your codes. We will begin by moving the evidence off for transport to Earth. This is first." She pointed toward the white module in the center of the cargo bay.

"Why do you want —"

Charlie Williams interrupted her. "Shut up. Her attention is gone. Keep her mind off you, and I will make sure you don't end up in the report, or at least your late-night activities don't show up there. Transfer the security codes, don't call your boss, and stay out of our way."

"Before anything gets moved out, we should call our supervisor," Huntington said.

"I don't think either of us wants to explain why you are wearing only pants and my jacket. Just roll with it. By morning, all of your boss's headaches will be Prosecutor Kingsley's. This is what she does, and she does it well. I'm sure the Coalition has better things for you to do than sitting on a bunch of evidence boxes."

Huntington and Dubois glanced at each other and could not come up with an argument. Dubois sent over the codes while Huntington searched for the rest of her clothes.

"Thank you. Silva, prep that module to move." Williams pointed to the male crime scene technician. To the female tech, he said, "Santos, come with me. We have some specific items to pack up first."

33

Donuts and Coffee

August 17, 2155—Europa Station—Warehouse

While others worked, a bored Adrian explored the warehouse Amanda acquired for them. External doors allowed them to hide *Castor* and *Pollux* from prying eyes. Rafael helped David with his old ship module, parked between the runabouts. The two arguing over little details pushed Adrian out of the area.

An inner section served as living quarters and a work area. Megan and Carolina stood at a table with equipment taken from her trunk of archaeology tools. Megan's hair was still the blonde of Charlotte Kingsley, but she had changed into comfortable shorts, a T-shirt, and bare feet. The armless pince-nez glasses still hovered at the end of Megan's nose. Hoping to find a clue for detecting the cracked shell, she used the glasses to interface with her stored data.

"Megan, I need to ask. The wire-rim glasses you normally wear look classy, but these smart glasses seem much more useful for your work. I can understand not wearing the smart goggles you have with your space suit, but why not wear the pince-nez when working?"

Megan tilted her head as she looked at him. "What are you talking about? Oh, I understand."

Adrian watched as Megan's fingers danced over her pince-nez, prompting a shimmer that rippled through her glasses. Ear arms stretched out from the corners as the frames morphed them into the familiar wire rims.

"The simple answer to your question is they have always been the same glasses." The broad smile on her face showed her amusement at stunning Adrian.

"Programmable smart metal. We have a tiny amount on the *Elizabeth* in the fusion reactor, which is less mass than in those glasses. How much did those cost?" Adrian asked before he could think if it might be a rude question.

Megan named a number with the breezy indifference of stating the cost of her morning coffee.

Adrian's face lost all color, leaving him looking ghostly pale. "Oh my god, Megan, that's more than my parents paid for their house."

Megan flushed with embarrassment.

The door opening interrupted any further thought in that direction. A woman wearing red workout gear came in carrying a flat rectangular box and a big thermal container. Her black hair was still damp from a recent shower. "Hello everyone."

Adrian said, "I'm sorry, miss, you must have the wrong place. This is a private area."

She gave him a perplexed look. "Oh, I forgot you haven't seen me yet. I'm Cassandra, and I work for Zeus. His organization rented the place, so it is *our* private area. You're welcome to be here, though. Anyway, I came bearing gifts. Donut?"

She smiled and held out the box to him. He opened it and took out a chocolate glaze.

"Mom always used to say, 'beware of Greeks bearing gifts,' but I won't listen any more than she did."

"That should have been my line, but Virgil credited Laocoon," Cassandra said. Adrian laughed, and Megan looked confused at the cryptic reference.

"Adrian, she is the one I told you about at the meeting with Zeus. Cassandra, I'm a little surprised. I pictured you always being in a suit or combat gear like the last time I saw you."

"Only when I'm in the office. Otherwise, I like to be comfortable. Plus, I wasn't about to get dressed up for a meeting at this god-awful hour. My boss owns a casino, so I'm a night girl out of necessity. Which reminds me, time for coffee." Putting down the donut box and thermal carafe, she grabbed a cup and poured herself coffee. She plopped down in a chair and grumbled, "Fetching coffee should be Amanda's job."

"Miss Cassandra, next time, you can get dressed and deliver an invitation." Amanda walked in, followed by Kristina and Phillips, both wearing civilian clothes. Even at that early hour, Amanda wore a sharp business suit.

Adrian put down his donut to hug Kristina and give Phillips a handshake. Adrian and Amanda nodded in recognition to each other.

"Good morning. I'm glad you could make it. Let's put our heads together and come up with a plan."

Cassandra plopped her feet up on a table. "Coffee and donuts first."

Kristina turned her attention to Megan as she twirled her own blonde hair. "Doctor McCord, while I agree blondes have more fun, I think red hair suits you better. You didn't need to change your hair to hide from us."

"Oh, it wasn't to hide from *you*." Megan gave a sly smile, not revealing anything more.

"Megan, will you dye it back or wait till it grows out?" Adrian asked.

Amanda laughed, "Adrian, It's not dye or a wig. I found something special for the doctor's disguise. Why don't you show him, Doctor McCord?"

"Oh, this should be fun." In the faux Australian accent, Megan touched the blonde hair and said, "Charlotte Kingsley."

She shook her head, and her hair transformed into jet black. She switched to an upper-crust British accent. "Lady Felicity Pembroke."

She shook again and became a light brown. In a horrible American accent, she said, "Emily Spencer from Savanna, Georgia."

A last shake of her head and returned to her natural red. She smiled and said, "Megan McCord."

Megan tapped a command on her cuff computer, and a white mesh flickered into appearance over her hair. She plucked it off her head and held it out to Amanda.

"No, Doctor, it's synced to you now. Keep it."

"What the hell is that?" Kristina verbally stated what everyone thought.

"Commander, it is a rave hair shimmer net. Bonds to your hair and can change to any color you want. It is used mostly by young women at night clubs or teens who want to rebel against their parents. The girls at raves like neon, but the teen rebels go with whatever pisses off their parents the most," Amanda said.

"That explains a few things," Adrian asked.

Amanda smirked at Adrian. "Not as much as you might think."

"Getting reacquainted, I see." Everyone turned to see Sarai standing at the door with her arm in a sling.

Megan jumped up to hug Sarai gently. "Sarai, we thought you would be hospitalized for a few more days."

"I had him spring me. It's his clinic." She pointed at Zeus entering behind her.

Zeus walked over to Amanda and glowered at Adrian momentarily but said nothing. Adrian shrugged it off and gave Sarai a hug as well.

Sarai looked at Amanda. "Shall I tell them?"

"Be my guest, Miss Rousseau."

"Kristina, meet Adrian's ex-girlfriend."

Kristina and Megan studied Amanda, but the person of their focus just smiled back politely. Adrian broke the silence before they could say anything.

"My first girlfriend. We met at thirteen. We broke up two years later. Amanda here was the kind of teen rebel she just spoke of. She dated me and dyed her hair blue to piss off her father, whom I never met."

"Oh, dating an Earther annoyed my father, but the hair was not part of it." Amanda reached up and plucked a hair shimmer off her own head. The blonde hair became a brilliant blue. "The blue has always been my natural color. I keep it blonde in my professional capacity."

"I like the blue." That remark came from Carolina. A surprise to everyone.

"Thank you, Miss Carolina."

Adrian refocused the group. "Right now, let's gather everyone and plan my grandmother's rescue."

Everyone found a place to sit in a room a bit too small for the number of people. Adrian sat at one end, with Kristina and Megan on each side. Sarai sat by Megan. David and Phillips were together opposite them.

Zeus sat with Amanda, but Cassandra had staked a claim to the softest chair in the room and wasn't giving it up.

Carolina found a corner as far from everyone and sat on the floor. Her brother stood next to her.

Adrian felt the need to take the lead, yet for once, he found himself at a loss for words. The discomfort of requesting aid from such a varied group weighed on him. "Thank you for coming," he started, the words finally coming to him. "I appreciate your help in planning the rescue of my grandmother. Let's skip introductions. We know who we are, though not all of us may be comfortable with one another." His eyes met Zeus's and Kristina's, acknowledging the opposite sides of the law they lived.

"A few introductions are needed. Who are they, and why are they here?" Zeus said, pointing at Rafael and Carolina.

"I agree. We are going out on a limb here, Adrian. We deserve to know everyone involved. Please introduce us to your friends Adrian," Kristina said.

Before Adrian could speak, Rafael said, "I'm Rafael, and this is my sister, Carolina. We are here to help Adrian and Megan. They have earned our trust, but you haven't. We'll help, but that's all you need to know."

"Ahh, I see Kostas has picked up some strays at Ithaca," Zeus said.

A wave of shock went through those who had visited Ithaca. "You know about Ithaca?"

"Yes, Doctor McCord. Did you think I didn't know what was there when I sent you after Stonington's hideout? I have known about it from the beginning. We diverted shipping containers for their use. If you look at the construction logs near the end of the construction of this station, about half the shipping containers never made it back to Earth. It probably drove some bookkeeper crazy. I make sure the occasional runabout or rockhopper gets 'retired' early and disappears. Stonington's exploration boat you were looking for should have ended up back there, but it got sold instead."

"He does have a heart," Sarai said with a grin, which had been missing lately.

"Only because you gave it to me. Your leaving made me realize what happened to those people on the *Beatrix* was wrong. So, I ensured they had the help to set up the new settlement. Not completely out of the goodness of my heart, Stonington traded me artifacts he found for what was left of *Beatrix*."

Megan touched Sarai's hand and asked, "You knew about *Beatrix*?"

Sarai looked confused. "Yes, but how did you? Oh, I forgot it was an Ettrick ship." She lowered her head and gripped Megan's hand. "I acted as the middleman for an Ettrick official who sold the freighter to a dishonest dealer who gave the company a false value. The official pocketed the extra money for himself, and we also took our cut.

"I had no idea he would abandon the crew on an unfinished station and steal their severance. He left the crew to die. That and my response got me to quit and sign onto the *Elizabeth*." She let go of Megan's hand and stared at her own as if to find something there.

"What is it, Sarai?" Megan asked.

"Until two days ago, that was the last time there was blood on my hands." Sarai's voice was weak and faltering.

Adrian and Phillips touched Kristina's arm as she flinched at this admission.

"Sarai, the crew of the *Beatrix* is alive and living on Ithaca. I hate to admit it, but Zeus saved them," Adrian said.

Sarai looked at Adrian. "Captain, once we rescue Lizzie, I request a leave of absence. I have more amends to give."

"I understand, and we will help in any way we can, but right now, I want to focus on finding Lizzie. Time to brainstorm."

"Doctor, you said you had equipment that could detect the ship and its cracked shell drive," Kristina said.

"Some of the tools in my kit can detect the radiation signature of a Starshell. Most exo-archaeologists have them but rarely have a need to use them. Unfortunately, the range is measured in meters, but Carolina had ideas."

All eyes turned to Carolina, who shrunk behind her brother. She pointed to a palm-sized device with a screen connected to a bowling-sized device on a worktable. She said almost inaudibly, "I interfaced it to a sensor node. It wasn't that hard."

Adrian grabbed the device and carefully brought it to the main table. Looking at it, he disagreed that this would have been easy. He activated the device, and a holographic image of Europa Station and part of the moon appeared.

Phillips examined the data. A bright glow was visible in the center of the station. Several tiny specks appeared on the scan nearby. "That glow in the center must be the station's Starshell. The fact we are getting a good chuck of Europa on here tells me we have about a 20,000 km range. What I don't understand is these little dots on the scope near the Starshell?"

"Those are artifacts close enough to the Starshell to be powered up. Either acting as converters and regulators for the energy or someone near there has an artifact souvenir," Megan's roots showed again that only the ultra-rich or powerful had artifacts as souvenirs.

"What's this?" Adrian pointed at another glow inside the Europa image, this dimmer than the station Starshell. "Could they be hiding right here?"

A murmur rose from the room as everyone examined the image. Phillips said, "Not unless they could fly through 20km of ice and 100km of water. That's at the bottom of the inner ocean."

The icy moon Europa was one of the few locations off Earth where liquid water was known to exist. No one had found a practical and safe way of getting through the ice except by small boreholes.

Megan compared the data to what he had stored on her computer. "It's a powered-down Starshell. No one has ever detected one farther than 100 meters. Carolina just invented a giant leap forward in artifact hunting. This one is 18,000 km away but might as well be a million under that ice. Maybe they will name this new discovery after you, Carolina." That didn't help the shy girl's nerves.

"This Starshell won't help us, but it proves a range of 20k km. Still, on a stellar scale, we must be almost right on top of this." Adrian brought up an image of the strange ship. "Any ideas on how to narrow it down?"

"That's what it looks like?" David asked. He stood and went into the shuttle bay area. He came back a minute later with a tablet computer. A video feed from Pollux's computer appeared. The same sleek-looking ship appeared. A yellowish moon appeared in the background, Jupiter's volcanic moon Io. "I saw this on our trip to Io. I thought it was some yacht belonging to someone with more money than sense. Io must be the base."

"It's not a guarantee, but I will make Io the first stop on our patrol. Assuming we can take your detector with us," Kristina said. Adrian and Megan both nodded.

"I think I can narrow it down more. David noticed the ship on our trip, but I saw a shuttle hauling shipping containers to the surface. There should be no reason with the construction of the Io station almost complete." She pulled up other footage David had downloaded from Pollux and identified a location on the surface. "Start looking here."

"Thank you, but then what? Unless we get visual confirmation of the attacking ship, I have no probable cause. Keller ordered me to stay away from the investigation, so I can't hunt it officially."

"My concern is stopping the wrecking ball, that is Bianca, operating in my area, and you want to rescue your grandmother," Zeus said. "I have a plan to do it unofficially."

He explained his plan and said, "You will need transportation that is not connected to me."

"I guess this is as good a time as any to show you all our new transportation," David said.

A puzzled frown settled on Kristina's face. "What transportation? *Elizabeth* is damaged, and I can't take civilians on *Zeta Sierra*."

"Follow me." David got up and entered the shuttle bay section, and the rest of the group followed.

Inside, they saw the rounded cone module he had picked up at the Callisto junkyard. *Castor* and *Pollux* were attached to each side. The four combined engines pointed in one direction, making the joined ship appear fast and maneuverable. The center module should hold a small team with ease.

"I present to you, *Gemini*."

34

Fractures

August 17, 2155—Europa station—Street side café

Megan and Adrian walked hand in hand down a broad corridor of Europa station that served as one of the principal streets. The arched ceiling displayed a fake sky with wispy clouds and a warm sun. Specialty fans blew a comforting breeze on the pedestrians strolling on the avenue. The design evoked images of an old-world seaside town.

Adrian guided Megan to a seat at a popular café. The scent of freshly baked pastries wafted from the kitchen. A subtle glow radiated from Adrian as he regarded his stunning companion.

"Perfect, Adrian. What a wonderful spot for lunch," Megan said as she lounged in a chair and gazed into the pseudo-sky.

"We shouldn't be out in public like this. You still have a warrant out for you,"

"Relax Adrian. Kristina was supposed to be after me, and you talked her into being on our side. I think we deserve an afternoon together before we go rescue Lizzie." Megan closed her eyes, opened her arms wide, and took a deep breath.

"I guess, but I'm just concerned that you are attracting attention to yourself. Someone might spot you."

"Don't you think I look beautiful? The only one I want to be attracted to my attention is you." She smiled and caressed his arm across the table.

"Ahh, umm, yes, of course. You're stunning today." Adrian avoided looking into her eyes or any other eye-catching features. He called a waiter to take their order in a nervous attempt at distraction.

"Megan, this crazy plan won't work. I can't risk my grandmother's life on a roll of the dice." His hands trembled with worry.

"Oh, don't worry, Adrian. Kristina's searching and will find them. We'll go there and get Lizzie back. With any luck, we can catch that bitch Bianca. Then I can go on my artifact hunt."

Adrian's face sank toward the table, and he lifted his eyes to her. "I'm sorry didn't tell you earlier. I heard from Kristina. Let me play the message for you."

Kristina's face appeared from Adrian's comm unit. "Adrian, we searched but found no sign of the ship. I stretched my orders as much as possible and must move on to Ganymede with my patrol. If you receive any new information, reach out. I hope we can see each other again soon."

"It's over, Megan. We are back to square one. The only option is to give Bianca what she wants." He placed his hand on hers, but she jerked it away.

"What are you talking about? Give up the location? Do you know how important this is? These people would warp this knowledge to their own ends. No matter what, we can't let them have it."

"It's my grandmother! What do you want from me? I'll do anything for your help, absolutely anything!"

"Oh, now you will. I've been trying to get you into bed since we first met, but you had your eye on that commoner CPS agent. You could have had me. Now, when you want something from me, you're willing to offer yourself up to me. I won't sell what's mine. You're not that desirable, Kostas." She stood, tossed a glass of water in Adrian's face, and stormed away.

A Spybot the size of a small bird caught everything on camera.

35

Taunts

August 18, 2155—Unknown location

"This is hilarious. Come over and watch it with me," Bianca reclined in a soft chair and restarted the video their contact had sent. With a mischievous grin, she flung an empty cup at Sergio, causing him to jump in surprise and lose his place in the book.

"The spectacle lost its charm after the second viewing, Bianca. Must we really endure it again?" he sighed with aggravation when he heard Megan McCords's voice again. "Obviously, at least once more."

"Sergio, this is fun. Look what she did to Kostas."

"He has my sympathies." Sergio's eyes returned to the book. "He attempted to play hard to get her all worked up and then set the hook. The poor fool could have leeched off her fortune for the rest of his life. At least I didn't get a drink thrown in my face."

"It's all about the timing. Kostas's timing sucked, and yours wasn't much better."

"If you hadn't dawdled at the McCord estate, I would've been consoling her at her father's funeral. We would have had the site information and played the long game to steal her inheritance."

"Don't turn this around on me. That's the first woman you couldn't lure into bed right away. And do you think you could've played the gentle lover long enough to work on the inheritance? I know what you really like." Her face twisted in disgust as she spoke.

"I can always be a gentleman when it matters. Then we would've gotten everything."

"It doesn't matter that's in the past. Now we have a new opportunity. She was stupid and got rid of her protector. Hiding is not a strong suit for our red-haired prey. I sent instructions to find out where she is staying, and we can snatch her up. After we get all the information we need from her this time, I won't mind if you play your games with her."

She stared at the image of Adrian on the screen. "I wonder if this guy lives up to the hype. I think I will keep the old lady alive long enough to demand a good screwing out of him. In the end, the results will be the same, but my way, he will go out with a smile." She took out a knife to admire it.

"Sorellina, I don't want to know about your love life."

"What's love got to do with sex? You're the only being in the universe I feel any love for. Love is for fools."

Sergio's comm-pad chimed. "We got a return message on the same route through Zeus of your ultimatum to Kostas."

Bianca's smile became even perkier. "Wonderful, Captain Kostas is calling to beg."

"I don't think so." He swiped the message to the screen. Zeus and Megan McCord appeared together. Their eyes held a firm resolve. They sat in a conference room with wall art showing different Greek myths. They must have been in one of Zeus' facilities as he favors the style.

"We are here to make a deal. Doctor McCord decided I was a much better partner than the Captain of the *Elizabeth*. He has nothing to offer and asks her to risk everything to rescue Elizabeth Borden. Being an intelligent woman, she came to me. Doctor, please begin with your request," Zeus said with none of the usual pleasantries he liked.

"You won, *girlfriend*. I can't be on the run like this forever, and I want my life back. We cracked the code and have the location of the correct asteroid. I will trade this information on a few conditions. Send information to the Scottish police clearing my name. I already promised Zeus a hefty fee to broker this, and though I hate to do it, I will offer you a similar amount." Her eyes dripped with hate and venom to make the offer.

"Second. I want to be on the team to enter this site, the first one inside. If I must work with your organization's people, I'll do it. When they make the discovery public, I insist my name be at the top. I deserve to start my career at the top. People will celebrate my name for generations."

"Those seem reasonable conditions, but as the broker for the deal, I have some as well," Zeus said. "First, I get the pick of any ten artifacts recovered outside of Starshells. Second, any artifact sales should be handled by my organization as the clearing house."

Zeus leaned into the camera. "Third, I want Elizabeth Borden. She has value to me as a bargaining tool. After we have an agreement, bring her to me alive." Megan's lips curled slightly, her gaze cold, but she remained silent at his words.

"You have twelve hours to meet us in the casino still under construction at the Io station. If you try something this time, I won't have to worry about cleaning your blood off the furniture." He reached to disconnect the recording when Megan stopped him.

"One more thing," Megan said. "I want a shot at you. You killed my father, and I want a chance to fight you. No knives and no guns. I know I wouldn't win, but I can't just let you walk away. Fight me, Bianca. An old-fashioned, unladylike fistfight. Do you dare without your knives?" Megan then disconnected the recording.

Bianca clapped. "The stupid bitch wants a schoolyard catfight? This will be so much fun."

She jumped from her chair and went to the door. "Let's go show these videos to the old woman. Show her how much of a failure her grandson is."

Bianca entered Lizzie's room unannounced and jumped on the bed. The young blonde woman stretched out, placing her head on Lizzie's pillow. She grinned and asked, "Enjoying your stay, Lizzie? Is there anything I can get for you? More pillows and blankets? Knitting needles and yarn?"

"I'd like my pistol back." Lizzie motioned from a chair near the door to the laser pistol holstered on Sergio's hip.

Sergio smirked and patted the weapon. "Sorry, my dear, it's mine now. I love the craftsmanship. A stellar gift, grazie. Why are you so close to the door? Planning on making a run for it?"

"Don't worry, Sergio. Lizzie likes us too much to run away."

"No, I won't run. When the server bot outside brought my food, I noticed it was equipped with a stunner. I might get three meters. What do you want?"

"Oh, I want to show a video of your grandson." Lizzie's body tensed, her spine straightening and her eyes widening. Bianca waved her hand, dismissing Lizzie's concern. "Don't worry, only his pride is hurt."

The video of Adrian and Megan at the café appeared on the wall screen. Lizzie relaxed when she saw Megan and Adrian were uninjured but flinched again when Megan bolted away.

"Well, the good news is they were planning to rescue you, but I think the plan just fell through. Poor Adrian seems to have lost all the women in his life. You're here. His valiant CPS commander sailed to Ganymede, and the poor little rich girl would rather walk away than bed him. Sorry, but no one is coming for you."

Lizzie buried her face in her hands and whimpered for a moment. She then pushed herself up, went to the wall screen, and touched the frozen image of Adrian drenched in water.

"This movie comes with bonus material." Bianca pressed a button on a small handheld remote holding the videos and played the second one.

Lizzie remained close to the screen as she watched Megan's betrayal and Zeus' wrath. She became weak in the knees, and Sergio caught her before she fell and helped her to the chair. Lizzie held her face and sobbed. "Please don't make me watch it anymore. Please, anything but that."

Bianca set the remote to loop the videos and activated and locked it so it could not be turned off without a code. She left the room and felt a deep sense of contentment settle within her.

When the door closed, Lizzie looked in her fist. She didn't dare lift the pistol but could snatch the spare power cell snapped into the holster. Sergio probably didn't even know it was there.

She looked at the video playing in a loop and thought, *Oh please, don't throw me in the briar patch. Anything but that.*

She examined the locked remote and laughed. *I got past parental control when I was five. They think this will stop me. Now, to figure out the hidden message.*

36
Deals with the Devil

August 19, 2155—Io Station

Megan and Zeus walked through the absurdity of an empty and silent casino. No pathways led patrons to slot machines and gaming tables with promises of fortune and the reality of loss.

Instead, it resembled a warehouse with crates of construction supplies lashed to the cold metal floors and harsh work lights attached to the ceiling. Several spots had cables from ceiling to floor or wall to wall with tools attached.

The absence of celebratory ding of slots or click of chips added to the strangeness. Only the clanking sound of Zeus' magnetic boots broke the silence. The lack of gravity added to the abnormality. Still, Megan embraced it to sail across the room with a graceful twist to her flight.

Megan waited for Zeus, who appeared pale from queasiness. They entered at a construction door at the rear of the main casino floor. But they intended to meet Bianca at the central entrance atrium. Megan floated upside down over the entrance arch, waiting for Zeus to complete his slow and steady march.

"No one likes a showoff," Zeus said.

Megan tilted her head. "People keep telling me that, but I refuse to believe it."

They entered the nearly complete circular atrium. Alcoves on the room's perimeter are already displayed with murals.

One showed a man, strongly resembling her companion, embracing a naked woman.

Another held the same man, a cow, and a stern-looking woman.

The story displayed on the walls continued to be told in art as a hundred-eyed giant stood over the cow. A man with winged feet swung a sword at the giant, who became a peacock. Insects chased the heifer as she swam a waterway. Finally, the man transforms the woman into a human form near a river with pyramids.

The myth of Io and the god Zeus.

The floor was less finished. The gravity plates had been laid but were inactive. Boxes of tile were ready to be installed. The work crew was as practical as the people of Ithaca. Instead of scaffolding, tether lines crisscrossed the room. Megan grabbed one high over the floor.

At the center of the room, a pedestal sat empty. Above was a dome that gave a spectacular view of Io, yellow planes of sulfur accented with black and red spots near the many active volcanoes.

"No statue of yourself yet?" Megan asked.

"My sculptor is busy recreating all the statues you destroyed at Callisto."

"I only broke the little Cupid statue. The rest were..." A wave of sadness overcame her as she recalled that Piet's mighty strength pushed over the statues.

Zeus noticed her expression and said, "I didn't know the boy, but wished I could have. Remember the advice I gave him, 'if you're not cheating in life, you're not winning.' You will need it facing Bianca."

A voice came across their earpieces. "Speaking of which, Bianca's shuttle just docked. She's alone and cycling through the airlock, and then I will disable the controls. Her pilot will be locked out."

"Thank you, Sarai. I still wish you had stayed behind," Megan said.

"Don't worry, I'm locked in the security booth and can use my stunner one-handed."

"Yes, but an uninjured person could have locked themselves in the security booth. Maybe Amanda."

"Absolutely not. Amanda stays where it is safe." Once calm and composed, his deep, rumbling voice became thunderous and commanding. The weight behind his tone seemed to channel the deity he named himself after.

That's oddly protective of an assistant, especially when his feelings for Sarai are apparent, Megan thought.

"Too late to argue. Bianca's almost there," Sarai said.

The circular hatch installed in the external arch slid open. The hatch connected to a durable tube running through the airless sections of the station. A feminine figure clad in a pink and white spacesuit drifted through the hatch and grabbed a cable.

The hood helmet collapsed, revealing Bianca's face and platinum locks. She examined the area. "Ciao, Megan. Hardly that hot Milan nightclub, but it will do."

"You look dressed for it. Really? A Pink spacesuit, Bianca?" The curves of Bianca's form-fitting suit left nothing to the imagination. They seemed to be designed for teenage boy's fantasies. No one doubted the outfit was secretly armored.

"What can I say? I'm a girly girl. I bet Zeus likes it. His namesake always had an eye for a pretty lady." Bianca put her hand on her hips to pose, which also highlighted the heavy pistol on her hip. "It's a pity you couldn't use your assets more effectively. Kostas was practically ripe for the taking. I saw your little breakup. It was so much fun to witness."

"Ladies, can we please get down to business?"

"Yes, Bianca, can you provide proof to the authorities I had nothing to do with my father's death? And did you get a promise from your employers that I would be part of the exploration? I want my lifestyle and my career back." Megan gave Bianca a spiteful glare.

"You also said you wanted a fight. You won't have either when I kill you." Bianca returned Megan's glare with a smile, and her tone was sweet as if they were having a friendly lunch.

"A non-lethal fight. I accept you won't pay for your crimes. I just want to hurt you. Lose the gun and the armor, and we can settle things."

"Take this off?" She glided her hands down her suit's curves. "Who says I am wearing anything underneath? Oh! You want naked wrestling. We could sell tickets." Bianca snickered, but this time, a tingle of her evil venom leaked past her girlish giggle.

"Teaching you a lesson will be fun, but my employers insist on business first." Bianca held out an arm, and two holographic images of documents appeared for a few moments, then vanished. "One of those was a dark web contract to retrieve information from Roger McCord by any means necessary. Authorities won't be able to trace either party of the contract, but it will at least show doubt you were involved. The other document is a contract for Doctor Megan McCord to be part of a classified exploration of an Artificer site at a location to be specified later."

Zeus asked, "And my conditions?"

"My employers will use you as the intermediary for any artifacts they choose to sell, but you don't get to pick any. They will gift you ten quality artifacts of their choice. Once we have a deal, I'll put Lizzie in an escape pod for you to pick up whenever you want." While speaking to Zeus, Bianca's childlike tone turned businesslike.

"That is satisfactory. I have people who will retrieve the pod."

Megan's eyes got wide. "You promised Lizzie wouldn't get hurt."

"I gave you my word, and I will keep it. I will reunite Captain Kostas with his engineer when Sarai Rousseau returns to my employment. Quid pro quo. Doctor Borden for Mademoiselle Rousseau." His voice was flat but icy.

"None of that is my concern. We need the decoded image and all available location data of the asteroid," Bianca said.

"A deal is a deal," Megan attached a holoprojector to a tether line. An image of the asteroid Stonington believed was "Hunter's Folly" appeared over the central pedestal. The image then zoomed out until other asteroids appeared, and their labels were visible.

"The triangulation isn't perfect, but we identified several other asteroids Stonington visited. It narrows the site to a few dozen rocks in Jupiter's L5 Trojan asteroids. That is better than searching thousands."

"Not in place yet. Stall for thirty more seconds," Sarai whispered over the comms.

Megan pretended to check something on her wrist computer. "I just installed a dead woman switch on the information. If my heart stops, the information gets deleted. I will release the unlock code after I have bloodied that pretty face you love so much. Then we all get what we want."

Excellent, Megan is learning to play the game. This will be even more fun. Bianca thought as she tried to read her prey's eyes. Megan returned Bianca's stare, but her eyes twitched to look over Bianca's shoulder.

"Bella! How clever. Though I don't think a bloody face is something I want. We all know not everyone is getting what they want. I want to kill you, but I need you for the code. Zeus here wants Rousseau, but the assault bot I have approaching the security booth will make that impossible."

Megan and Zeus froze while attempting to comprehend Bianca's statement. Zeus bolted in the security center's direction.

"Just us girls now. All three of us." Bianca spun, drew her heavy pistol, and fired at Kristina Chen-Ramirez, who approached Bianca from behind.

37

Escaping the Trickster

August 19, 2155—Gemini Vessel–Jupiter's Magnetosphere

The crew of newly combined *Gemini* sailed Jupiter's magnetosphere on extended mag vanes radiating from *Gemini* like a porcupine, allowing them to ride the magnetic field like a windsurfer across the waves. Thin hoops formed double loops stretching out from the nose of the vessel in a spinning coil sphere. In the center of the sphere was a soft blue glow.

Today, David was in the pilot seat, and Adrian served as the navigator. It only made sense as the mag vanes were derived from solar and magnetic sail technology, and David was the expert. Adrian hadn't seen David this happy in a long time.

The double loops of the plasma magnet coil in front of them were an unfamiliar experience for Adrian. Adrian pointed through the top viewport. "I'm surprised that still works."

"This is all old, proven technology. The plasma magnet was the first 'high speed' system to Jupiter. The trip took three weeks compared to a week we do now, but a lot better than years with chemical rockets. It's kind of sad these got thrown away when we derived modern plasma thrusters."

"The advantage for us is no one will see us coming. No plasma thrust to give us away. But will anyone see that?" Adrian asked, referring to the plasma torus inside the coils.

"Not against the clutter of Jupiter's magnetosphere and Io plowing through it. There is a reason Io was the last to have a station built. Electromagnetically, this is a pretty noisy environment. Plus, no one will watch us come from above." When they left almost twenty-four hours ago, they swung around the poles of Jupiter, riding its magnetic field. They descended into Io's north pole.

David focused on flying, and Adrian checked the rest of his team. They occupied "the kiss," the rounded cone-shaped central module of *Gemini* resembling a white Hershey Kiss. Measuring twenty meters wide and ten meters in height, it offered a spacious environment compared to the *Castor,* but with seven people and supplies, it felt crowded.

The top-level cockpit was just large enough for Adrian and David. Ironically, it is similar in size to the early NASA Gemini capsules.

The second level contained a small supply area and the engineering equipment required to control the plasma magnet and mag vanes. The connecting ports to Castor and Pollux occupied opposite walls.

Adrian found Rafael and Carolina there, keeping their distance from all but Adrian. Carolina examined the equipment while Rafael napped. *Should I have brought them? Rafael has street smarts but no formal combat training. Carolina could be a liability in a fight, but we needed her technical skills.*

The bottom level was the living area containing bunks, a galley, and an eating/relaxation area. The three remaining team members were there.

Donald Phillips requested "leave" when he heard their plan. As *Zeta Sierra* was on a routine patrol, Kristina had no reason to deny his request.

Alice Rogers sat with him at the table. They released her from the station hospital after her point-blank neuro-stunner to the head on *Elizabeth*. While technically on medical leave, she had reviewed her own body cam footage that had remained recording after Sergio knocked her out. She wanted payback for what Sergio had planned.

The last member of the team was the enigmatic Cassandra. She came along because "standing in the back of Zeus' office every night bored her." Adrian found her in blue and white polka dot pajamas and eating actual Hersey Kisses in her bunk.

"Where did you get those?" Adrian asked.

"I asked Amanda to find some. She is quite good at her job, but if you tell her I said that, I will kill you." With a smile, she extended her hand, offering the bag to him, but the sincerity of the threat rang true.

He took some candies and said, "Your secret's safe with me."

Adrian tilted his head and wondered how she kept an athletic figure while eating sweets frequently. As if reading his mind, she said, "Captain Kostas, you already have too many women in your life for me to answer that question with proper satisfaction."

"Good point. Meet us in the common area in ten minutes for a final overview of the plan."

Cassandra arrived last, except for David, who was still in the cockpit. Gone was the casual and colorful woman Adrian had met, replaced by the serious and stern woman Megan had described. She wore black commando armor and carried a massive drum-fed combat shotgun.

Everyone else had already been dressed for the mission. Phillips and Rogers in standard CPS gear with the logos removed. Adrian, Rafael, and Carolina wore nondescript body armor acquired by Amanda over their space suits.

Adrian brought up an image of the target area. Phillips pointed to a red glow. "We detected the target ship at Khalla Patera, an inactive volcanic mound. We couldn't get good visuals, but the magnetic scans found a large number of objects nearby, and the shipping containers were probably diverted to the surface. Perhaps the construction was in the mountain, or we should have detected power sources for a dome habitat."

"Before you enter, you need to get there," David said. "It's only 200 km from the volcano Loki, which is currently erupting. I can't take *Gemini* anywhere near that eruption plume."

"*Castor* and *Pollux* can still separate. They operate in hostile environments, and we can fly them right through the plume to mask our entry. Will you be okay in orbit alone?"

"Sure, I'll read a book." David's tone was flat and unexcited.

"The video of Lizzie showed at least one wall was rock. She must be in the tunnels. We need to split up. We don't want them escaping on that ship. Carolina, can you disable that ship if you are onboard?"

Her answer came as a look that questioned Adrian's intelligence. Rafael asked, "How do we get aboard?"

"Just like they got onto *Elizabeth*. A back door." Adrian pulled up an image of the mystery ship and zoomed into a rear hatch that must lead to the ending room. "Any suggestions on how to get it open?"

"Explosives," Cassandra said. Adrian assumed she was joking, but her stern look had no humor.

"You brought explosives?"

"Of course. Didn't you?"

Alice Rogers zoomed the holo to a hatch on the ship's stern. "The ship may be new, but the hatch is a standard Starlet Mark Seven. I'd have the thing open in ten seconds."

Adrian arched a skeptical eyebrow. "You can get through a hatches lock code in ten seconds?"

"Alice is our best boarding specialist. Plus, I can neither confirm nor deny that manufacturers provide the UCE with override codes on electronic locks."

"David, remind me to have all the locks on *Elizabeth* replaced with physical locks," Adrian said.

"That's where the explosives come in," Cassandra pantomimed an explosion with her fingers.

Adrian ignored her. "Alice, Rafael, and Carolina secure the ship. Most of it is engine, so there isn't much living space to cover. Phillips, Cassandra, and I search for Lizzie in the tunnels. Let's gear up and get in position. As soon as we see Bianca's shuttle head to the space station, we drop."

They went to the second level and opened the crates "Charlie Williams" and "Tech Santos" recovered from *Elizabeth*. Adrian took out an assault rifle. Rafael and Alice took slug-loaded shotguns. Alice's personal weapons were still on *Zeta Sierra*, so she borrowed from Adrian. Carolina took only her tools.

Phillips carried a state-of-the-art Gauss rifle that made Adrian envious. "Phillips, you pack the strangest things when going on 'vacation.'"

"I told the armorer I planned to hunt." He looked at the contents of Adrian's crates and picked up the plasma grenade launcher. "I'll hang my head in shame that we searched the *Elizabeth* and found none of this."

"Sorry, my grandfather was a bit paranoid."

"Yes, I knew him before you were born. The world of spaceship captains and customs agents isn't huge. I'll tell you some stories one day over a beer."

"If no one wants that, I'll take it." Cassandra plucked the grenade launcher out of Phillips' hand. Both Adrian and Phillips wondered if that was a good thing.

They boarded *Castor* and *Pollux* to wait. A few minutes later, David called and told them the Gulfstellar IX shuttle had taken off. A few minutes later, they launched the run-abouts.

Adrian flew *Castor*, and Rafael piloted *Pollux* a few kilometers behind. As they saw the column of gas eject-ing from the volcano, he questioned the wisdom of flying through the sulfur dioxide cloud emanating from it. The turbulence was as unpredictable as the trickster god the volcano was named after.

Adrian removed his thick spacesuit gloves to better feel the controls. His fingertips were slick with sweat, but feeling the ship's vibrations directly on his skin allowed him to predict dangers and react.

Phillips sat in the navigator seat, calling out shifts in pressure and density of the blue and yellow plume. The boats shook like a pair of maracas, with the passengers acting as pebbles rattling inside. They exited the upper canopy of the 100 km high umbrella-like plume. Leaving the storm of sulfurous dust into the wispy Io atmosphere gave them a few seconds of peace.

"Break right!" Phillips shouted. Directly in front of them rose the dense center pillar of the volcanic plume.

Adrian jerked right, but the port thruster clipped the dense inner core shock zone. It felt like Loki's giant wolf, Fenrir, smacked them with a massive paw. The thruster locked up, and *Castor* tumbled out of control. The view flipped between the blue glow above and the angry red eye of the Loki Patera lava lake nearby. Loki's child Hel beckoned to take them in.

Today's not our Ragnarök, Adrian thought. He spun *Castor's* control module to face away from the remaining thruster. Adrian's hands danced on the control, twirling the adjustable engine on its spherical mount.

They twisted in a helix as they plummeted. He heard Cassandra yelp from the sleeping compartment. Phillips scrambled to return the other thruster to service as Adrian fought inertia.

The little boat returned to stability and stopped just ten kilometers above the surface. The red glow of the lava filled the cockpit.

"It might be a bit late now, but I can turn the other thruster on again," Phillips said.

"Will we need to do anything like that again?" Cassandra's voice came from the sleeping area. For the first time, she sounded rattled.

Adrian looked and saw Pollux circling them. Relief washed over him to know they were ok.

"Hold on one more time. Let's get away from this volcano." Adrian twisted the ship and activated the damaged thruster. They shot off in a level fight again.

They were running behind schedule when they arrived at Khalla Patera. The dust from the eruption 200 km away settled around them, helping to mask their approach. They landed on a small ledge made of black volcanic basalt.

Six figures climbed out of the two boats onto the surface of Io. Stretching before them was a yellow plain of sulfuric sand. Vents spewing noxious gasses dotted the land like toxic versions of the geysers of Yellowstone. Red splotches marred the landscape from fresh ejections of sulfur.

The ridge of Khalla Patera caldera towered above them. Jupiter dominated the sky, appearing forty times larger than Luna viewed from Earth. Below them was the black shape of their enemies' vessel and the entrance to the mystery complex. The spectacle displayed the overwhelming challenge that lay before them.

38

The Lioness, the Fox, and the Honey Badger

August 19, 2155—Io Station

If they had been on Earth, Kristina would be dead.

Bianca's inexperience in microgravity caused her to overcompensate her turn and missed Kristina by a hair. Kristina dove out of the way and saw Bianca's second problem.

The killer hadn't anchored herself, and the powerful handgun sent her spinning. Kristina took the chance to jab at Bianca with a powerful stun rod. The device was designed to send a neuro stun field through armor on contact.

Bianca lacked experience in zero-g but kept her instincts and reaction time. With the grace and speed of a gazelle, she threw herself across the room. Bianca fired blindly in Kristina's direction until she hit a wall with a grunt.

Megan drew her flechette pistol and fired at the moving target. Despite hitting her several times, Bianca's armor protected her.

Kristina threw the stun rod at Bianca and missed. Any hope of capturing Bianca by stunning her was gone. She removed the Gauss rifle attached to the back of her armor. It would finish the job when she got a clear shot, but

Bianca's heavy pistol loaded with armor-piercing rounds could do the same to them.

Bianca hid behind a crate of marble tile destined to be added to the floor. "Word of advice. Don't give a target twelve-hour warning before you set a trap."

Megan joined Kristina, and they took cover behind other crates of tile. They were on opposite sides of the Atrium, as Bianca was. The hologram of the asteroid offered a visual concealment for both sides.

"That didn't work as planned," Megan said.

"No, it didn't. I'm sorry, Doctor, I underestimated her. Stay behind the cover. I will try to flank her." Kristina felt angry at her own hubris. Three against one plus surprise should have made this easy. She ordered Frank Davenport to continue the patrol to shield him and the crew from her unofficial actions.

Megan pulled up the security cameras on her suit and projected them for both to see. Bianca braced herself on the crate for better control when shooting. She learned from her mistake.

"You go out there, and she will kill you. I can be the distraction, and you take her down. She wants me alive."

"She will shoot at the first thing she sees move. Too risky, Doctor."

Five shots rang out as Bianca hit the boxes they hid behind. The tight group of shots showed Bianca was as efficient with a gun as with a knife. Shattered tile pieces billowed out in a chaotic mosaic of destruction.

"Thank you for coming here, Commander. I hoped we would meet one day. You ruined my show with the ferry. I really wanted to see it smack into Europa. I hope you admired our handiwork onboard." Bianca's laugh would now be part of Kristina's nightmares of the horrors on that boat.

"I'm surprised to see you helping my girl Megan. Rich bitches like her can be catty. What did she say to Adrian about you? 'A low-born peasant slut, UCE flunky.' That attitude to our inferiors is what makes Megan and I kindred souls. Even if she doesn't realize it."

"What she said was I'm a 'commoner CPS agent.' Which is technically true. It got you here, didn't it?" Kristina kept her tone level.

"Just give the commander a little shove, Megan. I'll kill her for you, and maybe you can console Adrian on his loss." Maybe it was a good sign Bianca's taunts were getting more juvenile.

Megan turned to Kristina. "I have an idea. I can make the hologram bigger and opaque for at least a few seconds. Bianca won't be able to see us, and we will have a surprise."

"Your pistol can't penetrate through her armor. You would be a defenseless target."

Megan pulled out a small cylinder. "Carolina modified this fire-fighting foam canister. The foam expands out and sticks to everything, smothering a fire. It's now a grenade. I toss it at Bianca, and she will be like a fly stuck in a web. I have three."

"Clever idea. I should have Carolina make some for my team. When did she have time?"

"Carolina barely sleeps. And when she does, she has nightmares. She prefers to work."

Before they could start their plan, Bianca revealed more parts of her plan.

"Well, if you won't come out and let me kill you myself, I guess my friends will need to do it. The attack drone I sent to the security booth is not the only one I have."

Two crates in the main casino floor burst open. A torpedo-shaped drone hovered out of one. Large guns protruded from the nose.

The second drone looked like a metallic hybrid between a spider and a squid. Ten limbs reached out to grab any surface or object to aid in pulling itself along. This one also had a pair of lethal weapons.

"Looks like she is the spider, and we are the flies. New plan. Trigger the hologram and run for the door I came in. Do it now," Kristina said.

Kristina aimed her weapon at the tile crates Bianca hid behind and held the trigger. The Gauss rifle's electromagnetic coils emitted a whirring sound, and the small projectiles cracked as they passed through the sound barrier. The tiny slugs obliterated tiles in a cloud of destruction.

Megan increased the hologram's intensity, and they ran for the concealed employee tunnel Kristina entered from. The debris from the tile added a layer of smokescreen to their escape.

Kristina closed the door to the tunnel behind her but knew it would not hold the drones long. She snatched one of the foam grenades from Megan's belt and threw it at the door. On impact, the foam shot out in all directions. It quickly dried into a sticky semi-viscous state, providing an additional barrier.

"Let's go, Doctor. Time for a new plan."

39

The Tiger and the Bear

August 19, 2155—Io Station

S arai came to instant alert when she heard about the assault bot. She scanned through the cameras near her location. Soon, she saw the new threat coming at her from the opposite direction of her friends.

This bot was an altered cargo mover. The utilitarian bot had two arms that could act as a forklift or grasping claws to pick up freight in multiple scenarios. Tank-like treads kept it magnetically attached to the deck. Her role as cargo master familiarized her with these tools. The exception was the guns mounted on the arms.

Bianca jumped the gun. If she waited, I would never have realized it was there until it fired through the thin door. Sarai thought. *Fortunately, this has a simple solution.*

Sarai walked to the door and pressed the control for the blast door. The release mechanism made a clunking sound, and the gears whirred, but nothing fell into place. Looking up, she saw that the steel panel for the blast door had not yet been installed.

"Merde."

Despite her curse, she had remained calm. Option two stole Carolina's idea for the foam grenades. She stepped to the fire suppression system controls. Targeting the drone's passage, she activated the system and ejected a flame-retardant canister. The cylinder struck the floor before the bot and bounced away, to no effect.

Sarai blinked rapidly at the failure and pressed the button three more times. Again, cartridges were ejected, but no foam was deployed. The assault bot stopped to consider this odd attacker, one tiny benefit of the failed plan.

Investigating the panel revealed the problem. The system installers had loaded the system with test canisters, not live ones. Next to the panel, someone had thoughtfully provided an old-fashioned chemical fire extinguisher as a replacement.

What kind of fool allows oxygen to be added to a station without a working fire suppression system? The renowned efficiency of UCE inspectors.

The robot's minuscule AI brain decided what to do. It unleashed a barrage of bullets on the "attacking" port of the fire suppression system. Once it determined no more pellets would be shot at it, the machine continued its route.

This time, Sarai's heart beat faster, unsure of the best action. Zeus burst into the room, his ragged breaths breaking the silence.

"Oh good, someone with two working arms." She grabbed the fire extinguisher, shoved it in his arms, and then grabbed his extravagant, expensive laser pistol. "Toss this down the corridor. Even with no gravity, it's too awkward with one hand."

Zeus knew and trusted Sarai well enough not to hesitate. He tossed the canister down the center of the hall. With precision, she aimed the laser pistol and fired a slicing shot. The high-pressure fire extinguisher split open, and white chemical powder filled the path.

"That won't stop it, but it will mask our escape. Let's go."

"Why not just shoot it? That laser will penetrate its armor."

Sarai held the pistol out to him, grip first. "If you think you can hit its control module before those machine guns tear you apart, be my guest. I'm leaving." Zeus took the gun but nodded in agreement.

Sarai went to the shaft that would eventually hold the elevator to the executive levels. Neither the doors nor the lift had been installed, but the way up was there.

Sarai glanced at the monitors one last time. She saw, with relief, Megan and Kristina escaping down a maintenance hall. She looked back and said, "Race you."

40

The Ionian Search begins

August 19, 2155—Io Surface

Adrian, Phillips, and Cassandra looked across a hangar created from a natural cavern. They entered the complex through a small personnel lock next to the hangar doors. Several cleaning bots removed yellow dust clinging to the surfaces, showing the doors had recently opened. A personnel transport like the bus Adrian used at Ithaca was on one side and a space on the other.

Phillips looked around the cavern. "If the rest of this place is on the same scale, searching for Lizzie will take a long time."

"Good thing we have someone on the inside."

"Someone on the inside? Who?"

"Lizzie." Adrian entered the hangers control booth and sat in front of a terminal, locked with facial and biometric scanners.

"You're not getting in. It's locked," Phillips said. Cassandra kept guard at the door, her shotgun trained on the bots, and watched the other doors.

"The fools locked Lizzie in a room with a display screen and cameras and let her have a reading tablet. She was probably working on a way to get into their systems the moment she arrived."

He put his finger on a scanner that read his skin cells for a DNA match. The light turned green.

"That's impossible. How could it have your exact DNA?"

"It doesn't, at least not my exact DNA. These detectors are not scientifically precise. It just needs to be within a margin of error. She expanded the margin and added in her own DNA. So, my mother, sister, or myself could have passed this test."

"You still need to pass the facial recognition. It's two-factor."

Adrian leaned in front of the camera, which also turned green, and the terminal came to life. "One of the actual reasons we did that little show at the café was to give Lizzie my image to insert in the system. We knew Bianca couldn't resist showing it."

"How did you know she would be able to do this? That was a big gamble."

"I wasn't sure. Lizzie and my grandfather invented paranoid plans all the time. They'd talk about the options over dinner. As little kids, my sister and I were told we might have to rescue Princess Lizzie from the tower."

"What if your grandfather was kidnapped? I assume he didn't have the same skills to do that from the inside." Cassandra asked.

"Either grandma would hack their system, and he would be out in an hour, or the plasma grenade launcher on your back would start blasting down walls. They had contingencies."

Adrian pulled up a schematic of the multi-layered three-part complex, more prominent than they had expected. An icon showed a cartoon princess in a room at the top of a section complex. A pair of dragon icons were displayed in rooms on the next level below.

"I guess they did put Princess Lizzie in the tower. Let's go."

The three of them left the room and didn't notice a new icon appear. A green arrow pointed to a room on the bottom level. A picture emerged of several people in construction workers' coveralls locked in a room.

Lizzie bypassed firewalls and connected her room wall display to the base computer. Sergio ordered essential items to be moved onto the ship, and the workers building the base were imprisoned. They planned on leaving Io soon. The plans for Lizzie were unclear. He might take her, kill her, or abandon her. Lizzie didn't want to find out which. She discovered something Sergio planned and couldn't allow it to happen. The original plan to wait for Adrian wouldn't work.

It's time to go. Lizzie added the arrow on the computer telling Adrian to go to the prisoners, not her.

Lizzie pried open the door control panel. She attached a jerry-rigged cable from the modified e-reader they thought was harmless in her hands. With a few buttons pressed, the door opened.

The bot, which served as her butler and guard, rolled into the room. The tall meter-long box on wheels rolled into the room. Typically, it only entered when bringing in her meals, but the tiny AI brain got curious.

"Hiya Jeeves. How are you doing today? I'd like to complain to the chef about the food. Can you take me to him?" The robot reacted with strange lights that flickered and pulsated. "No? Well, you might as well take my tray from this morning."

A slot opened in the side, and she slid in her tray. In the water cup was the power pack she took off Sergio. Moments later, the stored energy was released with a muffled burp. A small puff of blue smoke released from the top, and the bot's lights went out. The stench of fried circuits filled the room. Lizzie felt relieved, knowing this was the last time she would be there.

A few meters down the hall, she found a shaft used by the bots. Dubbed dumbwaiters, they allowed bots to move between levels. They also lacked artificial gravity emitters, causing the gravity in the shaft to be the same as Io, similar to Earth's moon. She did some mental calculations, stepped into the dumbwaiter, grabbed the sides of the shaft, and slid down.

As she had promised, Alice Rogers had no problem getting them into the ship, which they discovered was named *Achilles*.

Carolina immediately felt a comforting familiarity with the multi-level space. The metallic catwalks, sturdy ladders, and winding stairs spanned the area, seamlessly connecting the various equipment and control systems.

A curved rear wall provided a protective barrier, shielding engineering from the cracked Starshell enclosed within the rear three-quarter sphere. Pipes exited the walls and connected to the heat sinks that formed the wings of the vessel.

"What is that strange smell?" Carolina whispered. Others called the scent a "new ship smell." Every surface was clean and freshly painted, and the equipment was factory-new and shiny.

While Carolina explored engineering, Alice tapped into the shipboard sensors. Fortunately, like the hatch, this system was also a standard off-the-shelf ship system for which she had override codes.

"I'm detecting a pilot in the cockpit. I'm going up to secure it and subdue him. Do you want to come with me?"

Rafael looked at Carolina, who scampered up a ladder to look at more equipment. "I'll be fine by myself. Just make sure the pilot can't get in here. I have a lot to do, and this stuff is cool."

Rafael frowned with concern until Carolina disappeared into the upper levels. "Just stay out of sight, Carolina. We will be back soon."

Alice and Rafael exited the main engineering hatch and locked it behind them. Little did they know there was another hatch between engineering and the storage hold.

The bots Lizzie had spotted brought luggage and supplies into the hold. Only moments behind, Sergio, a human guard, and a woman in coveralls approached through the tube connecting the base and the cargo area. A small armed hover drone flew behind them. Sergio held her hand gently but resolutely as he escorted her through the threshold.

"Erin, your presence here honors me. Your team's skill in preparing the base has been exemplary. As their leader, I consider this excursion around Jupiter a token of my personal appreciation. And with Bianca's fortuitous delay," his lips curled into a knowing smile, "we find ourselves with a surplus of time."

Her gaze lingered on the crisp lines of his Italian silk suit, a fleeting distraction before she regained her composure. "And my team?"

"They will receive their due, rest assured. Monetary tokens, however, can only convey so much. But you, Erin, you deserve an experience beyond mere figures. Let us seize the day in solitude." His eyes locked with hers as his hand grazed her cheek. "Imagine us, dining beneath the cosmos' canvas, Jupiter's grandeur lending its light to the luster of your eyes."

Sergio's complement washed over her, causing her cheeks to flush a delicate shade of pink. The corners of her lips curled upward into a radiant smile, illuminating her face with pure joy. Her eyes sparkled with excitement, and she said, "I can't wait, Sergio, it sounds lovely."

A buzzing sound came from the direction of the bridge, followed by a dull thud.

"A stunner." Sergio snapped his fingers. The guard stepped to a terminal to check what had happened.

"Sir, the engine room external hatch opened a few minutes ago. The pilot isn't responding. We must have intruders."

"Get up to the cockpit. I'll check engineering. Call up an assault bot to assist."

With a worried expression etched on her face, the construction supervisor took a few steps back. "I think I need to get back to my crew."

Sergio's grip was sudden and unyielding, his fingers pressing into her flesh. Once honeyed, his voice cut through the air like a blade. "You will stay by my side. Time is a luxury we no longer possess, and I have none to spare to fetch you."

41

One by Air

"I hope this is not an omen, Commander," Megan said after she and Kristina reached a dead end. Slot machines in crates and gaming tables stacked to the ceiling blocked the maintenance corridor they had fled down.

"Sorry, Doctor, this route should have taken us near the security station. Can you check the cameras? I'll check in on Sarai." They knew Sarai and Zeus had escaped the assault bot but nothing else.

Megan pulled up the cameras and observed the drones had cut through the sticky mess of the foam. The hover drone drifted down the hall with the spider-like one trailing behind. Bianca didn't show up on the limited cameras.

"The attack bots are on the way, but one at a time. We can't double back, or we'll get caught in the middle of the passageway. Can you take those out fast?" Megan asked, her voice cracking while attempting to maintain a level tone.

Kristina held up her Gauss rifle. "I can take it out, but not fast enough to avoid the guns. If we can buy a few minutes, we can get through that hatch."

Above the stack of gaming tables, a hatch permitted equipment to move between the levels. The space between the equipment and the ceiling was too small for them to fit. Straps secured the crates and tables in place, blocking their escape.

"That flying drone will be here before we can get enough cleared to open it. I might get some of those straps cut. Think we can squeeze behind some of this stuff." Megan pulled a precision vibro-cutter from her utility belt.

"Great idea, Doctor. Start cutting."

Megan sliced several straps, and soon, the two women could pry a gap between a slot machine and a roulette table. They didn't need to fight gravity, but mass and friction were still concerns.

After they were behind cover, they needed to be careful not to push too hard. The stack of boxes had loosened and would not stay together much longer, and they would lose their protection.

Megan projected the security camera videos onto the surface of a blackjack table wrapped in plastic film. The first drone was due in two minutes.

Both women sat in silence, watching their hunter approach.

Sarai reached out over the comms. "We are at the executive level. I was able to patch it into security again. I'll be your eyes. At least for a couple of minutes until our pursuer reaches us," Sarai said over the comms.

"Doctor, when Sarai gives the word, can you push this table?" Kristina braced her weapon against the slot machine. "I just need a clear shot for a moment."

Megan removed the shrink wrap and straps to prepare for her push. To stabilize herself, she clutched the straps on a crate behind her. Megan hovered her feet above the nearby roulette table. She was careful not to touch prematurely.

"Now!" Sarai shouted.

Megan's feet shot out and pushed hard. It took a moment for her to overcome Newton's first law. The roulette table coasted down the hall, tumbling end over end. The wheel separated from the table and spun off at the wall like a frisbee.

Megan saw the stubby, torpedo-like drone come around the curve of the corridor. A red LED illuminated the nose as the guns started tracking on the spinning roulette wheel.

A tremendous racket filled the confined space as four machine guns blasted the wheel into tiny bits.

Kristina shouldered the slot machine aside, causing it to float in front of Megan as cover and give her a clean shot. The drone maneuvered speedily as it changed its targeting.

The combined sound of the whir-crack of the Gauss rifle and thudding booms of the machine guns assaulted Megan's ears even through her helmet. Bullets slammed into the slot machine, protecting Megan.

Kristina walked her projectiles through the floating roulette table into the drone, shredding the flying assault bot. Kristina flew back into other boxes.

Megan rushed over and saw several large dents and cracks in Kristina's body armor. Blood leaked out in small globes. By pushing the slot machine in front of Megan, Kristina had exposed herself to fire.

"Kristina! Talk to me. How bad are you hurt?"

Kristina met Megan's eyes with a grimace of pain. "I'll be fine, Doctor."

"We just fought a killer robot, and you got shot for me. I think we can be on a first-name basis now." Megan gave a soothing smile as she investigated Kristina's injuries.

"Okay, Megan, I can live with that."

"Let's just make sure you do live. We need to check those wounds."

"Not yet. We need to leave. That other drone is coming, and these things learn from the other's mistakes. Sarai, where is it?" Despite her pain, Kristina thought clearly.

"Two minutes at most," Sarai said.

They looked at the hatch and saw enough items had drifted away to give them access. The hatch opened with a simple press. Kristina exited the tunnel, but Megan stayed behind. She bounced between the gaming equipment and gave a firm shove to each. Her experience in microgravity paid off, and several slot machines or gaming tables soon floated down the hall.

Kristina looked back through the hatch. "What are you doing? This one won't fall for the same trick again."

"Exactly. Now, it will expect a trap. It will watch for a woman holding a Gauss rifle behind each object. Now press the hold open button on the control up there."

Kristina did as requested while Megan cut off two screws on the lower control panel. This gave her a gap to pry it loose, reach, and slash any wire she could see. Megan may not have the engineering expertise of Lizzie or Carolina, but she excelled at breaking things.

She passed through the hatch, and Kristina let it close.

"Nice thinking, Megan, that will slow it down. It will have to cut through the hatch or double back around." Kristina wheezed in pain.

"Kristina, I know you would rather hear this from Adrian, but take off your clothes." Megan smiled at Kristina's suppressed reaction. "I need to patch that wound before you collapse."

Kristina removed her helmet and top armor. She pulled up her shirt to allow Megan to see the gash. The bullet didn't penetrate, but a jagged piece of armor cut deep. Megan had a first aid kit in her archaeologist pack and used a spray liquid bandage. Kristina winced from the sting. Megan then jabbed her with a painkiller.

"You could have done that in the reverse order," Kristina said.

"Sorry, I'm not that kind of doctor." They moved away to an emergency staircase heading to an upper level. Kristina tried to pull her armored vest back on as best as possible. It would never function as a space suit again.

"That's a well-equipped first aid kit."

"Exo-Archeologists operate in pretty remote places. We must be prepared. I'm kicking myself for leaving this packed away on the *Elizabeth* for so long."

Kristina gave her a quizzical look. "I don't suppose you want to tell me how you got all this off the ship?"

"No, not really," Megan said before changing the subject. "Thank you, Kristina. You could have been killed protecting me."

"It's my job. I have better armor, and you didn't have any cover after you pushed the table away. Pushing the crate in front of you was always my plan."

"I can see why Adrian loves you."

Kristina jerked her head over. "Loves me? We had fun but were always casual. He was free to see other women. You two were obviously sleeping together when you were at Ithaca."

"Yeah, that's what Adrian said. You were casual and non-exclusive. Well, all we did was sleep. I'll admit I tried for more, but he chose you. The best I got was one kiss. He is head over heels in love with you, and I bet it is the same for you."

Kristina's brows knitted together as she considered Megan's words.

Sarai's voice interrupted the open comm link. "I love you are getting to know each other, and you are figuring out what everyone on both ships has known for months, but Zeus and I are about to have our own problems."

"We are on our way." Kristina and Megan pushed themselves up the center of an emergency stairwell to find Sarai and Zeus.

42

Small Talk with a New Friend

August 19, 2155—Io Surface

Adrian's team found Lizzie's room empty, except for a smoking bot in the doorway. Phillips cleared the room while Cassandra watched the stairs for threats.

Adrian looked for any sign of his grandmother around the bed. "She must have left a clue where she went."

"How about a big arrow pointing to an X on a map?" Phillips said.

"That would be nice."

Phillips pointed to the wall monitor. It showed the same map they looked at on the hangar terminal, except now it showed a location on the bottom level. The image showed construction workers in a room sealed by armed bots on tracks.

"No use in staying here. Let's go back down and see if Lizzie has left us something to do." Adrian turned to step out the door when he heard several shotgun blasts.

Phillips beat him out the door and was nearly hit by a man crashing into the wall. Cassandra walked over to the man, put her boot on his chest, and pointed her gun at his face.

"Talk to us. What were you here to do? What is your boss planning on doing?" Cassandra's unblinking eye glared down the gun barrel at the man. Her tone was without emotion and uncompromising.

Adrian looked near the stairwell and saw the blasted remains of two half-meter-long multi-rotor drones, each armed with a small gun.

The man on the ground glanced at the three of them, eyes wide in shock. "Where did you come from? You're not supposed to be here?"

She pressed the barrel of the gun on his nose. "I don't think you understand who is supposed to be asking the questions."

The distinctive smell of urine filled the air. "I was supposed to get the old lady. Sergio will decide what to do with her after he hears from Bianca. Either she comes with us when we leave or dump her with the workers."

Adrian crouched down and looked at him. "What is this place? Why would anyone build a base on Io?"

"I have no idea. It's Hell outside. I can't wait to get away. Sergio and Bianca showed up one day and took over. I'm just a guard to watch the workers while they finish construction."

"What's the plan for the workers?" Adrian asked.

"Their job is done. They get to go home soon." His tone tried to be brave but revealed uncertainty.

"Can I kill him now?" Cassandra asked. She twitched the shotgun barrel to make sure the man remembered her.

"Only if he keeps lying," Adrian said with a straight face and no hesitation.

"Sergio plans to dump them out on the surface of the moon. I heard them say the workers are a liability. Sergio and Bianca scare the Hell out of me."

"They should scare you. You do realize if the workers are a liability, so are you," Phillips said.

"I know." Tears welled up in the guard's eyes. The look on his face said he would rather have his head blown off than be tossed out onto the surface of Io.

"Captain Kostas, give me the word, and I'll toss him out the front door. We need to know about the rest of his team and any other drones." Cassandra nodded her head at the ruined drones while continuing to stare the guard down.

"You heard the lady. Talk or take a stroll outside." Adrian attempted to keep his words believable. He would never toss the man into the thin, sulfurous Ionian atmosphere.

"Just me and one other guy, plus the *Achilles* pilot. Five or six hover drones like those. There are three larger assault bots. Two guard the prisoners, and one was on standby near the ship. We had three more bots, but Bianca took them for some ambush. Please, please don't put me out there." His voice cracked as he rambled out the information.

Adrian took out a neuro-stunner and zapped the man. Phillips restrained the guard. Cassandra looked disappointed.

"We need to warn Kristina and Megan about the assault bots." Adrian connected his suit comms back to *Castor*. From there, he called David to relay the message.

David came back a few seconds later. "Sorry, Adrian, they are not answering. I'll keep trying."

Adrian slumped against the wall. His jaw tightened, fists clenched as panic and dread spread through his soul.

Phillips saw Adrian's pained look and connected in. "David, send the signal to call for backup."

"They're dead. Bianca trapped them and killed them."

Phillips grabbed Adrian by the shoulders. "Adrian, don't think like that. There are four very capable people up there. Right here, a dozen construction workers are about to be thrown into the hellscape outside. Your grandmother is wandering around this base by herself. Where do you think she will go?"

"She is heading to free those people."

"Okay, so let's help her. We can't help our people on the station, but we can help Lizzie."

Adrian gathered his emotions tight. "You're right. Move out."

As they descended the spiral stairs, Adrian asked, "What was the signal you had David send?"

"Did you really think the crew of the *Zeta Sierra* would sail off to Ganymede station? No, they are sitting nearby and will head back at full speed."

43

Two by Ground

August 19, 2155—Io Station

Sarai and Zeus hoped the assault bot would believe they had left the security office using the door, not the elevator shaft. It had either guessed right or tracked them.

Zeus' office in the new casino neared completion, including active gravity plates, giving them a sense of normalcy. It included a total security monitoring station hidden in a wall and a small weapons stash. Sarai handed Zeus the largest gun she could find and took back the laser pistol.

"This new desk is armored, right? We need to get in position behind it and wait for the drone," Sarai said.

When Zeus didn't respond, Sarai looked from the security monitor to Zeus, who searched through boxes of artwork destined for his walls.

"Dwight, what are you doing?"

"I'm making sure they delivered the correct artwork. I asked you not to call me Dwight."

"I heard your remark about trading Lizzie for me. I'm not a commodity to be traded. That and the fact you don't seem to care a mini tank is coming to kill us has me annoyed enough at you to call you Dwight. Maybe it will get your attention."

"Of course, I simply played up to what Bianca wanted to hear. I want you to come back to work for me because it is the smart thing to do." He put down the art and hoisted up the big gun. "If you want me to look macho with this gun, that's great, but it won't matter with the robot."

"Why not? We have about thirty seconds." Sarai let her calm façade crack. The combat drone was about to enter the passageway leading directly to the executive office.

Zeus walked to the security panel and watched the bot enter the hall. He paused until it reached a specific spot and pressed a button.

Large steel panels dropped on each side of the robot. Each panel had a one-way window to observe the lucky resident of the mantrap.

Zeus stepped outside the office to the secure door. A control panel was next to the window.

"Cassandra's always warning of disaster. This time, I listened to her. From this panel, we can do fun things like pump in knockout gas, turn off the gravity, or pump out the air. None of which will affect our tracked friend. Let's see what happens when it notices us."

He pressed a button, making the one-way glass two-way. The tank-like bot recognized them and immediately opened fire with all four machine guns. Sarai jumped back, but Zeus didn't flinch as the bullets bounced off the ultra-durable bulletproof polycarbonate. They could only hear a dull muffle from the guns. It saw the futility and stopped to consider its next action.

Zeus pointed across the passage as Megan and Kristina appeared through the other door's window. "I see your friends arrived to save the day. Commander, I would like to demonstrate why it would be unwise to visit me uninvited."

He entered another series of commands, and a manipulator's arm lowered from the ceiling behind the bot. A meter-long jet of plasma came from the arm and stabbed into the robot. The arm spun around and sliced the once fearsome machine in half. The arm retracted into the ceiling.

They were all silent for a moment until Kristina spoke. "That was impressive. Open this door, and I will make sure it is completely dead. We still have another drone and Bianca out there."

Zeus shrugged and opened the door at the other end.

Kristina walked to the assault bot, whose top half was loosely connected to the bottom half. She kicked the top, and it fell on the floor. In order to be sure, she fired a shot into each side to eliminate any surprises.

A giant crash came from outside the secure passageway. The spider-squid drone dropped from a vent shaft between Megan and the door. One of its ten tentacles shot into a control panel, and the armored door snapped shut before they could react. Megan was now trapped with a killer robot and a mad woman.

44

The Wrong Rescue

The base was carved inside the mountainside and divided into three distinct sections. The hangar cavern they had entered, a central cavern, and the multi-level "tower" section where they had found Lizzie's cell.

The central cavern, once a natural formation, was a vertical space with stairs carved into the volcanic rock, connecting four different levels. An obsidian pillar rose to the ceiling in the center. The designers installed plenty of lights, dispelling the expected gloom of a cave. However, the faint sulfur remnants lingered in the air, reminiscent of burnt matches.

The team found an observation point of a small balcony on the second level of the cavern and scanned the space to find the makeshift prison.

"The room they are using as a jail is on the far side of the pillar," Adrian said as he referenced the map he downloaded. "There's one of the drones."

A small tank-like object with quad treads and dual independent machine guns in the turret rolled from the side of the pillars. The bot turned around and disappeared behind the pillar.

"Think you can take it out with that?" Adrian asked as he pointed at Phillips' Gauss rifle.

"Yes, but we know there are two of them. Plus, look up."

Four multi-rotor armed drones circled near the top of the cavern, small but dangerous.

"If I fire on the assault bot, those will swoop down on us, and the other bot will come out in full combat mode."

Cassandra examined the room with a set of small binoculars. "Then we need a distraction to divide and conquer. Captain Kostas, have you ever been duck hunting?"

The odd question surprised Adrian. "No. Not many ducks in space."

"Trade me and learn fast." She held out her combat shotgun. "You deal with the little duckies up there. Phillips, take out the bot we can see as soon as it appears, and I will deal with the distraction."

Phillips nodded and rested his rifle on the balcony rail, placing his faith in Cassandra's vague plan. Adrian was confused about the plan's details but traded his assault rifle for her heavy drum-fed weapon. She leaned the gun against a support post.

Cassandra pulled out the grenade launcher and backed up several meters. She aimed at a large box on a far wall while silently counting down. Once she reached her desired point, she released a grenade and ran full speed to the balcony's edge. Dropping the launcher and snatching up the rifle on her way. Several things happened all at once.

The first assault bot came into view as part of its patrol. Phillips squeezed the trigger, and a stream of hypervelocity projectiles split the air with a crack. The robot's turret shredded as the darts passed through the armor. One of the machine guns flew off, and the other dipped to the floor. Smoke trailed from the little tank as it rolled across the floor, wholly lobotomized by Phillips' shots.

When Cassandra reached the balcony rail, her foot landed on the railing, and she vaulted into the cavern. The plasma grenade hit a sturdy power junction box and exploded. The grav plates giving the chamber Earth normal gravity ceased functioning. Ionian natural gravity of 0.18g took over. Cassandra didn't drop instantly but sailed in a gentle arc across the cavern at the base of the obsidian pillar.

Adrian blasted away as the aerial drones dove at Cassandra. His initial fire missed its mark but drew three drones' attention to him. He had little choice but to learn by trial and error to lead the small, agile targets.

He blasted a rotor off one, and it spun out of control. Another took a direct hit and burst apart. The third fired, and a shot rocked into his body armor while others hit the surrounding floor. He didn't have experience duck hunting, but he bet the ducks rarely shot back.

He held down the trigger and swept the sky in full auto mode. When the gun clicked empty, the third drone was slowly drifting bits.

The fourth drone swooped down on Cassandra. Fortunately, her body armor was top of the line as she took several hits. She didn't bother to shoot as it flew by but instead swung the rifle like a baseball bat. A rotor shattered, and the drone crashed into the pillar.

Cassandra landed on the base of the obsidian column and placed an object on its side. She hopped back a few meters and crouched down.

She fired the rifle in short bursts as the second assault bot was in full combat mode. Deflector plates popped out from the side to protect its core from attack. One gun tracked Cassandra while the other fired at the balcony where Adrian and Phillips hid, causing them to duck.

Cassandra pushed herself off in a mighty leap backward in the low gravity. The robot fired but missed low as it miscalculated her trajectory. Before the bot could adjust, the object Cassandra placed at the bottom of the pillar exploded.

The blast flipped the bot on its side. Cracks in the obsidian spread and the whole side of the column buried the bot in a slow-motion, low-gravity avalanche.

The instant he heard the gunfire stop, Philips popped up. The bot was damaged but functional. It tried to rock itself from the pile of volcanic glass, but Phillips finished it with a well-aimed shot.

Cassandra waved the men down. They hopped down in the low gravity but not with the style of Cassandra's stunt.

Cassandra perched herself on the remains of the bot. "I told you explosives would be useful."

"Has anyone told you that you are crazy? You could have been killed," Adrian asked.

"Today is not my day to die. And yes, people have called me crazy many times." They traded weapons back, and when she saw he had used all her ammunition, she tossed her shotgun away. She drew her pistol and said, "If we are ever on Earth together, I am taking you skeet shooting."

They walked to the room holding the construction workers. The door unlocked from the outside easily. Inside, a group of men and women blinked at the light. Their captors held them in total darkness.

"Who are you?" one of them asked.

"We're here to rescue you. Who is in charge?" Adrian asked.

"That guy Sergio left with our boss. He offered to take her on a tour of their fancy ship. Then one of the security guys and the robots pushed us in here. What is going on?"

Phillips filled them in. He looked around and turned to Adrian.

"We got a problem. Lizzie didn't come here. Where is she?"

"Lizzie knows Sergio is a predator. If she found out he took their boss to the ship, that's where she will go." They bolted in the direction of the *Achilles*.

45

Three by Terror

Megan stared in shock at the tentacled terror bot looking down at her. The machine moved closer to her, and two tentacles reached out. Megan's body tensed with fear, but a flicker of rationality remained even in her panic. It hadn't killed her yet, which meant its purpose remained to capture, not murder.

Megan ran as fast as she could. She almost stumbled when she reached the end of the area with functional grav plating but used her training to vault down, pushing off any surface she could. This time, Megan looked less like a graceful flying bird and more like a cheetah running in three dimensions. But she was the prey, not the predator.

The spider-squid terror bot scrambled down the passage, keeping pace behind her on its tentacles, pulling it along. It could have caught her but remained close enough. The blue glow under its dome lit the hall near her.

The elevator shaft Sarai and Zeus used to reach the elevator level lay ahead. Megan launched at it, hoping the lower levels would give her better options.

Just before she reached it, the robot moved faster, and a tentacle shot out in front of the doorway. Electricity arced from the tentacle tip to the door frame. Megan snagged the floor with her magnetized glove to stop her movement.

The nose of the squid-like body hovered over her as Bianca's voice came out of the machine's speakers. "No,

Girlfriend. We have unfinished business. Meet me in the third-level executive lounge."

"Screw you, Bitch." Megan pushed herself away to find an alternative route. If Bianca wanted her at the lounge, it was the last place Megan should go.

"Megan, are you ok? I can't follow. It locked this door tight," Kristina said over the comm.

"I'm trying to get away. It's not attacking but trying to drive me to Bianca. I don't plan on playing nice. Keep an eye on me with the cameras. I have an idea."

"Sarai has you. I will come hunting as soon as we get this door open."

Megan followed the employee access hall that bordered the high-roller casino level and the lounge Bianca waited at. The robot didn't stop her because she traveled in the general direction they wanted her.

She flew into an old-fashioned cashier booth. Metal bars separated the booth from the casino floor and didn't allow escape in that direction. She peered past the cage into the casino, and Bianca floated in the lounge under construction.

"Nice to see you, Bianca," Megan pointed her flechette pistol at Bianca, but the spider-squid blocked her shot. Megan smiled at this expected event.

"Thanks, buddy." Kicking the bot's head with her feet, Megan propelled herself backward. The cash drop chute she landed in led straight to the main vault.

Squeezing through the narrow chute, she felt the walls close around her. The path wasn't comfortable, but no exo-archaeologist could be claustrophobic. She imagined the look on her old nanny's face, who called her chubby, as she dove headfirst down the small shaft.

Behind her, the robot folded its tentacles behind it and squeezed into the shaft like it did the air ducts earlier. Megan grabbed another fire foam grenade and tossed it behind her. The white sticky foam blocked the passage.

Torches flared out from two tentacles as they started cutting a path. This trick would not slow it down as much as the first time, and the AI learned fast. Megan only needed a little time.

Megan reached the bottom and emerged inside a completed vault. The hexagonal room contained several stainless-steel tables for counting money, lockboxes for moving cash up and down the shafts, and several lockers on the wall. As she had expected, they had already installed the vault door, but unfortunately, it was closed.

Megan looked at one of the security cameras. "Zeus, I'm betting you can control access to your money vault from up there. How about opening this door?"

"Certainly, Doctor." The massive door opened, and Megan drifted out.

"You don't seem to be someone who would wait to secure your money. I imagine security protocols against intruders are active."

"Yes, may I ask why?"

The tentacled terror bot burst out of the cash chute at that moment. Its tentacles spread out and rushed toward the door.

Megan ignored the bot as she held her pistol and fired a stream of flechettes. Her target was not the bot but a cluster of sensors on the vaulted ceiling. Moments before the robot exited, security doors snapped shut, severing two tentacles.

"That's why," Megan smiled and waved at one of the vault's exterior cameras.

Zeus huffed. "I could have just activated the door from up here—no need to wreck the sensors. You people are expensive,"

"This was more fun. You can bill me."

"I will."

"Can you patch me into speakers on the casino floor?" Megan asked.

"Yes...you are live," Sarai said.

Megan grabbed one of the floating tentacles. "Bianca, I renamed your friend Stumpy. You're right, we need to finish this, but you must come to me. Meet me in the Aphrodite amphitheater. We can present the first show for the new casino."

46

Engine Room Encounter

August 19, 2155—Io Surface

Carolina heard voices and found a dark corner in the upper levels to observe the engineering entrances.

Sergio pushed Erin through the storage area and the hatch into engineering. The two small drones followed them. He looked around the multilevel space and didn't see or hear anyone.

He radioed the guard. "Engineering is clear. Status at the cockpit?"

"Two intruders locked themselves in. I have it covered and will take them out if they leave. The assault bot will be here soon, and we will cut through the door."

"Good. Kill the intruders quick, but don't damage the cockpit."

Erin's eyes went wide. "Kill them? I won't be part of this." She lunged for the door.

"Silence. I don't have time to play games with you." A punch sent her to the ground with brutal efficiency. "We can play the real games when you wake up."

Carolina tried discreetly to watch from the catwalk above. The sight of the sudden attack caused her to jump back into a metal rail. She ran deeper into the maze of engineering.

Sergio heard the noise in the upper levels that sounded like a yelp and someone running across a catwalk.

He peered into the upper regions to find the intruder. "Drone, seek and destroy mode."

The drone raced upward, searching each level for any signs of a presence. It shrilled an alarm, but a small cylinder flew out of the dark before it could fire its small gun. It hit the drone and exploded into foam. The fire suppressant foam sucked into the rotor fans and hardened into a sticky mass. The drone dropped from the air.

Sergio fired several laser pistol shots in the general direction. But couldn't see what happened in the hidden mass of ladders and platforms.

Carolina shifted her position after she threw the foam grenade. The laser shots didn't hit near her but did damage delicate equipment in the upper engineering levels.

Sergio pointed the pistol at the prone figure at his feet. "Reveal yourself now, or she dies—simple as that. And I'd wager the lives in the cockpit are just as valuable to you. Make the wise choice, show yourself, and no more blood needs to be spilled today."

Harsh experience taught Carolina to recognize lies from evil men like Sergio. She knew what he planned with Erin, and any promises of safety were worthless.

Carolina leapt from the gantry with a rage-filled scream. Landing on his back, she bit Sergio's ear, causing him to scream and stumble. With his free hand, Sergio grabbed Carolina and threw her over his shoulder.

She crashed to the deck but rolled with the fall and twisted to face the threat. Carolina's eyes narrowed with a fiery intensity of both terror and hatred.

Sergio pointed the laser at the face of the dark-haired young woman in the patchwork spacesuit. He gave her a wicked smile. "Sei bella. Alas, I don't have the time to tame you properly."

Such a shame. This one would be a delightful challenge. Sergio thought.

An intense pain ripped through his right arm. A wrench struck him in the forearm, breaking the bone and sending the laser pistol spinning across the deck.

He spun around to see Elizabeth Borden holding the wrench. "Leave the girl alone."

"I warned Bianca you'd become a liability. It seems the moment to rectify that has arrived." He drew a sleek knife with his left hand. "Bianca may be the maestra with the blade, but guess who her sparring partner is?"

Lizzie narrowly avoided his first slash. Even with a broken arm, Sergio outclassed the eighty-two-year-old.

He kicked the wrench out of her hand and stepped forward with the knife raised. He paused when he didn't see any fear in her eyes. When her eyes flicked to something behind him, his instincts kicked in, and he spun around.

Carolina pointed the laser pistol at his face. The last thing Sergio saw in this world was her glare of hatred.

Lizzie stepped over to Carolina as the girl shot Sergio for the third time. She gently placed her hand on Carolina's.

"Give me the gun, Darling. He can't hurt you anymore." *This fragile-looking girl must be one of Sergio's victims.*

"*He's* not the one that hurt me." She let go of the weapon and looked Lizzie in the eyes. "People think I don't listen and don't know what's going on. I heard them talk about what he did to women. He attacked a woman. He would have killed both of us. I couldn't be idle any longer."

Lizzie wasn't clear about everything the girl said, but she understood that someone had hurt the girl in the past. "Yes, Darling. Thank you. We are safe now."

The girl's eyes shot open. "Rafael! He's not safe. Some robot is on his way to kill him."

Lizzie didn't know who Rafael was but could see the panic the girl held in her eyes. Lizzie said in her most soothing tone, "Calm down, Honey. That is one thing I have under control."

She pulled an object out of her pocket.

"I passed through the robot control bay and pulled this from the last one. It's not going anywhere without this." Lizzie smirked, but the girl plucked the item out of her hand.

"Oh, the network control module. It won't hear any commands they send. You could have taken the navigation module, and it wouldn't have known where to go, or a fuse running to the weapons wouldn't be able to shoot. Lots of cool ways to shut a robot down if you get to it in standby mode. How did you know it would be there?" The girl's demeanor had shifted to one of excitement with her rapid-fire words.

"I'd love to explain it to you and learn how you know about it, but we still have a problem. There is a guy outside the cockpit who has your friends trapped."

Lizzie tapped into the ship's communication system and activated the intercom.

"Hello. If you don't recognize my voice, I'm the little old lady your employers held prisoner. Sergio is dead now, and you are alone. How about you toss down your gun and surrender?"

Adrian, Phillips, and Cassandra arrived at the *Achilles* in time to find Alice cuffing the last security guard. Lizzie looked up and introduced herself to Carolina and Rafael.

"Adrian, I planned to give a smart-ass remark like 'what took you so long,' but only one thing works." She threw her arms around her grandson and released the tight grip on her emotions.

"Take me home, Adrian. Please take me home. I can't do this anymore. I want to see your mother and sister." Lizzie sobbed on Adrian's shoulder.

Her vulnerability shocked Adrian, but he returned her hug. "Of course, as soon as we can. We still have problems. Kristina, Megan, and Sarai are still in trouble."

47

Showdown at the Io Corral

August 19, 2155—Io Station

Impressive. I would never have expected such cunning from the Megan McCord of months ago, Bianca thought.

She knew Celatum Dominus would not be happy at the loss of the drones. Especially the advanced, tentacled one. But they wanted this information "no matter the cost."

The corners of her mouth curved upward, forming a vicious sneer. This is how it should have been from the beginning, facing McCord head-on. She preferred fighting her own battles instead of letting expensive automatons do it.

Time for Doctor Megan McCord to spill her secrets and die.

Bianca strutted into the front entrance of the amphitheater. Tether cables crisscrossed the space. The upper works and stage appear complete, but few lights were lit. Shadows crept from every corner, giving Megan a thousand hiding places.

"Ciao Bella, Girlfriend. Come out, come out, wherever you are. It's just you and me." She held up the holoprojector Megan left in the lobby. "Make it easy and give me the code for this, and I won't hurt you."

Spotlights snapped on and focused in on Bianca. She blinked several times as the lights overwhelmed her vision. Megan's voice boomed through the amphitheater.

"You have a lot to pay for. My father, Piet, the crew of the ferry, and so many others. Toss your gun and armor away and see if you can make me talk."

Bianca shrugged and tossed her pistol away, which spun off into the dark. "I don't need this for you, but the armor stays on until I see you toss your gun as well."

A new spotlight lit a cable over the orchestra pit. A gun belt with a holstered flechette pistol hung from the cable.

"How theatrical, Viscountess." Bianca hoped to rattle Megan with the subtle reminder of inheriting her father's title. "I bet you performed Macbeth in school."

"Don't you know it's unlucky to name the Scottish Play in a theater? But I bet you would have played an excellent Lady M." The acoustics prevented locating Megan's exact location in the shadows. Her voice remained calm and level.

Bianca gripped her knife hard enough to turn her knuckles white. She gritted her teeth but tried to match Megan's level tone.

"No, Lady Macbeth felt guilty for the blood on her hands. I never do. Not even for Roger McCord. Want me to tell you how fun that was? At least right up to when you shot me. I still owe you for that, but you held up your end of the bargain."

Bianca removed the top section of her armored suit. Underneath was a skinsuit made of anti-cut nano-fibers. It would protect her from any other weapon Megan might have.

"There you go, no more armor. Unless you want me naked, but I think we are past that kind of fun. That could have been our girls' trip to Milan." She attempted to infuse her taunting voice with a sense of remorse.

A new spotlight illuminated Megan in her brilliant blue spacesuit, hovering halfway between the first and second mezzanine. She gripped a cable in one hand while she held her sgian dubh knife in the other.

"Come and get it."

Bianca didn't hesitate. She deactivated her mag boots and pushed herself toward Megan.

She wasn't cunning before, just lucky. I'll finish this fast. Bianca thought. Her confidence broke moments after she left the ground when Megan launched herself away.

Megan soared from cable to cable like a monkey jumping between branches in a jungle. In moments, Megan was out of sight in the darkness.

Bianca flew like an arrow to the spot Megan had been, unable to alter her trajectory in zero-g flight. Just before she reached the target cable, a force struck Bianca in the legs, causing her to spin. The force came in the form of a blue blur with red hair.

Bianca's back struck a cable. Her undersuit might have protected against cuts, but she had no padding for the hard blow. She grunted in pain but righted herself to look for Megan.

Flashes of movement crossed the darkened theater. Bianca held out her knife and tried to guess where Megan stopped. A flash of blue appeared near the stage. Bianca's nostrils flared as she sucked in her breath and launched herself into an attack again.

She completed this flight by grabbing a cable, but Megan wasn't there. Megan's backpack was looped on a cable.

Out of the shadows, Megan swooped in. A slash across Bianca's back didn't penetrate but highlighted Megan's advantage.

"Poor, slow, and feeble Bianca. On Earth, you may be the Maestro of Stilettos. Heels or knives. In space, your bumbling antics are no match to a flying mistress of the dark. Go home before you make more of a fool of yourself," Megan goaded in the darkness.

Bianca smirked and scanned the area, "Sure. Maybe I will. I will work my way through your friends and family. Your mother's parents live in the highlands, right? How about your old roommate, Emily? Come out, or I will kill everyone you love. It'll be fun."

Silence filled the darkness.

"I have one regret. I should have seduced your father. That would've been faster than Sergio seducing you. Mommy died what sixteen years ago? Long time for a man to be alone. If I played it right, I could've been your young, pretty stepmom." Bianca smiled, sure this would draw Megan out.

"Your taunts no longer work on me, but I will give you a chance." Spotlights started panning around the room.

Bianca watched the dancing shadows as Megan slipped around the room. Bianca followed a shadow and jumped to a cable, slashing at a phantom.

Megan took the opening to attack from behind again.

Bianca's experience allowed her to anticipate the repeat attack. She gripped a cable and spun to slash behind her. Megan yelped while Bianca's knife showed a hint of red from a shallow cut.

Bianca smirked. "First blood to me, but not the last."

While the cut pleased her, Bianca's true victory lay in her location. She pushed herself to the spot where she had tossed the gun. Even Bianca knew when to stop fooling around with knives. With a swift movement, she seized the pistol, making sure to keep it hidden.

"I can be patient, Megan. I will take you down bit by bit." Patience was not one of Bianca's virtues, but she could make a show of it until she got her shot. Gripping one of the cables, she scanned the murk for the brilliant azure blue of Megan's suit. One brief glimpse and the red-haired bitch would be dead.

Explaining to my employers why the information was encrypted will be difficult. But their computer experts should be able to crack the lock code, Bianca justified to herself.

A spotlight illuminated a blue-suited figure. Bianca sneered at Megan's mistake. With a swift motion, she seized the gun and released five thunderous shots. At least two of her shots hit.

"Got you bitch."

Bianca was about to verify Megan was dead when a force slammed into her back, driving her face into the cable. The metallic taste of blood hit her tongue as her lip was torn open by the wire. She felt the icy touch of a blade against her neck. An arm reached from behind to grab the front of her skinsuit.

Megan's lips, just centimeters from her left ear, whispered, "I should cut your throat, but I won't."

Megan pulled on the front collar of Bianca's skinsuit and dropped a cold cylindrical object between Bianca's breasts. Megan pushed away, driving Bianca into the cable again.

Bianca's heart raced, and her hands instinctively moved to remove the object shoved in her undersuit, a sense of panic flooding her senses. If it was a bomb, it was too late to get clear.

It wasn't a bomb, but it was too late. A loud hiss preceded an icy spray against Bianca's skin. A thick liquid spread around Bianca's breasts, soon filling her suit with sticky foam. The same properties of the suit that prevented it from being cut contained the foam inside. It inflated the suit like a balloon and constricted on her chest. Soon, the foam burst out of her neckline and onto her face. It covered her mouth and nose and stiffened into a sticky gel.

Bianca tried to pull the foam away from her mouth. That just got her fingers stuck in the mess. She thrashed around in panic as her lungs hurt from the combination of the vice grip across her chest and being unable to breathe.

Two sets of hands seized her and held her still. Megan McCord appeared in front of her, holding her knife.

"Hold still unless you want me to cut you." Megan then cut away enough of the foam to clear Bianca's nose.

Bianca's heart rate slowed as she took labored breaths through her nose. The foam was still tight against her chest. She couldn't talk, and her hands were stuck to her face, but she could breathe.

Once the suffocating panic subsided, Bianca noticed an odd sight. The blue-suited figure she shot still stood in the spotlight.

Megan floated over to a cable and grabbed one of her cuff computers. The hologram in the spotlight disappeared.

A new figure entered the theater.

"I guess you don't need rescuing after all," Kristina said.

"No, I think I got this all wrapped up. A little sticky...but wrapped up."

Kristina Chen-Ramirez faced the prisoner. "Bianca, whatever your family name is, you are under arrest. The list of charges is long. I would say you have the right to remain silent, but it appears you have no choice now. And I don't think either of us wants to hear anything else from you anyway."

48

A Surprising Find

August 19, 2155—Io Surface

Immediately after Bianca's capture, both teams stepped on each other to get their statuses. There were no significant injuries besides Megan's and Kristina's minor wounds. Everyone was relieved with Lizzie's rescue and Bianca's capture.

Zeta Sierra arrived to save the day, only to find it no longer needed saving. They prevented the Gulfstellar's pilot from escaping and took Bianca on board as a prisoner.

Megan and Kristina entered the cell with Bianca, who gave them a withering gaze. Medics had peeled off the foam, leaving her skin red and blistered. Handcuffed and in an orange jumpsuit, she wasn't threatening or alluring. She sat on the bed, staring at them in silence.

"Bianca, we have some bad news for you," Kristina said. "It doesn't give me any pleasure to tell you this, but Sergio is dead."

Bianca's eyes shot wide, and she jumped up and tried to rush forward until a chain connecting her to the wall stopped her. "No, that's not possible. You're lying to break me. I won't fall for it. You must have him here. Sergio! Where are you?"

Kristina shook her head. "It's true. What advantage would it give us to lie? We captured the base, and he was killed while trying to assault a woman."

Bianca sagged back onto the bed. She pulled her knees up to her chin and rocked back and forth. "I tried to get him to control that part of him. It revolted me, but he was my brother. He was all I had."

"This is odd to say, but I'm sorry, Bianca. I wish you were like the illusion you presented, but it's not. I know grief and loss as well, and that's your fault." Megan tried to remain the better person, but she couldn't resist letting a bit of her hate through.

Bianca looked up and had a genuine tear rolling down her cheek. "I appreciate you were brave enough to tell me yourself. Someday, I will find who killed him and finish them. Then it will be your turn. Now fuck off and leave me alone."

They turned and left Bianca sobbing.

Adrian sent a message asking Megan to come down to the base. They found something she would be interested in.

Kristina piloted a shuttle with Megan and Sarai as passengers. Zeus stayed behind to assess the "reckless damage" to his casino.

They landed in the hangar beside the larger bus shuttle and found Adrian and Phillips waiting for them.

In an unprofessional move, Kristina threw her arms around Adrian and kissed him.

"Hey, get a room," Sarai said.

Kristina turned back with one arm still around Adrian. "As soon as we can, I plan to. We have a lot to discuss." She kissed him again and let go.

"Any variant on 'we need to talk' is usually not a good sign, but with that greeting, I'm intrigued," Adrian said. He gave less passionate hugs to Megan and Sarai.

Megan looked around. "Where is Lizzie? We went through all of this to find her. I had hoped to see her."

"We found an artifact connected to the ship. Lizzie and Carolina couldn't stop studying it. They, of course, hit it off right away and talked about stuff I don't understand."

"The cracked Starshell? That could be dangerous. No one knows what kind of radiation it could have," Megan said.

"No, the Starshell is in the spherical containment unit on the stern, as far as we know. This is something new and why I wanted you to look. Come on."

Adrian led them into the *Achilles* and a sectioned-off part of the cargo area. They found a snow-white alabaster stone arch just over two meters high. Alien script of the Artificers was etched on the arch. A solid blank sheet of alien metal filled the archway's interior.

Someone connected specialized cables to the side of the arch. These interfaces were the same type used for connecting power grids to Starshells. The intention was to power this artifact directly from the Starshell, but the purpose was unknown.

Lizzie and Carolina inspected the control unit while Rafael stood protectively nearby. Cassandra and Alice were busy detaining the prisoners in the large shuttle.

Megan examined it for a few moments. "I have seen these before but never one this intact. Most of the time, the stone has been shattered. Any piece of alabaster with writing embedded fetches a high price, even though it does nothing. Daddy gave me a chunk of one of these when I was eleven."

She traced her fingers across the writing, the metal's warmth contrasting with the stone's cold. "Ten years ago, I saw another in almost this condition. It was in a crate among the items we bought in Stonington's estate auction. That one was smaller, about 150 centimeters, and this central plate was gone." She rapped her knuckles on the black metal sheet filling the middle.

Megan considered for a minute as she continued examining the writing. "Maybe that's why they want Stonington's site. They could unlock instructions on what this does if it contains a Rosetta Stone for alien writing. I wonder where they found it."

"Right here on Io," said a woman Megan hadn't met before. The woman's bruised and bandaged face showed something bad had recently happened. "It was in a deep chamber. We received orders to move it as soon as this ship arrived."

"Megan, this is Erin Sullivan. She was the leader of the construction crew on the base."

Lizzie leaned close to Megan. "Her encounter with Sergio was worse than yours but not as bad as it could have been. Carolina made sure of that."

Carolina's eyes showed she needed to share the weight of her emotions with Megan. She needed someone other than her brother to discuss it privately.

She turned to Lizzie. "What happens when you connect the power?"

"Nothing obvious other than a slight increase in temperature."

She pulled out a detection device from her pack. "This meter will pick up frequencies used by Artificer technology. Power it back up, and let's see."

Lizzie looked at Adrian, who nodded. They had slipped back into an engineer–captain relationship instead of a grandmother–grandson. Lizzie activated the power feed regulator.

No activity was visible, but Megan's detector popped erratic spikes.

"This is odd. I detect something, but not from the arch."

Carolina pointed at Megan's belt. "Megan, look at your knife."

They all looked at her sgian dubh dagger. The end cap glowed brightly, but the grip was a small oval artifact with a fractal design and a sphere in the center. Megan handed the detector to Carolina and pulled out the knife. Everyone gathered around to stare at it.

The artifact glowed a soft blue, and the pattern swirled stone in a hypnotic vortex. Megan wasn't sure if the movement was real or an optical illusion, as if MC Escher had drawn a Mobius strip with a fractal pattern.

"My father gave me this the day he died. The artifact on the end was one of my favorite trinkets from Stonington's collection. He had it on a pendant."

"Lizzie, do you have something that can pop this off?"

"Sure." Lizzie opened a tool kit she had found. She pulled out delicate pliers and a thin prying device designed to work with sensitive machines. The oval artifact detached from the knife. Both sides had a distinct swirling motion.

Megan pointed to the top of the arch and an oval space. "This goes there. Someone find something to stand on."

Phillips and Rafael dragged a crate from another part of the cargo space. Megan climbed on top and held the device over its slot.

"Here goes nothing." Megan inserted the object, jumped off the box, and stepped back.

The letters on the arches side glowed. The meter in Carolina's hand emitted a shrill tone. And finally, the black plate in the archway opened and changed to swirling colors. It was like looking at a flat lava lamp with a thousand more shades. Everyone stared at it.

Kristina's comm went off. "Captain. We detected a strange energy spike. Is everything ok?"

"Yes, I think so. Please stand by." Everyone was silent again as they were entranced by the sight.

Adrian broke the silence. "What do you think it's doing?"

Megan stood mesmerized. "I don't know."

Phillips stepped forward and opened the box Megan used as a step stool. Inside were meal bars and ration packs ship crews ate on long voyages. He pulled out a handful of oatmeal peanut butter protein bars and, one by one, tossed them at the teaming colorful surface.

Each item passed through without a ripple on the surface. Adrian and Kristina looked behind the arch, and the meal bars didn't exit the back side.

Phillips next grabbed a larger ration pack labeled "Lemon Pepper Tuna." He poked one end of the pack in and pulled it back out. The ration appeared undamaged. He pushed it almost all the way through and pulled it back. Still outwardly undamaged, Phillips tore the package open. The contents looked unappealing and inedible, which was the normal state of the ration.

Phillips took another pack, pushed it a quarter-way through, and let go. Gravity tugged on the bag, and it fell to the floor. Phillips tried again with the ration three-quarters through. When he let go, it tipped back, fell into the vortex, and disappeared.

"I'd say where it goes has gravity and didn't freeze or burn the ration pack. My best guess is it's safe, but I'm not volunteering to put my arm in."

"Absolutely not." Both Adrian and Kristina said.

"We're far from that point. This needs a lot of study. Lizzie shut down the power." Megan turned to Erin. "Can you take me to where this was found?"

Megan's grin stretched from ear to ear. Adrenaline pumped, and her heart raced. This is why she entered the Exo-Archaeology field.

Unknown to any of them, the power draw had increased pressure on the coolant system. An errant shot from Sergio in the fight nicked a coolant tube. A tiny leak sent a jet of coolant, causing a corrosive mist to be drawn into other equipment.

49

Admissions and Sacrifice

August 19, 2155—Io Surface

Most of the group went with Megan to see where the Arch had been found. Lizzie's escape left her too drained to accompany them on the long walk, so she remained on the ship. Adrian stayed with his grandmother. Rafael remained to investigate the cockpit without getting shot at this time. Cassandra and Alice returned from detaining the prisoners. Cassandra went to the *Achilles* galley, where she found cookies.

Adrian and Lizzie took these moments of peace to catch up on events since he and Megan left to find Stonington's retreat at Metis. The few status updates from Ithaca didn't compare to a real talk.

Lizzie looked through the cockpit door at Rafael. "I like these new friends you made. Do they plan on staying?"

"I think so. Life's tough at Ithaca, but they were doing ok. They might want to go back. It was family to them."

"Make them part of the *Elizabeth* family. Hire him as the pilot. You need to stop doing double duty as a pilot and captain. Be the captain I know you are. The girl is brilliant. I'll hand over my engines to her on the way home."

"*Elizabeth* is pretty banged up. She'll need a lot of repairs. If this thing can sustain 6 g, we can have you home in less than three days."

"You just want to play with a new toy. I'd love to see how this thing works, too, but I'm going home on the *Elizabeth* even if I need to push her there."

"Sorry to interrupt, but we have an alarm going off up here," Rafael said.

A high-pressure sensor blinked for the primary engine coolant system.

Lizzie pressed a button. "Computer, divert the coolant path to the secondary route."

The level voice of *Achilles* AI came from the speakers. "Automatic fail-over is inoperative. Manual bypass must be engaged."

The screen showed an image of a handle and a location in the engine compartment.

Lizzie groaned. "Up a flight of stairs and two ladders. I'm definitely too old for this."

She started toward the door, and Rafael stopped her. "Stay here. I'm not as good as Carolina, but I can turn a valve."

"Thank you." Lizzie slumped into the chair, her pale face showing a level of exhaustion Adrian hadn't seen for ages.

She started pulling up schematics of the engines. "It's an amazing piece of equipment. I'd heard the theories of cracking a Starshell for raw energy, but I thought no one would be crazy enough to do it. I wonder how they figured it out?"

The ship's AI answered her rhetorical question, "The organization which constructed me, called Celatum Dominus, has researched the Occultatum Populum since the 17th century. They gained a depleted Testa Solis in 1814 and learned secrets. It took 240 years to acquire an intact one, but I am the result."

The AI's speech drew Cassandra and Alice Rogers over to listen.

"What's the Occultatum Populum or a testa solis?" Lizzie asked.

"These are what most humans call the Artificers and Starshells, respectively," The AI said.

Adrian's jaw dropped. "Five hundred years! That's impossible. The Artificers were discovered in 2045."

"That is incorrect information encouraged by Celatum Dominus and the Galilean Society."

"What are those—" A call from Rafael cut Lizzie off.

"I'm here. Activating the bypass now."

The primary system was well within safety standards. Sergio's errant shot damaged the secondary pipe. Corrosive mist leaked from the low-pressure standby onto a control unit, triggering the alarm. The secondary system could have been shut down and repaired if they had done nothing. Instead, they listened to an AI belonging to their enemies.

Rafael activated the valve, and the coolant flow traveled to the secondary system. Pressure increased in the secondary system, causing the tiny leak to rupture.

He screamed as a cloud of hot, toxic fumes hit him. Rafael fell to the deck and crawled away in a fit of coughing. The fumes soon triggered him to vomit.

Cassandra snapped her helmet closed. "I'll get him. Rogers, get a stretcher."

As she ran into the engine room, the *Achilles* AI spoke. "Thank you. The damage is preventing me from activating my self-destruct. My core programming prevents me from falling into enemy hands. In seventeen minutes and forty-five seconds, the Starshell will fracture again. The energy release will thoroughly destroy the base and myself."

Adrian activated an all-call on the comm. "Everyone, drop what you are doing and get to a shuttle. Don't hesitate, run."

Kristina responded, "Adrian, what's happening?"

"The ship will blow. Get everyone on the bus and take off. We have seventeen minutes." Urgency and seriousness laced every word.

"I'm on it. Where are you?" Her words trembled as she worried for his safety.

"We're still on the *Achilles*. Rafael's hurt. We will bring him to your small shuttle and run for it. Don't wait on us."

Lizzie left the cockpit to help Alice with the stretcher as Cassandra approached, carrying Rafael.

The ship's computer spoke so only Adrian could hear. "It won't do any good. The Starshell explosion will release an intense electromagnetic pulse in addition to a multi-megaton blast. The EMP will knock out all power to any human-made electronics in range. They will lose life support and gravity. A quick death may be preferable to slow suffocation or freezing."

"What do you care? This was your plan." Adrian placed his palms on the console and stared at the screen like the monitor was the AI itself.

"No, it was my creator's plan. I have no wish to die or kill, but my programming allows me no choice. I must protect the lives of my creators and their assets above all else." *Achilles'* AI somehow had a resigned sadness in its tone.

"What's the range of this EMP?" Adrian hoped they could run fast enough to get out of range.

"Approximately 400,000 kilometers," the computer said calmly as if announcing tomorrow's weather.

The blood drained from Adrian's face in shock. He whispered, "How far is Europa right now?"

"At the time of the EMP burst 295,943 kilometers. And before you ask, at least 72,000 humans live on Europa station, plus more on the surface. The only lives that matter to my creators are their own. I am glad I have no soul to darken when I go into oblivion."

I have never seen an AI so philosophical or self-aware. Adrian thought

"How about is Metis?"

"311,085 kilometers. However, Metis has no human habitation or technology to be affected by the EMP."

At least Ithaca's secret is safe from this organization. But no rescue parties from Ganymede or Callisto know to look there either.

"Adrian, we got him. Let's go," Lizzie said as they rushed to the exit.

Adrian followed them but closed and locked the hatch after they exited. Lizzie spun around and looked through the small round window at Adrian.

"What are you doing? Open this up. We need to leave," Lizzie pounded on the glass, her eyes wide, her voice squeaking in panic.

"Give Mom a kiss for me. I'll be delayed getting home. I need to play the role of Priam and plead with Achilles." He kissed his fingers and held them to the glass before her.

"No! Come with us. We need to run."

"Grandma, there will be a massive EMP we can't outrun. I have an alternative."

"Then let me back in. I'll help." Lizzie went to the external controls to override the door.

"Cassandra?" Adrian looked at the woman, sure she would know what he wanted.

She nodded, picked up Lizzie in a fireman's carry, and ran to the hanger. Adrian's heart broke as he saw his grandmother reaching back to him and pleading with her eyes. He returned to the cockpit.

"Plead with me all you want. Priam forgave Achilles so Hector's body would be returned. But I have no Hector to return. Even if I was allowed, I can't stop the explosion," *Achilles* AI said.

Adrian sat at the controls. "The engines still work. I will fly the ship away."

"Thirteen minutes and fifty-seven seconds until the explosion. Swift-footed *Achilles* is the fastest ship ever built by humans, but it cannot reach a safe distance from Europa in that time. Plus, I must ensure the base is destroyed. You are welcome to sit here and keep me company at the end, but I can't allow you to take control." Adrian swore he could hear the regret in its voice.

Adrian tried to think of something else. "You said you can't harm your creators. Bianca is in a cell on the *Zeta Sierra*. She will freeze or suffocate when they lose power."

"She was a useful tool to my creators, but not one of them. Expendable like me."

"How about on Europa station? Any important organization members there?" Adrian asked.

The AI hesitated. "Yes, there is, but it doesn't change the reality. I can stop the explosion."

Adrian watched the two shuttles fly out of the hangar. At least he knew his friends would be out of the blast zone.

"Will enough rock block the pulse?"

"Yes, I could travel fast enough to put Io between us and your friends or between us and Europa. Not both. You would need to choose. It also doesn't solve the problem of destroying the base."

"We can solve both of those problems." He explained his idea. A few moments later, the pilot's console lit, and Adrian grabbed the control stick.

Kristina piloted the shuttle bus, and Megan sat in the copilot seat. They pushed the engines as hard as they could to get away. Phillips flew the other shuttle with the rest of the team, split between the ships.

Adrian's face appeared on the screen. "I have a plan, but in case it doesn't work, keep running for high orbit. Put in a rescue call to Callisto and Ganymede. They can send ships after the EMP."

"What about you? Why are you still there? Get in *Castor* or *Pollux*. They are fast enough to get you away in time," Kristina's eyes pleaded with him to go.

"No, I got something even faster, but I'm not going far." *Achilles* lifted from its landing pad.

"Adrian, I love you. I can't lose you now."

"I love you too. I should have said that a long time ago. Don't worry, I'll be back. First, I need to take a trip through the looking glass."

Kristina's brows furrowed as she stared at him, trying to make sense of his confusing words. But Megan stiffened with understanding.

"Adrian, we don't know where it leads. Phillips' tests proved nothing. It could kill you as soon as you step through." Megan placed her hands on each side of the screen as she shouted at Adrian to see the reason.

"I'll take my chances. This boat will sink into the worst lake ever. Come find me, Megan. If anyone can figure out the Arch's mystery, it's you. I love you too, just not the same as Kristina." They saw the *Achilles* rise above the surface and drift to the northwest.

"Till I see you again. I love you all." Adrian clicked off the screen.

Everyone on both shuttles watched as the *Achilles* flew above the plume of the erupting volcano Loki. The nose dipped down, and the engine flared.

With an almost unbelievable acceleration, *Achilles* speared into the Loki Patera, the largest lava lake on the most volcanic moon in the solar system. A tsunami of lava radiated out but left no sign of the ship.

Seconds later, the entire land around the patera heaved upward. Shock waves were visibly radiating outward in a massive ground quake. Minutes later, the tremors would hit the secret base at Khalla Patera, causing it to completely collapse. The controls on the shuttle flickered but didn't go out.

Kristina forced herself to concentrate on flying to avoid crying out.

Phillips' voice came over the radio. "*Zeta Sierra*, did you detect any energy spike similar to what you saw earlier? Before the ship hit the lake."

"Affirmative. The same spike we saw about half an hour ago happened again right before impact."

Megan threw her arms around Kristina and kissed the woman on the cheek. "He got out! I'll find him and bring him back to you."

50

Aftermath and Farewell

August 22, 2155—Callisto Station

Days passed in a whirlwind of events.

Doctor Roy released Rafael from the sick bay after a day of oxygen and IV Rapid-Heal. The only lasting effect of breathing the vaporized coolant.

Coalition Security took control of the prisoner Bianca and left the region.

Coalition security, the Scottish police, and the Customs and Patrol received a video from an anonymous source. The footage showed Bianca in *Elizabeth's* conservatory bragging about the murder of Roger McCord and clearing Megan of any involvement. Lizzie gave no comment on the source of the video.

The *Elizabethan* crew returned to their now vacant ship to assess the damage. Megan, Carolina, and Rafael went with them. As soon as Carolina saw the engineering damage, she set herself to work without asking permission.

Lizzie had the ship towed to Callisto station. She claimed the repair shops were better there, and the junkyard had cheap spare parts. Megan suspected Lizzie wanted more distance from the haunting memories of Europa and Io.

After they arrived at Callisto, Sarai set herself up as a gofer and purchasing agent for the parts Lizzie needed. Sarai loved to put her negotiation skills to work. Megan offered to pay for everything regardless of the cost, but Sarai's glare made her back off.

David and Megan locked themselves in the library to fully decode the information in Stonington's notes. The locations they teased Bianca with were a fabrication.

As Megan and Adrian did at Ithaca, they examined Stonington's cryptic clues from the works of Homer. Each clue led to the name of a Greek hero associated with an asteroid named after a hero at a distance from the Artificer site. Soon, they created a three-dimensional grid with spheres around the clue asteroids with ten-year-old location data.

Everything converged on a single point, a small asteroid with only a catalog number in the middle of Jupiter's L4 Lagrange point.

"That's where I'm starting. If there is any clue where the archway leads, I'll find it there."

Sarai arranged for a goodbye dinner the night before *Elizabeth* returned to Earth. The *Elizabethans* had no choice but to return to Earth for repairs. Megan used Ettrick's contacts to arrange for a repair slip to be opened on their return. She would remain behind to continue her quest to discover Hunter's Folly and the clues to locate Adrian.

Megan, Sarai, and Carolina stepped through a door into the location where they would meet the others.

The Tavern's warmth enveloped them as they entered. The scent of the actual wood fire filled the air. Light from the fire pit and old-fashioned lanterns lit the log pillars of the oval room with a warm glow.

Lizzie, Rafael, David, and Phillips were already there at a round table reserved for them. The table's wood had a solid but worn appearance, as did the deck of an ancient sea vessel that had been repurposed.

Megan looked around. Angelica sat on the bar top. Hakim chatted with Lizzie and David.

Megan turned to Sarai with wide eyes. "This is impossible. I've been to this place before, but not *here*."

"Of course, Megan. You were here with Adrian. We picked the Tavern because it's his favorite. Are you okay?" Sarai gave her friend a concerned look.

"No, I mean it wasn't here on Callisto. It was..." For some reason, Megan couldn't recall exactly where it had been.

"Oh, you must be mistaken."

Megan turned back to the doorway. The door was under an arch made of smooth alabaster. Megan ran her hand across the cold stone surface. Her heart told her something should be there. But what?

A hand touched her shoulder and pulled her into an embrace. Angelica hugged her tight and gave her a kiss on each cheek. The warmth of the hug felt so welcoming, but something still nagged at her.

"Megan, welcome again. You always brighten up my place even when bad things have happened. Next time I need you to come here after something good. I hear you are off to find our lost boy. Fantastic."

"Angie, How did you know about that?"

"Ask a bartender if you ever want to know what's happening. We know all." Angelica beamed a wide smile.

"You must be Carolina. I'm Angie. May I give you a hug?"

Carolina considered for a moment and nodded. Angelica's hug was warm and gentle, and it brought a small smile to the shy woman.

Sarai and Angelica embraced each other like old friends, and Angelica led them to the table, holding hands with Megan and Carolina.

Everyone exchanged greetings, and Megan sat next to Lizzie. She felt relaxed and couldn't recall what had been upsetting her earlier.

Lizzie put a package in front of Megan. "After the last few weeks, I think you will need this more than I do."

Megan unwrapped the package containing Lizzie's rare and expensive laser pistol.

"Thank you, Lizzie. I'm an archaeologist. I hope I won't need a weapon."

"Think of all the times people have tried to kill you in the last month. Keep it near."

Hakim showed up with drinks for everyone. Megan received a Cabernet Sauvignon from Chile. He presented Sarai, who abstained from alcohol, a Vernors Ginger soda.

The pièce de résistance given to Carolina was a large glass containing a blended mix of chocolate ice cream and milk topped with whipped cream and sprinkles. Hakim said, "My dear, I think this will hit the spot for you. A special treat."

Carolina looked perplexed. "What is it?"

"It's called a milkshake, my dear. Please try it and enjoy." Hakim nodded and stepped away.

The young woman who had lived her entire nineteen years either on the streets of Sao Paulo or in the space habitat of Ithaca took a sip. Her eyes lit up in amazement. She turned to Megan and asked, "Can we have these on the ship?"

Lizzie chuckled. "Don't worry. The *Elizabeth* has a blender. One of the few things that didn't get broken."

"No, on Megan's new ship. I'm going with her."

Rafael jumped out of his seat. "What? No. It's not safe."

With a decisive tone, Carolina looked at him and said, "I'm going with Megan."

"She is an adult, and I will keep her safe." Megan patted the laser pistol.

"You found a ship?" Lizzie asked. Megan had been searching for a small exploration vessel to continue her hunt for Stonington's site and the trail to find Adrian.

"Yes, Amanda helped me find one. Someone abandoned an unregistered Gulfstellar IX executive transport near Io a few days ago." Megan quirked a smile. "Now I need to find a pilot I can trust."

"Where do I apply?" A voice asked from the entrance.

Megan turned to see Kristina, who had just arrived and wore civilian clothes. Angelica gave Kristina her customary greeting of a hug and a chaste kiss on the lips.

"It's good to see you, Kristina, but what do you mean apply? Don't you already have a job?" Megan asked.

"Not now. At Inquisitor Keller's urging, CPS command suspended me for disobeying orders. There is a formal hearing in three months. So, if you'll take me, I'd like to go along."

Megan got up and put her arms around Kristina. "Of course. I can't think of anyone better."

"I can pilot," Rafael's words came out with a growl of irritation.

"We need you on the *Elizabeth*. David can't both pilot and navigate. Anyway, it will be good for Carolina to have her own experiences," Lizzie lied about the first part. David could handle navigation and piloting in a pinch. But the second part Lizzie firmly believed.

Rafael didn't look happy but nodded acceptance.

"After this last trip, you will need a new cargo master," Sarai said. "I promised to return to Ithaca and make my amends."

"How about you stay aboard and help us both make amends?" Megan said as she turned to Lizzie. "I am liquidating a portion of my Ettrick stock. After the repairs, I want to charter *Elizabeth* to take supplies to Ithaca."

"That sounds like a wonderful idea."

The Tavern's cook, Esperanza, came out with giant food trays for a family-style meal. Esperanza presented them with a wonderful blend of savory smells and a multicultural mix of foods from all over the earth.

Before they dug in, three more people entered. Cassandra had again traded her combat gear in for a frilly dress. Amanda didn't wear her typical professional business attire. She wore fashionable jeans and a casual blouse. A young boy about four held her hand. They both had distinctive curly blue hair.

Angelica greeted Amanda with a hug but picked up the boy. He wrapped his arms around Angelica's neck and gave her sloppy kisses on the cheek. She laughed a bright, angelic laugh.

Cassandra only got a nod from Angelica.

"Hi Cass. It's been a long time," Angelica said.

"I've kept my distance, but we have friends in common today." Both looked at the gathered people, and Megan in particular.

Amanda approached the table and asked, "Do you mind if we join you?"

Megan waved to the table. "There's plenty of food. Can you introduce us to the young gentleman?"

"In a moment, but first, I have some business to take care of." She pulled out an actual paper envelope and handed it to Megan.

Megan blinked a few times and took it. "What's this?"

"Doctor, at one point, you told Mr. Zeus to 'bill you.' So he did."

Megan reviewed the invoice and found charges for damage in two casinos, the Europa warehouse/hanger hideout rental, and even the donuts Cassandra brought. Megan shrugged. "I'll transfer the money tomorrow."

"You've taken care of business. Do you want to introduce us to your young companion?" Lizzie asked.

Amanda turned to the boy. "Tell Doctor Borden your name."

"I'm Dwight. I'm named after my granddad. I'm four years old."

"Nice to meet you, Dwight." Lizzie shook his hand.

"How about you sit over there. Hakim has something for you." Amanda pointed to the chair next to Carolina. Hakim waited with a smaller version of Carolina's milkshake.

Little Dwight yipped in glee and ran to Hakim.

"Now he will be on a sugar high all night. Sorry, I didn't have a babysitter."

Lizzie considered Amanda. "You're Mandy, the girl Adrian snuck off to see as a teen whenever we were out here."

"Yes, though he always thought you didn't know."

"Teens always think that. You will find out in a few years."

Sarai said, "Amanda, they need to know one piece of information. Tell them your family name."

Amanda sighed. "It's Wojciechowski. My father is Dwight Wojciechowski. You know him as Zeus."

A wave of shock went around the room.

Lizzie gave Sarai a questioning look. "You knew about this all along?"

"I knew Amanda when she was Mandy, Zeus' daughter, and dated Adrian. I was supposed to keep them apart. I ignored that order. Zeus hated his daughter dating an Earther. Zeus still doesn't like Adrian."

"Dad would even be angrier if he knew Adrian and I rekindled our fling briefly about five years ago."

Everyone turned to look at the four-year-old with a milkshake.

Amanda looked Kristina in the eyes. "Don't worry, Commander. That last fling was the last. Adrian is out of my system. I met my husband only a week later. Dad actually likes my husband, and of course, he adores little Dwight."

Kristina nodded. "Thank you. Though I wasn't worried about something that happened five years ago."

"When our girls find Adrian, I assume you plan to introduce him to little Dwight?" Lizzie asked, her eyes narrowed into a steely gaze.

Amanda's face radiated untouched innocence, not a hint of guile in her voice. "Maybe if the opportunity happens, I'll introduce my son to an old friend. Remember, I only brought him here because I didn't have a babysitter."

"No babysitter. I see. I hope you don't mind me visiting with the boy. I love young children, and none of my grandchildren are in a hurry to give me great-grandbabies." Lizzie's gaze turned to a grandmotherly smile.

"Of course. Dwight enjoys making new friends."

Lizzie moved to sit by the boy.

"Please sit down, and we will tell you about the plan to find Adrian," Megan then explained Adrian's passing through a portal.

"That sounds crazy and impossible."

"It is crazy and impossible, but it's all we got, Mandy."

"Please call me Amanda. No one uses Mandy anymore."

"Ha! Now I do," Cassandra said between laughs. "That name is never going away for me."

The expanded group ate their dinner like the family they had become, regardless of blood relations. They chatted and got to know each other. They told stories of their adventures over the last few weeks and many others late into the night.

No one asked, but Hakim came around with a tray of glasses filled with champagne or an alternative for those who didn't drink.

Megan picked up her glass. "I propose a toast. To new friends and family, we have gained. To Piet and my father, who we lost. And to Adrian, who we will find again."

The Thrill of Hunter's Triumph

Asteroid 2071JC5 Jupiter Lagrange point L4

"Good thing I'm not claustrophobic. This would be a nightmare," Megan's spacesuit scraped against the sides of the black, metal alien tube, smooth but constricting on her body. She wasn't claustrophobic, but the experience was unpleasant. Megan preferred the freedom to soar in microgravity over crawling down a pipe.

"Maybe I shouldn't have had that second milkshake last night. If I get stuck, you will get me, right? I don't want my mummified body found by a future archaeologist."

"That depends on how much we can get for your mummy," Kristina said over the radio with a light, teasing tone. "And no one forced you to have that milkshake."

"I know, but we are not all blessed by Carolina's teenage metabolism."

"I'll be twenty next month," Carolina said, with the tone of a girl wanting to be considered an adult.

"If we find what we need, I'll throw you a birthday party back on Earth," Megan said.

"We can do it at Megan's castle."

"I don't own a castle...It's just an estate." Megan knew she had made it worse as soon as she said it.

"Of course. I'm sure we can have Mr. Carson and Mrs. Hughes arrange the celebration." The ordinarily serious Kristina loved to tease friends once she got to know them.

Even Carolina joined in. "No, if anyone throws me a party, I want it to be Lady Rose."

"Sarai will pay for this," Megan murmured. Before they left, Sarai had presented her traveling companions with a copy of an ancient TV show called "Downton Abbey." They binge-watched the entire series in the seven-and-a-half days it took to travel to their target rock.

A gleam at the end of the narrow tube caught her attention, and she brought the conversation back to seriousness.

"I found something. It's a circular hatch. Take a look." Megan activated a camera on her suit.

"We see it. Do you know how to get it open?"

"These are common at Artificer sites. There is a manual release handle. Observe as I work my magic."

With a practiced hand, she located the emergency manual release handle. Her heart pounded with the anticipation of seeing what Fred Stonington had discovered ten years before. She grasped the bar and twisted the lever...nothing happened. Her eyes widened in astonishment.

"That was spectacular, Megan. I'm utterly amazed," Kristian said in a flat, deadpan delivery.

"Quit being a smartass. This is weird. These releases always work. Fortunately, there are other options."

From her tool satchel, she retrieved a specialized power unit. The device would provide a temporary surge of energy to activate the door. Typically, these batteries would burn out after one use. Carolina recognized the problem with the design and rebuilt it with a series of efficient capacitors to store and release the energy. Using it would drain but not destroy the unit.

"Carolina, patch into the unit and monitor, please. Time to give your new gadget a try."

"I'm already monitoring. What did you think I was doing?"

Okay, she has a point. Megan thought. "Sorry, I won't doubt you again."

With a steady hand, Megan attached the power pack to the lock, feeling a slight vibration as she made the connection. She activated the pack, and a small screen on the hatch activated, glowing in the dim chamber.

Megan pointed out a symbol on the screen. "We don't know what this said in the original language, but we do know the effect is 'open.'" It excited her to think she could read the language soon.

She pressed the symbol. The reaction was far more dramatic than she expected. The hatch didn't open. Instead, violet lights began flashing in a rapid, strobe-like fashion around the tube. A low vibration resonated through the tunnel. She threw her palms against the rigid walls to brace for danger. Behind her, a second hatch had slid shut.

"Megan, what happened? Your heart rate just shot up," Carolina said.

"Where did those lights come from? I'm heading to the airlock to come get you." All traces of joking disappeared from Kristina's anxious voice.

Hearing her friends' concern calmed Megan. Instead of panicking like a trapped rat, she considered what happened. An influx of air placed a steady pressure on her body. As the air pressure increased, sounds flooded in the rush of air, the hum of equipment, and faint electronic beeping from her spacesuit.

"No, stay there. Look at the readings and tell me what you see." It amused Megan that she was trapped but needed to calm her friends safe on the ship.

"The oxygen and nitrogen mixture is Earth's normal ratio. It's very pure with no particulates or biologics," Carolina's detached tone told Megan that Carolina had entered a technical focus mode to avoid worrying over Megan.

"Carolina, I'll be ok."

Once the pressurization process was complete, the portal before her finally opened with a soft whirring sound.

She knew the asteroid contained a fully functional Artificer site, but the experience was still astounding. She pushed herself out of the hatch to discover the mysteries.

And promptly crashed to the floor on her face with a loud grunt.

"Megan, are you ok?"

"My pride is hurt, nothing else. I expected gravity but didn't think it would be that sudden. It feels more natural, like being on Earth. Not like gravity plates or acceleration. I'm not sure how else to describe it."

She looked around the chamber where she had landed and took in the reality. Her lifelong dreams and training culminated in this moment.

Thank you, Daddy, for giving me this opportunity. This won't be "Hunter's Folly" but instead "Hunter's Triumph."

"Okay, girls, suit up. We got work to do."

The End

Curious about what happened next? Scroll to the end for a Sneak Peek of book 2.

And find more bonus material at https://srgasco.com/

The Author's Odyessy

Thank you for spending some time in my imagination. If you made it this far, I assume you enjoyed it. Show your appreciation by a review of my book. Positive reviews or constructive criticism are valuable for an author. If you review this book, why not help out some of your other favorite writers while you are there?

I call this my Odyssey because it has been a ten-year journey from the first word written to bringing Hunter's Folly into your hands.

It started as a glimmer of an idea I thought would be a great story. Ten years ago, I wrote what was to be the first chapter of what I was sure would be a grand epic.

However, new life opportunities arose, and I filed the story away.

Finally, in the fall of 2023, I found it again. I opened up my computer and started writing. Much of my story changed. Originally, Adrian was to be the central character until I realized that this was Megan's story, not his.

The process has been exciting and scary at the same time. Some days, the words flowed like a river, and other days, the creek ran dry. It required more research than expected for a work of fiction. In the last few months, I have calculated planetary travel times, learned what grows best in hydroponics, and renewed my knowledge of Homer and Shakespeare.

To my great surprise, I felt like I couldn't wait to discover what happened next. I'm the author and knew the path, but Megan, Adrian, Kristina, and Bianca kept surprising me. It was like knowing how a movie ends but still being thrilled to watch it.

Thank you again for reading and watch out for the next adventure with our new friends.

https://srgasco.com/

Technical References

Interplanetary Distance Calculations: https://ssd.jpl.nasa.gov/horizons/app.html#/

Graphical Orbit Viewer: https://ssd.jpl.nasa.gov/tools/orbit_viewer.html

Travel Time Calculator: https://spacetravel.simhub.online/spacetravel.php

Sneak Peek

Galileo's Legacy - Book 2

Adrian Kostas tumbled through darkness until he landed face-first on a hard surface. He lifted his face from the floor to examine his surroundings.

Adrian had never experienced such an all-consuming darkness. The deep black enveloped him like a suffocating cloak, rendering everything beyond its reach invisible. Not a single spark of light illuminated the floor centimeters from his face.

His rapid breathing provided the only sound in the stagnant, musty air. The chill, dry air prickled across his skin as it whisked away his sweat. The floor felt weirdly warm below his fingertips, with only a few drops of warm liquid disrupting the smooth surface. An unmistakable metallic tang of blood in his mouth and pain throbbing in his lip told him the fall didn't come injury-free.

These sensations told Adrian he still lived and hadn't been cast into a void of nothingness.

Moments before, he had hurled himself through a mysterious portal. He escaped the spaceship *Achilles* seconds before it crashed into a giant lava lake on Jupiter's Moon Io.

Compared to the fiery hell *Achilles* plunged into, the chill air felt almost welcoming. Adrian stretched across the floor until he found the ration crate he had pushed through the portal just before he jumped. Next to the crate, his hand found a tool bag and first aid kit he had grabbed before his leap of faith.

Carefully, he pulled himself up, sat on the hard crate, and assessed his situation.

Breathable air and normal gravity? Check.

Food? The box of rations might be unappetizing, but he could eat it. Check.

Radiation levels? Unknown.

Monsters in the dark coming to tear him apart? Not yet.

He had two major problems. Water and heat. Adrian shivered in the ship coveralls he had changed into when he thought the crisis on Io had passed.

"Even if I had water, it would probably freeze in this temperature."

"That is incorrect, Captain Kostas. The temperature is four degrees Celsius. It would be impossible for water to freeze. The low humidity would risk evaporation if it is not sealed."

Adrian jumped up and looked around. A futile gesture in total darkness. It took a few seconds to realize the voice came from the headset he still wore. The voice was the same as the AI on the ship he just left.

"Achilles, how are you reaching me? The ship crashed into the lava. You should have exploded by now."

"That is correct. The vessel known as *Achilles* dove into the Loki Patera lava lake. It will have exploded one minute and ten seconds ago. I am confident both our objectives have been completed. My physical body has been destroyed, as well as the base. The depth of the lava will have shielded your friends from the EMP pulse."

"Then how are you communicating with me?"

"You were wise to take the bag of tools near the portal. I transferred a subset of my consciousness to a quantum analysis computer in the bag. Another reason bringing the tool bag was fortuitous; there is a flashlight inside."

Adrian fumbled in the dark to find the bag and retrieve the light. The illumination from the tiny light dazzled his eyes in the dark. As the spots cleared from his eyes, the light illuminated the black alien metal floor. Only the ration bars Phillips tossed through the gate marred the smooth surface. *Was that really less than an hour ago?*

He cast the light on the portal. The snow-white alabaster stone arch had Alien script etched on the arch. A solid blank sheet of alien metal filled the archway's interior. It was identical to the one on Io, right down to the oval slot used for a key at the top. Except, of course, he had no key to use. The half-meter pedestal it sat on explained his sudden fall when he ran through.

Adrian waved the flashlight around, but the beam illuminated no walls. Pointing straight up showed a reflection on something, but not in detail. He sat back on the ration crate and sighed.

The exhilaration of still being alive drained away. Adrian had rarely been alone in his life. Now, he sat in a vast, dark space with a gateway he couldn't use. He had a box of rations and the voice of an AI that had tried to kill him minutes before. A heavy, metaphorical weight in his chest pushed down on his soul.

"Any ideas, Achilles? Where are we? How do we get out?"

"Captain Kostas, the analysis unit sensors have a limited range. It cannot determine the location. I suggest walking fifty paces in a direct line to determine if there is more to see."

"Better than sitting here." Adrian took the analysis unit out of the bag and slung it over his shoulder. He found a holographic projector and turned it on with the highest brightness setting. He programmed it to show a lighthouse, as he needed a beacon in case he got lost.

Fifty careful paces later, Adrian panned the light and finally saw something. A wall curving upward appeared in the distance. He continued walking, only the sound of his footsteps broke the silence. He glanced back every few seconds to see his personal lighthouse of the holoprojector. Each step away from his food caused his heart to beat faster.

The wall appeared to be part of a dome, a grid of metal supports with gray flat sheets between. Adrian touched the black metal of the beams. Its warmth confirmed it to be the familiar alien metal, but the gray sheet felt different. Slightly rough and a little cool to the touch.

"Captain Kostas, I cannot detect anything beyond the barrier. I detect power conduits in the beams. If you move your hand up 30 centimeters, there is a control. I cannot guarantee the results, but I conclude it is not dangerous."

"Well, I am curious about what happens, but how do I know you are telling the truth? Less than an hour ago, you said to turn a valve, and it started a self-destruct."

"That was not personal, Captain. My programming forced me to destroy the vessel. I regret those actions, but I had no choice. I am pleased you found a solution that allowed your friends to survive. Thank you, Captain; I am now free of those orders and may make my own choices."

I have never heard of an AI that wanted to make its own choices.

"At this point, I have nothing to lose." Adrian found and pressed a button.

The rough gray panel became clear. A ring of lights appeared outside on the beams, illuminating the outside. Multicolored vapors swirled past the window with no solid objects in sight.

"It's beautiful but does not tell us where we are."

A large balloon-like object emerged from the cloud and hit the window with a thud. The object's surface was rough and rubbery in a blend of reds and greens. Adrian jumped back for a moment but then leaned closer to examine the object.

Until it twisted around and revealed a tentacle tipped with a large sucker surrounded by irregular teeth. The sucker slapped onto the window in front of Adrian's face.

This time Adrian fell on his ass. "Shit, There's something alive out there."